Waiting
for the
Other Shoe

To Denise

Best Wishes

Maggie Hardsley

5th August 2008.

MAGGIE HANDSLEY

Waiting
for the
Other Shoe

Matador
9 De Montfort Mews
Leicester LE1 7FW, UK
Tel: (+44) 116 255 9311 / 9312
Email: books@troubador.co.uk
Web: www.troubador.co.uk/matador

ISBN 978 1906510 558

A Cataloguing-in-Publication (CIP) catalogue record for this book
is available from the British Library.

Mixed Sources
Product group from well-managed
forests and other controlled sources
www.fsc.org   Cert no. TT-COC-2082
© 1996 Forest Stewardship Council

Typeset in 11pt Stempel Garamond by Troubador Publishing Ltd, Leicester, UK
Printed in the UK by The Cromwell Press Ltd, Trowbridge, Wilts, UK

Matador is an imprint of Troubador Publishing Ltd

To Jane Jansson
with love

ACKNOWLEDGEMENTS

Thanks to Jo Smith, Ian Lloyd and Beth Harrison for their generous help in proofreading and editing.

Thanks to my family and friends for encouraging me to get on with it.

Spring 1990

Chapter 1 – Annie

'Who is she, I wonder? Who will she turn out to be?' said Annie, as they drove through the nether regions of Bradford into Churchill Close and drew up outside a dumpy pre-war semi.

'How should I know?' David refused to get caught up in Annie's speculation. 'She'll be who she is, I expect.' Annie stored a catalogue of pictures in her mind, baby pictures, toddler pictures, little girls, little boys; the burgeoning tribe she never had. As far as she was concerned, even down-to-earth David should be dying to know the child that was going to be theirs. She was so tense she could hardly breathe. What was it that was so fundamental about wanting a child that you'd do almost anything to get one?

'Come on then,' he said, opening the car door, 'let's get it over with.'

'Get it over with? What do you mean, get it over with?'

'You know what I mean.'

He's like a cat on hot flags, she thought. Nervous, like me. Not that he'd ever admit it, not David.

An aging Escort sagged at the roadside under a spindly flowering cherry.

'Looks like our social worker's here,' she said, climbing out into the early spring air. They looked at each other across the roof of the Polo and exchanged a smile. That weary expression he'd taken to wearing cleared for a minute and the smile reached right up to his trouser-

3

button eyes. Annie felt a surge of love, an unfamiliar certainty.

The foster mother was older than Annie expected, very hearty though worn ragged round the edges. She waddled through to the back room followed by Annie and David.

'Just you look at her. Isn't she bonnie?' A scrawny child lay sleeping in a battered wooden cot with her social worker hovering like a second-hand guardian angel.

'I'm Ms Blackshaw,' she said, emphasising the 'Ms'. Her tight wool skirt rode up round her chunky thighs as she bent over the child.

'You should've seen her when she first come,' said the foster mother, 'poor little beggar. You couldn't see what colour she were under all the muck. Didn't know if she were black or white. First thing I did was give her a good wash down.' She smiled fondly, stroking her baby cheek with podgy potato peel fingers.

Annie and David's social worker, Mrs Whitehead, had said nothing to prepare them for the pungent furniture, the half-empty mugs on a ring-stained tabletop, greasy carpets melded into the floorboards and a child that looked as though she was reared by wolves. Annie gulped down her rising gorge and took a deep breath. *Muck and squalor.* She could practically hear her mam's self-righteous sniff. Not that she was all that particular herself.

'Shall we have a cup of tea?' Mrs Whitehead switched her smile to full beam. 'Then we can all have a chat.'

'Sit yourself down, love,' the foster mother waved towards an exhausted sofa. 'Make yourself comfy.' Annie perched on the edge of the seat, folding her long legs sideways out of the way. She wished she hadn't worn her new linen trouser suit. That's what comes of dressing up, trying to look like somebody who's fit to be a

4

mother. Annie smiled her big toothy smile just in case anybody noticed her reluctance. You can't go upsetting people in their own homes, can you? Anyway, she could always get it dry-cleaned. David sat beside her and held her hand.

The foster mother heaved herself into the kitchen and filled the kettle. Ms Blackshaw sat down next to Mrs Whitehead in stark relief, bottle blond and killer heels next to a neglected perm and Clarke's sandals.

'Mrs Smith's very good, salt of the earth,' said Mrs Whitehead. 'They thrive with her, you know. She loves them, you see. That's what matters. It's the love that matters.' She looked suitably sincere.

'Smith?' said Annie, 'That was my name before I married a Neill.'

'Well, there's a coincidence!' Was it? This was all so far from what Annie had imagined, in spite of Mrs Whitehead's hints about the problems of neglected children. There was still, at the back of her mind, a little girl, dressed in a pink gingham frock, who would totter towards Annie with her arms outstretched. Annie would fall in love with her and take her home forever. Well, something on those lines. Not this skinny little creature that looked like something the cat dragged in. The social workers had smiles on their faces, though. It could still work out, couldn't it?

'Smith's a very common name,' said David but was ignored all round.

'Would you like to hold her for a bit,' ventured Mrs Whitehead, 'until Mrs Smith brings the tea?' A moment of silence followed, broken only by the clattering from the kitchen.

'Yes,' Annie said, 'Yes, I would.'

When Mrs Whitehead placed Bethany in her arms she felt unsubstantial, like a bundle of blankets with just a suggestion of a child inside. Annie held her close as though trying to breathe life into her.

When the tea came, she held on to the child one-handed. She was going on eighteen months but felt hollow-boned as a bird and smelled of baby sick. Annie tentatively sipped the tea from a brown stained mug. *Crate sweepings,* her mam would say. She would be lucky to get away without a stomach upset.

'She's a little sweetie-pie,' said Mrs Smith, lowering her broad backside onto a scuffed leather pouffe, 'a good little sleeper. I can sit and nurse her for hours. I sometimes wonder if she's ever going to wake up!' She laughed.

'What does she like?' asked Annie, not quite sure what she meant herself.

'Let's see,' said Mrs Smith, taking it in her stride, 'she likes something going on. She doesn't want to be left on her own in the dark. She likes to be with people.'

'What about food?'

'That's a bit of a problem. There's not much she likes in the food line. But you can always give her jam. She will take jam.' She smiled a hearty smile. 'Have you any favourite names?'

'Hasn't she got a name?' Annie couldn't believe it. What if she died? She looked frail enough to expire just from sitting in a draught. *Whammy*, like her mam said. She could be condemned to eternal purgatory. You can't not have a name.

'Her name's Bethany,' said Mrs Smith, 'though how she come to have a posh name like that beats me. Expect you'll want to change it. Most people do.'

'Oh yes,' said Mrs Whitehead. 'You can choose any

name you like. On adoption.' The words hung sharp in the air. David looked at his watch.

After a lifetime of waiting, years of disappointments and months of interrogation, Annie's head was spinning. Their intimate secrets had been flaunted on public display. They'd been up before the Panel, like plaintiffs in a court, stripped naked to the bone. What if, after all, this was a big mistake? Or, what if this was their only chance?

'It's early days, though,' Ms Blackshaw chimed in, her Virgin RED lips pursed like a monkey's bum. 'You've got to be sure you're doing the right thing.' Annie noticed her nail polish was chipped. 'It's what's best for Bethany, that's the main thing.'

Annie felt the child move against her; she practically kicked her in the ribs. She glanced at the grey-blue eyes and found herself locked in their gaze. It was like watching the North Sea, those hypnotising ebbs and flows. If you watched them long enough you could drown.

'Hello, Bethany,' she whispered. The child closed her eyes and softened in her arms. Annie held her close while Mrs Smith enlightened them about her little idiosyncrasies.

'She'll be alright though. Give her time.' It sounded as though the poor little thing had a lot to learn.

'Next time, we'll take her out in the pram,' said Mrs Smith, 'see how you get on with her. It can take a bit to get to know each other, specially if you're not used to having bairns around.'

'I'm an Infant teacher. I'm used to little ones,' said Annie.

'But it's not the same, is it? Not like having your own,' said Mrs Smith. 'Don't you worry love, it'll be alright.'

'Take your time,' said Ms Blackshaw. 'You don't want to rush things, do you?'

'No,' said Annie, her heart lurching like a ship at sea.

I just 'ope you know what you're letting yourself in for, young lady.

'I don't know.' David shook his head as he unlocked the front door. The weariness had come back but that wasn't what unnerved Annie. It was what he said. David didn't say he didn't know, not as a rule. David's whole universe was divided into things that were worth knowing and things that weren't. He was usually very clear what was what. Most of the time, it didn't much matter. What mattered now was his dithering.

Annie put the kettle on to make fresh tea, Yorkshire teabags in clean mugs. Then she went into the living room and lit the gas stove. They sat down, one each side, like a set of hearth dogs.

Annie scraped wayward strands of tawny hair behind her ears and cupped her chin in her palm. David looked old all of a sudden with worry lines sketched across his fine features and little fluffs of grey in his black boot-polish hair. She had a vision of them sitting there next to the popping gas stove for the next thirty years, slowly decaying under shrouds of spiders' webs, knee deep in dust; would-be parents who never quite made it. A tear oozed from the corner of one eye and slid down her face, like a weeping Madonna.

'It's just that it's such a big decision,' David said eventually. 'It's not like going to a pet shop and choosing a guinea pig. Are you sure this is the one you want?' She nodded. 'Well, it's up you, you know. Mrs Whitehead made it quite clear there's no obligation on anybody's part. Something better might come up.'

She thought for a while, wondering how to put it. Then it just came out.

'But she chose me.'

'What?'

'She wanted me.'

'What are you talking about?' David gave her one of his looks. David's looks could be unnerving. There was the look that implied you were terminally stupid, a look of grudging respect and a look that verged on sympathy. This was the one that implied terminally stupid. Annie thought about the kick in the ribs and the feeling of quiet acceptance but thought it better not to say.

'If you're sure it's what you want...' said David, shaking his head as though it was against his better judgement.

Funny, isn't it? You want something all your life then, when it looks as if you might get it, you panic.

Annie knew what life was supposed to be like, right from the Mixed Infants. According to the omnipresent Ladybird readers, life first recorded in decades long gone was alive and flourishing in the suburbs. A family of four lived in a square brick house, father wore a Trilby to the office, Peter and Jane fed the cat and the dog, then mother took them to the park. Annie devoured them all from 1a to 12c before she moved into the Juniors. Peter and Jane, and Pat the dog, became her best friends. She could always go and stay with them when the going got rough.

It was a far cry from life on the Oldham Road. Her dad laboured in greasy overalls and spent his wages in the pub. Her mam couldn't abide pets of any description, never mind children, and hadn't set foot in a park since the Methodist Whitsuntide Walk in 1957. Annie only knew that because there was a snapshot to prove it. Looking back, they had a lot to answer for did Peter and Jane.

Annie spent her teenage years nursing an imaginary life, how things would be if she had anything to do with it. She had strict ideas about certain things and wasn't going to put up with any more than she had to.

For a start, her name was Ann. An indefinite article, for God's sake. It's enough to give anybody an identity crisis. Granted, everybody called her 'Annie'. It's easier to say with 'ie' on the end but it was still indefinite.

Then there was her dad. She wouldn't marry a man like her dad even if he looked like Harrison Ford. As a matter of fact she wouldn't marry a man like any of the men she knew, particularly if they lived in spitting distance of the Oldham Road. The Oldham Road was the pits, a world-class cultural centre of grossness and pig-ignorance. No Thank You. What she wanted was a man who would be a proper dad and help his kids with their homework.

And there was the house, piled up with rubbish, nothing ever getting done and nothing in its proper place. What she wanted was a brand new house where nobody could possibly have left their dirty habits behind. Annie found a lot of comfort in her Ladybird world while she waited for the future.

Well, she hadn't done that bad so far, considering. She renamed herself Annabel and made up her mind that any child of hers would have a name of at least three syllables. Mind you, Annabel didn't last long. Not when it could be so easily shortened to Annie.

Then she met David at College. It was early September and there was already a taste of leaves in the air. God knows what he made of her that first day at Leeds, a lanky girl in a too-small coat laden down with Co-op carrier bags and hair billowing in the wind like a yard of brown barathea. He was ahead of her, escorting a gang of Freshers to registration. But he looked back, caught her eye and waited.

'Have you had a good summer?' he said, as though he knew her already.

'Yes,' she lied. Her heart thumped.

'What's your name?'

'Annabel.'

'Pleased to meet you, Annie.' How did he *know*? She screwed up her courage to look at him. Brown eyes, strong teeth and hair that stood up in clumps, he oozed reassurance and she relaxed enough to manage a smile.

'Come on, then,' he said. And she went. She never regretted it. Thank God she hadn't panicked over David. As a matter of fact, she'd never been so sure of anything as she was of David.

The house was a different carry on. You see so many houses you dream about them and wake up in a lather. You can never find the right combination of a house you like and a house you can afford. It's alright people saying you're particular, *you should be thankful to have a roof over your 'ead*, but it's not that straightforward when you not only have to live there but pay for it as well. Who, for example, would pay to live in her mam's house? Nobody in their right mind. It was only fit for rodents. And David was used to living in huge uneconomic vicarages, surrounded by fields of turnip and other such arable crops. He wouldn't want to cramp himself into a cottage that was hardly more than a dog kennel. But Holmebridge had little to offer outside the cottage range,

11

not unless you were in the mansion bracket and, being teachers, they weren't. As it turned out, their cottage wasn't bad, nicely situated on the hillside with views over the valley enough to give you vertigo. It was just the thoughts of the generations of unwashed previous occupants that put her off, all those second-hand skin scales lurking in crevices and the stale breath of old ghosts. Anyway, David promised her a new house as soon as they could afford it.

Now there was chance of a child called Bethany, a name with three syllables. But, to be honest, something was amiss. It was like hovering on the edge of a crevasse. If you mustered your strength and jumped over to the other side you would be alright. If you didn't, you would be left standing on slippery ground and wish you had. It was David. What was the matter with him? It was what he wanted, wasn't it? They'd talked about it often enough. He deserved more out of life than work, work, work. She would make a go of it for his sake as well as her own. Either that or die trying.

Annie hugged herself in anticipation, or at least as best she could lurching about on top of a double decker bus. It was enough to make you sick, like pregnancy. She savoured the word. It was so full of hope. Admittedly, her pregnancy was what you might call virtual but, all the same, she was expecting. She couldn't remember a feeling like it. It took her some time to recognise it as happiness.

She was going to tell her mam and dad. There comes a point, doesn't there, when you have to face up to telling them, whatever it is? Otherwise you're just storing up trouble for yourself.

Going back. It was always the same. She usually got the bus from Huddersfield town centre down the Oldham Road. It was a great lumbering thing that managed to shake itself like a shaggy dog on every start, stop or bend. The shaking was worse if you sat upstairs but if you sat downstairs you got more than your fair share of diesel fumes.

She'd take the car only she would have to park it right on the main road. They all did. Those houses weren't built for people with cars. They were built for people with next to nothing. They had plenty now, though, judging by the vehicles jammed on both sides. It was a miracle the bus could still get through.

Whether it was the traffic fumes or what, Annie arrived with a queasy feeling in her stomach. She didn't know how her mam and dad could stand it, living in a permanent pall of pollution. They might just as well park their fireside chairs in the middle of the Aspley roundabout.

Annie's mam was the most miserable woman on God's earth. Madge Smith nurtured her misery and wrapped it round herself like a greasy old blanket. Somehow, she managed to create an atmosphere of unrelenting gloom that expanded to fill any space she happened to be in. She could fill the whole universe given half a chance. Lucky for the rest of humankind, and whatever inhabited the outer planets, she spent most of her life in the house, huddled over the gas fire.

And her dad, Johnnie, was permanently laid off. Green Street Mill gasped its last in 1979, worn out with a hundred years' production of fine worsted cloth, the best in the world. Only the world didn't want it any more. Ages ago, she remembered, he took to working nights. That kept him well out of the way of anything resembling family life.

Being laid off didn't make much difference to his comings and goings. He still kept odd hours and spent most of his time wearing out the bar in the Weavers Arms.

Their house, No. 39, was a mean little house whose door opened straight onto the street. She steeled herself and walked straight in. No use knocking on this door. You could knock for a month of Sundays and nobody would open it. You could knock your knuckles to the bone and be found in years to come, a rattling skeleton hanging on the doorknob like a novelty wind chime.

'Hello,' she called out, stepping from the promising sunshine into the familiar gloom. She didn't expect a reply.

When she was little, she noticed that other people's mothers came to greet you at the door. Most of them were permanent kitchen fixtures, ranked somewhere between the sink and the stove. They kept stocks of hankies, safety pins, Elastoplasts and boiled sweets in their pinny pockets. They had red-scrubbed hands, always in water, dried vigorously on a rough kitchen towel whenever they came to the door. They were the heart of the house. They kept it alive and kicking, made sure that fires were lit, clean knickers and vests warmed on the rack and hot dinners appeared on the table every day. They smelled of kitchen, carbolic and comfort.

Annie's mam played a different game. No welcome mat here. Funny, there was always a smell of wet washing although you never caught her at it. Through the clammy kitchen into the back room, there she was, eking out her existence over the cracked and blackened radiants of the aging gas miser, dragging on a cigarette and gazing at the telly flickering in the corner.

'Hello Mam.' Annie breezed. Madge cast baleful eyes briefly in her direction.

'Put t'kettle on, will you.' That was as much as you'd get.

'How are you, Mam?' Annie called over her shoulder, heading back into the kitchen.

'Badly.'

'Oh?' Annie took her cue, inviting a recitation of symptoms, including wracked chest, stranglehold bellyache and chronic veins, that hadn't changed since Annie, at the age of five, had been frightened to go to school in case her mam died behind her back. How could she possibly wield a half-inch paintbrush with any conviction ('a field of daisies' poster paint on sugar paper, circa 1962) with her mam slumped in a dead heap in the back room? How could she open her little-girl mouth and join in 'Praise Him, Praise Him, all you little children...' when her mam was simultaneously sounding her death rattle? She felt a leaden weight lodge in her chest and knew it was all her fault. It was a miracle she ever learned anything. Her teachers always said she was a quiet child. No wonder. It took all her energy just to get through the day, never mind anything else. But Madge wasn't dead yet, though Annie was sorely tempted to advise her to hurry up and get on with it.

'Oh, I'm sorry you aren't feeling up to much,' she paused for effect, 'just when you're going be a Grandma!' She listened intently at the kitchen door. No response. She filled the kettle and started rattling cups and saucers, blue striped ones from Woollies that had lurked in the sideboard for donkey's years. No response. Kettle boiled, she brewed the tea, poured it out, plenty of milk and sugar, and then, with a little glow of satisfaction, carried the tea tray into the back room. The little glow died an instant death as she realised that Madge, glued to a repeat of Dynasty, hadn't heard a word.

'Joan Collins,' she said, stabbing her fag end in the direction of the television screen, 'knows how to dress up, she does.' Not that Madge would know. She hadn't dressed up since the Queen's Silver Jubilee, then that was only for a street party.

'Mam,' Annie said, 'we're going to have a little girl!' That grabbed her attention alright.

'What? At your age? You must be wrong in your 'ead. Anyway, it might be a boy and then what?'

'No, Mam, we're adopting! Didn't the social worker come to talk to you about it?'

'Oh, aye.' Light dawned. 'So that's what it were about. I thought she wanted to put me in an 'ome.' She sounded disappointed. Annie sighed in exasperation.

'I'm doing it, mam. I've made my mind up. I'm thirty-two and if I leave it much longer I'll be past it.' Annie went on while the going was good. 'We've been to see her a few times and now she's coming for the weekend.' Madge's mouth dropped.

'You don't want to do that. You never know what you're getting. You can't send 'em back you know, not once you've got 'em.'

It was a good job David couldn't make it after all. Annie was none too pleased on Saturday morning when he remembered he was supposed to be supervising an inter-school chess match. It wasn't like him. He usually made lists weeks in advance, wrote Daglo Post-Its to himself and ticked things off in his academic diary.

Anyway, it turned out for the best; he couldn't see her spending. She hardly knew where to start, never mind where to stop. Browsing round Babycare was a revelation.

Did babies really need all this stuff? It was like a whole new industry had invented itself behind her back, what with plastic widgets and polythene gadgets, interchangeable this and convertible that, never mind Heath Robinson on wheels. Mind you, it all looked very hygienic.

She asked an assistant for advice and came away with a SafeleyGo car seat, a Cumfibaby buggy, a Kosikid cot, half a dozen sets of non-allergenic bedding, terry sleeping suits, knickers and vests, pretty frocks, frilly socks and a dozen nigh-time nappies. All for one weekend? *Come up on the pools 'ave you, madam?* No, on the credit card. Well, she wasn't going to have her kid looking like a ragamuffin.

'Wait a minute!' the assistant called after her as she went to bring the car round for loading, 'What about feeding?'

'What?'

'You'll need dishes, forks, spoons, and things, won't you?'

'I've got dishes and forks and spoons and things at home.' I mean, for goodness sake, who wouldn't?

'Yes,' said the assistant in a tone of voice reserved for crass amateurs, 'But are they *baby* dishes, forks, spoons?'

Annie swallowed hard. It was all getting out of hand.

'And what about a pot?'

'What?'

'You know, a pot.' The assistant explained, as though it were self-evident.

'You mean a cup?' said Annie, embarrassed by her shortcomings in the babyware department.

'I'm talking about the *other end,*' said the assistant, her voice taking on an edge of exasperation. 'A potty. For weeing on and that.'

17

'Oh,' said Annie, as light dawned, 'I haven't thought beyond nappies. How do you go about it? Changing over from one to the other?'

'What you want is one of these.' The assistant hustled over to a display stand and picked up what looked like a squat pink plastic jug, featuring a jolly cat motif. 'A musical potty. It plays a tune when they wee. Encourages them you see. They can't wait to do it again.' A new line in novelty musical instruments, whatever next?

'Alright,' Annie was bordering on desperate, 'whatever you think.' The assistant took this as license to add a set of plastic bibs, one for each day of the week, and half a dozen pairs of trainer pants.

Torn between rushing over to Bradford to get Bethany and going home to prepare everything first, Annie decided to take the practical option. Sometimes, the only way to deal with David was to act fast and face him when the deed was done. It could save him hours of agonising. She set off for Bradford, to Churchill Close.

By the time David came home, Bethany was sitting on a fresh towel, spreading a jam sandwich over her Saturday bib and pink gingham frock. Her baby shampoo hair sprang into bright copper curls round her dainty features and little ruffs of lace circled her tiny feet.

'Look at her, David, isn't she sweet?' Annie felt radiant. David couldn't help but agree.

They sat on the carpet and watched her hungrily; enchanted by the way she picked at the bread and spread jam over her face, as though revelling in its stickiness.

'Look at her,' said Annie, her heart melting like lard in a chip pan. 'I think she's going to be bright, don't you?'

'You'll have her reading in no time.'

'See how straight she's sitting,' Annie marvelled.

'Yes,' David laughed, 'she looks as though she owns the place already.'

'And she looks so serious.'

'And so superior.'

'She's beautiful.'

Annie felt a fierce force of possession that nearly took her breath away. If that's what they call mother love, then that's what she had. She would die for this child if need be. Although, she thought twice about telling David just yet, he might think she was a bit previous.

'I just love her, David, don't you? Even when she's covered in jam!'

'Why did you give her jam? She should be eating something more substantial, to build her up.'

'She won't eat anything else. She isn't used to proper food yet.'

'Right, then. We'll have to do something about that,' said David, standing up and striding purposefully towards the fridge. Annie smiled.

She gazed at the sleeping child, drew the non-allergenic cover over her little shoulders and tenderly stroked her head. So small, so perfectly formed, Annie could fancy there was something fey about her. She felt a shower of warmth inside her like she never had before.

She took the warmth with her back to bed and snuggled up to David's back to share it. He was tired, worn out with his first taste of fatherhood. She put her arm round him and held him close, wrapping him in her burgeoning love. She pressed her face against him feeling his body heat seeping through his pyjama top, and closed her eyes.

David shifted closer, looking for comfort. She nuzzled into his neck with little sleepy kisses, wanting to tell him how much she loved him but was too drowsy to get the words out. She breathed in his familiar David smell. You couldn't say what it was exactly but it made her feel good. He said she had her own special smell as well but she couldn't imagine what it would be like. Anyway, she always wore Right Guard, even in bed, just to be on the safe side.

David reached out backwards and found her bum. He squeezed the plump curves in satisfying caresses, like kneading dough.

They didn't make love much nowadays. They'd got out of the habit. It was not having babies that did it. There didn't seem much point in setting yourself up to fail time and time again.

When you first fall in love you need each other all the time. You just can't help it. It seems the nearest you can get to possessing somebody, apart from eating them alive. And it's not long before you need them all over again.

Then you settle down and start trying for a family. It's the trying that gets you. You end up going through the motions like some outlandish ritual you're obliged to perform. If sex hadn't already been invented, who would have thought of it? It would take an unprecedented leap of imagination to think up the things you have to do to have a baby. It's all very undignified, not to mention unhygienic, when you look at it in the cold light of day. It's as though loving each other is beside the point.

David turned towards her, seeking her mouth with his. His touch was light and questioning, enough of a kiss to mean it but not enough to lose face if she turned away.

Annie's heart went out to him. She folded him in her arms and opened her lips inviting his tongue into her mouth. He let out a low moan and pressed himself hard against her, his needy hands grasping, squeezing, hurting... She relaxed and let him take his fill. Before, she would have felt obliged to do something in return, kiss for kiss, stroke for stroke, or something over and above like sucking him off just to please him. Now, all she wanted was to give and give, in a frenzy of giving.

Afterwards, she lay with him heavy in her arms, savouring the stickiness between her legs. Before she would have got up to the bathroom but the moment was too precious to just wash away. Now they were free to love each other for the sake of it.

'Our social worker told us not to expect too much to begin with but, quite honestly Mother, I think there might be something wrong.' David was phoning an update of the weekend's antics whilst Annie collapsed in a heap on the tired settee. She heard Elizabeth's cultivated tones floating over the airwaves, saying something very sensible, no doubt. Bethany was lying in the Kosikid cot doing nothing in particular.

David, after failing to get a coddled egg down her throat, rather than down her clothing and all over the carpet, decided they needed help.

'Why don't you ring your mother?' he said.

'You must be joking. Keep her out of it.' Annie surprised herself, never mind David, with the strength of her feelings. It was one thing putting up with the poisonous old besom yourself but to inflict her on an innocent child? Not on your life.

'Well, who, then?'

'The social worker?'

'That would be admitting defeat.'

'Mrs Smith?'

'Jam. She'll say give her jam.'

'Well than, what do you think?' Mr Know-all David thought the answer to everything was in a book but, in this case, he must have got hold of the wrong book. Nurse Harvey's 'Guide to Bringing up Baby' he'd found in Second Hand Seller on Main Street told you what the infant should do, such as smile at three months, but not what to do if it didn't.

'Then I'll have to ring *my* mother.' Good. Annie was, truth be known, a bit scared of Elizabeth. She was all Country Casuals and confidence, and lived in a defrocked parsonage in Norfolk, but somebody like her would be bound to know what to do. David grabbed the phone for the first of a string of phone calls that got them through the weekend.

By Sunday afternoon Annie was exhausted. How the heck do they do it, other mothers? Some have three or four all at once. Annie's colleagues used to say it was easier to manage thirty at school than one of your own at home. They always felt sorry for mothers who complained their kids were out of hand. Well, Bethany wasn't exactly out of hand but the mess was.

'She's not remotely toilet trained, you know,' David regaled his mother. 'We got through the nappies in no time. When we sit her on the potty, she manages to spread it everywhere. Hands and face, everywhere, she's completely incontinent.' He listened patiently to the soothing sounds that followed before launching into the next complaint.

'She won't feed properly. She doesn't seem to chew. She spits everything out. Then she daubs it all over the place. I mean, how can she live if she won't eat?' Elizabeth seemed to have an answer for that as well.

'She's not even toddling. She just sits there like a doll. And she doesn't talk. She just sort of whinges to herself. Honestly, Mother, I'm not convinced she'll ever be normal.'

Annie listened with a sinking heart. It had looked promising at the beginning. Now she realized it was going to be much harder than she thought. But she wanted to keep her all the same. From the minute Bethany was washed and powdered and dressed in her new clothes Annie knew she would never let her go. It was more than a conviction. It was a baptism. A baptism of fire, as it turned out.

'You can't move for clutter. There's so much stuff in here. It looks as though we've been invaded.' David droned.

'Can I have a word?' Annie held out her hand for the phone.

'Annie wants to talk to you, Mother, I'll ring back later, OK?' He passed it over and shuffled through to the kitchen to put the kettle on.

'Hello dear, you are having a difficult time of it, aren't you?' Annie suddenly realised she wasn't overawed by Elizabeth's immaculate articulation any more. Her voice was warm and comforting.

'It's hard going at the moment. What do you think, Elizabeth?'

'I think that son of mine is expecting too much all at once. You know, every baby is different, they all develop in their own time.' She paused to let the message sink in. 'I know she's been neglected but she'll catch up. After all, she's been assessed for adoption and, if there were any major problem, you would have been told about it.'

'Are you sure?' said Annie, sensing a straw to grasp at.

'Of course I'm sure,' said Elizabeth with reassuring heartiness. 'All you have to do is give her a home and love her.'

'Yes, you're right,' said Annie, her exhaustion evaporating as she spoke. 'She just needs to be loved and cared for like any other child. It's the love that matters.'

Annie glanced at the clock ticking on the living room mantelpiece. Five forty. The social workers were due at six.

'David, I don't want to let her go back. Not to that filthy foster place. Couldn't she just stay on with us?' Bethany was swaddled in her baby pink coat with matching bunny bonnet, all packed up and ready to go.

'You mean you definitely want to keep her?'

'Yes.' Annie balanced the child on one hip like mothers do. 'I've never felt like this before.'

'After the helluva weekend we've just had? Are you sure?'

'I can't let her go.' Annie's voice quivered. 'I just can't. She's got to me. She's part of me now.'

'I know.' David sighed. 'She's got to me as well.' He circled his arms round them in a big protective hug. Annie smiled, surprised. It wasn't like David to go all soft on her. They snuggled together, enjoying the cosy bundle of child between them for a few perfect minutes.

The social workers arrived in tandem to find out what was what, and installed themselves on the settee to hear the edited highlights of the weekend.

'That's a positive step forward,' said Mrs Whitehead.

'But we don't want to rush things, do we?' said Ms Blackshaw, drawing on a well-worn phrase from her repertoire.

'You can have her again next weekend,' soothed Mrs Whitehead. 'Then, we'll see.' They left with looks of satisfaction on their faces.

'Well then,' said Annie, subsiding onto the settee. 'We'd better start making plans.

'Right,' said David. 'Erm... what plans?'

'We'll have to rearrange the furniture, to fit everything in, then sort out a routine...'

'Ah, yes,' David was cottoning on. 'Register her at the Doctors,' he offered.

'And the baby clinic,' she said, thinking of Bethany's babysoft neck that smelled of Johnson's powder.

'Sort out some kind of childcare.'

'What?'

'You know, baby sitting, nursery, that sort of thing.'

'What are you talking about?' Annie's voice came out louder than she meant. That was enough to rub David up the wrong way.

'What I'm talking about,' he said in the voice he usually employed for pupils with special educational needs, 'is someone to look after Bethany when you're at school. She can't look after herself, as well you know.' Annie's heart lurched.

'But I won't *be* at school. We told the social workers *I'd* look after her.' David looked astonished as if for all the world this was the first he'd heard about it. Annie stood up. 'What's the point of having a child if you're going farm it out to all and sundry? You can't... and that's that.' She noticed herself shaking as though she were suddenly

25

somebody else looking on. *Now look what you've got yourself into, lady!*

'People do it all the time. They have to. It's the way society's going.'

'Well, they can if they want to but I'm not,' she said breathing hard, steadying herself against the chair back. 'You can't take a poor little kid who's hardly had a chance and pass her round like a parcel...' She fought back tears, willing herself to be in control. 'Every time she stops somebody'll rip a layer off.' David sighed. 'You know what your mother said. Bethany needs love and care. She's right. You know she is.' It wasn't often Annie saw red but she was seeing red now.

'Mother doesn't have to pay the mortgage, does she? And you're the one that's always going on about a new house. Do you want to stay in this so-called hovel forever?' David turned his back to show her the conversation was over. Not on your life.

'I know I called it a hovel,' said Annie evenly, 'and I am always going on about a new house. But it doesn't matter now, not when it comes down to choosing between a house and a baby, does it?' She knew by the slump of his shoulders that she'd won. But she also knew why he'd given in. It was something that wouldn't be mentioned. But she knew, and he knew she knew, and there was no joy in that. She would just have to make it work the way it was. Show him that it could.

Chapter 2 - Annie

Annie pushed the Comfibaby buggy along Main Street, past the Organic Grocery, the Veteran Clothes Cellar, the Community Caff and Yesteryear's foisty antiques. She dawdled because she was in no hurry to get back inside four walls, cut off from the world and forgotten by the rest of humankind.

She turned the corner into Beechwood Rise, away from the traffic that perpetually crawled along the main road coughing lead-laden breath into Bethany's face, and walked up to the kiddie's playground near the top of the hill. It consisted of a patch of green with a set of three swings and a seesaw. Annie liked to sit and swing in the late spring sunshine with Bethany in her arms, the nearest to a baby she would ever have.

'Look, Bethany,' she crooned, 'look at the daffodils, pretty daffodils.' She tried to teach her new words every day, to make her aware of things. Sometimes Bethany looked so self-absorbed it was frightening, as though she might never emerge again. Annie tried to show her the world around; houses, trees, flowers, a passing moggy, but Bethany was more interested in picking at a stray grass cutting that had attached itself to her pink woolly coat. Funny, she had these pernickety habits as though, deep inside herself, she was older than her years. There was so much to learn about her, this little human being. Annie held her close and hummed a tune that came to mind from a long time before.

'When I was but a little tiny boy, with a hey-ho, hey-ho, the wi-ind and the rain...'

As the afternoon sun waned Annie started to shiver. She strapped the child back into the buggy and set off down the hill.

Holmebridge grew up in an uncompromising Pennine valley; the buildings constructed practically one on top of another. Things were never what they seemed. What looked like a two-storey house at the front could easily be a three-storey house at the back with a flying freehold underneath.

The terraced houses on Beechwood Rise were tight packed like slices in a loaf of bread. Lacking the courtesy of a garden, they opened straight onto the street. Some people put potted shrubs outside their door in a brave effort to upgrade the neighbourhood. The terrace was stepped to accommodate the gradient of the hillside, each house propping up the next, and the jagged roofline looking like a row of rotten teeth.

The pavements were cracked and packed with moss. At the first sight of a wet leaf or a hint of frost somebody would fall and break a bone and then try to sue the council. But there's only so much a pavement can stand. After generations of hobnail boots, bogey carts, prams and mountain bikes it was all worn out.

Just as she was passing No.7, near the bottom of the hill, the door flung open and a woman stepped out, right in front of the buggy.

'Oops! Sorry.' She apologised and smiled.

'It's alright,' Annie smiled in return. The woman was stocky and dressed in layers of shrunken woollies. Her long hair hung loose in a hotchpotch of greys and browns. Annie vaguely recognised her from her daily walks round town.

'I've seen you before,' said the woman. 'You're from round here aren't you?'

'That's right,' said Annie, 'I've seen you out and about.'

'Tell you what, come in,' the woman waved them towards the house. 'Have a cup of tea.' A bit sudden, wasn't it? When they'd hardly met.

'But weren't you going out?'

'Oh, that can wait. Come on.'

The room was warm and welcoming though uncomfortably untidy. The woman swept a stale bundle of clothes off a sagging armchair so Annie could sit down.

'My name's Maura,' She filled a battered kettle and lit the gas ring.

'I'm Annie, and this is Bethany.'

'That's a pretty name for a pretty girl. What made you choose it?'

'We didn't. We're adopting her. That was her name to start with.'

'Adopting?'

'Yes, although I'll be glad when all the legalities are over and done with.' Then she'll be mine.

'Can't you choose her name, then?'

'You can't go changing people's names can you? I tried it once but it didn't work. You can't change who you are.'

'That's a thought,' said Maura, 'I changed mine but I don't know if I'm any different for it.'

'Why did you do that?'

'I didn't like it. In fact, it was bloody awful.' She laughed but didn't say any more. Annie decided she liked this openhearted woman, odd though she was.

'So, where do you live, Annie?' Maura reached into a cupboard for an outsize teapot and two striped mugs.

'On West Lane. We've been there a few years now, since David came to work at the Oldroyd Comprehensive. He's a science teacher, deputy head of department.'

'It's nice up there, isn't it?' said Maura. 'Some lovely little cottages.'

'Back to back, two up and one down, they're little alright.' Said Annie. 'What about you? Have you been here long?'

'All my life. Well, not in this particular house, but I've always lived in Holmebridge. I've got a shop on Main Street. Earth and Spirit, do you know it?'

Annie did know it. It was just across the road from the Community Caff. But she didn't go in because it was so crammed with rails of assorted draperies you could hardly get through the door, never mind turn round once you were inside. Not that it was her sort of shop anyway, more what you'd call New Age.

The kettle let out a frantic shriek and Maura turned the gas off. She poured the steaming water into the waiting teapot, gave it a stir and put the lid on.

'We'll just leave it a minute to brew.'

Annie, who resorted to teabags years ago, smiled at the familiar ritual. But, in fact, the tea did taste all the better for it.

'I haven't enjoyed a cup of tea so much in ages,' she said, feeling warmed and suddenly content.

Maura smiled and fed Bethany a cup of milk. She gulped it greedily, her tiny hands reaching out for more.

'That'll put some calcium in her bones.'

'I know,' Annie laughed, 'we had a job getting her to swallow anything at first and now I can't fill her. She can eat and drink for the lot of us.'

She felt reluctant to leave. It was as though all her life

a conversation had been going on around her that she hadn't been allowed to join in. Like when she was a little girl. She would pull out a kitchen chair on sunny days and sit with the women on the street, rocking the rickety chair over the uneven paving slabs and listening to their gossip. They enjoyed a good gossip, these women, other people's mothers. They liked nothing better. She could never be part of it though. First she was a child, and then she was educated. Either was enough to have you excluded. She felt part of it now though, talking to Maura, part of the universal conversation, part of what was going on. But she had to be back in time to make David's tea.

'I'd better be going. It's been nice...'

'Right, then,' said Maura. 'Nice meeting you too. Come into the shop next time you're out. If I'm not there Hamid will be. He's my partner, for my sins.'

'I will,' said Annie, 'If I can get the buggy through the door.'

'Oh, don't worry. We'll get it through.'

Annie wasn't convinced but didn't want to argue, it wouldn't be polite.

She felt lighter as she walked along Main Street in the teatime bustle, then up Winding Road towards West Lane. She was beginning to realise that, even though she had David and Bethany, she was lonely. And probably always had been.

'You made it, then.' Maura came to the half open door pushing a rail of Indian silks to one side. She grabbed the buggy and manhandled it into the only available space in the shop.

'Hamid,' she yelled towards the back room, 'come and meet Annie.' Hamid poked his head round the door and grinned like a Cheshire cat.

'Pleased to meet ya,' he said then disappeared, leaving the warmth of his grin behind. Maura retreated to the back of the counter.

'I know my place.' She laughed. They would manage for space if nobody else came in.

'We were out for a walk and I thought we'd call in,' said Annie across the buggy and the counter. It wasn't that far, just a bit more than normal conversing distance, but she felt obliged to raise her voice to penetrate the bitterchocolate fragrance that hung heavy in the air

'Glad to see you,' said Maura. 'It's nice to have company, isn't it Hamid?'

'Right,' Hamid's voice returned from the back room. Annie wasn't sure what to say next so she looked round for something to admire.

Like most shops on Main Street, it was once the front room of a terraced cottage. The owners usually extended into what were the kitchen, pantry, cellar or any other available square inch but they obviously hadn't the means. The tiny room was packed with damp fabrics, mirrored cushions, embroidered bags, handmade cards, herbal soaps and scented candles, arrays of rock crystals, stacks of contemplative music and assorted ethnic artefacts. She chose an elephant. Although its leather skin made it alarmingly lifelike, it looked refreshingly plain sitting on a pile of gaudy silk scarves.

'That's a nice elephant,' she said, for something to say. 'There's something appealing about an elephant, isn't there?'

'Oh, yes. Very,' Maura nodded enthusiastically.

Annie ran out of remarks and thought they'd better go. She felt a gulp of disappointment. Things hadn't gone as well as she'd hoped.

'Let's meet up for lunch,' said Maura. 'Tomorrow? Community Caff?'

'Yes let's!' said Annie, relieved, 'That's a good idea.'

'Fancy something to eat?' said Maura, eyeing a chunk of carrot cake. Annie looked at the display on the counter with growing doubt.

Where Annie came from, lunch was something other people ate. You had three meals a day, breakfast, dinner and tea. Then, if you were lucky, you had a fish supper from the chip shop.

At college, Annie found out that lunch was really a dinner, then there was another dinner for tea and, if you had supper as well, you could finish up with three dinners a day. One dinner was enough for her, thank you very much. She wasn't brought up greedy. She was brought up to be thankful for every mouthful. Tripe and onions, cow heel, lamb's liver, pork brawn, scrag end of neck, however disgusting it was, she was made to sit there until she ate it. Mealtimes were a duty to your parents, who slaved to put the food on your plate, or a penance because children were starving in Africa. It was enough to make you vegetarian, if not anorexic altogether. It was a long time before she realised food was something you were supposed to enjoy.

Now, in the Community Caff, you'd have a job finding anything resembling either a lunch or a dinner. The greasy glass domes on the makeshift counter covered a selection of amorphous brown lumps. Good thing they

33

were labelled or God only knows what sort of nasties you could be pushing down your child's innocent throat.

'I'm not really hungry.'

'Everything's home made, and organic of course,' said Maura, as though it would make Annie feel better just knowing that.

'Yes,' said Annie. 'I can smell it.'

'What d'you want, then?'

'I'll have a coffee. Bethany can have milk, if it's pasteurised.' Annie avoided the homemade cakes because she hated the bits that grind between your teeth. Besides, you didn't know who actually made them. It's not as though they came from a factory that was required to maintain certain standards.

The tables were makeshift, aging card tables with rotting baize, dead Singer treadle machines and a couple of rickety school desks. The chairs were a random collection of bulging Art Deco and stoic Utility. It was comfortable and unpretentious. At least that's what Maura said.

'You look a bit peaky. Is everything alright?' Maura's face registered friendly concern.

'What makes you say that?' said Annie, taken by surprise.

'To be honest, you look like a wrung out dishcloth,' said Maura, whose own appearance showed no signs of bothering with whatsoever. 'Are you feeling down?'

Funny, isn't it? If somebody says you look awful you suddenly start to feel awful. And if they ask if you feel down, you straightaway feel down. Annie didn't quite know why but unaccustomed emotions that she couldn't name and had tried to ignore swelled in her chest, tears collected in her eyes and started to slide down her face.

'Oh, sorry,' Maura passed her a recycled paper

serviette. It was virtually useless, like wiping your bum on torn up pages of the Daily Mirror.

'I'm fine. I don't know what came over me. I feel really peculiar sometimes.'

'It's probably hormones buggering your system up. We'd all be better off without them. You should try St. John's Wort,' said Maura, biting off a great lump of carrot cake.

'No, I'm fine, honest. I'm happy enough. What with David and Bethany, I've got what I wanted out of life.' Before Maura could draw breath to question her any more, she continued with, 'What about you, what did *you* want out of life?'

'Me?' Maura said through her mouthful, 'I don't know what I wanted. I didn't think about it. Just took one day at a time. I suppose it saved me from being disappointed.'

'Oh, I'm not disappointed!' Annie protested, too loud, attracting the attention of the other patrons of the Community Caff, two lumpy women with spiky varicoloured hair and multiple ear studs. They soon looked away. There were so many odd folk around Holmebridge you had to be really outlandish to attract any lasting attention.

'One day at a time, I never got the hang of that.'

'Easy,' said Maura, 'when you were brought up like I was. You've no idea...' she leaned forward like a runner about to pass on inside information.

'Really?' Annie perked up. 'Go on, tell us about it, then.'

Chapter 3 – Annie

David stayed up late, as usual, marking homework at the rickety kitchen table. It was actually in the living room since there was standing room only in the cellar top kitchen, but it was still, strictly speaking, a kitchen table.

Annie settled Bethany down to sleep. That was the time she loved her best when, bathed and sweet, she'd stopped whinging and shut her eyes to the world. Annie was enchanted by her bright copper curls, her button nose and babysoft expression, once she relaxed and let go of her wariness. That was the time when Annie could die of love for her. That was the time when, gathered together with her little family, she felt hope for tomorrow.

She got washed and changed ready for bed. She couldn't watch telly because that would disturb David so she read until he came up. She liked Ruth Rendell. She kept her awake and gave her something to think about apart from her usual worries about Bethany, David and society in general. *You think too much, you do. More than what's good for you.*

At last David appeared, had a quick shower, got into his M&S pyjamas and flopped into bed. He turned away from her and started his deep breathing routine, a prelude to snoring. Now what?

She could easily have felt peeved, after keeping herself awake for his sake, but she didn't. Instead, she leaned over him and with gentle fingers started to stroke his brow. He snuggled into the pillow. She put her lips to his face and dropped soft kisses round his eyes and mouth like little blessings. Eventually, he turned over and lay his arm across her in a clumsy, sleepy gesture, then fell back into the deep breathing routine.

At one time she would have been upset. It wasn't often she took the initiative, although she did more so lately. To be met with disinterest could be hurtful if she let it. But being a mother was changing her; she could feel herself growing stronger. She slid a hand under his shoulders, eased him towards her and cradled him in her arms, smoothing out the little worry lines with her fingertips.

Was that what you'd call getting into a routine, then? Annie began to feel like she was haunting the place. If she didn't watch out, she'd be getting a reputation as the walking dead. She might get a mention in tourist information if she was lucky.

They made the same rounds every day, rain or shine, and today it wasn't either, just a heavy stillness in the air.

There's only so far you can push a buggy and have enough stamina left to get you home. You have to decide when you've used up half your energy then turn round and go back. So there you are walking the same old pathways until you meet with gradients threatening enough to make you realise it's time to give up and head back to the house.

There were times during the day when it was hard to hang on to the fact that there was more to motherhood than feeding, washing and walking. And, although Bethany had started toddling at last, she couldn't do much walking; Annie had to walk for them both. It was all in the name of fresh air. Or getting out of four walls. She kept hoping to meet somebody she could talk to, another mother or maybe somebody like Mrs Smith, but she hadn't. Except Maura. At least she had her.

She turned round and headed for Main Street. She knew she was a nuisance turning up at the shop, there was hardly room to move as it was, but then you need somebody to talk to, don't you? It's only natural. Human beings were meant to be social animals, weren't they? That is, if they were meant to be anything at all. She sometimes thought it was all a ghastly galactic accident that some higher being would live to regret.

Conversations with Bethany were exhaustingly one-sided. What you really need is somebody who listens and gives you sensible replies. Her respect for the likes of Mrs Smith grew every day.

It's wasn't that Annie didn't try. She wasn't an Infant teacher for nothing. She bought stacks of Early Learning books, polythene bricks, plastic shapes to hammer through plastic holes and tubs of playdoh to mess about with; anything suitable for active eighteen month to three-year-olds, to give plenty of scope for progress.

She worked hard at quality time, bouncing Bethany on her lap playing 'Ride a Cock Horse', tickling her with 'Incy Wincy Spider' or hiding her face to surprise her with 'Peek a Boo'. The fact that these infantile games had survived through the years meant they must have found some sort of success but if left up to Bethany they would soon die a death. Her response was lukewarm at best. Annie couldn't imagine *what* it would take to put a smile on her face.

But it wasn't all for nothing. They were getting

somewhere. Bethany was beginning to come out of herself. She would play for short spells, throwing bricks about and chewing her rag books. She made some attempt at talking to herself between bouts of whinging. It was progress. The health visitor agreed and had practically said I Told You So.

She reached Earth and Spirit just in time to avoid the shower of rain that had been threatening all afternoon.

Maura looked pleased to see her.

'The answer to my prayers,' she said.

'Oh?'

'You can watch the shop for a bit, can't you?'

'Can I?' Annie perked up.

'Course you can. I've got to go to Leeds, chasing supplies. Hamid's dropped me in it, the bugger. He thinks I can be in two places at once.'

'Alright, then. Tell me what to do.' It was easy enough, just a matter of sitting there in case the phone rang or anybody came in. In the unlikely even of a sale, everything was priced up. Maura went off in a rush, Annie settled herself and Bethany in the back room, opened a window to relieve the atmosphere and, after ferreting through the assorted teabags, made herself a cup of chamomile tea. She looked round at the poky room and marvelled how it could be made to serve as a kitchenette, stockroom and office all at the same time. When the phone rang, it took her a minute to find it under a soggy kitchen towel.

'Hello, Earth and Spirit,' she chirped. 'How may I — ?' A bone-dry voice, just about recognisable as female, asked for Maura.

'Sorry, she's out. Can I take a message?'

'Tell her Kath rang. Tell her I'm coming round. About five. Got it?'

'Certainly,' Annie hardly got the word out before Kath rang off. Funny woman.

As Bethany obligingly nodded off, Annie spent the next couple of hours tidying the stock. She couldn't sit there in a tip. Anyway, it was interesting poking about, seeing what there was. She went through a pile of junk on the counter, adverts, flyers, photocopied events, straightening them out and clipping them together in neat piles. One of them caught her eye, probably because it was in Daglo orange:

Mothers 'n' Toddlers
Meet Tuesdays and Thursdays
Holmebridge Methodist Church Hall
1.30 - 3.30 pm
For more information phone Jo on 01242 8974690
All welcome

In her professional capacity, she used to look down her nose at amateur set-ups such as this but it was different now. From her present point of view, it looked promisingly like a lifeline. She folded the paper and pushed it into the buggy bag along with the spare nappies.

Maura came back just before five. Annie barely had time to fill her in on the afternoon's happenings, such as they were, before Kath arrived. Kath was tall and lanky with hair like a mop head. Her look was what you might call androgynous and she peered through vintage wire specs as though you were a long way off. Maura was thrown.

'Sorry, Annie,' she flapped. 'We've got business to see to.'

'I see.' Annie took the hint. She began the laborious

process of packing up ready to go, feeling awkward and out of place.

So this was where it was all happening? Holmebridge Methodist Church was on the main road and fairly central, as opposed to All Saints C of E which was well out of town. It was as though the C of E wanted that extra bit of effort for you to be worthy of them. In fact, most churchgoing folk of Holmebridge opted for the Methodists out of sheer idleness. Annie had tried going to the services once or twice, in the hope of making friends, but there was nobody remotely within her age group in the congregation.

It was different now though, at 1.30 on a fine Tuesday afternoon. The church hall was fairly buzzing with mothers and toddlers. A clinically obese woman in floral leggings appeared to be trying to impose some semblance of organisation on the random goings on. Annie recognised her as the Minister's wife. Poor woman, that's what you get for marrying a Minister. Everybody knows being a Minister's wife is a job in itself, only you have to do it for nothing.

'Hello,' said Annie. 'Can we join you?' The Minister's wife looked flustered.

'Course you can. I'm just going to get the toys out then I'll make the tea.' There was no hope of introductions; Annie would have to fend for herself.

'Can I give you a hand?' The Minister's wife looked grateful and showed Annie a cupboard labelled 'Toddlers'. One look inside was enough to wipe the smile off her face. You never saw such a collection of tatty old junk. Not even at Madge's. The dolls looked like victims of pillage.

The pram was missing a wheel, the box of bricks was half-empty, the toy kettle had no lid and the buckets and spades were useless without anything to shovel.

'You haven't got much suitable for toddlers, have you?' she said, rude on account of being shocked.

'No, we haven't,' the Minister's wife looked embarrassed. 'For one thing, there's no money, and for another, nobody's interested.' She waved round the room to prove her point. 'They only come to gossip and swap smokes. They leave the kids to get on with it. Some of them haven't even got kids. They bring other people's.' She looked near to tears.

'I see,' said Annie, who didn't. Another disappointment. 'Can I help you with the tea?'

Bethany stayed watchful in the buggy while Annie assembled a collection of beakers and searched for teabags. The kitchen, although small, was bleach clean, thank God, and well enough equipped. The Minister's wife was called Jo, she said, and was glad to meet Annie and please would she come again?

'Alright,' said Annie, feeling a challenge coming on. Maybe she could do something about those toys.

Handing out mugs of tea was a good way of circulating and she took the chance of introducing herself whenever she could get a word in edgeways. You have to, don't you, or you'd never get to know anybody? Then she saw somebody she recognised.

'Kath, hello,' she said in surprise. She wouldn't have put Kath down as a mother.

'Oh, hello,' she said in that bony voice. Well at least she remembered her.

'Which one is yours?' asked Annie, looking at a group of three scruffy youngsters sitting at her feet.

'None of them,' said Kath.

Well, what are you doing here then? Annie wanted to say.

'That's Doe's,' said Kath, pointing to a dark skinned child with wide-set black eyes. Annie was at a loss.

'And there's Doe,' Kath enlightened her as a big woman with a crew cut hove into view.

'Hello,' said Annie, 'I was just admiring your baby.'

'Right,' said Doe. 'Kath here looks after him. I've got M.E. you know.' That proved to be a conversation stopper. Annie felt she'd laboured hard enough as it was, never mind trying to find out how two single women like Kath and Doe came to have a child of unknown ethnic origin.

After the tea round, Annie lifted Bethany out of her buggy and stood her up, watching to see how she would react to other children. Bethany looked around intently, as though taking stock, then started toddling about from mother to mother looking quite self-possessed. Such confidence in one so small. Then Annie noticed the women's reactions. As Bethany approached them, reaching out her dainty little hand, the women left off talking and began to coo at her. Bethany looked up at each of them, graciously accepting their attention. Then she set off to work her charm on the next. Looking at the other toddlers, sitting on the floor banging things in boredom or clinging whining to their mams' legs, Annie thought how much more mature, in command, Bethany appeared, in spite of her elfin proportions. She thrilled inside and wished David was there to see it.

She helped wash the mugs and tidy the dusty old hall as best she could.

'Will you come on Thursday?' said Jo.

'Course I will. Look, I know it's interfering, but would you like me to do something about the toys?'

'Can't do a lot without money,' said Jo.

'We could raise some money.'

'I'm a Methodist remember. I'm a past master at raising money. But, there are other priorities. And when all's said and done, most of these women never set foot in church.'

'I'll think about it.'

'You do that. See you Thursday.'

Annie set off at a brisk walk, making a mental list of toddler's requirements and trying to work out how much they could get away with charging for a mug of tea.

Walking down Main Street, she decided to stop off at the Second Hand Seller to see what she could find in the child development department.

Annie was spreading mashed banana on toast for Bethany's tea when the phone rang.

'Hello, Elizabeth, how're you?' she said.

'I'm very well, dear. How are you faring?'

'We've had a good day, thanks. Bethany was a star at the Mothers 'n' Toddler's and I've got myself a job sorting the toys out. Honestly, they've no idea what to offer little ones.' Her voice was bright and brittle. 'And I've found a couple of books on child development to check on Bethany's progress. I was really pleased with her this afternoon,' she said, cutting the toast into four with one hand and arranging it on Bethany's Humpty Dumpty plate.

'Oh, really?'

'She's such a little darling. She was far and away the brightest toddler there.'

'That's good. She must be coming out of herself. How did she react to the other children?'

'She didn't, not really, but do they, at that age?' She lifted Bethany onto a kitchen chair one handed and gave her the plate of banana toast.

'She's too young to play with the other children but I would have thought she would react to them in one way or another.'

'Well, I was pleased with her. She looked so confident.' Annie wasn't about to make light of Bethany's achievement.

'I can't wait to see how she's getting on.' Elizabeth sounded very hearty all of a sudden. 'I'll come up for a few days in the school holidays. Could you book me into a hotel?'

'That's nice. It's getting busy now with it being tourist season. I'd better get you booked in soon.'

'Yes, do that dear, won't you?'

Annie didn't feel as pleased as she might have done. In fact, she felt like a tyre with a case of slow puncture. Course she wanted Elizabeth to come and see them. It was good of her to go to the expense. It was just that it seemed a bit contrived. As though she wanted to check up on them.

She put the phone down and turned to Bethany just as she was stuffing the last bite of toast into her mouth and looking round for more.

'Hello, Maura?' Annie was a bit tentative. She didn't want to interrupt if there was any early evening trade going on but she took the chance to ring Maura after tea whilst Bethany was glued to the telly.

45

'Annie, it's you. How are things?' She sounded pleased enough.

'Fine. I thought I'd give you a ring to catch up.'

'How did you get on in the shop? Was everything OK?'

'It was very quiet, actually. I didn't sell anything. I know it's rude to say so but I was wondering how you manage to make a living.'

'Tourists. It busies up no end in the summer.'

'Oh, I see.' Annie paused, feeling awkward.

'And you met Kath. How did you find her?'

'A bit strange, to be honest. I met her again at the Mothers 'n' Toddlers. She was there with a baby that looked distinctly foreign.'

Maura laughed. 'Bengali, s'matter of fact,' she said. 'It's a long and unlikely story about a Bangladeshi cook from Frizinghall who boldly went where no man had been before.'

'You mean Doe?' Annie's curiosity cranked up a notch.

'I mean Doe. It wasn't half a shock to her system. She's had M.E. ever since. I don't know what she'd do without Kath.'

'I see,' said Annie. 'Doe and Kath.' It suddenly seemed to her that human society was more complex in Holmebridge than anywhere else. Interesting though that was, it made her feel more out of it than ever.

'Anyway,' said Maura. 'Whatever made you go to the Mothers 'n' Toddlers? Didn't you know it's a lesbian outfit? You won't have much in common with them.'

'No, I don't,' said Annie in a small voice. 'I don't have much in common with anybody any more. I feel like I'm the only person left on the planet.'

'Sorry. Didn't mean to upset you.'

'You didn't. I was upset to start with.'

'What about exactly?'

'I don't know. . . I didn't think it would be like this. I feel as though I don't live in the real world any more. I do keep trying but the more I try the worse it gets.' Annie's voice broke in a sob. She grabbed a handful of tissues and clapped them to her mouth.

'Look,' said Maura. 'How d'you feel about minding the shop on a regular basis, say once a week? It'd give you something to do, chance to meet people.' Annie was glad she had something in reserve, or she might have felt patronised.

'Well, I could, if you like, so long as Bethany doesn't get bored. But not on Tuesdays or Thursdays. I'm committed to the Mothers 'n' Toddlers.' Maura didn't pass an opinion on that but graciously accepted Annie's offer to help out on Fridays.

Annie picked Bethany up and tried to cuddle her but Bethany stiffened in her arms She wasn't having any of it, as usual.

Chapter 4 - Maura

In the back room of Earth and Spirit Maura eased her poor feet out of battered Birkenstocks and sipped her decaffeinated Lady Grey. It was her quiet time, between the daytime and evening customers, time to take stock. But she couldn't settle. There was this free-floating anxiety around her since she talked to Annie. How would they manage her involvement in the business? Minimal though that would be, she might be around at awkward times. Maura sighed. She'd been too impulsive. She did what she usually did when she felt nattered, phoned Hamid. After six rings the ansafone clicked on.

'Hamid, are you there? Answer the bloody phone, will you? Come on you...'

'OK, OK, give us a chance.' Hamid did his usual impression of somebody in a very important hurry, 'I just walked through the door, in'it?'

'Aren't you coming in? You said you would.'

'Yeh, yeh,' he was thinking rapidly, she could tell by his tone.

'Hammy, love,' she got in before he had chance to frame an excuse, 'I need you. Come on. I need to see you.' The ploy was ambiguous enough to interest him.

'OK, I'll be there.'

She saw him arrive about seven when she was in the middle of a Tarot reading but he knew better than to interrupt when she was with a paying client. Maura eventually found him in his black BMW, on the double yellows across the street, scoffing a fish butty.

'You took your time.'

'Yeh,' he said through a great mouthful, 'had loadsa stuff to do.' He opened the passenger door. She took it as an invitation and climbed into the vinegar atmosphere.

'Ya know what?' said Hamid, waving the remains of his butty towards the shop window, 'It doesn't look nice. It's not smart.' He wrinkled his face in distaste. 'Needs more class.'

'What d'you mean?' Maura said, sharpish, looking at her shop front with new eyes.

It was characterful. The building was over a hundred years old and looked well settled on its foundations. It would stand for at least another hundred, probably more. The shop window was in keeping and although the woodwork was painted purple it was a nice subdued shade that hadn't been challenged by any of the local conservationists. It was what was in the window that was the trouble. She could see that now she took a fresh look. It was such a mish-mash. Too much in too little space and tatty condensation-soaked felt-tip notices stuck all over the glass advertising Tarot readings, crystal healing, head massage (ladies only) and relaxation techniques. It screamed AMATEUR and Maura was no amateur, she was brought up to it.

'Right,' she said, 'What d'you think?' Hamid was busy considering alternatives when it struck Maura that he was hijacking her agenda again. She wanted to talk to him about Annie and there they were planning alterations.

'Whatever, you want,' she said, so long as you pay for it. Now Hammy, I want to talk to you. Come on in.'

Once inside, Hamid made for the back room to rinse

49

his greasy hands. Maura followed. She drew up a stool to the scrubbed oak table that stood in as her office, expecting him to join her. Instead, Hamid came up behind her and draped his arms insinuatingly round her neck.

'Ya need me, Plum. Ya said ya need me,' he wheedled. He always called her Plum when he wanted sex.

'I want to talk to you, Hamid,'

'Yeh, yeh,' he said, moving his hands over her copious unfettered breasts. 'What about?' he said, squeezing her nipples.

'Hamid, you bugger!' her protest was only token. She wouldn't resist. Maura never resisted anything. She didn't see the point. He pushed her forwards onto the table, hoisted her skirt up round her backside and slid a familiar hand up through the leg of her outsize interlock knickers. He'd won again. But it was just as exciting as usual. Besides, let's face it, where else would she find such a sexy man to fuck a woman like her?

Things were looking up. Give Hamid his due, whatever he made his mind up to do, he made a good job of it. Maura leaned against the doorjamb in the sunlight, catching her breath after a hefty bout of window cleaning. Hamid was up a ladder attaching the new price board to the back wall with a couple of six-inch nails. Bugger the plaster, thought Maura, so long as the bloody thing stops up.

As he stretched and hammered, Maura took the chance to relish his body. Fine boned, sleek, tight, made in manageable quantities, he was everything she wasn't. She was fascinated by the way his skin changed colour in different lights. In the spring afternoon it was golden syrup. She could lick him all over for tuppence. Then, later, come the evening, he would look as though he were dusted with cocoa powder. His abundant hair was strong and black as espresso and stuck out like a charge of electric. She liked to pick out the little hairs round his nipples with her teeth. It gave her an illusion of control.

'Shit!' after hammering at the nails with fervour, Hamid suddenly reached a full stop. They refused to go in any further.

'Probably got down to the stone,' said Maura.

'This fuckin' plaster should be at least six inch thick!'

Well, it obviously isn't, she could have said but didn't.

'Never mind. It'll do like that,' she said. The nails stuck out at least an inch but it wasn't that noticeable if you didn't get too close. Hamid sighed, resigning himself to imperfection. Then he turned his attention to the display stands.

'Too much,' he decided. He was probably right.

By the time a good half of the stock was packed up in boxes and piled up in the back room a stylish emporium had emerged from the chaos, a credit to Main Street. Hamid definitely had what it took in more ways than one. Besides, as the so-called sleeping partner, he had to protect his investments.

Maura was restacking the herb-scented candles when, for no particular reason, she started thinking about Annie. She was miserable. Anybody could see that. But why? She had everything she wanted. It was something Maura wanted to get to the bottom of. Not that it was any of her business. It was just that Annie was so needy. Then there was that scrawny little kid to think of.

Hamid wasn't much help. He never was much good at anything you might call personal. She sometimes wondered why she kept on trying.

'Not your problem.' He flashed a grin over the counter. 'Ya got me to worry about, in'it?'

'I don't know,' her face puckered. 'There's something wrong and I can't put my finger on it.'

'Ask them cards.'

'No need for sarcasm,' said Maura, knowing he had no time for what he called 'that magic crap'. 'Anyway, they can't tell you anything you don't know.'

'Why do folk pay, then, if they already know?'

'Perhaps they don't realise what they know, or hope they've got it wrong.'

'Well, how can cards tell the future if *they* don't know?'

'They can't. You have to work it out yourself. From what *you* know.'

'All *I* know is - fuck all.' Hamid grinned, ripe with self-satisfaction.

'Oh, go on then. Let's have a go.'

The little bag was dark blue velvet, embroidered with silk and mirrors. Maura slipped out the familiar cards and shuffled them. She laid out a three-card spread on the counter top.

She turned the first card. The Emperor. Maura smiled. Strength, wisdom, where would she be without them? Good job she was a spring baby, an Arian, living as they did on the hillside with nothing but the rotting carcass of a caravan between them and the bitter Pennine weather. She was named Bird of Paradise. God knows why. Any sensible bird of paradise would die an instant horrible death in those conditions. Anyway, it was soon shortened to B, a letter of the alphabet, uninspiring but useful.

Her most abiding memory was of cold. Not the ordinary cold that people moan about at bus stops but a searing cold that paralyses nerves and crystallises muscles. Her mother hardly noticed it; she was stoned most of the time.

The next card was the nine of swords. Anxiety, despair, what's this about? A woman in torment? Maura could honestly tell herself that, in spite of her many problems, she was not exactly in torment. Somebody around her was suffering. But you could say that about most folk.

With heart racing she turned the third card, The Reaper. A surge of fear; it always has that effect on her. But the Reaper brings change and that's not always bad is it?

So, her wisdom and strength would help a woman in torment through a serious change. That was the best she could do in making sense of the reading as a whole. More cards from the Major Arcada, two to one, nothing you could do about it.

'What did it say, then?' cheeked Hamid.

'Nothing I didn't know already.'

Maura finished late after a prolonged head and shoulder massage. Doe wallowed in her weekly massage like some folk wallow in a hot shower. It was good exercise for Maura and regular cash in hand. Doe also had a regular order for Hamid's Organic H, raised with natural fertilisers and free from synthetic chemical additives, and that kept him sweet.

After locking up, she glanced across the street and noticed the Community Caff was open. The hours offered to the Community by the Caff were variable, depending on who could be persuaded to remain in a fit state of mind to function past teatime. She went into the fluorescent gloom and found Horace in charge. Horace was one of the founders of the Community Caff and the most loyal since he didn't mind that it never made a profit. He was Maura's long-term ex and she still had a soft spot for him.

'Nowthen, Horace, how're you?' she said. He lowered his Evening Post and looked over the top of his specs. Most of Horace's hair grew on his chin, the rest was pulled back in a scraggy ponytail. He wore a permanent scarf round his throat to keep colds at bay.

'Champion,' he claimed, taking a swig of something out of a yellow mug. 'So long as I have roof over my head and food in my belly, I'm a happy man.' He was given to philosophy was Horace.

'I know,' said Maura, 'and the rest.' She dropped a kiss on his bald patch and caught a whiff of wintergreen. 'Anyway how's business?'

'This is not a business,' he pronounced. 'What this is - is a community service.' Maura smiled. Everybody needs something to get up for.

'Well then, what've you got?'

'Not a lot,' said Horace cheerfully. 'You can have a drink if you want.' He indicated his stash of booze with a wave of the hand towards the defunct ice-cream freezer. It was hidden on account of him not having a licence.

'What've you got to eat?'

'Dunno,' said Horace. 'Tell you what, go get us a curry.' Maura smiled and did as she was told.

Good old Horace. She could talk to him. No silly games with Horace. Pity they split. Well, drifted more like. Call it a combination of circumstances, like chronic idleness combined with brewer's droop.

Later, she disturbed their mutual contentment by remembering to worry about Annie.

'Horry love, do you think I'm interfering?'

'Interfering? Course you're interfering,' said Horace, rolling a fag of some description and daintily licking the paper's edge with a long wet tongue. 'That's what women are for. How would we manage if nobody interfered?'

Maura made her way up to West Lane and knocked at the door of No. 3 with a firm sense of purpose. If there was anything she could sort out then she would sort it out. There was no reply.

'Annie,' she yelled. The sense of purpose wouldn't let her leave until she was absolutely sure nobody was in. 'Annie, are you there?' She heard movement and then the sound of the key in the lock. The door opened to reveal Annie draped in a much-washed pale blue dressing gown.

'Sorry,' said Maura. 'Were you in bed?'

'No, no, it's just that I haven't had time to get dressed.'

Then what have you been doing all morning? she felt like saying but didn't.

'Come in.' Annie's voice was flat. Maura strode into the living room and parked herself in a fireside chair without waiting to be asked. The sense of purpose was working overtime.

'Are you going to put the kettle on, then?' she prompted in what she thought was an encouraging tone.

'You sound like a social worker,' said Annie, from the cellar top kitchen.

Maura looked around. You could do with a social worker, she thought. And hasn't that Health Visitor been yet?

Nothing in Maura's life so far could be said to have prepared her for childcare but even she could see that leaving a toddler sitting in the middle of the floor, unattended and surrounded by hazards, was not a good idea. She started collecting the nappy bags Bethany might suffocate herself with, the pots of cream she might knock herself out with, the Q tips she might choke herself with and any other object that could conceivably be used in the process of self-annihilation children of that age go in for.

'I was going to tidy up,' said Annie, eventually appearing with two mugs of tea.

'I thought she might hurt herself.'

'She won't. She'll just sit there doing nothing. She does it for hours at a time. It's as though she's watching you, only you never catch her at it.' Maura felt a twinge of alarm.

'Tell you what,' she said, in her social worker voice, 'we'll have our tea then I'll help you get sorted.' Coming from Maura, who rarely sorted anything, that was a generous offer.

'I'm aright. Just a bit behind with things. It doesn't matter really.'

'What does matter, then?' Annie sighed and indicated the child development books accumulating by the side of the chair. With the likes of Professor Ronald Illingworth and Dr Miriam Stoppard, Nurse Harvey was in good company.

'It's Bethany. There's definitely something wrong with her. She makes no effort to communicate. David was right, she'll never be normal.'

'She looks alright to me. I know she isn't toilet trained but you don't want to get hung up on that. You'll give her a complex.'

'But she doesn't even smile, never mind talk. And she's supposed to look at you. I think she must be backward. Unless there's something wrong with her eyes.' Maura looked closely at the child sitting on the carpet. Granted she didn't do much but she looked well enough. Maura stood her up. She toddled a few steps across the room. Then Maura called her name and Bethany turned and looked at her.

'Look, she's alright.' At that point, Bethany stretched out her arms scarecrow style and toddled, gurgling, back to Maura who picked her up and hugged her. Annie winced and looked away.

Chapter 5 - Elizabeth

Elizabeth sat in the warmth of The Old Parsonage's conservatory, recovering after a bout of gardening. She poured herself a cup of Darjeeling and sipped it gratefully, enjoying the fragrance of muscatel. There was so much to do at this time of year; forking manure, planting out the first of the annuals, raking the lawn ready for feeding and tending the little lavender hedge. She wondered how long she could keep up to it all. What with the garden, the house and the church, she was run off her feet.

Elsie appeared in the doorway holding a yellow duster at arm's length as though she might eventually get round to doing something with it.

'Yourn 'right there Mrs Neill? she said. She was small and plump, and swathed in a cloud of Coty L'Aimant.

'Yes, thank you, Elsie dear,' said Elizabeth. 'I don't know what I'd do without you.'

Elsie was thoroughly reliable. She 'did' for selected houses in Little Ellingham; having a monopoly in the 'help' market, she made it her career. The only problem was that Elsie, being born and bred in these parts, shared the local sense of time and consequently worked at a pace that was barely productive. By the time she'd taken her coat off and filled the kettle, it was practically time to put her coat on again. It was the same with tradesmen. 'Same day service' could just as well mean the same day next month, or next week if they were in a mood for granting favours.

'Very well, then. I'll just get on, shall I?'

'Yes, thank you Elsie,' said Elizabeth, thinking how nice it would be if she *did* just get on. The house was in definite need of somebody just getting on. All the same, she counted herself lucky to have a house at all, snapped up for a song at a time when the Church was liquidating its assets. With not much demand for a clay lump property in rural Norfolk, she was in with a chance. That was shortly before Francis disappeared and died of a guilty conscience.

How like his father David was, self-assured, dogmatic, argumentative. Fortunately, he had his mother's saving graces; he was intelligent and capable. And he had, she suspected, an underlying sensitivity that would make him a good father once he got into the way of it. As for Annie, there was no substance to her; it was as though she lacked essential nutrients. Maybe that was why she hadn't conceived.

They'll be fine, she thought. They'll manage. She planned to invite them down for the summer holidays. Bethany would grow up with the benefit of Norfolk summers, hearty food and country air. She would buy her a pony when she was old enough.

Feeling better, Elizabeth made her way upstairs to shower and change before crossing the lane to refresh the altar flowers at St. Michael's. The staircase was generous with plump polished banisters and a spacious half-landing. This was where she housed a small walnut writing desk and hung family photographs so she was often tempted to linger on her way upstairs to rearrange ornaments, perk up the seasonal flower arrangement or look at the pictures.

The wedding group caught her eye. It took place at St. Michael's, of course. There was no question of a registry office in Huddersfield. David looked happy and relaxed.

Annie looked anxious. She must have been worrying about her father. He was dreadful, he and the person they called Uncle Ted. No matter they were vulgar. One could cope with that. It was their drunken behaviour that marred the occasion. Luckily, the mother didn't attend.

There were other photographs of course; David and Annie looking happy and relaxed on holiday in Greece; David standing proudly by a second-hand Metro, his first car; Annie surrounded by little ones on a school picnic; and others in and amongst that supported the notion they were a happy couple.

The latest was a studio portrait of Bethany, by Greaves of Halifax. She was enchanting, no doubt about it. Elizabeth was a cultured woman with refined taste and could look beyond the fond imaginings of a grandmother to see a lovely little girl who would one day be beautiful. There was something, though, that wasn't quite right. What was it? That guarded expression? Was it to do with the eyes? The way she refused to look at the camera? Maybe she was shy of the photographer.

Elizabeth decided to phone when she got back from church. It was usually Annie who answered and she seemed to appreciate the support. Not that Elizabeth would give advice unless she was asked. Oh no, she would never be so ill mannered as to interfere.

Chapter 6 - Annie

There was a well, Annie remembered, in Great Auntie Janet's front yard. It was right at the bottom of the front doorsteps, of all the places to be. In the days when Shelley village was a law unto itself, Auntie Janet used to pump well water and boil it on the stove in galvanised buckets. That was quite a feat, considering she was barely five foot tall and skinny as a rake.

After the Second World War, civilisation, in the guise of the County Borough of Huddersfield, caught up with Shelley and Auntie Janet was connected to the mains. Course Annie didn't remember all this, that was before she was born, but she remembered the tales that were told. Her dad and Uncle Ted took to reminiscing in a big way during the sixties. It was as though they wanted to order and record their lives so they would eventually mean something in the great march of history that was fast leaving them behind.

One summer, when she was about six, for want of anything better to do, they took Annie up to Shelley for a day out. Nowadays you could drive there in twenty minutes but then it took all day to get there and back on the bus.

The well was covered with paving stones but, since they were rectangular flags covering a round hole, they left gaps that you could peep through.

'Watch,' said Uncle Ted, showing Annie how to drop a stone down the well and listen for the plop. 'You can work out how far down t'water is by timing how long it takes to plop.' Trouble was, he couldn't remember how. Typical when you come to think about it.

Annie crouched down with her eye to the gap and concentrated hard until she could make out the rough stone walls, the rusted remains of an iron grating and, far below, the oily glint of water; a huge lizard eye, hypnotic and enticing. She was overcome by a sensation of falling, plummeting down the dank drop, down to the inevitable plop. She laughed sharply, a laugh she did when she was scared, a laugh that was really a shout.

'What's up, love?' her dad said mildly. He looked happy that day, she remembered. 'Alright?'

She couldn't remember much about Great Auntie Janet, except she was little and old, but she remembered that well alright. In her dreams it became a Vortex, a malevolent force that made her feel like the bottom of the world was falling out.

That was what Annie was feeling now, and not for the first time. She held on to the back of a kitchen chair and took deep breaths. It was just a matter of keeping her nerve until the panic passed.

Elizabeth climbed down from the railway carriage into a determined drizzle of rain. What a shame, thought Annie, knowing Elizabeth liked going hill walking when she got the chance. There wasn't much scope in Norfolk, there not being any hills to speak of.

'Hello, how're you?' Annie came running, pushing the buggy along the platform.

'Hello, dear,' said Elizabeth, dragging a green leather case down the steps. No wonder it looked battered. 'I do hope this rain clears up. It was perfectly fine as far as Leeds and it hasn't stopped since.'

We are in the Pennines, you know, thought Annie. What do you expect? 'Come on, let's go home and have a cuppa and you can have a play with Bethany.'

The weather didn't improve at all that day. They got drenched walking to the cottage and just about got dried out in time to get drenched again on the walk to book into The Crown Hotel on Main Street. Except Bethany, of course, she sat in her plastic buggy tent immune to the elements like a princess in a palanquin.

Elizabeth said she was wet enough for one day and decided to stay put at the hotel.

'David'll come and see you after tea,' offered Annie, wishing she'd dropped him off at school and kept the car. At least it was just for today. He'd be on holiday from tomorrow. She set off once more in the wet, pushing the buggy up Winding Road and onto West Lane. All this to-ing and fro-ing, packing and unpacking, dressing and changing, it was enough to wear you out. One of these days she'd be nothing but a shadow of her former self, whoever that might be. She hoped it would be better weather tomorrow. Elizabeth's stay was beginning to look like a washout.

As it happened, the next morning dawned fresh and dry and Elizabeth appeared at the cottage in time for coffee. David was out buying new laces for his fell boots and Annie was scrabbling round trying to make the place look fit for human habitation. For some perverse reason, toddlers take up more space and need more possessions than the rest of humankind who, in turn, need more than any other living creature on the planet. Anyway, Elizabeth didn't seem to notice the chaos but made herself at home in a fireside chair.

'She's a lovely child,' she admired over her mug of Co-op freeze-dried coffee, 'so dainty and pretty. She looks almost like a little flower fairy.' Annie was intrigued. It wasn't like Elizabeth to be so twee. Well here goes.

'Do you think she's normal?' The question came out in a relatively neutral voice, as though she hadn't been rehearsing it for days.

'You can't expect her to be normal, dear. Not yet. She's got a lot of catching up to do. But don't worry, she'll get there in the end. Love is what she needs.' Elizabeth spoke in such cultivated tones; that alone gave authority to anything she might happen to say. Annie felt a huge surge of relief. She had, after all, been making too much of things.

Elizabeth lowered herself onto the floor and took Bethany onto her lap. On the floor was not her natural milieu but, never mind, she was making the effort.

'This is the way the farmer rides, clip clop, clip clop,' she recited, jigging Bethany in rhythm. Bethany was unimpressed at first. Then she stiffened and squawked; that was a sure sign she'd had enough.

'This little piggy went to market' was marginally more successful. Bethany watched carefully as Elizabeth wiggled her fingers one by one. 'This little piggy stayed at home' earned a suspicious glare. 'This little piggy had roast beef' and 'This little piggy had none' brought a fleeting look of amusement. But when it came to 'ran all the way home!' into Bethany's armpits, she screamed in rage.

'I must be losing my touch,' said Elizabeth, trying to sooth the thrashing child.

'Just leave her alone until she gets over it,' said Annie wearily, trying to ignore the commotion.

'Do you want to see Bethany's book?' Annie got up and reached over the table to the bookshelves behind. 'Her social worker made it for her. She's supposed to add to it,

as and when she wants, to make a record of her life.'
Elizabeth took the big scrapbook, carefully covered in
stickyback plastic and labelled in large print:

My Life Story
by
Bethany Neill

The front page displayed a small photograph of a baby
shaped blob clasped to the bosom of Mrs Smith. At least
it looked like Mrs Smith, going by the knobbly cardigan.

This is me age 1 year.
My birth mother loves me but she can't look after me.
So I went to live with a foster mother for a while.
Then mummy and daddy adopted me.
They love me.
They will always look after me.

On the next page was a relatively recent photograph of
Annie and David standing outside the cottage.

It was a shame there wasn't a dog, thought Annie,
thinking back to Peter and Jane.

This is mummy and daddy.
This is my home.

Photocopies of Bethany's birth certificate and adoption
papers were pasted onto the next page. The social worker
had apparently decided they were self-explanatory. Then,
bizarrely, there was a photocopied handprint.

This is my hand, aged 1 year and 6 months.

Then there was the Greaves of Halifax studio portrait of Bethany looking downright suspicious, in spite of Mr Greaves's best efforts.

'It doesn't amount to much, does it? But I keep taking more photos for her to choose from,' said Annie. 'She'll need to make some sort of sense of her early years. If she chooses things herself she might feel more... in control.'

'I've been meaning to ask,' Elizabeth hesitated, 'do you know much about her background? Other than that she was neglected, I mean.'

'No, not much,' said Annie replacing the book on the shelf. 'It was like getting blood out of a stone. Mrs Whitehead warned us we might not be told any more than the basic facts. We learned more from the foster mother than the social worker.'

'Doesn't it feel like working in the dark? I mean, you just don't *know*, do you?'

'No,' said Annie, sitting herself down. 'You don't.' She pushed any nasty possibilities that presented themselves to the back of her mind. 'It's supposed to be a fresh start.' She scraped her straggling hair behind her ears then started picking at her cuticles.

'You could put some of her drawings in the book,' Elizabeth suggested. There were several dotted about the place, although 'drawing' was hardly the word since Bethany's wielding of her Jumbo colouring stick was a random affair and any contact with paper was incidental. Annie felt warmed by her kindness.

'It's difficult not knowing,' she said, 'specially if you're the worrying kind.'

'Are you the worrying kind?' asked Elizabeth.

'I was brought up to be the worrying kind. I don't know how not to be.' Annie was surprised. She didn't know she knew that about herself. She could hardly believe she'd said it. But she decided not to mention the recent panic attacks. It might be said that the kind of woman who goes in for panic attacks isn't fit to be a mother. That's hardly fair, of course. There are natural mothers who go in for all sorts of bizarre behaviour, Madge, for example. Nobody ever threatened to remove Annie from her dubious care and place her in a foster home. In her bleaker moments, she could wish somebody had.

'A lot of young mothers feel exhausted, you know. You expect to be in a state of permanent bliss once you have the baby but it doesn't work like that. Having a child turns your life upside down and it can take a while to readjust.' Elizabeth sipped her coffee, a picture of calm.

'I feel so useless sometimes... I can't seem to shape myself. I don't want to be like this, it's pathetic.' Her voice was barely a whisper.

'Annie, you're a grown woman now. You can be who you want to be. I know from my own experience. You have it in you, believe me.'

You can be who you want to be? That was a revelation. Did you have a choice in the matter? Like choosing from an identikit personality? 'I'll have the cheerful disposition, if you please. Don't give me anything bordering on misery, not if you know what's good for you.' Anyway, it was food for thought, wasn't it? A change from worrying about humanity, the ozone layer or the prospect of the world being swallowed up by the sun. In fact, the idea, once you got hold of it, with a bit of thought, could promise to be quite liberating.

'I'm beginning to see what you mean.' Meanwhile, Bethany's rage spent itself and she settled down to a steady whinge.

'Oh, look,' said Elizabeth, smiling. 'The sun's coming out. We can go walking after all.'

'So, how did it go?' asked Maura in a dutiful sort of way. 'How did you get on with the Mother-in-Law?' She made it sound like an encounter with somebody from remote foreign parts.

'Great, I enjoyed having her,' Annie smiled. 'She's so capable, she makes everything seem so much easier.'

'That's nice.' Maura was a bit acid. 'It's a gift we could all do with.' She was sorting out the mess on the office table. 'I've got to do these bloody accounts this aft, if you'll watch the shop.' Annie took this as a thinly disguised order to get out of the way and leave her to it.

Friday afternoons were turning out to be quite entertaining now the tourist season was under way. Annie often thought Holmebridge attracted an odd sort of inhabitant, but the folks who chose to visit were turning out to be downright peculiar; a crackling procession of androids encased in cagoules, leggings and boots as though they were just about to board a space ship. It was an endless source of fascination.

'You wouldn't believe what happened today!' she regaled David on a weekly basis with stories of tourists up to no good.

'Wouldn't I?' he said, as though nothing surprised him any more. But Annie was constantly surprised. They stocked endless knickknacks that were neither use nor ornament but she found tourists cheerfully stole them by the dozen. She even went off the leather elephant she used to admire. She'd seen too many of them.

Maura was kept busy as well. She handled the

tobacco side of the business and Annie didn't interfere. It was strictly under the counter, being from 'alternative' suppliers. Horace seemed to have a stake in it. He popped in from time to time with old sweet jars packed with the homecut Virginia he grew in a little greenhouse in his backyard. He also supplied brown paper packets of 'special' grown in his airing cupboard, but didn't specify what. Hamid supplied the 'Afghan' that came in sturdy office envelopes sealed with Sellotape, the 'Dutch' that was wrapped in greaseproof and his 'Organic' line that came in small white packets. Annie didn't want to even think about the nature of the various products or their legal status. She left it to Maura to do that.

'What's Bethany up to?' Maura called from the back room in what sounded like a suspicious tone of voice.

'What d'you mean?'

'She's quiet. What's she doing?'

'She's always quiet.'

'No she's not. She whinges.'

'Not all the time. In fact she's getting much better at not whinging.' What had got into Maura for goodness sake? 'She's playing with magic markers if you must know.'

'That's a good sign,' said Maura, 'so long as she doesn't mark the stock.' Annie was a bit put out. Bethany was improving, thank you very much, and there was no way she was going to start making excuses for her. Particularly now she was taking herself in hand, reinventing herself.

'Right, that's a good job done,' said Maura eventually. 'Pity the Miracle Mother-in Law can't come and wave her magic wand over us.' Before Annie could frame a reply,

Maura said, 'When d'you want me to babysit, then?' throwing her into a state of total confusion.

Annie strapped Bethany firmly into the SafelyGo car seat. There was no way she was going to take her on the bus. Even if a bus deigned to stop for you, by the time you folded the buggy up with one hand, hung on to the toddler with the other, and staggered your way up the steps into the clammy interior, the bus driver was already letting out the brakes with a spiteful hiss. And by the time the buggy was stowed, child sat down and you found your purse, you were practically at the next stop. The other passengers sat there as though you were laid on for their particular entertainment. They'd rather drop dead than lend a helping hand. Then, when you got where you were going, you had the whole rigmarole to go through again only backwards. No way. Annie decided to drop David off at work and then take the car even if she had to double park and terminally constipate the whole of the Oldham Road.

As it happened, she found a space in the front yard of the Weavers Arms. There was a notice saying 'Patrons Only' but she considered her dad did enough patronising for the both of them, if not for the whole neighbourhood. She didn't bother to see if he was in his usual spot in the taproom. He would either be there or at home in bed.

She unpacked Bethany from the car seat and repacked her in the buggy. It was only a short walk to the house but walking a toddler across a busy main road is just asking for trouble, especially when the toddler was as perverse as Bethany. She could loll about the house all day saving up her energy for a screaming match in the middle of a main road.

Annie knocked on the door as usual, opened it as usual and stepped into the usual dank atmosphere with the usual sinking feeling in her stomach. Bethany didn't seem to mind the gloom. Once released from the buggy, she toddled round the room exposing herself to hazards such as the array of multicoloured tablets Madge kept on a little table by her side, the unprotected gas flames hissing through broken filaments, the wire trailing across the carpet because the plug was at the wrong side of the fireplace for the telly, and abandoned mugs of brew. You might just as well leave agar plates strewn round the place to support the incumbent germs in their mission to take over the world.

'Put t'kettle on,' said Madge, sucking on a tab end. 'I'll watch 'er.' Annie was torn between protecting Bethany and showing naked distrust of her mam. She compromised by leaving the kitchen door wide open and bobbing back and forth as she performed the tea making ritual. Once that was done with she persuaded Bethany to sit down and drink her milk.

'Well, what do you think of her?' Annie said brightly. 'Don't you think she's grown?' It was only for form's sake. Playing at families. Madge wouldn't notice any difference if she turned up on the doorstep with a baby elephant in tow.

'I don't know about that.' Madge shook her head. 'She looks on the sickly side, if you ask me.'

Something in the way she said it took Annie straight back to her childhood, on the receiving end of that same malevolence, a victim of petty power and control. *You're not going to school in that state, young lady. I'll get the doctor.* The doctor came and went, leaving a prescription for tonic. What else could he do? Matter of fact, he could have said there was nothing wrong with Annie and wasn't it time she got herself out of bed and off to school before she got behind with her learning? He could have told Madge she was an over-anxious, manipulative woman intent on ruining her child's prospects altogether. No, don't be daft, course he couldn't. It would have precipitated the world's biggest tantrum since Mount Etna last blew her top. And he wasn't up to dealing with that. Nor was her dad. That's why Madge always got away with it. Nowadays, you'd call it child abuse.

The anger welled up inside her, scalding her insides. Annie swallowed it down, like she always did, like she'd been brought up to do, and made up her mind there and then that it wasn't going to be like that for Bethany.

Why don't I just strangle her and have done with it? she thought. No, she couldn't face the prospect. Leave her to it. Madge never was a proper mam, what hope was there of her being a proper gran? She'd better finish with her now before Bethany got contaminated. Elizabeth was a much better grandmother even though she did live in the back of beyond.

'Better be off, then,' she said briskly. After Bethany was parcelled up and strapped in the buggy, it struck Annie that, if she was going to shake the dust from her feet, she ought to make some move to say goodbye to her dad.

'Where's Dad?' she said. Madge looked confused for a second, then remembered.

'In bed.' Oh well, he was probably fast asleep. Annie pushed the buggy through the kitchen door, gave her feet a good wipe on the doormat and stepped out into the street.

The Mothers 'n' Toddlers project wasn't exactly a roaring success. Annie's attempts at fundraising were thwarted at every turn. She made jolly posters to stick up round the room proclaiming 'Toddlers' Toys' as a Good Cause but nobody took any notice. The Quality Street tin she'd labelled 'Toy Fund' and stuck in the doorway, stayed stubbornly empty and her efforts at charging 15p for a cuppa met with subversive Thermos flasks being brought to meetings. She made dainty butterfly cakes that would appeal to little ones and tried to sell them at barely more than cost. But the women turned their noses up at anything less than organic and wouldn't allow the poor little mites to eat anything that might remotely take their fancy. Jo looked sympathetic.

'I see what you mean,' Annie told her and admitted defeat.

The idea came to her in the middle of the night, or in the early hours of the morning to be exact. David had got up to the lav and just sighed his way back into bed, a ritual that woke her at least once every night, when she experienced a brainwave. Well, it was just an idea really but, at that time in the morning, it felt like a divine revelation.

'David!'

'Mmmm.'

'I've got an idea!'

'Mmmm?'

'If you can't join 'em, beat 'em!'

'Mmmm.' Poor lad, leave him be. Annie got up, while the spirit moved, and spent the next half hour at the kitchen table getting something down on paper before the idea faded to nothing in the cold light of day.

THE HOLMEBRIDGE PLAYSCHOOL PROJECT

She made a list of things that needed looking into, like grant funding, premises, insurance, legal requirements, staffing, equipment and so on, wrote copious notes and jotted down where she might find information. Her project, she felt, had taken its first tottering step. Now she had a purpose. And it wasn't only for Bethany; it was for her as well, for the both of them. It was their comeback to the real world, an end to their social isolation and, she felt sure, a way forward for their relationship. She would use her skills to help Bethany grow and develop in a healthier situation than the claustrophobic twosome they had now. It would, she hoped, take the anxiety out of it. She practically skipped back to bed.

Next morning, after getting up and swallowing a bit of breakfast she phoned Jo who was relatively impressed.

'Good God,' she said, 'I haven't met anybody so organised in a long time.'

'D'you think it'll work?'

'In theory, but not with the lot that comes here. You'll have to find a different clientele.'

'I want to appeal to mums of two-to-four-year-olds who care about their kiddies' learning,' said Annie hopefully.

'Well, you can hope, but I think you'll have to look further out of town. Try the new developments', was Jo's solid advice.

Holmebridge was busy sprawling outwards like everywhere else. Being in a narrow valley, it tended to sprawl at the ends with only tentative efforts at construction on the near-vertical hillsides. The modern builders didn't have the same tenacity that the older generations had. So, the new developments, housing the aspiring up and comings, were where Annie would begin.

David looked relatively interested as she told him the

details. He even made encouraging remarks over the remains of his Weetabix.

'It'll do you good to go out to work again.' He smiled at her enthusiasm. What she didn't tell him though was that she wouldn't be getting paid. Annie was making her own decisions now.

Summer 1995

Chapter 7 - Annie

Annie wallowed in the bath foam that, being a present from Maura, smelled predictably of patchouli and ylang-ylang. How wonderful she thought, looking round the glossy ceramic fittings, to have a brand new house that couldn't possibly have been polluted by other people's rubbish. Whether it was something physical, like flakes of dandruff or nail clippings lurking in corners, or whether it was something less substantial, like anger or misery ingratiating itself into the fabric, didn't make any difference. Living in somebody else's house was practically sharing a bed with them. You could never get away from their stale sweat or bad breath, never mind the dubious thoughts that might be going through their heads. Annie did not want, never did want, other people's rubbish. She lingered a bit longer, feeling better than ever.

What should she wear? It was something of a non-question really because her clothes were all alike, black, white or beige. She decided on the just-above-the-knee length black linen dress that showed off her legs and her strappy stilettos. She wanted to feel mature, in charge, *arrived.*

She climbed out of the bath into a fresh white bath sheet; not just any old towel with green stripes across, or pink floral motifs sprawling round the edges, but a great sheet of Egyptian cotton towelling that felt better than a mink coat and dried her without even trying.

Annie sang as she dressed, 'be it ever so humble...'

which, of course, it wasn't. What it *was* was her brand new brick palace at No. 13 Brackenbed Drive, on the highly desirable Riverside development. When they got the chance to buy an affordable newbuild house in the Holmebridge area, after years of controversy over green field sites, they grabbed it with both hands. Not that they were green fields as such, being the strips of land between the road and the river that wouldn't be much good for anything but bog plants. The cottage on West Lane had made a tidy profit and David's promotion to Head of Department was a good help even though it meant he was working harder than ever.

She squirted Chanel No.5 behind both ears and down her understated cleavage. Not that she liked Chanel No. 5 very much, she found it a bit challenging, but David had bought it for her and, anyway, she felt in the mood. She brushed her hair and scraped it up into a banana clip. The spikes that bunched out at her crown put her in mind of a palm tree. Never mind, it was supposed to be the fashion. She just hoped David realised that. She smiled to herself. He would appreciate the effort.

She hummed as she clomped downstairs, admiring the mellow tones of the newly varnished wood. And, as she heard Bethany playing in her room and the scrape of David's key in the back door, she felt a pulse of pure happiness somewhere deep in her insides. At last, everything was as it should be.

Maura arrived late. You could rely on Maura to be late. Time Form could take bets on it. That's why, if Annie wanted her at seven, she told her half past six. Well, now it was seven, and here was Maura.

Honestly, she got worse as she got older. You'd think downtrodden workers in third-world sweatshops manufactured retro Oxfam rejects specially for the bottom end of the Holmebridge market. What's more, in a last ditch effort with herself, she'd taken to henna-ing her hair. It looked like a yard of unravelled jumper.

'Come on in,' said Annie, ushering Maura through the archway into the lounge. Maura looked around sharp-eyed. She hadn't seen the house since it was furnished.

'Very nice,' she said, her voice echoing round the room. 'Nice and light,' she added, nodding reassuringly. Annie winced as she strode her sturdy boots over the flokati rug and dropped her bulky backside on the unstructured beige sofa.

'Where is she, then?' Maura looked round as though Bethany might be lurking somewhere in the soft furnishings.

'She's upstairs, playing with her dolls. You know, pretending. She does all their voices. She has a brilliant imagination.' She allowed herself a glow of motherly pride. She'd earned it. After what they'd been through with Bethany's unsociable and incomprehensible behaviour it was a miracle they'd come out the other side. They'd hung on when anybody else could be forgiven for murdering her. Now she was going to meet the Year 2 teacher to discuss how well she'd done in the assessment tests. She did right to be proud. As a matter of fact, the world would be a better place all round if more parents could put themselves out to be proud. If hers had, she wouldn't have been forced to resort to threats before they let her go to college.

'What time does this 'do' begin?' Maura seemed to think it was some kind of social. Not that she'd know anything about schools, the way she was brought up; almost accidentally.

'We're due to meet Mrs Clough at quarter past seven.

Then we'll get a cup of tea in the parents' room. We won't be late back, half eight at the latest.'

'Have you left me something to eat?' As if she wouldn't, for goodness sake.

'Course I have,' said Annie. 'The freezer's full of readymeals. Just waft one in the microwave. And there's a bottle of wine in the fridge.' Annie always had wine in the fridge. She liked to be hospitable.

'I don't suppose it's organic.'

'As a matter of fact, it is.' Annie wasn't keen on the organic Bergerac but she felt obliged to pander. Anyway, it wasn't as though there weren't teabags on the counter top and water in the tap.

'Right then,' said Maura, 'go just as soon as you're ready. We'll be fine, Bethany and me.'

'You can leave Bethany upstairs if she wants. She's quite happy with her own company.'

'She'll be looking after herself next, I suppose.' Maura sniffed. Annie handed her the television controls.

'Here's the remote,' she said. 'We've got Sky if she wants to watch TV.' Maura started flicking through the channels. She looked oddly out of place. Maura never watched TV on account of all the violence creating negative energy that beamed into the atmosphere. It struck Annie that she might feel awkward in the new surroundings, or jealous even? Maura's own house was the same as ever, down to the same piles of washing hanging about in the kitchen, she shouldn't wonder.

David strode into the room, struggling with his tie.

'Hello, Maura. I can't get this bloody thing right.' Annie smiled and reached out to him, catching his tie in a movement resembling an embrace.

'There,' she said, 'you look good enough to eat.' She

growled deep in her throat and made as if to bite him. He laughed. You didn't often see him laugh. Still, he had a lot to put up with.

Annie clattered into the hallway to fetch her trendy oversized cardi.

'This laminate floor's so noisy,' she said. 'I'm beginning to think we should have it carpeted.'

'It was your idea,' said David. 'And it cost an arm and a leg.' He shrugged into his jacket and fished about for his car keys.

'Come on,' he said. 'Let's be having you.' Annie dropped a kiss on top of Maura's head and trotted after David who was already striding through the door.

'Put that thing on, will you?' he said, 'It might be July but that doesn't mean it's warm enough to go out without a cardigan.'

'Bye,' said Maura.

'She's a bit touchy, isn't she?' said Annie as David started up the Golf and eased it out of the pristine tarmac driveway onto the new made road.

'You mean Maura?'

'She's been like that lately. I've an idea she might be jealous?'

'Jealous? Of what?'

'Bethany, the new house, everything. We've got a nice life, thank God, after all our ups and downs. She hasn't got much when you come to think about it. Hamid's never there and the shop's going downhill. And I think she's feeling well and truly middle-aged.'

David grunted in reply, concentrating on turning right onto the main road into town.

'I'm glad we moved further out,' said Annie. 'It gives you a feeling of space, *and* it's on the flat.' Course, being on the riverside, it would be.

It wasn't only that though, it was a new start. It gave her a feeling of normality living in a development with families around them, like Rod and Lynda next door with their two little girls and a miniature poodle. In Holmebridge itself, you never knew what to expect in the way of houses, or their occupants. Like Kath and Doe with their unlikely child who occupied a converted corner of the old Co-op. It was very unsettling.

Society was becoming seriously undermined like a worked-out colliery. If you didn't keep shoring it up, it would collapse in on itself and become yet another black hole in the universe.

Annie glanced sideways to catch David's profile. In spite of his middle-aged wrinkles and badger hair he was still a good-looking man. She laid a soft hand on his thigh and thought how she might please him later, when the time was right.

'It's been good for us having Bethany, hasn't it? Made us stronger. D'you remember how worried we were when she first started school? She was so little and hardly spoke a word.'

'Now look at her,' said David. 'She's like a talking beanpole'

'She'll have a good future as a Supermodel,' said Annie. And keep us in the manner we'll make sure we become accustomed to.'

'I hope she does something more constructive than that,' was David's predictable reply. Annie smiled and felt content.

They turned into the Holmebridge primary school

carpark at about the same time as a faded woman in a purple Corsa.

'Hello,' called Annie, climbing out of the car, 'You're Jessica's mam, aren't you? I'm glad the girls have made friends.' She was as well. Bethany didn't go in for making friends. It was a relief to see that side of her developing. The woman drew herself up to the full extent of her below-average height, gave Annie a dirty look, slammed her car door, and stalked off. Oh well.

As they walked across the playground in the early evening sun Annie felt the warmth on her shoulders; she straightened her dress and was glad she'd left her cardi in the car.

'Come in. Sit down will you?' Mrs Clough was the kind of teacher you could call dedicated. She wore loud colours to keep her pupils cheerful, perfume to calm them, bright red lipstick to attract their attention when she spoke, and lace-up pumps for running about after them. The soft evening sun flowed through the window, across the desk piled up with children's workbooks covered with yellow Post-Its, and lighted on her like a benediction.

Her light-brown-going-grey hair fell round her shoulders in rats' tails because Mrs Clough spent all her time thinking about her pupils and had none left over to think about herself.

'I'm glad you came.' She smiled as though she meant it. She was the sort of teacher Annie would have liked to have been had things been different. Mrs Clough, she knew, had no children of her own.

Annie and David perched on child size chairs. David looked awkward but Annie was used to it, bringing herself down to Infant level. She was constantly amazed by people who address small children through the tops of their heads. Poor little kids have enough to cope with, trying to make sense of what's going on around them, without verbiage raining down from above. No wonder they ignored it.

'I was going to have a word with you,' said Mrs Clough. 'But we don't seem to find time when you're helping out in school. I thought it better to wait for this evening to have a chat.'

Annie felt confused. Wasn't that what parents' evenings were for?

'How's Bethany doing?' she said politely.

'Well, now,' said Mrs Clough, 'let's see.' She opened a blue folder labelled 'Bethany Neill' and leafed through the pages with her busy teacher fingers.

'We're very pleased with Bethany's progress, you know. When you look back you'll see she's done very well.' She pushed the record book towards them, including them in.

'Remember what she was like when she started, and now she's well within the average range. I think you should be proud of her.'

'We are,' said Annie. 'We really are.'

'I suppose there's more room for improvement?' David's question came out more like a statement of fact.

'There's always room for improvement,' said Mrs Clough. 'But let's give her credit for what she's achieved.' She picked up a felt marker, as though she was about to do a quick presentation.

'Looking back,' she went on, 'her Reception teacher, that was Mrs Murgatroyd at the time, she left last year you know, when she had her second set of twins,' Mrs Clough looked sympathetic as though two sets of twins could be classed as an affliction, 'well, she was worried about Bethany's social skills. She was clingy with adults and took no notice of the other children. Mrs Murgatroyd put it down to insecurity.' She leafed through a couple of pages attached with a paper clip. Annie recognised her own handwriting.

'You say here that she spent two years at Playschool before she started Reception. I would have thought that would give her confidence.'

'It did,' said Annie. 'I started the Playschool for her benefit. It did do her good but she regressed when she started school. Mrs Murgatroyd asked me to stay for a bit in the mornings to give her more security.'

'Did that help? Oh, yes. The end of year report says she was settled and learning steadily. Now, let's see how well she did in Year 1.' She turned the pages to check what Miss Sykes had said.

'There, you see, she made good progress in her learning. She finished the year at the lower end of average. Miss Sykes was very pleased. But...' she paused, skim reading the report, 'there seem to have been some behaviour problems; spitting, kicking, throwing dirt... and frequent 'accidents'. Do you remember what that was about?' Her face registered friendly concern.

'She went through a bad patch,' said Annie. It all came flooding back. 'I came to see Miss Sykes. We thought it was attention seeking, you know.' Her voice faltered. The spitting, the daubing, the frequent soiling, the deliberate bedwetting, she thought they'd put it all behind them. 'But she got over it in the end.'

'Actually, there's something I wanted to mention,' said Mrs Clough, in a voice that you might adopt to tell somebody they needed a very serious operation. 'She settled down very well this year, behaviour wise, but there was an incident yesterday lunch time, involving Bethany and Jessica.'

'Oh?'

'Yes. It seems Bethany was calling Jessica a baby. She took her Telly Tubby and tried to flush it down the toilet. Bethany denied it but there were three other girls in the toilets at the time, and a lunchtime supervisor, and they all say it's true.' Mrs Clough's face arranged itself into an expression of genuine regret. David, for once, said nothing. Annie found herself sliding down an all-too-familiar slope that led from hope to disappointment. She had been down that slide too many times, each time hoping it would be the last. No wonder Jessica's mam had been funny with her.

'I suppose I'd better replace the Telly Tubby,' she said.

'That might be best,' said Mrs Clough. 'And an apology?'

'Oh yes, of course I'll apologise.'

'No, no,' said Mrs Clough. 'Not you. Bethany.'

'Do I take it, then,' said David, 'that Bethany *hasn't* apologised?'

'No,' regretted Mrs Clough. 'In fact, she still denies doing it.'

Annie was feeling a horrible sense of recognition. David was squirming like a ferret in the too-small chair.

'The most worrying thing is,' Mrs Clough paused as though drying to decide how to put it, 'before she flushed the doll in the toilet she, well, I'm afraid she weed on it.'

'Are you sure?' said David.

'As sure as we can be.' Mrs Clough lowered her gaze like somebody at a funeral.

David unfolded himself upright. 'Come on Annie. That little madam needs sorting out.' He nodded a 'thank you' to Mrs Clough and marched out of the room.

'Sorry,' said Annie, following, although she wasn't quite sure who she was sorry for and what exactly she was sorry about.

'Will you come back and see me?' Mrs Clough called after them. 'You will, won't you?'

His feet crunched across the car park like guerrilla gunfire. Annie ran to keep up, teetering in her stilettos. Her head was a whirlpool of worries. One of them surfaced. Don't let David drive. When David's feeling bloody minded he's not fit to let loose in the streets, never mind take charge of a lethal weapon like a motor car.

'David,' she yelled. He took no notice. She knew he wouldn't. To hell with it. What if she did break her heels, her ankles even? She could run on stumps if need be. She went full pelt and pasted herself to the driver's door.

'Let me drive.' She was breathing heavily because of the running. Perhaps that made her look menacing. Anyway, he unexpectedly handed over the keys.

She took a few deep breaths to calm herself down and got in the car. David sat down heavily in the passenger seat and looked straight ahead. She concentrated on the driving, keeping her thoughts at bay, until they approached the Riverside development. She found a quiet stretch of road and pulled up alongside the river.

'D'you want to get out? Or shall we talk in the car?' David didn't answer but opened his door and turned away from her, sitting half in and half out. A swarm of midges swirled above the clumpy cow parsley verge. Annie opened her window, letting the pollen-laden breeze fan her face.

'I thought she'd got over all that,' she said. She had hoped against hope that the behaviour problems were something Bethany would grow out of like other kids grow out of asthma. Now she felt sick at the stomach. What can you do? Where do you start? How can you make her understand what's right when she can't even see she's in the wrong? And it's no use making her promise not to do it again. She'll go and do something else instead.

'You didn't make a very good job of it, did you?' said David. 'Bringing her up.'

'You mean *we*.'

'It was you who insisted on staying at home with her. You could have done better than that.'

'She needs me at home. She needs security. You don't know what she remembers from before... ' Annie chanted the well-worn mantra, 'It could be *anything*.'

'What she needs is discipline and guidance. And not before time.'

'She needs *love*.'

'Love, huh. Fat lot of good that's done for her.'

Annie could have told him how hard she worked, in case he hadn't noticed. Bethany got more thought, time, love and care than a whole class full of kids. You can only do your best. She could have said he hadn't a clue what went on in his own home because he was never there. But he was in no mood to listen. There was no point in carrying on.

She closed her window and started the engine. David took the hint, swivelled his legs round into the car and slammed the door. As she drove off, she tried to keep a quiet mind but, however hard she tried not to, she heard insistent little voices telling her what she already knew and didn't want to hear.

There have been lots of incidents, haven't there? Far too many when you come to think about it. Things put down to delayed development, insecurity, emotional upheaval, any handy excuse?

'You're back early,' said Maura. She was in the kitchen poking about in the freezer. 'I haven't had my tea yet.'

'We had a very upsetting talk with Mrs Clough,' said Annie. David stalked off upstairs.

'What's up? Isn't she doing as well as you thought?' said Maura.

'You could say that.' Annie's voice quavered. Maura gave her a long look.

'Perhaps I'd better go,' she said and started gathering things into her floppy patchwork bag.

'Annie! Come here!' David bellowed from the upstairs landing. She ran, frightened. Maura followed.

'Just look at this.'

Bethany's room was next to the house bathroom. A trail of smudgy footprints led from one to the other like trodden-in dog dirt on a pavement. And shitty handprints adorned the bathroom walls like some primitive work of art. So, it was back to her muck-spreading phase. That was supposed to be in the past, left behind in the old cottage with the rest of their unwanted baggage. Annie retched with disgust. It was a desecration.

Chapter 8 - Annie

'She swore it wasn't her,' said Annie, shredding a recycled paper serviette. 'She looked me right in the eye and said she didn't know anything about it.'

'That's funny,' said Maura, blowing on her filter decaff, 'she never looks you in the eye. She's a bashful beauty, like Princess Di.' If that was meant to be sarcastic it didn't sound it.

The Community Caff was busier these days. Its recent improvements included reclaimed Formica tables, a mix and match collection of second-hand earthenware and the smell of Fair Trade coffee. Horace was in the process of rebuilding a defunct Jukebox but, in the meantime, Classic FM added a touch of class. The main improvement, though, was in the quality of the food. It was, at last, recognisable as such and made fresh every day by somebody with a certificate in hygiene. But Annie was too upset to eat any lunch. It didn't take much to put her off and now she felt as though she might never eat again.

'You're just going to have to talk to her. Make her realise that sometimes she needs to find alternative outlets for her self-expression,' Maura advised, biting into a fig roll.

'It's alright you saying that now. You were telling me to encourage her self-expression for long enough.'

'Well, she *was* withdrawn, wasn't she?'

'That's why I started the Playschool. It did her a lot of good.' She took a grudging sip of the muddy cappuccino.

'I miss it, you know. But Jo was ready to take over and I was ready to move on.'

'Helping out at school twice a week, is that what you call moving on?' Maura sounded doubtful.

'It's a step in the right direction.'

'What direction?'

'Back into teaching.'

'Right,' said Maura, helping herself to Annie's unwanted fig roll. Annie's insides weren't as sturdy as Maura's.

'Bethany's not a baby any more,' said Maura darkly. 'She's vulnerable. She needs to learn how to mix with people and look after herself. You don't want her running wild and getting in with the wrong sort.' Good advice, coming from her. You might well ask who the 'wrong sort' could possibly be. And how come she's an expert all of a sudden?

'You sound like David. He's cast me in the role of gaoler.'

'Trust him. Just like a man to go for a mechanical solution. Anything to avoid getting involved.' Maura's voice was sour.

'How's Hamid these days?' said Annie, before she had chance to think twice. 'I haven't seen much of him lately.' She immediately regretted it when Maura pulled a face and rolled her eyes. She wasn't particularly wanting half an hour of Hamid's shortfalls. Anyway, she hadn't finished with Bethany yet. 'We thought she'd be alright now she's a bit older. The teachers love her. I don't know what gets into her.'

'Everybody loves her. That's why she gets away with it.'

'How d'you mean 'gets away with it'? Gets away with what?'

'She just – you know - gets away with it.'

Yes, Annie thought. Like that time at Scarborough last summer. Bethany wanted to go on the Viking Longboat. It was a huge monster that heaved itself up on one end then swung down in a sickening drop ready to repeat the performance in the opposite direction. Annie's one and only experience of the so-called ride had been enough to put her off for several generations. Bethany was told a firm 'No' and distracted with a disgustingly gaudy candyfloss that melted in the heat. But not for long. Annie, queuing at the tea stall, looked round and found her gone. Terror grabbed at her throat and the Vortex threatened.

'Are you alright, love?' said the woman behind her. She was wearing a too-tight pink cardigan that clashed with her sunburn.

'My little girl...'

'Oh, she's alright,' said the woman. 'She's over there with her dad.' She pointed to the Viking Longboat. Bethany was sitting herself down next to a tall young man who wasn't her dad because David had gone off by himself to find the Rotunda. Annie raced over to the ride but it was already starting up. She had to wait an agonising four minutes before it stopped.

'What do you think you're doing?' She accosted the man who wasn't Bethany's dad.

'Oh, is she yours?' he said vaguely. 'She said she hadn't enough money so I gave her a pound.'

'You should know better than to give money to strange little girls!' Her fear turned to anger. 'I could have you arrested, you know.' The man looked bewildered. 'Is that what you do? Go round enticing little girls? There's a name for people like you.' Annie looked round desperately and saw they had attracted an audience. 'Can't somebody get the police?'

'What's up, love?' said the woman in the pink cardigan. 'She's alright isn't she?' The spotlight shifted to Bethany who was standing there as though butter wouldn't melt in her mouth.

'I don't know what you're on about,' said the man. 'It was her that spoke to me. I was doing her a favour.' He was beginning to sound aggrieved.

'Jason? There you are.' A young woman with a blond ponytail emerged from the crowd and attached herself to him, where evidently she belonged,

'You owe us a quid,' she told Annie. As the spotlight shifted back to the young couple, Bethany pointed her finger. 'He touched me,' she said, 'on my bum.'

'You little liar,' said the blonde ponytail. 'I was there all the time.' She turned to Annie, 'She's a little scrounger, she is. You want to teach her some manners.' She pulled Jason away, threw Annie a dirty look, and marched him off into the crowd.

'Well, I don't know. I must say,' said the pink cardigan, turning away.

Annie was left shaking and near to tears. 'Come on,' she said, 'lets go find your dad.'

They found him back at the car. Annie dragged Bethany along the north pier car park to the ice cream stand they'd parked alongside. David was sitting with both doors wide-open reading The Independent.

'Hello,' he said, 'Back already? Had enough?'

'You could say that,' said Annie, pulling the passenger seat forward to let Bethany in the back. David sighed.

'I want an ice cream,' said Bethany.

'You're not having one,' said Annie.

'I'm hungry.'

'You can't be.'

'I am.'

'For God's sake,' said David, scarred by many a such fruitless argument, 'you'd better get her one or we'll never hear the end of it.'

'She doesn't deserve one. And she's already had a candyfloss.'

'I'm hungry,' Bethany whined.

'Oh, for crying out loud. Stop that noise, will you?'

'I want an ice cream.'

'Will you get her an ice cream?'

'Alright,' said Annie, 'But I'll have you both know it's against my better judgement.'

'What better judgement?' muttered David. Annie ignored him and went off to buy a small cornet.

While Bethany was enjoying the spoils her victory, Annie told David about the incident.

Bethany denied everything at first. David, thank goodness, didn't believe her. Eventually, she conceded.

'Well, Daddy, he said I could go on the Viking Longboat with him if I let him touch me. I was frightened and he said he'd kill me if I told.' She stuffed the last of the ice cream cone in to her mouth and chewed it with evident enjoyment. David turned to Bethany, startled.

'Where did he touch you?' he asked cautiously.

'On the Viking Longboat.'

'She's lying,' said Annie.

'How do you know?'

'Believe me, I know.' Violated little girls don't brag about it whilst stuffing their greedy mouths with ice cream. Violated little girls are forced to keep secrets and feel too sick to eat.

'Well,' said David. 'I don't know what to believe. I only hope you're right.' He shook his head. 'It's your

96

fault, you know. You shouldn't let her wander off.' Of course it had been her fault. Somehow it always was.

Annie sighed and pushed the Fair Trade cappuccino away. It was a mistake. Like so many other choices in life, including ones that hadn't been hers to make.

'You're right,' she told Maura. 'She does get away with it. Have another fig roll.'

Annie rang up and made an appointment to see Mrs Clough but she waited until Bethany was in bed before she told David.

They were sitting in the dining area at the Scandinavian birch table set with blue checked placemats and white porcelain tableware. David was eating a late tea after a long and tedious departmental staff meeting. Annie poured herself a glass of South African Chardonnay.

'Funny, isn't it, having a separate space just for eating in?' Her voice sounded hollow since they hadn't got any curtains up yet. She was planning another trip to Ikea when she could get hold of the car. David didn't respond. Well he wouldn't, would he? Not with his mouth full, he'd been brought up better than that. She took advantage of that to tell him what she knew he wouldn't want to hear.

'I'm going back to see Mrs Clough tomorrow,' she said lightly. 'I want her to refer Bethany to the Educational Psychologist, to get to the bottom of whatever it is that's wrong with her.' There was a short silence as he swallowed a mouthful of pasta salad.

'There's nothing wrong with her that can't be sorted out with a bit of discipline,' he said, exasperated, like an old man airing a well-worn grievance. 'There's no need to involve the psychologist,' he said, waving a fork in her direction. 'It'll cause nothing but trouble. She'll be labelled for the rest of her life.'

Well, he's been told, Annie thought. And he can like it or lump it. She'd had enough of trying, hoping, waiting and trying again. She was exhausted with loving and getting nothing to sustain her in return. There has to be a time, doesn't there, when you stop making excuses, face up to the fact that you've bitten off more than you can chew, and get on and do something about it?

David threw his fork down with a clatter, scraped his chair back from the table regardless of the laminate flooring, and stood leaning over her.

'I'm warning you,' he growled, 'if you carry on like this, contradicting me at every turn, then we're not going to last much longer.' He drew himself up, red in the face and breathing heavily. 'It's hard enough holding your own at school these days without being undermined by a daughter with *special needs*. How do you suppose that would go down? Heh? A teacher with a daughter who has *special needs*?' he said, marching out of the room.

'It's up to you!' he threw the challenge over his shoulder as he went.

Annie heard the front door go. She sat staring at David's discarded plate.

Mrs Clough met her at the door. 'I'm glad you decided to come back Mrs Neill. I must say, I was worried. Let's go to my room, shall we?' She strode along the corridor with Annie trotting after her.

The chairs were tipped up on tables and everything tidied away, waiting for the cleaner. Everything, that is, except Mrs Clough's desk. She had enough work on there to keep her going until the caretaker shut up shop and went home. Whatever was left she would take with her to keep her company for the rest of the long summer's evening.

'What do you think about referring her to the educational psychologist?' Annie was abrupt because she wanted to say it and was afraid she might not. Mrs Clough took it in her stride.

'As a matter of fact, I was thinking about putting Bethany on the Special Needs Register. We could call in an adviser to help us deal with her behaviour. It's not that she's all that disruptive, it's just that she seems to be, well, to be honest, a bit disturbed.' She looked apologetic, as though she was sorry to have to mention anything so delicate.

'What good will that do?' said Annie. 'Doesn't she need somebody more qualified? A professional psychologist?' Or God himself, if they could only get hold of him. She was that desperate. She wondered whether to tell Mrs Clough about the shitty bathroom episode. That was disturbed behaviour in anybody's lights. But then, so was weeing on a Telly Tubby.

'We'll try first things first. See how we get on. The psychologist is run off his feet anyway. It would be weeks before he could see Bethany.'

Mrs Clough was an expert in Special Educational Needs and all kinds of unmentionable problems passed through her hands. She should know best.

'Alright,' Annie agreed, but wasn't altogether convinced.

'I'll get on to Mrs Kaur, then, shall I? She's an adviser in behaviour management.' She smiled a reassuring smile.

'Behaviour management? Isn't that just treating the symptoms? What about the root cause?' Annie felt the carpet being swept from under her feet.

'It could take forever to find that out, Mrs Neill, particularly since Bethany was going on for two when she was finally adopted.' She twiddled a pen in her fingers as though getting ready to write a report. 'It's probably very complex and even if you could understand the ins and outs of it, you would still need behaviour management to deal with it.' She paused for a moment as though to let the idea sink in.

'I see,' said Annie.

'But, you know, that often does the trick even when we don't know what's at the bottom of it.'

'Yes,' said Annie quietly. 'We'll do that. Thank you, Mrs Clough.'

Was that all? Was that what she had put her marriage on the line for? Behaviour management. She'd been hoping for something more radical. Like a miracle, for example.

The traffic was slow. It always was at teatime. The Holmebridge road wasn't up to the volume of traffic that heaved and spluttered its way through Main Street like a chronic case of irritable bowel syndrome. And parking, well you might just as well forget about it. Annie stopped the car on double yellows outside Earth and Spirit to collect Bethany, thinking she'd be in and out in no time. As it was, she walked into an atmosphere.

Maura was standing mournfully behind the counter. Bethany and a child that Annie recognised as Doe's little boy were sitting cross-legged on the floor, one either side of the door.

'What are you playing at?' said Annie.

'You might well ask,' said Maura, shaking her head.

'I *am* asking.'

'Well, don't ask me, ask her.' She sighed heavily. Annie looked at Bethany. The smirk on her face was enough to make you want to slap her.

'She hurt me,' piped up the little boy. With his big black eyes and thick mop of hair he looked like a cartoon child on a birthday card, designed to melt your heart. In fact, he was a dab hand at melting hearts.

'Tell Annie what happened,' said Maura. Bethany ignored her. She had a way of looking at you that wasn't so much looking *at* you as *through* you as though you didn't exist. It was infuriating at the best of times, making you feel not only invisible but useless as well. Like a ghost trying to haunt somebody who didn't believe it was there.

Annie suddenly realised the procession of traffic outside the shop had shuddered to a halt and overheated drivers were leaning on their horns, looking for somebody to blame. A siren wailed into hearing distance and stubbornly carried on wailing even though anybody with any nowse could see that it was impossible to move out of the way because there wasn't anywhere to move to. It dawned on Annie that the situation might have something to do with her. She ran out to see a police officer abandon his car to investigate the hold up. Even if she could start the Golf before he reached her she couldn't get away with it. There was nowhere to go.

The police officer sorted out the logjam by sheer bloody-mindedness, eventually waving Annie into the traffic stream, reclaiming his car and wailing off into the distance. Annie felt a surge of relief that she'd got away without an on the spot parking fine but at the same time there was a vague sense of panic. She was driving slowly but steadily away from the shop and from Bethany. Part of her felt like carrying on, as far away as she could possibly get.

It was a good few minutes before she found somewhere to stop, on the forecourt of Ormandroyd's hardware shop. By the time she got back, she felt like spitting feathers.

Kath was there, berating Bethany. Omar lurked behind her, his pants draped round his ankles and a look of self-satisfaction on his face.

'What's going on for God's sake?'

'Sorry, Annie,' said Maura. 'You won't like this.'

'It's sexual harassment,' said Kath. 'You can be sued for that, you know.'

'What?'

'I don't think so,' said Maura. 'Not at that age.'

'What are you on about?' Annie was feeling exhausted and thought she might faint.

'Bethany assaulted him,' said Kath, in a challenging tone.

'She grabbed his willie,' said Maura, 'and wouldn't let go. Poor little bugger.'

Whatever next? 'Why did you do that, Bethany?' said Annie.

'I don't think she knows,' said Maura, regretfully. 'I think there are some serious issues here that need sorting out.'

Annie gave Bethany a hard look. Her face was a blank mask. As far as she was concerned, they might just as well be talking to the doorpost. It was frightening. If somebody won't listen, how can you make them hear? No wonder parents resort to violence. It's sheer desperation. They have to find some way of getting through.

'Look,' said Kath, displaying Omar's genitals as evidence. His little willy did look a bit red and there might have been the beginnings of a bruise.

'What are you going to do about that, then?' Kath demanded.

'OK, Kath. Leave her to me. I'll sort her out,' said Annie, although *how* she would sort her out was anybody's guess.

'Aren't you going to get him circumcised?' said Maura, unexpectedly. 'Isn't he supposed to be Muslim?'

'I'd never thought of that,' said Kath, suddenly winded.

Annie thought it was a good time to go.

'Sorry about all that, Maura,' she said. She found herself shaking. If she didn't get out she'd fall apart and finish up scattered over the floor like half a pound of cherry lips.

She grabbed Bethany by the hand. Luckily, Bethany consented to being heaved to her feet and frogmarched through the door and up the road to Ormandroyd's.

'What was that all about?' said Annie, once they were installed in the car.

'Don't know.'

'Why did you do that to Omar?'

'I didn't.'

'What was Maura upset about, then?' Bethany shrugged her shoulders and gazed straight ahead. Annie knew she wouldn't get any more out of her. They drove home in silence.

As soon as they got in, Annie went through to the kitchen and poured herself a glass of chilled white wine. She felt the need to fortify herself for the motherly chat that, she knew in advance, would make as much impression on Bethany as prescribing vitamins for somebody who'd just died of starvation.

David was in a mood to start with. He came home late. He was behind with his departmental planning and had a pile of marking waiting. Annie could sympathise. When your time is taken up sorting out the problems of youth you don't want to come home to yet more of the same. Not when you're behind with your work. She left him to get on with it, kept Bethany out of the way, made mugs of tea to keep him going and waited until he was ready for bed before she said something.

Looking back, it could have been left for the next day. Or the day after that. But how many days can you leave these things before you just can't say them any more?

They kissed softly. Annie knew he was exhausted and didn't make demands but his kisses became more searching. He was reaching the point where his body would decide whether to carry on or call it a day. He paused for breath.

'David, I've got something to tell you.' You could say she picked her moment. But you have to pick one sometime don't you?

'Bethany,' he said, voice heavy with resignation. She wondered, briefly, what to say and what not to say. It dawned on her that she was beginning to be selective with the truth. On balance, it seemed more important to tell him about the behaviour management than the incident with Omar. Maybe that could be swept under the rug. The behaviour management couldn't. Course, it was like a red rag to a bull. He rolled off the bed, stood over her, fists clenched.

'You've done it now, haven't you? What did I tell you? She'll arrive at Oldroyd with a label round her neck. How d'you think that'll make me look?' he grabbed her arms, shaking her as though she'd done something horribly wrong. 'Don't you think I've enough to put up with? You've no idea... I don't *need* that. I don't need any more.' He sounded desperate. It wasn't like David. David was capable. Not now, though, he was losing it. He pushed her down onto the bed. Annie felt fear rise in her throat. It wasn't as if she didn't want him. It was just that she didn't want him like that. His anger scared her. He'd no need to force his knee between her thighs. She would have opened them anyway. Then he rammed into her as though it was meant to be some kind of punishment. She thought he would never come.

Afterwards, he left her on the bed and thumped downstairs. She heard doors slam, then she thought she heard sobbing but couldn't be sure.

In the morning, she found him in the kitchen getting ready for school just like any other day. She decided to let it go. Say nothing. Forget it. He'd enough on his plate. Didn't they both for God's sake?

Annie picked up the phone in the lounge. She used to like phones. They were comfort objects that you could hold onto for hours at a time if you wanted, so long as you had somebody at the other end. This one looked like something invented by NASA to facilitate interplanetary communication. You could never be quite sure who you might find on the other end.

She pressed number three, the code that told it to sort Elizabeth's number out of its memory and dial it for her, thank you very much. One of these days there would be a phone that talked back, doing away with need for somebody on the other end altogether.

'Morning, Elizabeth, how are you?'

'I'm fine, dear. How are you?' Elizabeth sounded weary. Annie thought twice about burdening her with her worries.

'I'm OK...' But her voice gave her away. Tears appeared from nowhere and once they started, they wouldn't stop. She had to mop them up on her M&S combed cotton sleeve. It was a bit before she could say anything.

'It's alright, dear. Don't worry. Whatever it is, it's not the end of the world.'

Dear Elizabeth, sensible, capable, put-things-in-proportion Elizabeth. Why couldn't she be her mother? Why was she wasted on David? David could have done without a mother with no noticeable difference to speak of.

'It's Bethany. She's uncontrollable I just don't know what to do with her. The harder I try the worse it gets. How can you love somebody if they won't let you?' she wailed. Her sleeve was sopping.

'There's nobody on this earth that doesn't need love. It's a basic need like food and drink,' soothed Elizabeth. There was nothing in her tone that might suggest 'pull yourself together'. Annie was grateful for that.

'I try to be a good mother but she won't let me. She won't let me near.'

'You are a good mother dear, believe me. I know how hard you try.'

Try but don't succeed, thought Annie.

'You *are* coming for the holidays, aren't you? It will do you a world of good. The rooms are ready and waiting. You can come as soon as you like.'

'I want to come,' said Annie, wiping her eyes with the back of her hand, 'but David won't commit himself because he's not sure if he'll be needed for appeals.'

'Then come without him,' said Elizabeth. 'It will do him good to fend for himself. He'll realise how much he takes you for granted.'

'But he's stressed out of his mind. I don't know about leaving him on his own.' She picked at the skin on her fingers. It looked like she was getting eczema.

'He's a grown man now and it's you that needs help with Bethany.'

It had never crossed Annie's mind to go without him. And, what's more, since it was Elizabeth's idea, not hers, maybe she could go without feeling guilty.

'You know what,' Elizabeth got down to making plans, 'I think Bethany's old enough to learn to ride. As a matter of fact, I have my eye on a suitable pony. What do you think to that?'

After a good old chat, things looked brighter. Annie said goodbye, went through to the downstairs cloakroom to swill her face and give her nose a good blow on the triple-ply quilted 'look after your bum' toilet paper.

James huffed and puffed over 'The Oxford Reading Tree', making the adventures of Biff and Kipper sound like the Labours of Hercules. He took deep breaths, blew his cheeks out and applied himself to the next paragraph as though instructed to translate from the Greek. Annie smiled. His pudgy face puckered up in concentration and he rubbed a grubby hand over his close-cropped head as though his brain ached. She heard James read two afternoons a week, Tuesdays and Thursdays. He tried so hard, poor lad, and never gave up. He deserved all the help he could get.

It's a strange business is literacy. Some kids take to it like ducks to water. Look at Bethany. You only had to waft a book in her direction and she could read it off pat, she practically hoovered the words off the page. For kids like James, though, it was like wading through treacle. Annie got a lot of satisfaction from teaching children like James. She found the longer she spent in school, the more she felt at home there. It gave her a sense of purpose, pride in her expertise and a little glow inside. She'd made her mind up to go back to teaching just as soon as she could get Bethany sorted out.

Sometimes it got to her. She could spend an hour with James and know that she'd done him some good. Yet, here she was giving up years of her career for Bethany and getting nothing but bother for her pains. It wasn't fair. She gave and gave of her love and got nothing in return. In her bleaker moments, she felt cheated. She hadn't got what she'd bargained for.

A Year Six girl came clomping down the corridor towards Annie's workstation. Actually, it was two tables pushed together with a couple of plastic chairs in a corner that, in summer, got so hot you could die of hyperthermia. Nevertheless, this was where Annie gave her reluctant readers their individual tuition.

The Year Six girl's name was Stephanie. She was the child who was always chosen to do things that required somebody sensible. Judging by her air of cultivated boredom, the status was going to her head.

'Mrs Neill,' she deigned to say without actually looking in Annie's direction, 'you've got an urgent phone call in the office.' With that she turned on her heel, possibly to drop in on one of the Year Six lessons.

Annie's heart thumped. It couldn't be Bethany since she was here at school. It must be David. She hustled poor little James back to his teacher and practically ran to the school office.

She passed a student teacher on the corridor, a blond young man called Mark, with a group of pupils bearing tape measures and metre rulers, evidently intent on a maths project. As she negotiated her way past them, she saw one of the girls reach out and take Mark's hand. Annie was startled enough to look back. It was Bethany, wouldn't you know? Mark smiled, she noticed, but had the good sense to remove his hand.

The school administrator raised her eyes over the top of her half-moon specs.

'Mrs Neill, there's a man on the phone for you.' She was one of those women who try their best but don't have time to exercise or have their roots touched up.

A man. Well, that narrows the field. Annie didn't know many men worth knowing. In fact, she didn't know many men of any description.

'Hello?'

'Hello, is that you? Annie?' The voice was thick and rough. She hadn't heard it for ages. Her heart thumped against her ribs.

'Dad? What's the matter?' There had to be something the matter for him to go to all the trouble of finding her. Or, come to think of it, go to any trouble at all.

'Annie, love,' his voice broke, 'It's your mam. She's gone.'

Annie was amazed. She would never have thought Madge had it in her to pack up and go. At the same time

109

she wouldn't blame anybody for leaving her dad. If he was looking for sympathy he'd come to the wrong shop.

'Really?' she said. 'When did she go?' It might have taken him a day or two to notice.

'Other day.'

'Where's she gone, d'you know?'

'You what?' he said. "Ow am I supposed to know where she's gone? She's dead in't she?'

Annie's mind reeled. How many years was it since she'd left Madge hunched over the gas fire? That's where she thought she'd be if she thought about her at all. Now all she could imagine was the empty chair.

'What was it?' she said. 'Lung cancer?' The rate Madge smoked you could lay odds on lung cancer.

'Oh, no, not that.' He sounded put out by the very suggestion. 'There was nowt wrong with her, you   know.'

'I see,' said Annie, who didn't. 'What did she die of then?'

'Poison. They think she were poisoned.'

'*Poisoned*?'

'Aye.'

'What kind of poison?' Her mind raced through the possibility of somebody lacing Madge's tea with rat poison. Her dad perhaps? But, then again, he didn't have enough about him to do anything like that. Then there was a chance that Madge had poisoned herself. Not on purpose of course, that would be asking too much, but perhaps by drinking one of her brews that had been left hanging about cultivating bacteria for God knows how long.

'Fumes,' was the answer. 'Gas fire were faulty.'

'Yes, Dad.' She remembered the smell, as permanent as the wallpaper. 'It's been faulty for years. For as long as I can remember.'

'Well, I knew nowt about it. She should've got it mended.'

What could you say? Annie decided not to get involved. She hadn't been involved for years and she wasn't going back to all that.

'Are you coming over, then?' The question seemed to expect the answer 'yes'.

'What for?'

'Funeral.'

'When?' Annie's heart sank.

'Some time next week.' That's helpful.

'When did she die?'

'Day before yesterday. Or was it t'day before that? Anyhow, she's still in hospital waiting for a post-mortem. I don't know how long t'waiting list is for post-mortems. We can't book a funeral till we know when.'

Annie didn't know whether to laugh or to cry. Only her Dad would make an urgent phone call to say her mam had died and would she come to the funeral without knowing the date and time of either occasion.

'Alright.' Why did she say that? Why couldn't she just say No? 'You'll have to let me know.' She made her way back to her workstation with her heart like a lump of lead.

To cap it all, when she got home, she found a letter from the West Yorkshire Police. It was a fine for parking illegally and causing an obstruction.

Sometimes, she thought Justice must have her scales on upside down.

When you think about it, in the scheme of things, she didn't deserve it. Those who did deserve the wrath of the

111

West Yorkshire Police, or even that of God himself, usually came out smelling of roses.

On a scale of one to ten with, say, murder at number one, rape at number two and so on, never mind terrorist activities in foreign parts, causing an obstruction must be at about number zillion. Why her?

Why not Madge for being an abusive mother? Why not Johnnie for being a careless father? Why not Uncle Ted for being a paedophile before the term was ever invented? Why not Bethany for being a little witch? Why not all those people in Africa who caused untold suffering to pot-bellied babies by grasping for ex-colonial power? Why not the so-called benevolent western powers for creating a wealth that most of the world just couldn't compete with? Why not? Who? Why should Annie, of all people, deserve it?

Chapter 9 - Maura

Maura was sick and tired of the way Hamid treated her lately. If he told her in advance, she could get Annie in to help out. But to ring up at the last minute and tell her to shut up shop, on a busy afternoon in the tourist season, to meet a contact in Leeds was asking too bloody much. She'd been asked enough lately and might not take kindly to being asked again.

Hamid had taxi-drivers on his payroll; why not send one of them? Mind you, he was given to crises of trust. Maybe he was losing the confidence of youth. Anyway, she set off to drive to Leeds railway station where she was supposed to meet Kay Leigh, a young woman with five little kids all to different fathers.

She got as far as the Armley Giratory when she realised she had time to spare. It wasn't like Maura to have time to spare. She was usually well short of it. So she made a quick decision, took the Inner Ringroad to Moortown and made her way up Fairview Drive to the pebble-dashed semi that was Hamid's home. She didn't really expect him to be there but she felt like making her presence felt.

A petite woman answered the door. She was dressed in a dainty pink shalwar-qameez that flattered her heavy pregnancy. How much better, thought Maura, than having a great belly hanging out for all to see, like they do nowadays. Her eyes were wide and expressive and her thick bouncy hair was cut short. Maura, coming from the Holmebridge background, where such things were not politically correct, had never seen anybody so beautiful.

Two little kids with big eyes and grimy faces hung around her legs.

'Hello, I'm Maura, Hamid's business partner,' she said less stridently than she was going to. 'Is he in?'

The woman smiled, showing a perfect set of teeth.

'No, I'm sorry he isn't,' she said, her voice like golden syrup.

'Can I leave a message?' Maura's brain was busy framing something suitably cutting. The beautiful woman smiled again.

'No,' she said. 'You can't leave a message. What you *can* do is tell him to go fuck himself.'

'Is that possible?' said Maura. The beautiful woman gave her a pitying look and shut the door.

Then, on top of all that, Kayleigh never turned up.

'Fuckin' bitch,' said Hamid, when Maura called him from the station. 'I don't like being let down.'

'Maybe she got arrested,' said Maura, 'along with her kids.' She even went so far as to think it might be a good thing. She was sick of this side of the business. Why carry on taking risks? It was not as though the market was all that brisk. The small-time action had moved out of Holmebridge, taken over by a dealer in Huddersfield. And, on top of that, there was the swing towards synthetic designer drugs that any self-respecting whole-food health disciple wouldn't be caught dead with. That was the trouble nowadays, too many synthetics. Folks were losing touch with nature. No wonder everybody had allergies.

'Anyway,' she declared, 'I'm having nothing more to do with it. From now on, you're on your own.' Course he wasn't on his own. He had legions of hangers-on. In fact, if anybody was on their own it was her.

Maura realised she hadn't passed on his wife's message. But then, she could always save it for later.

She was just locking up at teatime when she saw a familiar figure striding towards her, his jacket flapping like jackdaw wings.

'David,' she said.

'Oh, it's you,' he said, stopping. That, thought Maura, was an answer that would be guaranteed correct every time.

'How're you?' She asked out of habit more than anything.

'OK,' said David. Then, 'Actually, to tell the truth, I'm not. Definitely not OK.'

Now what? Maura didn't have much experience of men who were not OK. They either *were* OK or at least pretended to be.

'D'you want to come in?' she said. David hovered, briefly.

'Thanks. No, I won't. But thanks all the same.' He walked away. Maura watched him down the street and then bob into the Big Bytes Internet Café, which was what the Second Hand Seller had reinvented itself as. That's weird, she thought. Why hang out with the teenage techno nerds when he's got a computer at home?

Then she decided to call in at the Community Caff just in case Horace was there. She could do with a friendly face, not to mention a listening ear. Horace was the only person she could think of that might offer both at the same time.

***

Maura spent the evening thinking things over. Consequently, when Hamid turned up on the doorstep, she was in a state of self-righteous fury. Typical. She sees neither hide nor hair of him for weeks on end, then he has her running round like headless chicken all afternoon and, to crown it all, he turns up at ten o'clock at night expecting sex on tap, no doubt.

'What are you doing here at this time of night?' she said.

'Come to see you, in'it?' he grinned. 'Aren't you gonna let me in?' He stretched out and leaned against the doorframe in the late evening sun. She caught a whiff of Armani on the evening air.

'Matter of fact I was just going to bed.'

'That's OK by me.' He looked so self-satisfied that Maura was tempted to slap him round the face.

'Say what you've come to say, and then you'd better go,' she said, folding her arms. His face fell.

'What's up now?' he said, aggrieved.

'You know bloody well.'

'Am I supposed to be mind-reader, or what?'

'You're supposed to be my partner. That's what you're supposed to be.'

'We're not still on about that are we?'

'What we're on about is the fact that I don't see you from one month end to the next, then you turn up and expect me to drop everything, including my knickers. It's not on. Not any more. I'm not your bloody servant, you know. I deserve some respect.' She scowled.

'Aw, come on!' Hamid protested, a pained expression on his face.

'Come on, nothing. When did you last do anything for the shop? When did you last do anything for me?'

116

'Listen. I've got a fuckin' business to run, you know. Big business. And I mean mega. Shop's nothing to me now. And, you know something else? Neither are you.' He glared at her, breathing hard. 'You're not the only one to drop your knickers, you know. I don't go beggin'. I have any fuckin' bitch I want.' He balled his right hand into a fist and thumped it into his left palm. It crossed Maura's mind that he might well be capable of hitting her. She took a deep breath.

'Is that what you came to say?' she said quietly.

'No.' He paused and changed his posture, letting the tension go. He stood casually, hands in pockets and his weight on one hip. 'I came to say I'm finished with the shop. You can buy me out if you want.' It took a while for his words to filter through.

'But, why?'

'It's fuckin' losing, that's why. It was only my side of the business that kept it going.'

Maura knew in her heart of hearts that this was true. But, all the same, she'd put so much of herself into that shop over the years. It was more than a job; it was the centre of her universe.

'It's past its sell-by date, in'it? Look around, there in't no more bric-a-brac shops left. You have to specialise to survive.' Specialise to survive? A soundbite he must have picked up off T.V.

'What d'you mean? I do specialise. I'm New Age.' Maura felt put out.

'New Age nothin'. It's a mess. You want to sort yourself out. You know, your niche market and all that?' Niche market? Bloody hell, what next?

'I'm in wine bars now,' he said. 'I need my capital, in'it?'

117

'I can't afford to buy you out,' she said, turning away.

'Is that so? How much is this place worth, then?' Hamid called after her as he turned to go. 'Think about it, eh?'

Sell her house to buy him out? No way. The smarmy bastard had obviously got it all planned. Who did he think he was, using her like that?

Hamid got into the BMW and set off with a throaty roar, showing off in front of the neighbours. Maura remembered the beautiful woman he had at home and thought he did nothing to deserve her either. She shut the door and locked up for the night.

She woke up with a start. There was something wrong but she couldn't think what. Then it hit her. Hamid. The shop. She sighed, then dragged herself out of bed and down to the kitchen to fill the kettle. She looked at the clock. Twenty past six. It wasn't like her to be up so early. But, by the time the kettle boiled, the morning sun was sneaking through the kitchen window and she was beginning to feel better. At least things were out in the open. Hamid didn't give a shit. Well, that was no surprise. In fact, in a way, she would be better off without having to run round in circles just to please him.

She spooned tealeaves into the big brown pot and scalded them with boiling water before giving them a stir and leaving them to brew. What to do? With ten years to go before pension age, she'd have to get by one way or another.

There'd always been somebody to keep an eye on her, whether it was a spaced out mother, lascivious employer or temporary lover, there'd always been somebody there.

She'd always made do with whoever she could get. But who would be there for her now?

She felt suddenly lonely. It was the thought of old age that did it, living on a pension with nobody to turn to except herself. She poured the tea through a strainer into a yellow striped beaker and savoured its fragrance while she considered her options.

Even if Hamid sold the shop as a going concern, which it wasn't, but Hamid could make it look as though it was, a new owner wouldn't keep her on, not if they wanted to make a profit. If it was sold as vacant it wouldn't fetch all that much so, once Hamid recouped his investment plus interest, there'd be nothing much left for her. It looked as though she'd have to find something else. Weird, she thought, it was quite exiting to be threatened with unemployment. She could start again, do something different, but what? Specialise. Niche market. Hmmm. She sipped her tea and pondered.

Horace appeared at teatime carrying a bulky brown paper parcel. He approached the shop looking this way and that as though wary of being followed.

'What's up with you?' said Maura as he whipped through the shop doorway and shut it behind him.

'Nowt,' he said. 'Just wanted to surprise you.'

'Well,' said Maura. 'I'm surprised. Now what?' Horace put the parcel on the counter.

'Open that,' he said, with a look of self-satisfaction all over his face. Maura picked at the brown paper bit by bit, framing various replies in her mind, depending on what she might find.

'Bugger me!' was what she said in the event. Nothing

had prepared her for the sight of a parrot in a cage. Horace grinned, obviously expecting overwhelming gratitude.

'Bloody hell,' was Maura's response. Horace seemed satisfied with that.

'You like it, then?'

'Oh, yes,' said Maura convincingly. 'Er, what gave you the idea?' Bless him.

'Well, you were lonely, weren't you? I could tell. It'll be company for you.' He looked at her indulgently like an old grandad. Well, well, had it come to that? A parrot for company. She didn't know whether to laugh or to cry.

'Right then,' she said. 'Thanks. I'll have to think of a name.' Horace chuckled. Maura locked the shop door and went through to the back to boil the kettle.

'Come on,' she said. 'I'll make a brew.' Horace parked himself on one of the wooden stools and propped his elbows on the table. Maura stood hovering over the kettle.

'Sit yourself down, lass,' said Horace. 'Don't you know a watched pot never boils?'

Maura perched on a stool. She didn't know what to think. It struck her that she'd never been in charge of a living creature before. Not even a goldfish. A feeling of responsibility was sneaking up on her.

'Horry, love, how the heck do you look after a parrot?'

'Food and drink,' he said, 'same as anybody else. Plus a bit of T.L.C. They're no different to people, you see,' he went on, getting into his stride. 'We're all the same under the skin. Animals get exactly the same problems as us when the poor buggers are treat bad, neurosis, psychosis, inferiority complex, the lot. It just goes to show.' He scratched his beard thoughtfully, 'Aye,' he said, 'it just goes to show.'

'But why a parrot?' There must be thousands of pets more convenient than a parrot. And more cuddly.

'You get your money's worth with a parrot.' Horace's face spread in to a smile. 'They last a long time and, what's more, they talk back.' So, she'd be stuck with it for the rest of her life, a pet that talks back. She might just as well have kept Horace in the first place.

'But where did you get it?' The local shops weren't exactly bursting with parrots. And Horace never went as far as anywhere like Leeds. His smile widened.

'Internet,' he said, with evident satisfaction. Bloody hell, whatever next?

'Internet?' She could hardly believe it.

'Aye, Internet. Down at the Internet Caff. You should try it. You'd be surprised what you can get on the Internet.' He chuckled as he fished about in his pocket for his cigarette papers and tin of God knows what. Maura tried to digest her amazement as she went about brewing the tea. Then curiosity crept in.

'Tell me, Horry,' she said, 'd'you ever see David in there? Y'know, David Neill?'

'Schoolteacher? Oh, aye. I see him sometimes, round about teatime. You'd think he'd no home to go to.'

'Is he usually with somebody?'

'No, on his own. Though what he's doing there, I don't know. You'd think they'd have computers at school.'

He's got a computer at home, never mind at school, thought Maura but, at risk of being thought nosy, decided not to say.

Horace first took a shine to Maura when she was about nineteen, half a lifetime ago. Weird, he looked much the same then as he did now, sitting at the table smoking and ruminating as he did. He always was a thinker, was Horace. She knew him for months before she finally took him on. He crept up on her, like he was doing now, undermining her resistance with his insight and dependability. He was always there. That was the trouble. She hadn't wanted to be tied to somebody who was always there. Particularly when that somebody didn't see the need to exert himself unduly. He seemed quite happy just to exist without feeling obliged to do anything about it. Still, maybe time had proved him right. She had never known Horace to be unhappy.

'Horry, love,' she said, pouring the tea into two big mugs, 'I'm in a quandary. Do I sell my house to buy the shop, or do something completely different?'

'Now you're asking.' Horace nodded pensively for several seconds then came up with, 'What you want to do is think about the pros and cons. Aye, that's it, pros and cons.' Fat lot of help that is, thought Maura.

'But, what you have to remember,' he added sagely, 'is that once you've sold it, that's it. There's no going back.' He took a thoughtful drag of his fag and shook his head 'No, there's no going back,' he said through a cloud of exhaled smoke.

The parrot, left behind on the shop counter, started squawking.

'There, you see,' said Horace, 'he doesn't want to be left on his own. They're no different to people, you know.' He went to fetch it. 'Come on boy, come on then. Come to your dad.' Maura rolled her eyes. She could see him turning out like one of those old folks who communicates with the rest of the world through a pet. She found herself trying not to laugh.

'I know,' she called after him, 'I'll open a pet shop.' And sell the bloody parrot.

***

Maura made a half-hearted attempt to tidy the kitchen before Annie arrived. Normally she wouldn't bother tidying the kitchen even if the Queen herself sent word she was coming to tea. But there was something about Annie lately that made her feel nervous. It wasn't the same. Something had altered in their friendship and Maura couldn't help thinking that it was Annie, not her, that had changed. But it doesn't do to go dumping friends willy nilly, not if you don't want to be left high and dry in your old age. So she was making an effort.

Annie arrived about seven with a family-size pizza that smelled of garlic mushrooms and a litre bottle of organic Chardonnay. David had obviously exerted himself and got back in time to babysit.

'Hello,' she called, 'Nice evening, isn't it?' She stepped into the kitchen, put the pizza and wine on the table and started opening cupboards and drawers, looking for plates and cutlery. Granted, it was good to see her feel at home but on the other hand it was a bit of a cheek.

'Sit down,' said Maura. 'I'll see to that.'

'OK.' Annie sat in the armchair that had just been cleared in readiness. 'Well, where is it then?'

'What?'

'The parrot. The one Horace gave you.' Annie looked round as though expecting it to fly out of nowhere.

'Oh, that one,' said Maura, smiling. 'I put it upstairs out of the way. Honestly, Annie, it's a liability. It squawks and nips and stinks to high heaven. I daren't let it out. I'd never catch it.' She started hacking at the pizza and placing random lumps of it on two plates.

'Let it out!' Annie almost squawked herself. 'You can't let it out. What about the mess? The germs?'

'I know,' said Maura, pulling a face. 'The last thing I

need is that little bugger shitting all over the place.' Then she thought better of herself. 'It was nice of Horace though, wasn't it?'

'I suppose so,' said Annie, unconvinced. 'But what inspired him to do it for goodness sake?' Maura was struggling with the wine cork and finished up extracting it with her teeth.

'He says I'm lonely. But I'm damned if I want a parrot for company.' She poured the wine into two mismatching tumblers. 'Here,' she said. 'You can have the biggest. Sorry about the bits of cork.'

Annie took the wine and helped herself to pizza. Maura sat at the kitchen table and picked up a piece with her fingers. It must be something about the texture of pizza, she thought, that made it so satisfying to chew. You could say what you like but a mouthful of quorn and brown rice just didn't hold the same satisfaction. That's why she allowed herself once in a while. It wouldn't do to be virtuous all the time, would it? Annie was picking at hers as though she was scared of the calories.

'*Are* you lonely?' she said.

'Don't know, I never really thought about it. But I am worried about the future.'

Annie looked surprised. 'It's not like you to worry about the future,' she said. 'That's more like me. I worry about the future all the time. I envy you, how you take things in your stride.'

'Well, I'm getting on, you know. And I've got big decisions to make. How am I going to manage for the next ten years? I'm not used to forward planning. You're the expert at that.' She took another lump of pizza and chewed it thoughtfully. The room was filled with the tick of the kitchen clock and the parrot squawked upstairs.

'It's alright forward planning,' said Annie, 'if things work out like they're supposed to. Otherwise it's a wicked waste of your life.' Here we go, thought Maura, the Bethany litany. You'd think any woman with half a brain could bring up a child without all the wailing and gnashing of teeth that Annie went in for.

'You've got David,' she said, '*and* his income. You don't have to worry about a roof over your head and food on the table.' She swigged her wine and suddenly remembered David striding into the Internet Café.

'David hasn't a clue,' said Annie. 'He's no help at all with Bethany. As far as she's concerned, I'm on my own.'

'How're you doing with the psychologist?'

'There isn't one. He's gone off with stress. Don't think he's coming back.'

'Good thing too, if you ask me.' Maura had no truck with psychologists. All up themselves as far as she was concerned.

'What about the behaviour modification?'

'Nothing yet. I'm still waiting for an appointment.'

'Look, just think about it,' said Maura in a tired 'we've been over all this before' sort of voice. 'What is so bad about her behaviour? It really doesn't matter what she does so long as she doesn't harm anybody else. She needs her own space, you know, space to be herself. We all do.' She sighed. 'That's the trouble with parents these days. They want designer kids. They know exactly how they want them to turn out and, when they don't, they start yelling for a psychologist to give them a diagnosis.' She was just about to launch into her 'just because you have kids you needn't think they belong to you' routine when Annie burst into tears. Maura sighed. For God's sake, there's only so much you can do. The woman was as wet as a soggy dishcloth. If anybody needed a psychologist it was her.

'By the way,' ventured Maura, after several minutes of Annie's snivelling, 'I bumped into David yesterday, going into the Internet Café.' She watched Annie's expression change.

'Are you sure?' she said, 'Why would he go in there? He's on the Internet at home.'

'Really?' said Maura, innocently.

Course she felt guilty later on, after Annie had gone. She scraped the plates and realised Annie had hardly touched the pizza. Maura scoffed the remains and drank the rest of the wine.

She had no right to comment on David's comings and goings. They had trouble enough without her stirring things up. All the same, this friendship was turning out heavily one-sided. Annie hardly spent five minutes on Maura's problems whilst she'd had years of Bethany. She filled the kettle to make some tea.

Her mind went back to the parrot. She really ought to give him a name. She went upstairs to rescue him, to bring him down to join her in the kitchen.

'Nowthen, my lad,' she said. He scratched at the sandpaper on the floor of his cage and gave her a mean lob-sided stare.

She was surprised the next morning when Horace popped in the shop. Not that he didn't pop in from time to time, but never at nine o'clock in the morning. Horace could usually be relied upon to be out of circulation until lunchtime at least. But there he was, large as life, and grinning from ear to ear.

Maura didn't often look at Horace very closely. She'd

known him too long. There was that taken-for-grantedness in their relationship that saved them the trouble of bothering with themselves. But she looked at him now. His beard shone soft and clean. His teeth were scrubbed and his eyes sparkled. His sweatshirt appeared to have been recently acquainted with soap and water and he sported a fresh scarf round his neck.

'Good God,' she said.

'I've come to ask you to dinner,' he said, like somebody in a film. 'Tonight. At my place.'

'Horace, what's come over you?' This was not the Horace she knew and loved. He was up to something.

Dinner at Horace's place was something well beyond Maura's experience. Horace had never been known to cook a meal in his life so where the dinner was coming from was anybody's guess. And the last time she'd been in his back kitchen, she couldn't see across it for lines of tobacco leaves strung out to dry before he hung them in the green house to brown off. Still, he was trying.

'Well, thank you,' she said, trying not to let the doubt show. No, not doubt. What she felt was more like downright disbelief. So much so that she couldn't resist.

Later that evening, after a surprisingly nice microwaved vegetable pasta readymeal served in Horace's hardly ever used and recently dusted living room, they were enjoying a bottle of Australian Shiraz when Horace put his glass down, leaned over towards her and softly kissed her on the lips. Maura's heart skipped a beat. Must have been twenty years since they kissed like that. She was in a state of shock when he took the wineglass out of her hand, held her by the arms and pulled her to her feet.

He cupped her face with gentle hands. 'My little

treasure,' he murmured. Maura felt her eyes flood with tears. When had anybody ever said that? Not since Horace last said it all those years ago. As she held him close in gratitude she got yet another surprise, a definite bulge in his crotch.

'Horace?' she said pressing her hand over his cock. It was there alright, up and working.

'It's amazing what you can get on the Internet,' he smiled and kissed her in a way that left her breathless.

After that, she decided to call the parrot Viagra.

Chapter 10 - Elizabeth

Elizabeth decided to go for a lie down. She didn't approve of lying down as a rule. She usually left that to the kind of woman whose sole mission in life is to prevent herself from wearing out. But Elizabeth was realistic. She knew she was wearing out. Her joints told her so. She also knew there was nothing she could do about it.

So she lay down on her big double bed and pulled the patchwork quilt over her so as not to feel chilled if she nodded off. She settled her limbs into the least painful position and took deep breaths, willing herself into a state of pain free relaxation.

She closed her eyes, inhaled the smell of the lavender hedge beneath her window and listened to the trees rustling soft leaves in the breeze. She heard the busy little scuffs of small animals and the baby cries of piglets from Beale's farm. A distant tractor droned across the warm afternoon and, eventually, she fell asleep.

She dreamed about Francis. He still came to haunt her, though not as often as he used to. He was never quite there, though, it was as though he was always in the next room. She could get as far as the door then he would disappear again. Sometimes, she caught sight of his face, fleetingly, in the shadows as he went. His soft smile, his luminous eyes, she loved him body and soul; she shouldn't have let him go. But what could she do? Nothing but follow him through layers of tissue paper dreams and wake up exhausted.

Elizabeth sighed, knowing she would never find him. She had dreamed that dream so many times she knew very well how it would end.

'Thought you'd like a cuppa, Mrs Neill. Before I go on my way.' Elsie was standing by the bed with a tea tray. Three o'clock already.

'Thank you, Elsie dear.' Elizabeth struggled to raise herself on her pillow. Then Elsie put the tray down on the bed beside her.

'I'll be off now,' she said. 'Yourn got everything you need? I'll see you tomorrow, then. Bye.'

Elizabeth poured herself a cup of tea and sipped it gratefully. She tried to shake off the sadness that pressed down on her. She should have got over Francis by now. It must be thirty years or more. She made herself think of David, Annie and Bethany, the living not the dead.

To tell the truth, Elizabeth didn't like the sound of what she was hearing in her recent phone calls. She was never one to pry but she was adept at reading between lines.

David was her one and only beloved son but even the fondest of mothers couldn't blind themselves to the fact that he was hardly ever there. And, as she well knew, an absent father was not much better than no father at all.

Annie, poor thing, was struggling. What could one expect of a girl from her background? But then she had done very well for herself, considering. She deserved better than to be left holding the baby. She deserved a husband.

And Bethany. Well. What was she supposed to make of Bethany? From the sound of it, she was getting out of hand. There were problems of course, over the years, but that wasn't unusual. Most children went through messy stages, playing with dirt and so on. And the frequent squabbles could be said to be a matter of testing her boundaries. But her recent behaviour was quite bizarre. Annie said she disappeared for an hour at a time then, when she was on the point of calling the police, came back laughing at her. Then there was the stealing that she always denied; things constantly turning up in her room, other children's toys, Annie's make-up, felt markers from school, even parcels of food wrapped in kitchen paper. She was fast becoming a kleptomaniac by the sound of it.

It was a mystery. Bethany had a good home, love and care, endless time and patience, good schooling and a healthy proportion of the things she wanted. What was wrong? What was it, exactly, that was wrong?

Elizabeth didn't have much experience of bringing up children. Only David. But he was easy enough. He usually did as he was told and didn't have enough imagination to get into trouble. What she did have was a lifetime's experience of raising horses and dogs. It was purely and simply a matter of consistency. Carrot and stick and a firm set of ground rules. Elizabeth had her doubts about Annie. Too much carrot? Not enough stick? And what were the ground rules? Of course, she couldn't blame Annie altogether. It was David, after all, who left her to it.

Elizabeth decided the time had come for her to do something. She found herself looking forward to the summer holidays with a newfound sense of purpose.

Chapter 11 – Annie

Annie arrived in good time, and on her own. David and Bethany didn't want to take time off school. Anyway, she didn't want to drag them into anything she might regret.

MacNess's funeral parlour was situated on Primrose Hill, off the Oldham Road. The street crawled up the steep valley side and, if you carried on far enough, you might well, at this time of year, find primroses growing wild on patches of land deserted for decades amongst the crumbling relics of mill workers' cottages.

As it was, the funeral parlour had established itself at the bottom of the hill nice and convenient for comings and goings, particularly in the days of horse-drawn hearses when they had to give the horses a certain amount of consideration.

She parked the car in the very small carpark; two more cars and the hearse wouldn't get out. Then she made her way upstairs to the stuffy waiting room, furnished in the Post War Utility style with a vintage upright Hoover standing in the corner. Next to that was a foisty viewing chapel where bodies were laid out on display, along with arrangements of plastic chrysanthemums and a recording of 'Abide With Me' droning in the background. The ground floor of the building, what used to be stables, was taken up by the garage, which doubled as an office.

At five minutes to eleven, Mr MacNess and his assistant laboured upstairs to greet the mourners. They were both well beyond retirement age but determined to carry on the MacNess tradition as long as they lived and could manage to breathe.

'Good morning,' intoned Mr MacNess to the assembled mourners. There were three of them, Annie, her dad, and Frank Dyson, one of her dad's mates. They muttered a subdued reply.

'If you would care to come this way,' said Mr MacNess, his arm outstretched, indicating the way back down the stairs he'd only just succeeded in climbing up.

A sorry procession, thought Annie; two wheezy old men in funerary garb, followed by Annie's dad in his shabby double breasted suit, Frank Dyson in his all-weather tweed jacket and flat cap, and Annie, wearing a hypocritical black trouser suit. Her dad hadn't seen the need for a funeral car so Annie found herself following the hearse in the Golf with her dad beside her and Frank Dyson in the back. Her dad lit a Woodbine and passed one to Frank. They smoked in silence, tut-tutting from time to time, as befit the occasion.

They didn't exactly crawl along, like funerals used to do in the days when the neighbours closed their curtains as a mark of respect and peeped through them so as not to miss anything. But they could travel at a slow enough pace just by keeping up with the traffic. A casual passer-by would be hard put to say what was a funeral and what was a regular commuter on a generous expense account. Not like back then. Funerals were important then. You could talk about the deceased for weeks, reworking their lives to make a passable story. One that was fit to remember them by. Now they hardly got a passing mention.

'You know,' said Annie's dad. 'I think it's going to rain.'

***

133

Weather forecasting came readily to folk in Annie's street, she remembered. Weather prophets were like pigeon fanciers; they had a genetically inbred ability. The whole of Annie's childhood was hemmed in with qualifying phrases like, 'Look at them clouds.' 'Mark my words...' 'Bet you any money...' Then the first few inevitable drops would be greeted with cries of 'It's spitting! It's spitting! Get your washing in!'

So, whenever Annie had broached the great outdoors she'd been laden down with a gabardine mac and an umbrella that she usually left on the bus. It was bad enough carting her bulging school bag to and fro, giving her scoliosis, without any additional paraphernalia. The neighbouring women made do with rainmates concertinaed over their headscarves but she wouldn't be seen dead in one of those. You might as well cover your head with a Co-op carrier bag.

Course she worked it out eventually. It was always going to rain, wasn't it, whatever anybody said? It was only a matter of when. And, so what? You could only get wet.

They arrived at the crematorium in good time for their eleven-thirty slot. Annie discovered you have thirty-minute slots at the crematorium. A bit tight, wasn't it? What if you were held up by road works?

'Sorry Mrs Neill, we can't do your mother today. Nowthen, how are you fixed for next Tuesday? Let me see, we have a window at nine thirty.'

Thankfully that didn't happen. They were ushered through into the chapel dead on time. The oak-effect coffin, with gilt-effect handles, was already in place on its pedestal as they took their seats in the front row. The silence was heavy. Annie looked around admiring the restrained décor and little stained glass window that caught the light. She felt peaceful in a way that she couldn't remember feeling before, a feeling you could say was next to relief.

Mr MacNess approached her dad and whispered discreetly. Her dad shook his head. What now? Mr MacNess scuttled out breathing hard. A minute later, a priest came striding down the aisle, adjusting his cassock as he walked. The silence lasted as long as it took him to climb into the pulpit, take a deep breath and gather his wits.

'Dear friends,' he intoned, with every indication of sincerity. 'We are here before God to remember May Smith, a dear wife, mother and good friend, to commend her into God's loving care and to comfort one another in our grief. We do this in the hope that is ours through the death and resurrection of our Lord Jesus Christ.' He paused to draw breath before launching himself into John chapter eleven, verses twenty-six and twenty-seven.

'Who's May Smith?' whispered Frank but was ignored.

'Jesus said, I am the resurrection, and I am the life; he who believes in me, though he die, yet shall he live, and whoever lives and believes in me shall never die.'

Annie was busy trying to figure out how that worked when she happened to glance at her dad. His expression was uncharacteristically serene. Frank was picking his nails.

The priest turned towards the organ. As there was nobody there to play it he took a deep breath, opened his mouth and ploughed on. With no knowledge of the deceased whatsoever, he was obviously obliged to ad lib to the best of his ability.

'Mavis was a kind-hearted woman who enriched the lives of all who came into contact with her.' Well, whoever he was talking about, you could bet your life it wasn't Madge.

'...a remarkable woman indeed, busy with life, always on the go, sewing and knitting, cooking and baking, washing and cleaning. A kind word for everybody. She will be sorely missed.' He was starting to sweat and ran his hand over his brow and thinning hair. Then he took a sip from a glass of water left over from somebody else's eulogy. Having exhausted his knowledge of womanly virtues he resorted to prayer.

'Let us join together in prayer for the soul of our dear departed friend.'

Annie had a hard time keeping her face straight.

'Merciful Father, hear our prayer and comfort us in our distress and strengthen our faith that Mavis, and all who have died in the love of Christ will share his resurrection. Through Jesus Christ our Lord, who reigns with you and the Holy Spirit, One God now and forever. Amen.'

Annie fervently hoped Madge would keep well out of the way of any resurrection planned for the foreseeable future. The priest made the sign of the cross in the air and bowed his head. The mourners took it that the service had ended. Probably the shortest in local history. But why was the coffin was still sitting there, large as life? Surely that should have gone somewhere? Trundled off to the Everafter? Nobody moved.

Mr MacNess broke the tension. Striding to the front of the chapel, he indicated the coffin with a theatrical flourish and invited the congregation to say their farewells on the way out. The congregation stood and started to shuffle towards the exit. Annie's dad stopped in front of the coffin and shook his head in a 'well, fancy that,' sort of gesture. Frank Dyson took his cap off and held it for a moment over the region of his heart. Annie felt a bubble of hysteria bursting in her throat. Not the way to behave at a funeral. Anyway, she'd said her farewells years ago.

The priest shook hands with them at the door and Annie thanked him politely.

'It was a pleasure,' he said. 'I'm glad I could help out. Mr MacNess nobbled me just in time. Another minute and I would have been on my way home.'

'So you were here for the previous funeral?' said Annie.

'And the one before that. In fact, I've been here all morning.' So Annie's dad wasn't the only one who forgot to book a priest.

It was kind of him, she said, and felt grateful. More than you could say for her dad who was heading for the car, intent on the Weavers Arms no doubt.

Annie's dad slotted into his usual pitch at the bar next to Frank Dyson. Although several of their mates appeared, a respectful space was left where Uncle Ted and Billy Greenwood belonged. Not that they were likely to turn up to occupy it. Uncle Ted disappeared years ago and Billy Greenwood dropped dead with a heart attack in that very spot whilst celebrating his sixtieth birthday.

'Now then, Johnnie,' said Jack Bickerstaff, a hairy man with a chest like a barrel.

'Johnnie,' nodded Walter Shaw, his scrawny mate.

Two other men who Annie also recognised as fellow ex-millworkers nodded a solemn greeting. They were soon joined by Eddie Rothary and Don Morgan.

The barman pulled pints of Webster's best bitter with the clinical concentration of a brain surgeon. Hardly a drop of the precious stuff was spilled as he handed them over the crowded bar. Annie was offered a half but she could hardly bring herself to drink it.

'It were a good do,' said Frank Dyson, breaking the ice.

'Oh, aye,' said Johnnie, 'a good send off.'

'Respectful, like,' said Frank.

'Aye.' Johnnie nodded.

The other men shuffled their feet and murmured their condolences.

'Aye,' said Johnnie with a sigh, 'we did her proud. She'd 'ave been pleased.'

It crossed Annie's mind that it would have been a better 'do' altogether if the funeral had been held in the pub.

'What'll you do now, Johnnie?' said Jack Bickerstaff, as though Madge's passing would make much difference.

'Carry on. You know. Just carry on.'

Annie didn't know whether to laugh or to cry. Watching her dad there where he belonged, jawing with his mates, she felt the pressure of passing years bearing down on him. It seemed like yesterday when she brought David home for the first time and Johnnie took him out for a drink. About nine o'clock in the evening, Madge started clutching her chest and moaning. Annie recognised that as a cue to fetch her dad before things got much worse. She ran across to the Weavers Arms and stood at the door peering through an atmosphere of smoke and sweat. Women weren't encouraged in the taproom in those days.

David was sitting in the far corner looking detached

and middle class. He used to wear his body like his clothes, slender and close fitting, you could hardly tell where one turned into the other. You couldn't imagine him getting undressed; he might disappear altogether.

He was obviously not putting himself out to make conversation, just drinking his beer, not in great mouthfuls like the other men, but meted out in well-moderated sips. He could probably make a pint last all night. There was a moment when she wondered who he was.

Johnnie and Ted slouched at the bar in their usual places between Billy Greenwood and Frank Dyson, their drinking arm holding their pints aloft and the other arm propping them up. You could almost see dark wood grooves they'd worn with their elbows. Unlike David, Johnnie and Ted didn't fit their clothes. The ex-army shirts and rough overalls didn't do justice to their hard tempered bodies. Decades of physical labour had shaped them until their backs were broad as an ox's and their fists like muttons. They didn't lurk in corners, not them, they were in the thick of things, talking and laughing with their mates. That's what brought them together.

Frank Dyson noticed Annie in the doorway. He nudged Johnnie and jerked his head in her direction. They looked round and the laughter died away.

'What's up, love?'

Annie looked at Johnnie, then across to David, her eyes measuring the distance between them. Is that what you call going out for a drink? They might as well be on different planets.

'It's Mam,' she said. 'You'd better come.' Frank and Billy nodded knowingly, tut-tutted in sympathy and applied themselves to their beer. Johnnie gulped down the rest of his pint and thumped the glass down on the bar. As he walked to the door, his shoulders dropped and he suddenly looked smaller. David followed, but only at a distance.

Seeing her dad now, with his mates, Annie felt the tears behind her eyes. It would be alright to cry. In fact, it was the right thing to do. Somebody was supposed to cry at a funeral and you couldn't expect Johnnie to do it, not in a public house. But she wasn't really sure what she was crying about. Something about what he used to be and what he might have been, given the chance. The usual feelings she had for him, the impatience and frustration, were softening with a grudging respect and maybe even a bit of sympathy.

Life had passed them by, men like Johnnie. The skills in his fingers and his sheer brute strength, everything he used to take a pride in, didn't matter now. The textile industry had died and his pride along with it. Perhaps David had an inkling, when he sat there all superior in the corner of the bar, that he would succeed in a future where men like Johnnie would finish up on the scrap heap.

And what about her? What was left for her? The life she'd wanted out there in the suburbs didn't seem to exist any more, if it ever did. Everything was in a state of flux. It was like wading through treacle. How was the ordinary person supposed to cope with that?

'Annie, love,' said her dad, turning towards her. 'Why don't you go across to the 'ouse and see if there's owt you want?' Was he being kind or did he just want her out of the way?

'I'll be over in a bit,' he said. Maybe he wanted to talk.

'Alright, Dad.'

***

The sideboard was a Victorian hand-me-down that Madge had refused to part with. Parting with anything never came easy to Madge, you'd think she was sacrificing her last ounce of flesh. So there it stayed, the most unlikely piece of kitchen furniture in Huddersfield, its vast mahogany flanks filling half the kitchen and its sturdy mirror surround propping up the ceiling with its flamboyant curves. There was a kind of holy aura about it, probably on account of its size. It had its uses, mind. It had the only mirror in the house. You could at least make sure you were half-decent before you went out into the street.

Annie peered into the black spotted expanse and wondered what that mirror might have seen in its time.

There was a vague memory at the back of her mind, one that she hadn't entertained until now. The accommodating surface of the sideboard had once held a child's cardboard coffin. Its reflection in the mirror made you see it twice. Annie, as a little girl, was scared of it. She wouldn't believe it held her little brother and refused to look at all.

Another memory that surfaced was that of Uncle Ted, his huge looming image possessing most of the mirror while hers was a frightened little face in the corner. For some reason he was much more scary in reflection than he was in real life; the threat of what he might do being worse than what he actually did.

Then there was Johnnie on his way out, abandoning his responsibilities, pausing to give himself an admiring glance or a cheeky grin.

On the whole, she'd rather remember the sideboard covered with its usual array of dusty items such as syrup of figs, odd buttons and pens that had run out of ink.

Its drawers were party to a lifetime of correspondence of one sort or another. Anything really important, such as the TV licence, was kept there so they would know where to find it. The cupboards stored the eternal blue striped crockery, not that there was much left. And they stored the family history, including every photograph of every relative never seen in the flesh. Annie wasn't allowed to rummage in the sideboard. She might mix up important papers and then where would they be? She went rummaging now though. Not that she had anything particular in mind. She was just looking for something, anything, that would make some kind of sense.

Eventually she found a small black and white photo, a deep dark memory from way back, as though from another life. A child was toddling through Shelley Woods, hands held out like lollipops, his hair a halo of light, and he was laughing.

'When I was but a little tiny boy, with a heigh-ho, heigh-ho, the wi-ind and the rain.'

Where did that song come from? She must have learnt it at school. It always came to mind when she thought about her baby brother. Not that she thought about him all that much. The baby hardly impressed his little self on Annie's young life. Maybe she was too young to take much notice. At the time he seemed more like one of her mam's accessories than anything else, like her mock crocodile handbag. As it happened he didn't last long, poor little thing. He caught pneumonia and died. You'd have thought they could have done something for him by the sixties. Maybe medical progress hadn't caught up with Huddersfield yet. It was probably too far north. Anyway, he died and that was that. Edward, his name was. No doubt shortened to Eddie. Looking back, it must have been about then when her mam took to nursing the gas fire.

Was that where the longing came from, then? The

longing for a child. Was it the loss of her brother or was it something even more basic than that?

'Hello, love.' Her dad staggered through the kitchen door. 'Found anything you want?'

'Yes,' she said.

'Well, come and sit down, then. It's been a queer sort of a day.' He walked unsteadily through to the back room and lowered himself into a fireside chair. The other chair was Madge's. She'd sat in it for so long that the boundary between her and the chair wasn't altogether clear. Significant amounts of Madge's organic material could still be there, integrated into the uncut moquette. Annie couldn't bring herself to sit on it so she perched on the pouffe instead.

Johnnie fished in his pocket and found a cigarette. As he lit up, Annie noticed his hair stained round the edges with decades of nicotine, and a dead cigarette tucked behind one ear. She didn't mention it. He'd probably find it later.

'I'm alright lass, don't you go worrying about me.' Annie hadn't planned to. She had enough to worry about. But surely he was worth a passing thought? There must have been a time, right at the beginning, when they were happy?

'Will you be stopping here, Dad?'

'Stoppin' 'ere? Good God, no. I'm off on my travels soon as this lot's over and done with.' He paused for another drag. 'I've made a bit. Now I'm off to spend it. Can't take the bugger with you.'

'Made a bit?' the words welled up Annie's throat like vomit. 'You haven't worked in twenty years, Dad. You spent your dole at the Weavers Arms. What was left for Mam, or me for that matter?' Had it all been for nothing, the too-small clothes, the scrappy food, the state of the house? When he'd 'made a bit'? She noticed tears gathering in the crinkles at the corners of his eyes. She sighed, her

143

anger seeping into the furnishings leaving a bitter resignation in its place.

He took another drag of his cigarette and went on. Annie could see it wasn't easy. 'I gave 'er money. I gave 'er plenty. It's just... well, she were wrong in 'er 'ead.'

It was a relief to hear him say that. As though an eminent doctor had just made a diagnosis that relieved her of blame forever. Madge was wrong in her head. It wasn't just Annie who thought so. Other people did as well.

He wiped his eyes with the back of his hand. 'We 'ad a taproom syndicate, you know, invested the winnings. I gave her plenty. But she couldn't manage, you see. It were losing her little lad that did it.' Time hung heavy for a minute or two and the silence was loud in her ears.

'But what about me? She still had me,' she said in a little girl voice.

There was no answer to that.

'It's time I went. I've got some jobs to do before I pick Bethany up from school.'

'Eh, lass, don't go.'

'I have to,' then something, she wasn't sure what, made her say 'don't worry, Dad, I'll come and see you soon.'

Now, for God's sake, why did she say that?

Heavy raindrops began to fall as she stepped out into the street and she breathed in that fresh cleansing smell of rain on hot pavement.

'Brilliant! At last, someone thinks these kids are worth investing in.' David was in a better mood. He'd managed to get a grant to update the school's science equipment. Annie had every sympathy. She wanted the best for them all, including Bethany. She congratulated David on his

144

successful bid and praised his plans for improving the department.

They drank a bottle of Australian Merlot with their braised steak and broccoli and, after Bethany went to bed, decided to go upstairs for an early night.

David snuggled up to Annie, pleased with himself. She was pleased for him and tried to show it. She cradled him in her arms, breathing his special David smell and feeling the familiar love. David was moving in with urgent kisses and she was glad to respond. He drew back for a moment and said 'Sorry'. Whatever it was, it didn't matter. He hadn't asked about the funeral. That didn't matter either. What mattered now was that they should make it up. Whatever 'it' was.

His kissing became more searching. He reached his tongue deep into her mouth and moved his belly hard against hers. His hands grasped her breasts, sending surges of want coursing through her insides. On a sudden whim, she rolled over him and sat herself on top. It wasn't often she did that. But now, feeling him hard inside her, she felt in control. She bore down on him, again and again, making him push up against her, groaning. She'd never felt such heady power before. It was like the feeling she got when she dreamed she was flying. And, if she was honest with herself, in her omnipotence, there was a perverse feeling of paying back. Paying back her dad and Uncle Ted, and David.

Chapter 12 - Annie

Jasbinder Kaur was a slender young woman under a mass of dense black hair. She looked as though she might go under with the weight of it. Her piercing eyes, laden with heavy-handed mascara, were compelling. A good thing too, when you think about it, in her job.

'Hello, Mrs Neill,' she said, striding towards her, hand outstretched. 'Sit down, will you?' She indicated Mrs Clough's vacant armchair whist she perched her neat backside on a child size plastic chair.

'As you know, Mrs Clough referred Bethany to me,' she said. 'I'd like you to tell me about her.' She smiled a stunning smile.

What could she say? Where to even begin? Have we got all night?

'It's difficult. There's just so much...' Her voice trembled. 'I feel so useless... a failure... giving my life all these years... going through all that. And she's as bad as ever. If only it wasn't so near the end of term.' There she was in tears again. She'd have to get a grip. You can't go grizzling to everybody, can you? They just get fed up in the end.

'Take your time,' said Jasbinder, still smiling. 'Take all the time you need.' She opened her briefcase and took out a packet of Kleenex.

'I do love her, you know,' sobbed Annie, 'I do try. But it's hopeless trying to bring up a child who doesn't give a shit.'

***

146

'Look Bethany, I've brought you a game. It's called Consequences.' Bethany, slouching at the dining table, looked unimpressed.

Annie was feeding her before David came in, whenever that might be. There are times when you have to be pragmatic. For one thing, she wanted to avoid David's nattering about Bethany's greedy manners and, for another thing, she wanted to pin her down and food was the best way to do it. She piled a second helping of Spaghetti Bolognaise onto Bethany's plate, poured herself a small Semillon Chardonnay and carried on.

'There's no choice about this game, Bethany. We both play it. And even if you don't play fair, I will.' Bethany slurped and chewed but looked as though she was listening. Annie fished in her bag and brought out two plastic containers and a bag of marbles.

'It's easy,' said Annie.' You see this pot has a smiley face. Well, whenever you do something good we put a marble in it. When the pot's full, you can choose a treat. Whatever you like up to ten pounds to start with. OK?' Bethany's eyes narrowed as she continued chewing.

'This pot,' Annie went on, 'has a glum face. If you do something bad we put a marble in it. If that pot gets full, you don't get any pocket money. It's as easy as that.' Bethany paused to run her tongue round her mouth, then carefully loaded another forkful of spaghetti.

'So what we have to talk about, you and me, are what are good things to do, like cooperating with your mam and dad, sharing your things and taking care of your friends, and what are bad things you're not going to do to other people, like being rude or hurting them. Then you can start thinking about your first treat.' Bethany chewed impassively.

147

'We're going to play this game, you know. There's no choice. You need to think about it.' Annie felt more in control than she had in a long time, now that she had a strategy to work with.

'When you've finished your tea, you can decide what you can do to earn your treat.' After that, she thought she deserved her glass topping up.

She was pleasantly surprised when Bethany, having scoffed the last of her meal, took a notepad and pen into the lounge and for probably the first time in her life started grappling with the notion of good and evil; a big enough job for anybody but Bethany had it sorted in five minutes flat. Annie's surprise soon evaporated when she saw the results. Maths, PE and going to bed were on the bad list, whilst good things to do included eating ice cream, watching TV, painting pictures and killing. Annie's heart lurched.

'What do you mean? Killing?'

'Just pretend,' Bethany laughed. Annie knew that Bethany's dolls were dismembered more often than not but they were occasionally resurrected whole. Was that what it was about? Pretend killing? She shivered, remembering an incident on Bethany's fifth birthday when she sliced through her new doll's head with a vegetable knife. Then Annie realised that what she was seeing told her what she already knew. To Bethany, 'good' and 'bad' simply meant what *she* did or didn't want to do, never mind anybody else. She had no idea of right and wrong.

Annie poured herself another glass of wine wondering, not for the first time, what to do.

In the end she had an early night. Bethany was lounging in her bedroom, watching University Challenge.

David was still not back. It got to nine o'clock and there was no wine left in the bottle. The only thing she could think of to do was to go to bed.

The morning sun shone bright and Annie reluctantly opened one eye to squint at the bedside clock. Half past seven.

'Oh my God! We've overslept.' She turned to David to give him a shake but the mound of duvet on his side of the bed covered nothing but his empty pyjamas. Funny. Had he got up without waking her? Or, she sat bolt upright as a horrible thought struck her at exactly the same moment as a sledgehammer headache, had he been out all night?

She called Bethany and made her way downstairs to find the Panadol she kept in a kitchen cupboard. She hesitated for a moment then decided to take three. As she gulped them down she heard a noise like a steam train coming from the lounge, the familiar sound of David snoring. Sure enough, there he was, fully dressed and flaked out on the unstructured beige sofa.

'David.' She shook his shoulder. He stirred but didn't wake. 'David!' She poked him in the ribs. 'David, wake up. You'll be late.'

'What?' he said bleary eyed.

'It's gone half past seven. You'd better get moving.' David sat up and rubbed his eyes, gradually coming to.

'I must have dropped off,' he said, answering the question that hung between them. 'I sat down for a minute when I came in and that's the last I remember.'

'You must have been tired,' she said. 'What time did you come in?'

'About eleven, I think.' Annie didn't ask what he was

doing out until eleven. She knew full well that Oldroyd School wouldn't be open so late. The Internet Café might well be but she didn't have time to go into all that. It would have to wait for later. Now she had all on to get them up and fed and off to school.

'I'll take you to school if you like. Then I can have the car. I ought to go and see how my dad's getting on.'

'OK.'

'You'd better get in the shower,' she said, hurriedly filling the kettle. 'I'll get Bethany moving and make some toast.'

Annie didn't have time to think until later when, wearing a cardi over her nightdress, she'd dropped off both David and Bethany in the nick of time.

Going home, the air was light and fresh. She decided to brew a pot of tea instead of going back to bed. After the third cup she phoned Maura and asked her to meet for lunch to talk things over.

'I don't know,' said Maura, 'I'm quite busy. I don't know if I'll have time for lunch today.'

'You can't go without lunch,' said Annie. 'Why should you? Just to line Hamid's pocket?' That was enough to make Maura rise to the bait.

'You're absolutely right, the ungrateful bugger.'

'Right, then. Where? The Internet Café?' Now why had she said that?

'You're bloody joking. All those dirty old men and spotty youths who ought to be at school. No, we'll go to the Community Caff. We're practically part of the furniture.'

You speak for yourself, thought Annie. 'Alright, then,' she said. 'See you there. About one o'clock?'

***

Course, it was busier than ever. The Community Caff that had been so lovingly nurtured as an alternative space for those who embraced an alternative lifestyle, or for those who wanted cheap food and didn't care much what they ate, was becoming an ideological monster. It was making money. And that was down to the tourists.

Tourists always want a cup of tea. You can't call it an outing if you haven't had a cup of tea. So there they were, a constant stream of middle-aged ladies wanting toasted teacake and a pot of tea for two. At the same time, there was a growing interest from folk who came out of curiosity. Holmebridge had recently won the 'Crazy Cultural Capital' competition on Radio Yorkshire and people were dropping in from all over the place to admire the retro Formica furnishings and the renovated Juke Box. It was also very convenient for the Back Door Theatre that was known all over West Yorkshire for staging experimental works by the Black Dyke lesbian arts group.

Annie and Maura made their way into the crowded space. Luckily Horace was there so he could give his seat up and bring another one out from the back.

'It's hot in here,' said Annie, wafting a serviette.

'Yeah,' said Maura, 'all these sweaty bodies. It's the price of success.' She picked up one of the menus Horace produced on his computer. It was decorated with flying veggie burgers and printed in three different colours. 'I'll have a mozzarella, tomato and basil roll,' she said. 'Wholegrain.'

'Right you are,' said Horace, happy to do the honours even though they now employed a waitress. Janie was stick thin which came in handy for squeezing between the tables. In fact, you could say it was an essential qualification for the job, except that would be discriminatory against people with ordinary bodies.

'I'll have the same,' said Annie, but regretted it when it arrived balanced on Janie's twig-like arm. 'Wouldn't it be better cooked?' she said, poking at the soggy lump of mozzarella with her fork.

'You can't cook that stuff,' said Janie scornfully. 'It turns into rubber bands.'

Annie applied herself to dissecting the roll and eating it with a knife and fork in manageable quantities.

'So,' said Maura, chewing energetically, 'how's things?' Annie was at a loss what to say. Why had they come here? You can't talk in a crowded café. It's like displaying your dirty washing in public.

'What I'm having to deal with is that Bethany can't tell the difference between right and wrong,' she said in a low confidential tone, mouthing the words as though Maura was deaf. 'She doesn't even understand what the words mean. I'm really worried about her. You know... the future. How's she going to manage... as a teenager? She could get herself into all sorts of bother. D'you think there's anything can be done?'

'There's lots of folk don't know the difference between right and wrong,' boomed Maura, causing several ladies to direct their gaze towards her. 'You have to reason with them. You know, help them to negotiate their needs against other people's, look for a win-win situation, you know?' It all sounded very profound.

'How?'

'Send her to me, I'll have a go at her,' said Maura. 'Let her stay over on Saturday then you and David can have a dirty weekend. You look like you could do with a break.' That sounded like a good idea. The two ladies on the next table seemed to think so as well. They adjusted the direction of their gaze from Maura to Annie and smiled at her in unison.

'Horace, love,' yelled Maura, and beckoned him over,

'we're having company this weekend. Bethany.' Horace's expression remained admirably neutral.

Bethany was looking pleased with herself when she emerged into the afternoon sunshine with her socks round her ankles and her cardigan and school bag slung over one shoulder. Annie's heart leapt with pleasure.

'Hello,' she said. 'What have you got there?' Bethany was holding a green backed exercise book as though it was the Holy Grail.

'My maths.' She looked smug.

'Why are you taking your maths book home?'

'Because.'

'Because what?'

'Just because.'

'Is it for homework?'

'No. My homework's in my school bag where it belongs,' she said with exaggerated patience.

Then what's all this about for goodness sake? Annie felt like saying but didn't rise to the bait. Instead, she turned and started walking towards the car park. The tactic worked.

'I got three silver stars today,' Bethany piped up, 'and an 'excellent' in my book. Mrs Clough told me to show you.' Annie stopped, surprised. 'Excellent' for maths? Bethany hated maths. Bethany had *always* hated maths.

'Well done,' said Annie, trying not to sound too amazed. 'What did you do to earn that?'

'I finished first *and* got all my sums right.'

'Did you?'

'Yes,' she said.

'How did you manage to do it all by yourself?'

'I just decided to.' Just decided to... Annie's mind

reeled. Was it purely and simply a matter of just deciding to? Had the conniving little monkey been holding out on them all this time? She took a deep breath.

'Wait till you tell your dad.' She could just imagine his reaction:

Good Lord, it'll be nuclear physics next. And Bethany wangled three marbles in the smiley pot, one for each silver star.

'Where were you last night?' Annie tried to keep her voice even. They were getting read for bed. It was nearly ten o'clock and still light but they were both well past it.

'With John.' John was a colleague from the science department. 'We got working on some Internet stuff round at his flat after school. I didn't realise how late it was.' He sat on the bed to take his socks off.

Why didn't you phone? She didn't ask out loud. She already knew the answer. It hadn't crossed his mind. Anyway, she didn't want to sound like a carping wife.

'Did you see your dad?' said David, heading for the en-suite in his underpants. At least he was making the effort to show an interest.

'No. I didn't manage to get. I might go on Saturday though. Bethany's going to Maura's for the weekend.' David didn't answer. She pulled her outsize cotton T-shirt over her head and got into bed. She wormed right down under the summer weight duvet and didn't bother trying to stay awake for him.

Saturday was dull in every sense of the word. You could put up with dull weather if you had good company and you could put up with dull company if you were doing something interesting. But, as it was, Annie found herself driving through a determined drizzle along the Oldham Road on her way to see her dad in the line of daughterly duty. Guilt, you might call it. How come parents always make you feel guilty even though, whatever it is, it's not your fault?

She found her dad in the kitchen, rummaging through the contents of the sideboard.

'Thank God you've turned up,' he said. 'This lot's beyond me.' He gestured hopelessly towards piles of papers and envelopes that looked as though they'd been lurking there since the turn of the century.

'Never mind, Dad,' I'll help you get it sorted.' Annie realised years ago that her dad was barely literate. She whipped through the piles of ancient correspondence like a human shredder. Johnnie, whose respect for the written word was practically medieval, hovered nervously as though she might accidentally dispose of a family fortune.

'Look, Dad,' you only have to keep things that are current, like insurance, and bills from the last five years.' Well, there wasn't any insurance and the only bill in evidence was one that was outstanding for electricity.

'That's soon sorted, then. You'd better pay that bill and tell them when to cut you off.'

'How d'you do that?' Johnnie looked alarmed. 'I've never paid a bill in me life.'

'What?' Annie was amazed that a founder member of a successful dog racing syndicate was unacquainted with the machinations of paying bills. 'Who paid them, then?'

'Who paid 'em? 'Er o' course. Madge.' Annie's mind reeled. She could honestly say that in the course of her childhood, adolescent and adult years she had never, ever,

155

witnessed her mam doing anything as remotely useful as paying a bill. So, she wasn't as black as she was painted after all.

'Alright. Give me the money and I'll pay it. When do you want to be cut off?'

'Err, next week,' he reckoned.

'What day next week?'

'Depends on Ted.' Ted? Uncle Ted disappeared years ago, after the row about her going to college. She felt an uneasy prickle run through her spine, right through to the nerve ends in her fingertips.

'How d'you mean?' she said.

'Ted's coming with me on me travels. Like old times.' He smiled an embarrassed smile.

'Where are you going?'

'Back to the Med.' Johnnie used to talk about Malta when he was younger. His National Service must have been the best part of his life. *All them plump Maltese lasses and a pint o' wine for 6 pence.* As a matter of fact, Malta was where he'd found Uncle Ted and then brought him home since he didn't appear to have anywhere else to go. It dawned on Annie that, in his own tin pot way, her dad was following his dream.

'You kept in touch with him, then?' Of course he had. He might well look embarrassed. 'You didn't believe me did you? What I said about him?' Of course he didn't, Ted was his mate. She wasn't too surprised; it was one of those things that nobody wants to know. Funny, if it weren't for Uncle Ted, and what she said about him, they would never have let her go to college. She'd been a nuisance they wanted rid of. All the same, she felt sickened.

'It was true,' she said. Was there anything more depressing than not being believed? Even after all these years.

156

'Aye, well. It were along time ago.' That was as much as she would get.

When the paperwork was whittled down to essentials, such as birth, marriage and death certificates, Annie stuffed it all into a brown envelope and labelled it 'Dad's papers' in black marker.

'Where are you going to keep it?' she said.

'I'm not,' he said, as though it might be contaminated, 'you can 'ave it.'

'Thanks.' There *was* something of a contaminated feel about the shabby envelope but it looked as though she'd have to take it. The house, being rented, had to be cleared.

'What are you going to do with everything, Dad?' There was a lot of junk to shift and not much time to do it in.

'Oh, leave it,' he said airily. 'There's nowt worth 'avin 'ere.'

'You can't just walk out, you know. It has to be cleared,' she said, an edge in her voice.

'Why not? There'll be nowt anybody can do about it.' He was probably right but, all the same, it was just so bloody typical.

'Walk out on your responsibilities?' she couldn't help saying, 'You? Never!'

As things turned out, she got £2000 for the sideboard from a dealer on Canal Street.

Back home, Annie made herself a hot chocolate and took out Bethany's book, her Life Story. What have we got so far? Photographs of Bethany playing, always alone; Bethany's school reports, a mixed bag but showing progress; a 'Pupil of the Week' certificate for excellent work

157

in maths; endless drawings in felt marker, all alike, abstract, you could say, without the usual progression through tadpole men to women with triangular skirts, with symmetrical houses and lollipop trees. Her latest, a drawing of the new house, showed some semblance of form but could have been drawn by somebody with x-ray eyes. You could see all the insides from the outside. Very odd.

And a grudging attempt at writing. Annie encouraged her to write, thinking it would boost her sense of self, otherwise she could be forgiven for thinking she'd been snuck in from another planet, like Superman. But the writing was deliberately dull and scanty.

'My name is Bethany Neill. I am seven years old. I live at 13 Brackenbed Drive. I haven't got any brothers or sisters. I haven't got any pets. I like watching TV. My favourite colour is red.'

She wasn't giving anything away. Annie wondered, not for the first time, what went on in her head. As far as Bethany was concerned, it was a closely guarded secret, a skeleton that would never be let out of the cupboard.

It was Annie who stuck things in the book, Annie who was inventing Bethany's life story, because Bethany refused to do it for herself. She shivered as she sipped the hot chocolate.

The Crown Hotel was the sort of place Annie used to stand outside looking in at the posh folk in fur coats who, having made their pile in the post war boom, could afford to go there for their dinner. Looking round now at the plush furnishings, starched linen and silver service, Annie felt a solid sense of achievement, a feeling of having arrived. Course it was past its best but who were they to say so?

They had a generous table for two. It could easily have seated a family of six. Not like these modern places where you get a few inches of laminated hardboard to juggle your meal on. The napkins were at least a yard square, though frayed at the edges, and the table setting was graced with a spray of fresh roses. You could tell they were real by the black spot.

David studied the menu. He'd made an effort, bless him, dressed up in his interview suit and a new M&S tie.

'I don't think this menu's changed since 1900,' he said. 'Don't they know Victoria's dead?' He ordered Mulligatawny soup, followed by lamb cutlets.

'It's nice to have something traditional for a change,' said Annie. She chose grapefruit for starters and then settled on the Yorkshire rabbit. You might as well have something you don't cook at home or else what's the point of eating out? They sipped a dry sherry whilst David studied the wine list.

'Have you seen these prices,' he hissed. 'You could buy Tesco's out with this wine cellar.' David, she thought, was getting tight in his old age. He eventually settled on the house wine.

'It's the best bet,' he said. 'It must have a reasonable turnover. Some of these wines cost so much they could have been lying about for years.'

'Aren't they supposed to?' Isn't that what wine cellars are for?' she said.

'Yes, but there's a limit isn't there? If it was laid down in the reign of Queen Victoria it'll be past its sell-by date by now.' There was a glint in his eye. He might have been joking. She took it as a good sign.

The first bottle, a French Sauvignon Blanc, was just about as acid as the grapefruit. Annie thought it must be a problem with her uneducated palate. David was struggling with the Mulligatawny and could have been drinking dishwater for all he knew.

'Chef's a bit heavy handed with the spices,' he croaked, but soldiered on. Annie tried to ask the waiter for a jug of water but he wasn't going to stir himself for something you didn't have to pay for.

What with the spicy aroma wafting off the soup, the acid of the grapefruit and the paint stripper wine, Annie was beginning to feel sick. She took deep breaths and tried to concentrate on mind over matter. Meanwhile, David managed to wave the waiter to within hailing distance. The waiter took him seriously as, by that time, he was beginning to look like a pickled beetroot.

'I don't know why you have to beg for water,' he gasped, 'in a temperate climate with above average rainfall.' Annie sighed. She had hopes for this evening, hopes about clearing the air, a fresh start, putting back the magic. Things were not going in the right direction. But, she'd spent good money on a black dress with a split up the back that stopped just short of her knickers and she'd sprayed the bed sheets with ylang-ylang and patchouli, just in case, so she was going to make the best of it.

After a few sips of water her stomach felt more settled and David's colour began to look more like. Annie felt they should be chatting, in a light hearted sort of way, as a prelude to an evening of relationship-building self-indulgence, but she couldn't think of anything to say that didn't include the words 'Bethany' or 'Internet.' David was obviously in no mood for chitchat either so they sat opposite each other in silence, like all the other married couples in the room.

The lamb cutlets and Yorkshire rabbit eventually arrived.

The wine waiter brought the Cotes du Rhone swaddled in a white napkin on a silver tray. He made a show of pouring it out in medicinal quantities as though dispensing laudanum. Annie suppressed an urge to laugh. She hadn't seen anything so ridiculous since her mam's funeral. As a matter of fact, she hadn't told David about the funeral yet, or about her dad, or Uncle Ted. She suppressed the bitter thought that David wouldn't want to know about any of them, or Bethany, or, perhaps, even Annie herself. She raised her glass.

'Here's to us,' she said. David raised his glass and sipped.

'Bloody hell,' he said. 'You wouldn't wash your feet in that.'

They didn't have to go to the bother of sending it back because, just then, Annie's handbag began to vibrate on her lap and the muffled tones of 'Rule Britannia' came seeping out from under the tablecloth. So much for a posh evening out.

'For goodness sake! Why didn't you switch it off?' David glared.

'Bethany. In case...' She dug the mobile out of her bag. 'Oh, God! It's Maura. What's wrong now?' She soon found out.

'You'd better come and get her,' said Maura, her voice like thunder, 'before I strangle her.'

'Why? What's matter?'

'I'll tell you what's matter. She's only set fire to the bloody parrot.'

It was something to do with the way she was sitting on his knee with her head insinuating into his neck and her thumb stuck in her mouth like a baby that made Annie's insides lurch. Horace looked as though he'd rather be somewhere else, preferably without a Limpet Girl attached. Maura was standing by the fireplace, arms folded firmly across her bosom. There was a sharp smell of singe in the air.

'How's the parrot?' said Annie. She followed Maura's gaze to the cage sitting on the tabletop. Viagra was sitting on his perch suffering from dented pride. You could tell by the slump of his shoulders that he wouldn't want to be seen dead in singed feathers.

'He's traumatised, he is. Poor lad,' said Horace pursing his lips and shaking his head.

'And so am I,' said Maura. 'He's my parrot you know.' She turned a tragic face to Bethany. 'I can't trust you any more, you treacherous little bugger.' She turned back toward the fireplace, her shoulders shaking. Annie's heart sank. Join the club, she thought. Horace looked as though he might say something then thought better of it. David's jaw was clenched. Bethany nonchalantly swung one leg back and forth over Horace's ankles.

'Bethany,' said Annie, calm as she could, 'get down off Horace's knee and say sorry to Maura.' Bethany looked round the room, assessing her audience, then staged a meek climb down and a soft voiced apology delivered from under lowered lashes. 'Right, madam,' said Annie, 'now get your coat on and come with us.' Bethany flounced over to the coat hooks by the door, grabbed her coat then flung the door open and swept out into the night. David, shaking with rage, went after her. Annie was left looking at her friend. 'I don't know what to say,' she said.

Chapter 13 – Annie

'I think I'll have a dog,' said Bethany as they crawled along an endless Norfolk lane behind a lumbering procession of farm traffic. The row following the parrot episode seemed to have made more impression on Bethany than any amount of straight talking and now she had enough marbles in the pot to earn her a treat. But Annie wasn't convinced about the Consequences game. She knew Bethany was manipulating it but had yet to work out how. She wanted a straight tale to tell to Jasbinder next time they met.

'You can't get a dog for ten pounds,' said Annie who, personally speaking, wouldn't give a dog houseroom.

'Yes I can,' Bethany insisted, 'if it's a dog nobody else wants.' Annie wasn't too sure about that. Even rescue dogs cost money. Funny, it cost more to adopt a dog than to adopt a child. Anyway there was no point in arguing about it now.

'Well, we'll see.'

The farm traffic turned off the lane up a dirt track towards Beale's pig farm. Annie sighed with relief and put her foot down. It wasn't as though there was any danger of breaking a speed limit. The lane was so narrow and winding you'd have a job to go much faster than walking pace without running the wheels into the ditch and rolling over into a field of turnips. Consequently, they'd been on the road a good five hours when they eventually turned into the pebbled drive of the Old Parsonage.

The Magnolia tree was in full bloom. It was a

venerable specimen that had spent the last century or so feeding on the rich arable soil. Its flowers were nearly as big as dinner plates and folk came from miles away to admire its magnificence.

'Doesn't it just take your breath away?' said Annie.

'No,' said Bethany, scanning the scene for action. A great black Labrador came lolloping round the corner of the house.

'There he is!' Bethany jumped out of the car and ran to meet him. Annie cringed at the sight but managed not to say anything about germs when he licked Bethany all over the face with a fair amount of slobber.

'I though I heard voices,' called Elizabeth, emerging from the greenhouse waving a watering can. 'I was watering the tomatoes. They get so thirsty in this warm weather, poor things.' She pecked Annie's cheek and then turned to Bethany but she was too taken up with the dog to notice.

'Bethany,' said Annie, 'say hello to Gran.' Honestly, she shouldn't have to be teaching her manners at her age. She should have learnt them long before now.

'Hello, Gran,' said Bethany, occupied with teasing the dog.

'We should send Blackie home,' said Elizabeth, 'he's not allowed to wander or he might get himself shot.'

Blackie belonged at the scrapyard on the far side of the village where he was supposed to earn his living as a guard dog but since he'd never been known to bark at anything other than a rabbit you could say he was something of a dead loss.

'I call him Gnasher,' said Bethany. 'It suits him better.' Annie raised her eyes heavenward and then went to unload the Golf.

'I'll go and ask Elsie to make us some tea,' said Elizabeth, 'then I'll help you with your things.' As Elizabeth turned to go indoors Annie noticed how stiff her movements were.

'Gnasher,' Bethany yelled, 'stop it!' Annie turned to see to dog's jaws clamped round Bethany's wrist. Bethany was trying to wrench her arm away.

'Keep still,' said Annie, 'he thinks you're playing. Just keep still then he'll let go.' Bethany yelled with rage and landed the dog a hefty blow on his windpipe.

'Bethany!' said Elizabeth, turning back.

'He bit me.'

'No he didn't, dear. He was only playing,' said Elizabeth. 'Look, he hasn't even broken the skin.'

Annie glared at Bethany through narrow eyes. She's at it again, she thought, as Bethany allowed herself to be led into the house for a dab of Dettol and slice of Elsie's all-in-one fruitcake, no doubt.

The dog, she noticed, laboured over his breathing for a good two minutes before he took himself off towards the scrapyard.

'Will you have gin? Or whisky?' Elizabeth opened the kitchen dresser and poked about in its foisty insides. 'I think there's something in here.' She found an unopened bottle of Glenmorangie and two half empty bottles of Tanqueret. 'I like a spot of gin myself,' she said, 'but I don't approve of drinking alone and I'm afraid Elsie won't touch anything better than cooking sherry.' She looked at Annie expectantly.

'Err, Have you got any white wine?' Annie felt put on the spot. She knew nothing at all about Glens and, where she was brought up, women who drank gin were practically whores. She remembered gruesome tales of desperate women driven to gin induced abortions. Those poor women got what was coming to them, although Annie could never quite understand how you could possibly get anything that wasn't coming to you. Funny, gin was so sinful yet something like port and lemon, for example, was considered quite respectable. And most folk would have a sweet sherry at Christmas time. Except Madge, of course, she never touched a drop. Well, she wouldn't, would she? She might start enjoying herself.

'Oh, now let me see,' Elizabeth looked a bit thrown. 'You know, there isn't a single wine merchant between here and Norwich,' she said, heading for the cellar stairs. She reappeared with a bottle of Chablis, dusted it down and put in the fridge. 'Ready in five minutes,' she said. 'Doesn't do to chill it too much.' Annie was relieved. What a carry on, just to organize a drink. Surely there was a Tesco somewhere in the county?

'*I'll* have a gin, Gran,' Bethany piped up. 'You can give *me* some gin.'

'Bethany!' Annie started. Elizabeth laughed.

'Oh let her have some. With lemonade, of course. It won't do any harm, I'm sure. I was practically weaned on gin and I'm no worse for it now.' Annie felt the ground disappearing from under her feet. It was, she thought, going to be hard going.

After a couple of glasses of Chablis, though, things felt better. It wasn't Elizabeth's fault that she'd been brought up posh and Annie hadn't. It wasn't her fault either. They would just have to manage like they always did.

Bethany slurped a tumbler of mostly lemonade, decorated with twirls of lemon and lime. She threw Annie a sidelong glance from time to time to make sure she was being noticed.

Elizabeth got busy cooking supper. It was what Annie would call tea, but never mind.

This is cosy, Annie thought lounging on the lumpy horsehair couch in front of the smoking log fire. Although it was warm for July, the evenings in Norfolk crept in cold underfoot. She sipped a glass of the brandy Elizabeth had unearthed from the cupboard under the kitchen sink.

'I never know,' Elizabeth said, 'where I'm going to find the next bottle.' Either she'd put them away and forgotten, or they were left over from the time when Francis planted his drink all over the place. If so, they must be thirty years old. 'Still,' she said, 'a good brandy can last a lifetime.' She sipped thoughtfully and then put her glass down on the little pie-crust table next to a photograph of six-year-old David cowering beside a Great Dane.

'Now Bethany's out of earshot,' she all but whispered, 'I wonder if we could have a chat.'

'Of course,' said Annie. 'I must say I was surprised when she took herself off to bed. Make the most of it before the novelty wears off.' Elizabeth's look made her feel mean. She didn't sound fit to be a mother.

'Sorry,' she said. 'She wears me out. All I want is a bit of peace and quiet.'

'Yes, dear,' Elizabeth said. 'We all need that. Tell me, how are you getting on with her behaviour modification programme? Is she making progress?'

'In theory.' Annie sighed. 'She's always earning treats but, maybe its just me, there doesn't seem to be any improvement in her attitude.' She took another sip of brandy, feeling it spread out through her insides, deep and warming. 'It's as though she knows how to do just enough to get her what she wants. Like a dog. God knows, the last thing we need is a big slobbery dog lolloping all over the place. *And* she'll probably end up murdering it.'

'Why do you say that?' Elizabeth looked shocked.

'She murders her dolls on a regular basis,' Annie found herself saying. 'Why stop there? She nearly finished poor old Blackie off this afternoon.'

'Tell me,' Elizabeth spoke cautiously, 'did you never want a pet when you were a girl?' Annie thought briefly of Pat the dog. But then he was a sterile character, like all the others who inhabited the Ladybird world.

'Not really,' she said. Thinking about it, given a choice, she would rather have had a functioning mother.

'I've been thinking,' said Elizabeth, that was the nearest she got to telling you what to do, 'Bethany might respond to the same sort of training as a pony. Lay down the rules, reward her, win her trust. It's just a matter of patience. What do you think?' Annie laughed.

'The last time anybody tried to win her trust she set fire to the parrot,' she said. Elizabeth levelled her a look that clearly meant she wasn't trying hard enough. 'Oh, alright. Let's give it a go.' Elizabeth smiled.

'Wait until you see what I have in the paddock.' She said, mysteriously. Oh God, thought Annie. Having practically won the battle of the dog, she was, she could see, being set up to lose the battle of the pony. She took another gulp of the brandy and watched the flames flickering in the hearth.

※※※

Annie woke early and drew back the curtains back on a lush green landscape set off to advantage by the bright morning sun. She could hear movement downstairs and guessed that Elizabeth was already up and dressed. Actually, it turned out to be Elsie working in the kitchen, her Coty L'Aimant vying sickeningly with the smell of frying bacon.

'Hello Elsie,' said Annie. 'I thought you were Elizabeth.'

'Good morning,' said Elsie, 'Mrs Neill was up well before you. Out in the paddock with her granddaughter. Couldn't wait to eat their breakfast before they went.' She looked as though she might be offended any minute now.

'I see,' said Annie. 'A pony?'

'A pony,' said Elsie. 'I've heard about nothing but pony for weeks. I hope it works out. That's all I can say.' Annie absorbed the implication. It was going to be important to Elizabeth that her project bore fruit.

'You can always hope,' she said. Elsie gave her a funny look then pointedly rearranged the rashers in the pan.

'I expect yourn want to see for yourself,' she said. 'I'll keep this warm until you're ready.'

'Thanks,' said Annie, heading outdoors to the paddock.

'Look at me, Gran!' Bethany was sitting astride a little brown pony that looked as though it needed a haircut, yelling at the top of her voice. Her face was flushed and her eyes shone. Annie had never seen her look so alive. She caught her breath in a moment of pure happiness.

'Just look at her,' said Elizabeth, 'Francis would have done justice to a picture of her like that.' Francis, Annie knew, was something of an amateur painter. She was all too familiar with a number of his creations that David

169

insisted on hanging around the place. He thought they were artistic. She thought they looked like biscuit tin lids (circa 1950) but, then, you have to compromise, don't you? She could see what Elizabeth meant, though, the angelic little girl on the cute little pony would be pure heartmelt to anybody who didn't know any different.

'Mum,' Bethany spotted her, 'look at me!'

'I'm looking,' she said.

'Hector is a Welsh Mountain pony,' said Elizabeth, bursting with enthusiasm. 'He's got just the right temperament for a beginner. She'll be safe enough with him.'

'Will she actually be able to ride him?'

'Oh, yes,' Elizabeth patted her arm in reassurance. 'He'll teach her himself.' That sounded all too far-fetched for Annie. Ponies that taught people to ride them? Whatever next?

Bethany looked surprisingly at home on Hector. She let him walk her round the paddock as though they had been friends for life. The sunlight caught her copper coloured ponytail and her cheeks were pink with excitement. Wonderful, thought Annie, something positive is happening. Bethany turned to her and smiled. The reserve she habitually wore on her face was practically gone. Annie smiled back and Bethany held her look. Annie felt dizzy with love. This was how it was supposed to be.

'Come along, Bethany,' called Elizabeth. 'It's time for breakfast. Elsie will be waiting.' Annie held her breath. What now? Refusals? Tantrums? Galloping off into the horizon? No, surprisingly enough, Bethany allowed Hector to return her to Gran who helped her down to earth again. She smelled of pony and fresh air.

'There now,' said Elizabeth, 'did you like that? If you

learn how to look after him and treat him properly, you can keep him. It's up to you.' Bethany laughed with pleasure. Annie and Elizabeth joined in.

'He will only come to you if he wants to,' said Elizabeth, showing Bethany how to hold out a piece of apple on the flat of her hand. 'The trick is, to make him want to. You can't bully him, you know. You must be kind then he will give you what you want.' Annie stood watching in the afternoon sun, enjoying the breeze on her face. She had heard the same thing said in different ways a few times during the last half hour,

'Imagine how he feels. Would *you* like to carry a big girl around on your back?' Now Bethany was practising giving him apple, held out on her palm so that he could stretch out his elegant little head towards her and nibble it with velvet lips. 'You are asking him to be good to you. You must be good to him in return.' It dawned on Annie that Elizabeth was teaching Bethany more than pony craft. She was using the pony to teach her consideration. Well, we'll see how long that lasts, thought Annie, watching Elizabeth with admiration.

Her eyes roved over the landscape. Not that there was much to rove over. It was so flat in Norfolk that the landscape reached an abrupt edge not very far from wherever you happened to look. You could imagine falling off on a dark night without a sensible torch. And there was too much sky. Annie was used to sky in jagged patches, framed by hillsides of solid rock, not this great expanse that left you feeling exposed to any passing bird of prey. Still, in good weather, she had to admit it had its attraction.

The fresh air was doing Bethany good. She hadn't

171

stopped eating since she arrived. Even Elizabeth, with her inbred manners, couldn't help but look surprised at the amounts she put away at mealtimes. It was like watching a JCB at work. She would be actively growing out of her clothes, no doubt.

Elizabeth set Hector off walking round the paddock with Bethany on his back. Then she came and stood with Annie, watching.

'David never liked domestic animals,' she said. 'Francis neither. They liked the natural world, small creatures in burrows where they belong. Francis used to draw very detailed specimens. David couldn't be bothered with that. He took photographs though.' Annie didn't quite know what to say.

'It's good to see Bethany's interested.' Elizabeth smiled. Then Annie realised.

'Yes,' she said. 'She might take after you.' Never mind if it was wishful thinking. God only knew who Bethany would really take after. 'I'm sorry Francis died young,' she said. 'It must have been hard bringing David up by yourself.' She felt herself shaking inside, surprised by her daring. She needn't have worried.

'Yes. It was.' Elizabeth thought for a moment then appeared to reach a decision. 'He took his own life, you know. But I understand the reason why.'

'Was it depression?' Annie said cautiously. She knew about depression, how it could eat away at your insides like maggots and leave nothing but an empty husk. That must have been what happened to Madge.

'No, not depression,' said Elizabeth. 'Guilt.' Maybe it was easier to say things like that when you were both looking at somebody else. They watched Bethany, relaxed and confident, for once, and thoroughly involved in her riding.

'He left us for someone else. Then I heard he had taken an overdose of aspirin with a bottle of Irish whisky. He always did have an over-active conscience. It comes with the job, I suppose. Vicars are supposed to be above that sort of thing.'

'It can happen to anybody,' said Annie who read enough novels to know. Whether it was Catherine Cookson or Charlotte Bronte, it was the same. The overwhelming passion was a universal phenomenon. It happened all the time; not that it had ever happened to her, thank God. It would be bound to end in tears.

'I know.'

Bethany came to a halt in front of them. At least Hector did, and Bethany with him. She was breathing hard and her eyes were shining. Annie couldn't remember her looking so relaxed.

'Wait a minute, will you?' said Elizabeth, I'm going to get my camera.' She hurried off with an awkward gait. Annie smiled at Bethany, wanting to share the moment. Bethany turned away, jabbing her heels into Hector's sides until he stirred his dainty feet to walk round the paddock yet again.

'Ask him nicely,' said Annie, trying to capitalise on Elizabeth's teaching. Bethany ignored her. As she watched her settling into Hector's stride, it crossed Annie's mind that the movement seemed to comfort her, like rocking a baby. Except she'd never allowed herself to be rocked. She looked set to go round and round the paddock forever.

'Here we are,' Elizabeth eventually appeared with her aging Agfa and started fiddling with the settings.

'Ask Hector to stop, dear,' she called. Hector carried on. 'You know, lean back a little, draw in the reins as I told you.' Bethany appeared to do as she was told. It made no difference to Hector. He carried on round the paddock, almost with a smile on his face. Bethany frowned. Annie smirked, then thought better of it. Bethany tried again.

'He won't stop, Gran.'

'Yes he will, if you ask him nicely.'

Bethany leaned back and hauled on the rains. Hector carried on.

'Whoa!' Bethany yelled, 'Whoa!' Hector ignored her. Annie's mouth was twitching with suppressed laughter but she knew something would have to be done to avert a crisis. Luckily Elizabeth summoned the strength to open the paddock gate and go after them. Even with her arthritis she eventually caught up.

'Whoa, there,' she sang out, touching his bridle softly. Hector stopped on the spot and started breathing his affection over her. Bethany scrambled awkwardly off his back then whacked him a hefty thump on his neck. It made no impression on Hector who was busy nuzzling Elizabeth. Bethany turned and ran.

'Come along Annie,' said Elizabeth calmly, 'help me will you?' They led Hector to his loose box where they brushed him down and gave him a bucket of fresh water.

'That's what Bethany should be doing, isn't it?' said Annie.

'Yes.'

'So what now?'

'Ignore her. Come on. Let's find a cup of tea. Then we'll let him out to graze.'

They walked back to the house in silence and went in through the conservatory door.

'Let's sit in here, shall we?' Elizabeth pulled a wicker chair away from the window into the shade. 'Sit here where it's comfortable,' she told Annie. 'Elsie will have gone by now but she's probably left the kettle on the Aga.' She headed towards the kitchen to brew the tea.

Annie perched on the edge of the sagging cushion that was the only defence between her and the spiteful spikes of wicker. The chair creaked. It's like everything else round here, thought Annie, on its last legs. She felt herself trembling inside, on the edge of panic. Try as she might to imitate Elizabeth's cool, she didn't know how much longer she could keep her nerve. God only knew where Bethany was. She could be lying in the undergrowth with her throat slit, or worse, much worse. She tried not to imagine the lurid blood spattered scenarios that she'd rehearsed to herself on other such occasions when Bethany tried her punishment by disappearing act. She took deep breaths to keep the Vortex at bay.

As it happened, they didn't have to wait too long. Bethany turned up with Blackie and his owner, Andrew, just as the tea was ready. In her relief, Annie forgot her initial unease at the sight of Bethany riding on Andrew's broad back, her head snuggled into the side of his bullish neck and a look of triumph all over her face. Andrew looked quite flushed. But then, due to his lasting affection for brown ale, he often did.

'Hello, Andrew,' said Elizabeth. 'Come and join us for a cup of tea.'

'That's alright,' said Andrew, unloading Bethany. 'Came visiting, she did. Had a grand old time with Blackie, didn't you?'

'Gnasher,' said Bethany. 'He's called Gnasher now.' Andrew forced a laugh, trying to be polite, no doubt. What was he doing letting her hang about the scrapyard? Annie thought. Had he no idea? Still, he'd had the grace to return Bethany in person so she thanked him.

'Oh, that's alright,' he said. 'No trouble. No trouble at all.' He turned to Elizabeth. 'I'll be on my way, Mrs Neill. Good afternoon, now.'

'Goodbye, Andrew,' said Elizabeth, rising to show him out. 'Thank you.' She didn't make a fuss, Annie noticed. She took it all in her stride. More surprisingly, Bethany didn't fuss either. She seemed quite happy when Elizabeth suggested she should take Hector a carrot to chomp and let him out to graze. Maybe that's the way forward, thought Annie. Ignore the bad behaviour for as long as you can keep your nerve.

Annie picked up the bedside phone. After a week of good weather, fresh air and exercise, they were all feeling much better and she was in the mood to talk to David before she settled down for the night. So far their conversations had been limited to words that didn't mean much; it was just staying in touch for the sake of it. Now she felt like having a good old heart to heart like they hadn't had for a long time. They say absence makes the heart grow fonder but Annie suspected the opposite. She felt as though the absence had lasted a lot longer than a week. You could say it had been going on for years, one way or another, and if she didn't do anything about it soon she would live to regret it.

She let the phone ring until the ansaphone clicked on. Her heart sank. Where was he at this time of night? Internet Café? John's place? Where? Why? Should she leave a message? She was just going to put the phone down when she heard his voice.

'Hello?'

'David, it's me.'

'Oh, hello. I was in the shower.'

'How are you?'

'OK. How are you?'

'Fine,' This is getting us nowhere, thought Annie.

'Can we talk?' she ventured.

'What about?'

'Anything, everything. You know, have a proper talk.'

'Right,' said David. Now, thought Annie, where to begin?

'Bethany's doing so well with her riding. You should see her. She looks really happy.'

'That's good. I dare say she'll be trying out for the Olympics next. What about you?'

'Me?'

'Yes, you. Are you enjoying yourself?'

'Yes I am.' Annie began to believe she was. 'But I'm missing you,' she added, just in case he got the wrong idea. Or was it the wrong idea? 'Will you come down next week so we can have a few days together?' Well, she'd said it. Put her cards on the table. He could only say no. He hesitated, but only for a moment.

'Alright. I'll need to find the train times to Norwich. I'll ring you tomorrow.'

'Oh good.' Annie felt a surge of relief and said 'I love you,' just before she put the phone down. David didn't say anything in reply but, then, men don't, do they?

Chapter 14 – Maura

The phone rang just as Maura was going to pour the batter into the smoking Yorkshire pudding tin. She put it down, turned the gas off and picked the receiver up. Why did she keep doing that? She was a slave to it. She should let the bloody thing ring.

'Hello, Maura?' Annie's voice came over the airwaves.

Here we go, thought Maura. Histrionics. Trust Annie to phone when she was trying to cook a meal for Horace, ruining her Yorkshire pudding. Now she had a private life she didn't want it invaded every verse end with tales of the blessed Bethany. She was buggered if she was going to let Annie come between her and Horace. Annie had a husband and no need to earn a living. Maura was facing unemployment and had nobody to live with but a parrot. It's alright when you're young but at her age, she realised, the price of freedom was high. Now she had chance of a settled relationship and she was going to grab it with both hands.

'Sorry Annie, I can't talk now. I'm in the throes of cooking. Horace is coming round.'

'I see.' Annie's voice was cold. Sod it, thought Maura. I don't see why I should feel guilty. I have my own life to think about.

'I won't keep you,' said Annie. 'Just to let you know we're all OK and David's coming down for a few days next week.' She sounded quite positive.

'Good,' said Maura. 'I'll give you a ring tomorrow, shall I?'

'If you like. 'Bye.' Course Maura felt guilty, jumping to conclusions like that. It was nice of Annie to go to the bother of phoning her, even when she had nothing to moan about. It made a change from the eternal wittering. Oh, well, she'd make up for it tomorrow. She went back to the Yorkshire pudding, lit the gas and gave the batter an extra whisk, hoping it would still rise. So David's going to join them, Maura thought.

Last time she saw David, he was acting furtive outside the Halifax with a smart young woman in a navy blue polyester suit. She was laughing, showing a mouthful of porcelain crowns framed by a border of lip-gloss that looked like an advert for superglue. Anybody who kissed her could be stuck to her for life. He looked to be talking earnestly until he saw Maura when he nodded a curt goodbye and strode off down Main Street. The girl turned on her trim little heel and disappeared through the Halifax doorway. Maura was left with a feeling that she'd seen something she shouldn't.

Horace turned up just as the Yorkshires were done to a turn and the nut loaf set enough to slice. She drained the peas and carrots, stirred the mushroom gravy and checked the plates were hot. Horace came up behind and put his arms round her, squeezing her breasts.

'Not now,' she said. This, she could tell, could become one of his annoying habits if she didn't nip it in the bud. 'Would you like to sit down? I'm ready to serve up.' He pulled up a chair to the table and smiled expectantly. Horace appreciated the luxury of being cooked for. It was worth the effort just to see his face.

The nut loaf was tasty, the mushrooms earthy and the Yorkshires melt in the mouth. Maura sighed a sigh of satisfaction and relaxed to enjoy the meal.

'I've been thinking,' said Horace, between chews. 'You should come and live with me.' He was probably anticipating a lifetime of hot dinners. 'Then you could sell up and buy the shop.' He looked at her as if to say, Aren't I the clever one? Transparent as glass, thought Maura. Yes, she could flirt with the idea; company, caring, sex. But old memories left her thinking it all might go downhill once she got installed. Better to let Horace come to her then *he* would have to make the effort.

'Actually, Horace,' she said, swallowing a mouthful, 'I'm not buying the shop. I'm having nothing more to do with Hamid, the self-seeking bastard. I'm not going to take over a dodgy business just to suit him.'

'Oh,' said Horace. He looked thoughtful but said no more.

'I've decided,' said Maura, 'to find my niche in the market and work from home.'

'Right,' said Horace. He looked deflated. Maura thought fast.

'But I'm relying on you to help me, you know.' She allowed a tremor in her voice. 'I don't know where I'd be without you, Horry love.' He brightened.

'What is it, then, your niche?'

'I don't know yet.' Maura smiled what she hoped was a fetching smile.

'You can rely on me,' said Horace, like she knew he would, bless him. She felt a warming rush of affection course through her insides.

'Wait 'til you see what's for pudding,' she said, smiling suggestively.

***

'You could always start an Internet business,' said David. Maura took advantage of him dropping into the shop the next morning to pick his brains about niche possibilities. He was sipping a strong black decaf in the back room and warming to his idea. 'On-line Tarot readings, cyber fortune telling, web sales of herbal medicines, some people will buy anything on the Internet.' She wasn't quite sure if he was being facetious. She suspected he was. All the same, there was the germ of an idea there. And Horace knew about the Internet.

'Of course, you couldn't do massages on-line but you could do them at home.' Yes, she supposed she could put a treatment couch up in the box room. 'But,' said David, smiling, 'be careful how you advertise yourself.' Well, if that was a joke it was a poor one. Maura had years of experience of weeding out creeps who thought they'd come to a massage parlour. That's what prompted her to specialise in ladies only. It was no problem in Holmebridge. There were plenty of women like Doe who relied on a regular pummelling to keep them going.

David swallowed the last of his coffee and got up ready to leave.

'Right,' he said, 'I'd better get going and check the train times to Norwich.' He paused in the doorway. 'I thought I'd take something for Annie. What do you suggest?' Maura thought for a minute.

'Nowthen, what about this?' She went through to the shop and picked out a dainty green bottle. 'Isn't it lovely?' It was shaped like a lily bud and sparkled ever so slightly where it caught the light.

'Does it smell nice?'

'Heavenly,' said Maura. She held a tester under his nose. It was a flowery fragrance with undertones of almond and camomile, not that David would recognise them as such. 'Annie will love it,' said Maura. She wrapped it carefully in tissue paper and tied it with Indian silk ribbon.

'Thanks,' said David. 'Thanks a lot.' Maura smiled to herself as he left the shop. He probably didn't realise it was massage oil.

Horace was replete. It didn't take much to make him happy. A satisfying fuck was enough to make him feel like he'd won the lottery. Not that he bought tickets. He'd rather spend his meagre cash on something more substantial, like teabags.

'Little treasure,' he murmured into Maura's hair that all but covered his face. It was debatable where her hair finished and his began, it was all pretty much the same. It was a long time since Maura could be described as little but, to Horace, she'd always been a treasure. She knew that now and sometimes grudged the years she'd wasted on independence. It was alright in one sense, showing that a woman can rely on herself, surviving without any old excuse of a man, but Maura's ideas were changing. She'd come round to thinking that a good man in her bed was better than any amount of ideas in her head. Hamid was never in her bed. All she got from him were quickies in unlikely places. Not that she hadn't enjoyed them at the time. The sense of urgency and the possibility of somebody walking in on them any minute now was as good as any aphrodisiac. But, she felt, as far as he was concerned, the pleasure was all his. Now she had Horace. Again.

Like everything Horace did, his lovemaking was slow and considered. No matter he was past his prime and his body bore no comparison to Hamid's; his flanks were skinny, his skin pale and, to be honest, his cock wasn't just as hard, but he made Maura feel like a sex goddess. She could feel his adoration through her skin. She couldn't get enough of him. The way he kissed her as though she was unbearably precious. He didn't try to gobble her up like most men do. (And Maura had a wide experience of men being, as she was, brought up in an alternative society.) He stroked her with gentle fingers, not grabbing and seizing like Hamid did. He waited until she was ready before he penetrated her. Then she wallowed in his measured rhythm before he finally thrust into her in a grand orgasmic finale. Maura was in love. Again.

She slipped out of bed leaving him to snooze. She thought she'd make a pot of tea before she woke him up. It was alright spending the evening in bed but then she had to get him up in time to go home to go to bed again. It would be easier to let him stay the night but then he might start taking things for granted.

She hummed as she waited for the kettle, mulling over her situation. She made a mental list of her saleable skills: Tarot, crystal healing, Indian Head massage, aromatherapy, and the latest addition to her repertoire, Hopi ear candles. She dabbled a bit in Feng Shui but wasn't really convinced there was anything to show for it apart from unlikely colour schemes and a bowl of wet pebbles. As far as she could see, the only one of those transferable to the Internet was the Tarot. But, the idea crossed her mind, she could do a crash course in Astrology and offer that as well. In fact, her mind raced on, probably very much affected by their evening of steady fucking, she could, with Horace's help, create an Astrological Internet dating agency for likeminded people looking for love, or sex, or both. Forget the rest. She had, she could feel it in her bones, struck gold.

'Horry, love,' she said, nudging him awake, 'I've found my niche!'

'Have you now?' he said. 'Well, so have I. You know what mine is. What's yours?' He smiled a lazy indulgent smile that made her slip back into bed and snuggle up to him again. He smelled of comfort, sex and sleep.

'It's a matter of finding appropriate software and building a website,' said David when Maura phoned him the next morning. 'You could talk to John. I'll give him your number if you like.' Maura thought she would like and thank you very much.

'When are you off to Norfolk then?' she said.

'Tomorrow morning. But it looks as though it'll take all day to get there.' He sounded peeved.

'Well,' she said, 'it'll be a break.'

'I suppose so.'

'David,' said Maura tentatively, 'is everything alright?' She held her breath for a moment.

'That depends,' said David, 'on what you mean by 'alright.'' Maura was worried by his attitude but didn't want to intrude.

'Well, you know where I am,' she compromised, 'if you want somebody to talk to.'

'Thanks.' She realised, of course, that men didn't go in for talking as a rule while, it could be said, that women were prone to do altogether too much of it. All the same, it wasn't like David to be unsure. He was never unsure. The world could collapse all around him and David would know exactly the right thing to do. This recent shilly-shallying was something that bothered Maura more than she cared to admit.

Still, she had things to do, her notice to give in to Hamid, a phone call to John, then she and Horace could make a start on building their future.

Chapter 15 – Elizabeth

Elizabeth watched Andrew saunter down the lane, scuffing the dust in the light afternoon breeze. Blackie was sniffing round his heels, enjoying a bit of attention no doubt. She smiled to herself. This would be the second time today, and about the fifth time that week, that Andrew happened to be walking his dog in their direction. Usually, Blackie's walks were taken on his own and on the sly when he wondered off from the scrapyard out of pure boredom. Now he was panting happily alongside his master who, Elizabeth knew, was up to something. She had never seen him so active, relatively speaking.

'Good afternoon,' she called, waving her outsize gardening glove in his direction.

'Afternoon, Mrs Neill, it's a warm un today.' he said. Elizabeth knew he would stop to admire the Magnolia. Then, she guessed, he would start a conversation and eventually work his way round to the subject of Annie. Men are so predictable.

'That Magnolia's looking better than ever,' he said, drawing to a halt and leaning his bulk on the gatepost as though preparing to stand there for some considerable time.

'Yes, isn't it?' she smiled.

'You put a lot of work into that garden. It does you credit.' He smiled and nodded. 'Yes, it does you credit. Me, now I have no garden worth speaking of. Mind you,' he said, I'm kept busy enough in the scrapyard.'

Yes, thought Elizabeth, busy with the Daily Mirror and a crate of brown ale.

'How's Bethany today? I thought she might want to play with Blackie here.'

'She's with her mother in the back garden. Sunning herself, I expect.' Elizabeth felt mean not offering him tea and the company he was so obviously searching out. But, she thought, it wasn't really up to her to invite him to visit Annie. Anyway, knowing him, he would probably invite himself.

'I'll just go and say hello then, shall I?' He didn't wait for an answer but headed for the back garden with Blackie close on his heels.

When, feeling hot and thirsty after clearing the drive of rampant weeds, she decided to break off and make a jug of lemonade, Elizabeth spotted them through the kitchen window. Bethany was throwing sticks for Blackie. Annie, watching, appeared happy and relaxed. Andrew, looking on, was smiling. They looked for all the world, she thought, like a happy little family.

David arrived after dinner when Bethany, sleepy after a day outdoors in the fresh air, was already in bed.

'The train was late and I'm starving,' he said. Annie had offered to pick him up in Norwich but he'd insisted on travelling by taxi and was thoroughly put out when it cost him a small fortune. Then, to his disgust, the remains of the lamb casserole were congealed and smelled of dead meat.

'Shall I cook you an omelette?' Annie said apologetically.

'I suppose so,' he said. 'But I *was* looking forward to a good dinner.' Annie hovered, undecided whether to try to resurrect the casserole or not. Elizabeth, reading the anxiety on her face couldn't help but contrast it to the serenity she wore when Andrew was around.

'Why don't you both have a drink,' she said, trying to sound more cheerful than she felt. 'You can have a chat whilst I rustle up some ham and eggs.' She bustled towards the refrigerator.

'Alright,' said David, turning toward the living room. Annie followed clutching the Tanqueret and a couple of tumblers.

Elizabeth tuned into Radio 3 and started preparing the meal. She could just about hear their voices through the second movement of Elgar's 'cello concerto but not well enough to be thought to be listening in. It sounded stilted though. Elizabeth's heart sank. Things looked as though they might be even worse than she thought.

David ate the ham and eggs in silence whilst Annie drank half a bottle of Chablis rather too quickly for her own good.

What remained of the evening was spent in small talk with Elizabeth feeling as though, in trying to draw David out and put Annie at her ease, she was flogging a dead horse.

They went to bed early but Elizabeth didn't, for a minute, take that as the positive sign it could have been. She cleared the dishes, locked the door and switched off the lights before climbing the arthritic old staircase to a night of troubled sleep.

Annie and David set off down the lane on a mission to Waitrose, armed with Elizabeth's shopping list. Being, as they were, in Little Ellingham, a trip to Waitrose was likely to take them some considerable time - time, Elizabeth hoped, to find their tongues and start talking to each other again. Meanwhile she was planning to give Bethany a riding lesson.

'You *are* making good progress,' she told her, 'and when Mummy and Daddy come back, you can show them how well you are doing.' Bethany preened. She was taking a pride in her riding skills and that, thought Elizabeth, was a good thing. It was high time David took a pride in her too.

Hector was in a frisky mood but Bethany, under Elizabeth's patient guidance, had learned how to calm him and take control without resorting to yanking and kicking as she used to. By the end of the morning, she was able to trot round the paddock with reasonable confidence.

'Well done, Bethany. Would you like to learn to jump him tomorrow?'

'Oh, yes, Gran! Yes! Yes!' Bethany jigged up and down in excitement.

'Well then, don't frighten the poor thing,' said Elizabeth, 'dismount and lead him to his loosebox.'

They were brushing him down when Blackie came running through the paddock towards them.

'Gnasher!' Bethany dropped her dandy brush and ran out to meet him.

'Bethany,' Elizabeth called, 'what about Hector?' But Bethany took no notice. She embraced the dog with enthusiasm and he reciprocated gratefully, licking her face as thoroughly as though it were edible.

As Elizabeth anticipated, Andrew followed along, breathing heavily from trying to keep up with the dog.

'I let him off the lead,' he panted, 'and away he shot like a bullet from a gun.' He paused to catch his breath, 'Eager to find Bethany here, no doubt.' Andrew smiled broadly in her direction. 'Your mother's around, is she?' The nonchalance he tried to affect was completely sabotaged by his puffing and panting.

'Gone shopping,' said Bethany, patting Blackie on the head then snatching her hand away to tease him.

Hmmmm, thought Elizabeth.

'Bethany has to finish brushing Hector, don't you dear? Then you can play.' Bethany took no notice, jumping up and down as she was, working Blackie into a frenzy. Surely Andrew could see that was not at all healthy for either of them?

'Andrew,' said Elizabeth, 'do call Blackie off. Bethany, you must let Blackie be. Do you hear me?' She raised her voice in pitch that changed from gentle to firm. Bethany turned to look at her in amazement, the 'Who, me?' expression on her face showing she was taking notice at last.

'Now, come and do your duty to Hector.' Elizabeth, determined to make her point, made it sound like a royal command. She gave Andrew a look that clearly put him in his place.

'I'll be on my way, then,' he said, looking embarrassed.

'If you don't mind waiting a few minutes,' said Elizabeth, 'Bethany will be free to play and Elsie will make us a nice cup of coffee.' Andrew obviously took this as an order. He attached the lead to Blackie's collar then propped himself up against the doorframe to wait for as long as it took.

'There we are,' said Elizabeth, when Hector was groomed and watered then let loose to graze, 'now you can play.' Bethany unleashed Blackie.

'Come on Gnasher, come on, boy.' She set off chasing round the paddock with the dog chasing slavishly after her.

'Now, we'll have that coffee, shall we?' Elizabeth led Andrew across the paddock and through the garden into the conservatory.

Andrew sagged on the creaking wicker as though exhausted. He took out a grubby handkerchief and wiped his face. It's not so hot, thought Elizabeth, maybe he's sickening for something. But, then, she reflected, there *was* his size to consider. She smiled what she hoped was a reassuring smile and went through to the kitchen to find Elsie.

Returning to the conservatory, Elizabeth noticed him watching Bethany and the dog. He started suddenly, as though caught doing something he shouldn't.

'Mrs Neill, there you are. I was just thinking how good it is for Blackie to have someone to play with. They get on a treat, don't they?' Elizabeth turned to the window.

The sun was almost overhead, lighting the scene with a short-lived brilliance that was only seen on the best of days. The house itself facing west, the paddock was framed by Beale's farm to the north and fields of sturdy green kale to the south and east. Next to the paddock, and bordering on the conservatory, was Elizabeth's garden with a neat rectangular lawn, annual flowerbeds, flowering shrubs and her French lavender hedge. The central focus of the picture was Bethany, slender as a reed and hair that sparkled like spun copper, dancing in the sunlight with an adoring dog her unlikely partner.

'She's a beauty, she is, and no mistake,' said Andrew.

'She is,' said Elizabeth, 'but, as you saw for yourself, she's also very wilful. She needs a firm hand.'

'Oh, I don't know,' said Andrew who, to the best of her knowledge, had no experience of child rearing whatsoever, 'I think it's a good thing to know your own mind.' Elizabeth sipped her coffee and decided the wisest course of action was to say no more about it. No need to involve neighbours in family matters.

A companionable silence settled on them, broken by the living room clock revving up ready to chime one o'clock.

'Will you stay for lunch, Andrew?' said Elizabeth.

'That's very kind of you, Mrs Neill,' said Andrew,' but I think I'll call Blackie and be on my way. Thanks for the coffee, now.'

'You're very welcome,' said Elizabeth, smiling. Andrew nodded a 'goodbye' and set off towards the paddock whistling for his dog. Elizabeth, glancing through the window, saw that neither Bethany nor Blackie were anywhere to be seen.

Andrew stopped, looking around, then walked towards the loosebox. Had he heard something? Elizabeth, poised to follow, hesitated, watching. He opened the loosebox door and went inside. The door swung shut and Elizabeth held her breath. She felt suspended in time. What was happening in there? Then a rush of adrenaline took her out through the door and across the paddock, as fast as the arthritis would allow. The loosebox door opened and Andrew emerged with Bethany clinging onto his back for all she was worth.

'What on earth...?' Elizabeth's mind was reeling. Andrew looked pained.

'That's enough, Bethany,' he said, weakly. 'You'd better get down,' Bethany clung tightly, shrieking with laughter bordering on hysterical.

'No, that's enough,' said Andrew, trying to free himself of her. 'Come on now, get down, will you?'

'Bethany,' said Elizabeth, in her firmest voice yet, 'Get

down. Here, let me help you.' She grabbed Bethany firmly round the waist and prized her off his back.

'Now go indoors and wash your hands ready for lunch.' Bethany, realising there was no compromising, turned her laughter into tears and sulked her way back to the house. Elizabeth looked at Andrew.

'I guess you're right, Mrs Neill,' he said, 'she does need a firm hand.'

'What on earth was going on?' said Elizabeth, feeling overtaken by the bizarre nature of the event.

'I heard noises from the loosebox so I went in to see if she was there.' He paused, looking away. 'She was there alright, crouching in the corner with Blackie. She held her hands tight round his muzzle, telling him to keep quiet. The next thing I knew, she climbed up the hay bail and jumped me.' He shifted awkwardly, embarrassed. 'It was all very odd. She was acting like somebody drunk. And, why was she hiding in the loosebox to start with?'

Why indeed? thought Elizabeth. To make sure someone came searching her out of course. She felt suddenly contrite as she remembered entertaining suspicions about him only minutes before. He was obviously more sinned against than sinning.

'I'm very sorry, Andrew,' said Elizabeth, smiling her most conciliatory smile.

'That's alright,' said Andrew, mellowing. 'Just high spirits, I expect.'

'Well, I hope you'll come and visit us again soon.' He nodded his goodbyes, called Blackie to heel then went on his way.

Elizabeth walked slowly back to the house. What was Bethany up to? Was it attention seeking? But why Andrew? No doubt he had many virtues but Elizabeth was at a loss to see what a seven-year-old would find attractive about him. Then it struck her. Jealousy. Andrew was attracted to Annie and Bethany was jealous. Right, now she felt she had something to work on. A good ticking off about inappropriate and embarrassing behaviour was called for. And more adult attention of the right kind, then Bethany would have no need to put herself at risk by seeking it out.

By the time Annie and David returned with a carload of groceries, the incident, as far as Elizabeth was concerned, was dealt with. There was to be no riding the next day. Then the situation would be reappraised. And Elizabeth would find an appropriate opportunity to remind Annie and David of their duty to praise as well as to criticise.

She was pleased to see Annie looked more relaxed and David was in a chatty mood, unusual for him these days. Things, she thought, were looking up.

'There you are,' said Elizabeth, when she came down next morning to find David in the conservatory reading yesterday's Independent. Little Ellingham was too remote for the average paperboy on a bicycle.

'Would you like breakfast? I can ask Elsie to cook something if you like.'

'Morning, mother.' He looked up from the paper and smiled. 'I'm alright, thank you. Annie made some toast and coffee.'

'Oh, good.' It was not so much the fact that he had eaten breakfast that pleased her so much the fact that Annie had felt moved to perform this small service for him.

'I was thinking,' she said, hesitating, 'that you two might like to spend some time together? Go to the coast, perhaps? Bethany and I will be quite happy here with the animals for company.'

'Are you trying to tell me something?' he said, his gaze firmly on the newspaper.

'Yes, perhaps I am.' For an awkward few moments Elizabeth felt she had gone too far. David sighed.

'I suppose it must be obvious that we're not getting on very well,' he said. Elizabeth said nothing, hoping he would continue. 'The thing is she doesn't see me as a person any more. The only role I have in her life is that of a provider. That's all I'm good for.' His voice was bitter, almost petulant.

'What role does *she* have in *your* life, David?' He thought for a moment.

'Bethany's mother. That's what it's come down to. Everything else has gone by the board. We have no relationship worth speaking of.' Elizabeth held her breath. It was so unusual for him to open up like this. It was a delicate moment not to be spoiled by any mistaken remarks on her part. 'It's too late. Things have gone too far,' he said.

'It's never too late,' said Elizabeth. 'Never.' The catch in her voice made David turn to look at her, then he realised.

'Father?' he said then reached out and took her hand.

'Don't let her go.'

'I won't.' He stood up, folding the paper carefully and leaving it on the chair. 'I'll go and talk to her.'

Elizabeth extracted a lace edged hanky from her sleeve, blew her nose and composed herself. When Annie appeared twenty minutes later, she was casually flicking through the pages of Homes and Gardens.

'David suggested a trip to the coast,' said Annie, 'do you mind if we leave Bethany with you?'

'What a good idea,' said Elizabeth, smiling. 'Of course you must go.' Annie's face lit up and Elizabeth felt her spirits lift.

'Can I play out, Gran?' Bethany asked airily, seemingly not the least bit bothered about the ban on riding.

'Yes, but you mustn't wander off. Stay in sight of the house, won't you?'

'Alright.' Bethany found an old football. 'Do you think Gnasher will come today?'

'He might, if he's invited.' Elizabeth smiled. 'Why not ring Andrew and invite them both for afternoon tea?' Bethany brightened at the idea then had second thoughts.

'Can't we have Gnasher by himself?' Feeling embarrassed about her behaviour perhaps?

'I'm sorry, we can't.' Elizabeth barely suppressed a chuckle. At last Bethany was having to face up to the fact that she couldn't have everything her own way.

'Huh,' she said and ran outside. Let her think it over.

The day was bright but cool and there was a smell of autumn in the air. That's ridiculous, thought Elizabeth. It's not even September. Yet it was there alright. It made her think of the young David, dressed in his too-big uniform, ready to start the new school year. Then the long slide into winter, punctuated by treats such as her birthday and bonfire night. Well, it wasn't winter yet and she had better make the most of whatever good weather was granted them.

She decided to tackle a job that had been on the fringes of her conscience for a while, painting the conservatory door and window frames. The woodwork was in a state and desperately needed doing before the winter.

In spite of her arthritis, Elizabeth tackled outdoor work with a zeal that rarely showed itself indoors. Even in the coldest of weather she would rather be out sweeping leaves or clearing snow than faffing around with a duster and vacuum cleaner. She was happy to leave that to Elsie. When it cam to faffing, Elsie was an impresario.

Elizabeth brushed paint stripper onto the peeling remains of old paint, which soon gave up the ghost, then got to grips with the heavy duty sandpaper in a merciless attack on the gently rotting wood. She was enjoying herself, she reflected, out in the sunshine, doing a worthwhile job of work, with her granddaughter playing nearby.

Bethany was playing football with herself. She could play five-a-side with no trouble at all. All she had to do was name the imaginary players and do the voices for them.

'To you, Kerry!'

'This way, Greg!'

'Come on Ben, you pillock!'

'Nice one, Georgie!'

Elizabeth, hearing the rough, guttural voices of players hectoring each other, against a background of squeals and grunts from the pig farm, could easily imagine a serious game going on behind her. Odd, she thought, but smiled all the same.

As the morning wore on, she methodically made her way round the window frames. Eventually, she stood back and cast a critical eye over the stripped wood. The most offending spots needed a chisel to them, she thought, and went indoors to find one in a kitchen drawer. She came back with the radio and set it on Classic FM. Music while you work, she thought, as the Ride of the Valkyries spilled out into the fresh bright air against the steady hum of Elsie's vacuum cleaner.

By the time the worst of the rot was chiselled out, the sun was high overhead and Elizabeth felt hungry. She decided to break off, give her hands a good scrub and then see what was for lunch.

'Bethany!' she called. 'Lunch time!' No reply. She switched off the radio and listened. She heard the usual background of leaves stirring, pigs snuffling and distant farm machinery. Not a sound out of place. Where was Bethany?

With surging heart, she hobbled into the house, quick as she could.

'Elsie, Elsie, have you seen Bethany? Is she in the house?' Elsie came through from the kitchen, wiping her hands on a tea towel.

'What is it, Mrs Neill? What's the matter?'

'Where's Bethany? Do you know where she is?' She was panting, more through anxiety than exertion. Bethany's previous disappearance had unnerved her more than she would admit.

'I'm sure she'll be around here somewhere,' said Elsie. 'Where else would she be?'

'Help me look for her, will you?' Elizabeth took a deep breath. She was overreacting, of course. Better pull herself together. She made off towards the loosebox, thinking she might be playing the same trick as before, but she wasn't there. She looked in the greenhouse, the dark corners of the shrubbery and along the lane. Elsie came running out of the house, her little plump body quivering like a jelly rabbit.

'She's not in the house, Mrs Neill. What shall we do?' Elizabeth took one last look down the lane.

'Wait,' she said.

'Are you sure, now?' Elsie looked unconvinced.

'Yes. We'll wait. Give her time to appear before we start

panicking.' Elsie, still waving the tea towel, looked well on the way to panicking but said no more. They walked into the house together. Elizabeth went to the bathroom to scrub her hands whilst Elsie set three places at the kitchen table, put the kettle on to boil and started buttering bread.

By the time the tea was brewed, the ham arranged on a serving plate and the salad freshly tossed in the bowl, both women had lost whatever appetites they might have had and hardly touched their lunch.

'I think I'll go for a lie down,' said Elizabeth, after picking unproductively at a lettuce leaf.

'Lie down?' Elsie couldn't contain herself any longer. 'Don't you remember that little girl who disappeared in Cossetti last year? They found nothing but her bicycle.' She burst into noisy tears.

'Elsie, dear,' said Elizabeth, reaching across the table to pat her, 'we'll have no more of that sort of speculation. She'll be back as soon as she's good and ready. You'll see.' She got up, ready to make her way upstairs.

'If it gets to three o'clock, I'm going to call the police. I can't go home until I know she's safe,' said Elsie, through her sniffles.

'Yes, dear,' Elizabeth felt by no means as confident as she tried to appear, 'do that.' She felt a great weariness closing in on her as she climbed the stairs, going through the motions as though there was a principle at stake.

She surprised herself by falling asleep. Not that she realised it until Elsie woke her up again.

'Mrs Neill, Bethany's here. She's back.' Elsie was all smiles, ready to kill the fatted calf.

'About time too,' said Elizabeth, feeling grim, 'Whatever time it is.'

'It's just gone half past two.'

'In that case, why don't you go home? It's been a difficult day and I do appreciate your support, Elsie.'

'Well, if you're sure... ' Elsie sounded a bit hesitant, hanging back like someone who was just about to miss the final act of a murder mystery.

'Yes, thank you, dear.'

'I'll leave you to it, then, Mrs Neill,' said Elsie and left in something of a huff.

Elizabeth got up and rearranged her clothes. Not that it made much difference. Her outdoor work outfit of shrunken jumper and baggy-at-the-knee tweed trousers was not at all up to her usual everyday standard. She scowled at herself in the mirror then braced herself to go downstairs and deal with Bethany.

She found her in the kitchen, wolfing a ham sandwich.

'Hello, young lady,' she said.

'Hi, Gran,' she mumbled through energetic chewing.

'Bethany,' Elizabeth's voice was stern with purpose, 'where have you been?' Bethany shrugged and turned away. Elizabeth felt a pulse of anger throb inside her.

'Don't you dare shrug me off.' Her voice was cold and heavy as ice. 'Put that sandwich down and look at me.'

Bethany turned round, her face showing nothing but faint surprise. Elizabeth glared at her until she put the sandwich down on the table and her chewing abated.

'You have caused Elsie and me a good deal of anxiety today. We were worried sick about you.'

'Were you?'

'Yes we were. What do you expect? You were nowhere to be seen for hours on end. What were we supposed to think?' Bethany shrugged again but his time it was merely a gesture.

'Went to see the pigs.'

'Why didn't you tell me you were going to see the pigs?'

'Don't know.'

'How long does it take to see the pigs?'

'Don't know.'

'Did Mr Beale know you were there?'

Bethany shrugged again. For the first time in forty years, Elizabeth lost control.

'Don't you see,' she shrieked, 'for all we knew, you could have been dead?' A moment passed whilst she regained herself.

'Sorry Gran.' Bethany smiled a paper-thin smile and her gaze slid away, unconcerned.

No she is not. Not sorry at all. She doesn't know what 'sorry' means. Elizabeth's mind flooded with cold certainty. She simply has no idea.

Then she noticed herself trembling. With what? Shock? Fear? She must go out into the garden to clear her head. She went out through the conservatory and started to pick at the lavender hedge, breathing the heavy fragrance released by her distracted fingers. There was an acrid smell in the air. Bonfire. Garden fire. Too early for that, she thought. The breeze was blowing cold, the sun waning and shadows creeping in. She shivered, allowing herself a dry chuckle. This was not like training ponies. A different matter altogether. How could she have been so stupid as to believe so?

She heard the car driving down the lane and the crunch of tyres on the driveway, the slam of doors and the sound of conversation. Annie and David. What should she say? What could she tell them? It struck her like a blow on the back of the head. She could tell them nothing they didn't already know.

'Mother?' David's voice rang through the hallway. She collected herself, put on a competent smile and went to greet them.

'Elizabeth,' said Annie, her face flushed, 'there's a fire at the scrapyard. The fire engine's there.'

'What?' Elizabeth's mind went numb. 'Andrew, is he alright?'

'He's OK,' said David. 'I stopped the car and called out to him. He's not hurt but Blackie's in a bad way.'

'I should go,' Elizabeth said but didn't move.

'It's alright Mother. You stay here. I'll walk over there and see if there's anything we can do.'

'I'll put the kettle on, shall I?' said Annie, leading the way into the kitchen. 'Where's Bethany?'

'She's here. Not far away.' Thank God. Elizabeth lowered herself onto a kitchen chair and tried to bring her mind into focus.

'I'll have a drink, dear. Gin, if you don't mind.' Annie reached into the cupboard for the bottle of Tnnqueret. It was almost empty. Annie gave Elizabeth a hard look. Elizabeth opened her mouth to protest but, realising how futile it would sound, shut it again.

'It's a bit of a shock, I suppose,' said Annie, pouring a drink and handing it to her, 'especially when it's somebody you know.' Elizabeth noticed the eczema on Annie's fingers was healing. Strange how you notice things like that in times of crisis.

'What a day!' Elizabeth sipped steadily as Annie closed the windows against the drifting smoke.

Bethany appeared, looking pale and bleary-eyed.

'Hello,' said Annie. 'Have you had a good day?' Bethany ignored her and opened the fridge door.

202

'We had a good time at the coast,' Annie tried again. Bethany took a slice of apple pie and started chewing while looking to see what else she might have.

'Did you know, there's a fire at the scrapyard?' Annie flogged on. 'The fire engine's there now.' Bethany hardly responded. Elizabeth was beginning to see everyday happenings in a different light.

'I'm afraid Blackie's in a bad way,' she said, testing her. Bethany barely glanced at her. 'You're very fond of Blackie, aren't you?'

'No, not Blackie,' said Bethany in a deadpan voice. 'It's Gnasher that I like.' Elizabeth's blood ran cold. She looked at Annie. Annie looked away.

Andrew came round the next morning, distraught. Blackie had died in the night. Elizabeth and David spent the next two days helping him. The house was in one piece but suffered smoke damage. The work shed was beyond repair, the fire having started in the lean-to where Blackie was stationed on guard duty.

'Police said there's vandals in the area,' said Andrew. 'But nobody remembers seeing anyone.' His face contorted in pain, 'Why would anyone set fire to my dog?' Elizabeth, looking at the remains of Blackie's den was asking herself the same question.

'What was their motive?' said David. 'What did they have to gain?' He shook his head.

'All I can say,' said Andrew, 'is that there's some sick people about.' He hung his head as tears rolled down his face and gathered under his chin. 'It's my fault,' he sobbed, 'I was snoozing after my lunch. I should have heard him barking, been there.' Elizabeth patted his shoulder and

David looked away. Any thoughts Elizabeth might have had about excessive amounts of lunchtime Brown Ale were suppressed by her compassion for the poor man.

'You are right,' she said. 'There are some very sick people about.' Then a though darted into her head. Bethany had set fire to a parrot. What if...? She barely had time to think it before pushing it to the back of her mind. It was too horrible to contemplate. Anyway, what evidence was there, other than circumstances? All the same, she couldn't entirely rid herself of the burden of suspicion and was glad when Annie and David decided to go home the next day.

Elizabeth waved them off, her head spinning in relief. She had expected tantrums at the prospect of leaving Hector behind but Bethany didn't give him so much as a backward glance. In fact she didn't look well at all when she got up that morning. She lolled about complaining of a headache and took little interest in anything, least of all poor Andrew and his departed dog. At last, they were packed up and off, back to Holmebridge.

Feeling exhausted, Elizabeth went into the kitchen and put the kettle to boil on the Aga. Then, breaking the rule of a lifetime, took her bottle of gin from the kitchen cupboard. It was empty. Oh, yes, she remembered. She had a drink the day of the fire, but then, she didn't think she had quite emptied the bottle. Oh well, there was the Blue Sapphire that Annie had bought at Waitrose. That had been opened too and at least a quarter of it gone. Elizabeth knew with a cold certainty that she hadn't opened that bottle and, as far as she could remember, neither had Annie or David. She put the gin back without touching it. She needed to keep a clear head, she thought, if she was going to be of any use at all.

'She was acting like somebody drunk,' Andrew had said. And he ought to know.

She took her tea into the conservatory and sat in the smoke tinged sunlight that was already on the wane. The house slowly settled itself around her and she found herself looking forward to Elsie coming in the morning.

Winter 1999

Chapter 16 – Annie

'What're you doing for Christmas?' Annie watched Kelly in the mirror, snipping at her hair like Edward Scissorhands. It seemed like a good idea at the time, coming to the hairdresser's, making an effort but she'd forgotten how exposed you are in a salon. It's like there's an unwritten rule, part of the unspoken contract you make when you walk in, you have to bare your soul.

'Nothing much,' she said, through the mirror, knowing that wouldn't be enough. People like Kelly saw Christmas as an occasion for 'doing'. The more you 'did' the better. What was she supposed to say? We'll have Christmas dinner at teatime? There'll be me, mother-in-law and Bethany? But it won't be the jolly, happy, family occasion it's always made out to be. Although, anybody who's been through anything resembling real life knows it's all a cruel myth, invented by the greeting card people, no doubt, and exploited by the churches.

Kelly looked at the haircut, screwing up her dainty face into a critical grimace. She flicked her fingers through the soggy strands and decided she was satisfied. Then she busied herself applying colour and encasing strips of hair in foil.

It was a toil of a pleasure. The process of wetting, cutting, colouring, washing, drying and tonging took all afternoon. The more colours you had, the longer it took. She settled for two, chestnut undertones and honey highlights. Some people had four or five colours. You could finish up looking like an over-ripe melon if you weren't careful. Still, if she'd made more effort in the past perhaps she could have stopped David going off to Altrincham with the girl from the Halifax; the one he'd met in a chat room for people interested in Near Earth Objects and it turned out she worked in Holmebridge. Not that 'girl' was the right word exactly. Beccy was at the desperate end of her thirties and the sort of woman who relied on gel filled bras to save her from androgyny. By the time she took everything off at night, there'd be nothing left but a skeleton. Annie knew she was bolting the stable door after the horse had gone but had decided to Pull Herself Together before it was Too Late.

Too Late for what, she couldn't put her finger on exactly. Something to do with being past forty, Bethany going to high school and a feeling that life had not only caught up with her but was frantically passing her by. And then there was always the hope that David might come back. Fat chance. She could look like Kate Moss and he wouldn't come back. Not while Bethany was around.

Anyway, here she was, looking like something from Startrek, pulling herself together. Ha, ha.

'How's Bethany going on?' Kelly's topics of conversation were limited. Not having got very far with Christmas, she was moving on to family. It was a bit early to talk about holidays. That would come after the New Year. The New Millennium.

'She's fine, thanks.' At least she hoped so. David's going last year seemed to have made no impression on Bethany whatsoever. She was settled at Oldroyd and was in Mr Kaye's top set for maths. Mr Kaye was the old fashioned sort who kept noses to grindstones so Bethany was doing well. She spent her spare time reading or watching TV and didn't seem to want to bother with whatever it was her classmates got up to. Mind you, it was perhaps as well. Some of the girls you saw out on town, wearing nothing but a cropped top and a pelmet skirt, were hardly more than twelve years old. Bethany still played pretend games with her dolls. She had an amazing repertoire of voices that allowed them to say all sorts of things she never said herself. Annie found it a bit childish and, if truth be known, a bit disturbing. Still, she'd put a whole term in at Oldroyd without any complaints.

Hope for the best. Annie didn't want any upset when she started work in the New Year. It was only temporary, a maternity leave, covering for Miss Sykes whose pregnancy was as much a shock to her as it was to anybody else. It wasn't so much that she was a dedicated single teacher that caused consternation as the fact that she was well on the way to fifty by anybody's reckoning. She looked well on it, though, and Annie was due to take over the Holmebridge Primary Year Ones in January.

Funny, isn't it? David finally got her to go back to work by leaving home. Never mind waiting until Bethany was sorted out, it was a financial necessity. Would it have been any different if she'd gone back before? They would still have had Bethany to deal with and one of them had to have the energy for that. Things could have been even worse she thought, eying her reflection in the worn-out mirror.

'Doing owt tonight?' There she was again, on about 'doing'. Kelly dragged the brush through her hair, pulling it as tight as it would go before it gave in and fell out by the roots.

'Not much,' said Annie, over the busy dryer, 'Just going out for a meal.' Kelly's face showed a flicker of interest.

'Where ye going, then?' She had an extensive and detailed knowledge of every bar and restaurant in the area. Going Out for a Meal was something she 'did'.

'A friend's.' Kelly wasn't likely to have come across Maura. You could say they moved in different circles. Maura's circle revolved round Horace and Astradate, their online astrological dating business. Kelly's revolved round her job and the local social scene. Depending on who there was to take her, she sometimes went as far as Maestro's in Bradford. What would Bethany be like at Kelly's age, she wondered. It was only a matter of a few years, then what? Didn't bear thinking about.

Kelly gave Annie's hair a good going over with the tongs and enough hairspray to keep it glued on to her head for a week.

'Have you thought about holidays yet?' As far as this conversation went, Kelly was scraping the barrel.

'Good God! What have you done to your hair?' Maura's eyes popped. 'It looks like a wig.'

'I know,' said Annie. 'It'll take a bit of getting used to.' Maura was always the same. She'd never been to a hairdresser in her life. Her grey mane was scraped back into a ponytail, like what was left of Horace's.

'You look smashing,' said Horace, smiling through the scraggle of his beard, and holding his arms out wide.

Walking into the coal fire warmth of Maura's house was like walking into a big hug. It always was. But it wasn't enough to thaw her through to the inside. Not these days.

'Where's Bethany, then?' said Horace whilst Maura got to grips with the corkscrew.

'Lynda's keeping and eye on her.' Annie said wearily. She didn't want them to know that, as far as Bethany was concerned, a meal round at Maura's represented terminal boredom. Anyway, Annie would rather go without her, given the chance.

'Lynda?' said Horace.

'You know,' said Maura, as though he should, 'Annie's next door.'

'Ah, that's alright, then. Let's have a drink.'

Maura poured out three mismatching glasses of Romanian Pinot Grigio.

'Here,' she said, as she always did, 'you can have the biggest.' It didn't make any difference. They all drank as much as they wanted. But it was nice of her.

'Come and sit down,' said Maura. 'I've got the starters ready.' Starters? Since when did Maura do starters? 'It's a Nigella.' So that was it. Horace's dedication to daytime TV was paying off. Not that he cooked himself, he just researched the recipes. The television in the corner of Maura's living room was something of an anachronism. It came with Horace and the computer. Maura was obliged to accommodate it as part of the package.

'Heard from David?' said Maura, dishing up the Mediterranean roasted peppers. They smelled like a Greek holiday.

'Last week,' said Annie. 'He's moaning about the stink in the flat. It gets into everything.' The flat was a one bedroom rented affair over the Beijing Diner on Manchester Road.

'Well, it's his own fault,' said Maura, a tart expression on her face, 'he was the one who left. And you'd think

213

somebody that works at the Halifax could find better accommodation than that.'

'I know,' said Annie, wearily. 'But at least we're still on speaking terms, that's the main thing.'

'I don't know why you bother,' said Maura, not for the first time.

'Come on now,' said Horace, probably worried that the Mediterranean roast peppers were going unappreciated, 'let's not keep going over old ground. Get stuck in and enjoy yourself.' He took a swig of wine and relaxed into his easy smile.

Annie returned the smile and put her mind to the food, appreciating the effort that had gone into it and that it was made especially for her.

She wasn't that surprised when David left. They'd been growing apart for years, their marriage eroding as fast as the Scarborough shoreline under the battering of Bethany's behaviour. In a way, she felt sorry for him. He'd reached the point where he couldn't stand the sight of her. Couldn't keep control. Said he'd strangle her as soon as look at her. So there she was left holding the baby.

'Are you looking forward to getting back to work?' said Horace, as though he knew anything about it. Horace hadn't worked for as long as anybody could remember. True, he sat in the Community Caff from time to time but he didn't actually *do* much, not since he renovated the Jukebox in 1995. All the same, it was good of him to ask.

'I'm looking forward to it,' she said. Hadn't she been looking forward to it for years? 'But, it's so long since I had a class of my own. You know?' Maura and Horace nodded sagely, their faces lit with sympathy and understanding.

'You'll soon get back into it,' said Maura. 'It'll do you

good.' Do her good? What was that supposed to mean? Take her mind off Bethany? Get things in proportion? Give her something else to think about beside herself? The way Maura was talking, you'd think teaching was some kind of therapy. Far from it. Teaching was enough to put you *into* therapy these days. All the same, she felt a twinge of anticipation, a forlorn hope that this might be her salvation.

Maura cleared away the starter plates then took a casserole dish out of the gas oven and set it in the middle of the table with a flourish.

'Wait 'til you try this,' she said. 'It's a Delia.' Delia? Well, fancy.

By the time they'd had the pudding, a curd tart Horace had fetched from the Corner Deli, they were stuffed. Maura opened a bottle of what she called pudding wine. Quite nice for Californian, thought Annie.

She didn't want to go. She could stay there all night in the fug of Maura's kitchen. But she had to get back for Bethany. And frost was forecast.

Bethany wanted to go to Meadowhall but Annie couldn't face it. It would mean an hour's drive on the M1 then a queue a mile long to get off, parking half a mile from the entrance then a foot-aching trail round all the same shops you could find in Huddersfield town centre, so that's where they went.

'What're you getting for Dad?' she said, turning her collar up against the biting wind. Bethany shrugged her shoulders but Annie didn't care. She'd done her duty just by reminding her.

'I'm not getting anything for Beccy,' said Bethany.

'Neither am I.' They looked at each other and giggled. Annie was surprised. She couldn't remember them colluding before.

'Let's go and look in Samuel's, I want to find something nice for Elizabeth.' They crossed the street and peered in the busy window. Watches, rings, necklaces, bracelets, earrings, that was only the start of it. You could buy anything from pot dogs to grandfather clocks if you had a mind to.

'That's nice,' Bethany pointed to a cast resin figure of a Labrador.

'It looks like Blackie. Do you remember?' said Annie, Bethany said nothing but when they went inside she bought a poodle instead. That's more Lynda's cup of tea, thought Annie but didn't say.

She chose a silver brooch shaped like an Egyptian ankh. 'That's for a long life,' she said.

'Gran's had a long life already. She's well old.'

'She can have a bit longer, can't she?'

Bethany's eyes were roving over a glass cabinet display.

'I want a watch,' she said.

'You would *like* a watch?' Annie prompted.

'Yeh.'

'Which one would you like?'

'That one.' Bethany pointed to a purple Swatch with jumbled up numbers on its face.

'That one, what?'

'That Swatch.'

'You're sure that's the one you'd like?'

'Yeh.'

'Yes, what?' I'll make her say 'please' if it kills me, thought Annie. It nearly did. The next thing she knew, she

216

was lying sprawled across the floor with her legs akimbo and her clothes up round her bum.

The Accident and Emergency Department was heaving.

'It's the Christmas rush,' said the triage nurse, as though it were the Borough Market. Annie was too upset to think about it. Her ankle throbbed like a sledgehammer and her whole body shook with the force of it.

They were eventually sent to a cubicle that smelled of iodine.

'What happened to you?' said the junior doctor whose name badge said Shaheen.

'I don't know,' said Annie. 'We were in the jeweller's, looking at watches... then... there were some steps behind me...' To be honest, she could have sworn she was pushed. It was all so quick.

She remembered a red haired shop assistant insisting she didn't get up. Wait for the ambulance, she'd said. Annie felt embarrassed through her pain. The shop was busy and she was sat there like a lump with customers climbing over her. The assistant was making a speech about health and safety regulations, exonerating them from blame in advance. It wasn't their fault. A big notice warned potential litigants to Please Mind the Steps. Bethany stood on the sidelines. A detached observer. That's what she was doing now, standing there in the cubicle as though she was nothing at all to do with what was going on. Had she pushed her? Annie remembered a dig in the ribs. That might have been all it was, just a dig in the ribs, punishment for picking her up on her manners. Anyway, here she was, hardly able to walk and everything to do for Christmas.

Sometimes, she could lie down and die.

'You will need an x-ray,' said Dr Shaheen, squeezing her foot to the point of agony, 'just to make sure there are no broken bones.' Her hands were tiny but she didn't half have some strength in them. 'You'll have to wait for a porter.'

So there she was, stuck in a cubicle with Bethany who fidgeted and sighed as though she were being put upon. It was no good trying to make conversation. That would be asking for trouble.

Eventually, a young man with a shaved head and earrings appeared and wheeled her dexterously down the corridor to join the queue in the x-ray department. Bethany followed.

'There you go,' he said cheerfully, whizzing the chair round and applying the brakes.

'Thanks,' said Annie, noticing at the same time the wide film-star smile Bethany bestowed in his direction. He strode off back down the corridor, glancing back at her over his shoulder.

The x-ray queue was quite fast moving. They probably want to get finished by Christmas, was Annie's sour thought.

It only took a minute to hold her foot in an excruciating position whilst the radiographer disappeared behind a screen, leaving her to the full force of the radiation. Then she was back in the queue, waiting for another porter.

To Bethany's evident delight, the same young man turned up again, all smiles, and wheeled her back to Dr Shaheen.

'It's only sprained. Not broken,' said Dr Shaheen, scanning the ex-ray on a VDU. Thank God for small mercies. It was strapped up and that was that.

Annie told Bethany to go outside and call a taxi on her mobile.

They called in at Samuel's to pay for the brooch and buy the blessed Swatch, then went on home. It cost a small fortune.

'What a nightmare,' said Annie, hobbling through the door.

'I told you we should've gone to Meadowhall,' said Bethany.

Horace came round to help.

'I'm not bothering with a tree and all that,' said Annie. 'I can't see the point.' So he brought some holly.

'You have to have *something* Pagan,' he said, 'or it won't be Christmas.'

'Can you meet Elizabeth?' she said. Elizabeth was due on Christmas Eve. She'd be arriving at the station and nobody to meet her. 'You could bring her in a taxi.'

'Aye, I reckon I can.'

'I haven't got a present for David.'

'He can do without.'

'Bethany hasn't got a present for David.'

'That's her lookout, not yours.'

'I haven't got a present for Maura.'

'Never mind. She's got you.'

'I haven't got a present for you.'

'Ah, well, nowthen,' said Horace, stroking his beard, 'that's serious, that is.' He chuckled and gave her a hug.

Thank God for Horace.

She sighed when he'd gone and poured herself a sherry. That's what you're supposed to do at Christmas. To keep the cold out.

Elizabeth sank unsteadily into the low-slung sofa. She wasn't used to modern furnishings and ambient uplight. She was used to perching on a horsehair couch, gazing into a glowing log fire. She smiled as Annie sloshed the after-dinner brandy into tumblers.

'I'm glad to be here,' she said. 'Christmas Eve is a bad day to travel.'

'I don't want to be rude,' said Annie, handing her a drink, 'but wouldn't you rather spend Christmas with David?'

'Yes, I would. If David were here with you, where he belongs.'

'It's not his fault, you know.' She sighed and picked up her glass. 'Bethany runs him ragged. He couldn't stand her any more. He had to get out before he did her an injury.'

'And what about you?'

'She runs me ragged as well.' You can say that again. Actually put it into words. Bethany's a past master at running you ragged. She taunts. She lies. She steals. She undermines everything you try to do. She makes a mockery. And you can't appeal to her better nature because she hasn't got one. She laughs in your face. She'd laugh in your face if you throttled her. To the last gasp.

What can you do? Nothing. Not a blind thing. Send her to bed, stop her pocket money, ground her, confiscate her computer, stop her going on the school trip; nothing bothers her because she doesn't give a shit. She's the Kamikaze kid.

There. She'd said it. Not out loud but she'd said it all the same. It was like the road to Damascus. There would be no going back.

'But you haven't given up on her.'

'No.' Not yet. She pushed her hair behind her ears and gulped her brandy, doubting her own sanity.

'So,' said Elizabeth, softly, 'what's going to become of you?'

'Me?'

'The three of you. The family.'

'I don't know.' Annie felt the usual dismal heartache but didn't have any tears left to cry. She was all dried out.

Bethany appeared like an Angel of the Nativity in her baggy white T-shirt, her long hair loose and curly from the shower, and smelling of lilies.

'Dad rang me on me mobile. He's promised to send me some money for Christmas.' Silence hung in the air, then

'At least he's trying,' said Annie.

'Very trying,' said Elizabeth.

Chapter 17 – Annie

'Another Christmas Day over,' said Elizabeth, stacking the dishwasher to the strains of the King's College Choir's 'Festival of Christmas Music' CD. 'How many more, I wonder?'

'What?' Annie was sorting out bits of turkey crown worth keeping for sandwiches.

'I'm getting on, you know. I'll be eighty four next year.' This was a revelation. Elizabeth never mentioned her age. It was one of those things she just didn't do.

'Eighty four?' Annie was amazed. She didn't look a day over seventy, in spite of her arthritis.

'I'm afraid so. I wasn't exactly a child bride, you know,' she said, twiddling her engagement ring, or what was left of it after a lifetime of wear and tear. 'To tell the truth, Francis was ten years younger than me.' She had a perky look on her face, inviting reassuring protestations of how young she looked.

'I told you Gran was old,' said Bethany, busy texting a message on her mobile.

'Bethany,' Annie warned.

'It's true. I *am* old.' Elizabeth sighed.

Trust Bethany. Any little balloon of happiness floating about, you could guarantee she would prick it. Bethany was a past master at pricking balloons.

'I'm off to Jessica's house tomorrow,' she said. 'Her mam says I can.'

'When did she say that?' Annie was surprised. Bethany

222

had been hanging about with Jessica since they went to Oldroyd together but her mam had maintained a dignified silence since the Telly Tubby incident all those years ago.

'Just now,' said Bethany, waving her mobile. 'Jessica asked her.'

'That will be nice, dear,' said Elizabeth, smiling.

'Yeh.'

We'll see.

Annie wrapped the turkey bits in foil and put them in the fridge.

'What shall we do? Watch television?' she said, washing her hands with mild green Fairy liquid.

'I'm quite happy listening to this lovely music,' said Elizabeth, sitting at the kitchen table. Bethany, still texting, said nothing.

Annie decided to hobble upstairs and phone David, just to make sure there was, however rickety, still a bridge between them.

'Hello.'

'David?' she said, as though she wouldn't know his voice anywhere.

'Annie.'

'I'm just phoning to wish you all the best for Christmas.'

'Thanks. Same to you.' His voice wasn't so much cold as ... hopeless. She felt a sharp pain in the middle of her chest. Something like longing.

'David. Are you alright?' It came out wrong. More like an accusation than a cry of despair.

'I suppose so.' He didn't say 'What about you?' He already knew the answer.

'Are you doing anything special for the New Millennium?' The fast approaching New Millennium felt

223

like something that was only for other people. She couldn't bring herself to believe in it.

'Actually, it's not the New Millennium until the end of the year 2000.' His voice was stronger, now that he was on firm ground, ground where he knew what he was talking about. 'If you stop to think about it...' She let him go on a bit. It did him good to think he knew best. Anyway, she couldn't be bothered with it.

'Yes, you're right,' she said. 'Well, whenever it is, I hope things change for the better.' She felt a prickle of tears at the back of her eyes. That was a good sign. She wasn't completely wiped out yet. 'Keep in touch.' She hung up. At least they were talking. Even though it was about something theoretical.

She limped back to the kitchen to find Elizabeth poking at Bethany's mobile. Bethany was smiling a patronising smile

'Look at this, isn't it marvellous? Bethany's teaching me how to send a text message!' Elizabeth hadn't looked so animated in a long time. 'There's life in the old dog yet!'

'It's all very well, you phoning to say you'll be late,' said Annie, 'but you'll be putting everybody out.'

'I won't,' Bethany's voice was peevish.

'Bethany, you've been there all day. Don't you think Jessica's mam's had enough of you by now? It is Boxing Day, you know. Give her a break.'

No answer.

'And it's bad enough me driving with a bad ankle never mind stopping up late as well. I ought to be resting it. Look, if it's just a matter of watching a film, you could watch it at home.' Annie heard the wheedling tone in her voice and felt cross with herself.

'I'll come and get you in half an hour,' she said, trying to sound as though she meant it. 'Half an hour. OK?' She hung up before Bethany had chance to contradict and filled the kettle. No good drinking anything stronger than tea until she'd driven Bethany home. Anyway, it was just as well, she was drinking far too much these days.

As it happened, she didn't have to wait long at all. The kettle had just about struggled to boiling point when the doorbell rang. It was only an ordinary doorbell, not one of these that barks like a dog or plays a popular classic, but even so, it could get on your nerves when it went on long enough.

'Who the hell is that that?' Annie snapped, loud enough to hear through the door.

'I'll tell you who it is!' yelled a voice on the other side. 'It's Jessica's mam. I'll have you know I've returned your daughter and I don't want to see sight nor sound of her ever again.' Annie had opened the door by this time so got most of the message at full blast. Jessica's mam was red in the face and doing her best to look down her nose. Not an easy feat with somebody who's a good six inches taller than you.

'What's the matter?'

'What's the matter?' shrieked Jessica's mam. 'Ask her what's the matter!' She turned the full force of her glare in Bethany's direction, made a sound like a tubercular cough, then stalked off, digging her stilettos into the tarmac as she went.

'You'd better come in and tell me what's going on,' said Annie, much as she felt like slamming the door in Bethany's face.

***

Neither Annie nor Elizabeth got much sleep. When they finally gave in and got up, Bethany could be heard snoring like a pig.

'I really think David should come home and deal with this.' Elizabeth's voice shook. With anger, if the look on her face was anything to go by.

'It would only make things worse.' Annie gazed out of the kitchen window, watching the early morning frost twinkling in the pale sunlight.

'How much worse could they get?' Elizabeth was not easily put off.

Much worse, Annie suspected. All that trouble over the years, it wasn't just isolated bits and pieces here and there. It all added up to something. Like a snowball rolling downhill, getting bigger and bigger, gathering random debris in its tracks. If it rolled on long enough, gained enough momentum, it could fly off the end of the earth and become a planet in it's own right. A deep-seated fear sent shards of ice through her nerves, right through to her finger ends.

It had been there all her life, that deep-seated fear. She was probably born with it. And her mother did her level best to make sure it was nourished and thrived. It was a control mechanism, you see. Push the right button and you're in charge. They all had their buttons to push. Madge might die. Johnnie might bugger off and never come back. Uncle Ted might ... Now Bethany. Bethany might drive her over the edge. If she let her. Only if she let her.

'I'd better go and see Jessica's parents,' said Annie in a voice like plate glass, 'I want to know what's going on and I'm not going to get anything out of Bethany.'

'I suppose you're right.' Elizabeth sat crumpled into herself, looking suddenly small. Annie turned to put the kettle on.

'I'll have a coffee first. Fortify myself.'

'What about Bethany? Isn't she having breakfast?'

'Never mind her. Let sleeping dogs lie.'

Bethany appeared half an hour later, moaning about a headache.

'What have you been drinking?' Elizabeth gave her sharp look. Bethany gave her a baleful stare.

'Gran asked you a question,' said Annie. Manners again.

'Nothin.' Bethany shrugged her shoulders and turned to the fridge, grabbed a tub of Cherrylicious, found a spoon and disappeared into the lounge.

'Ice cream for breakfast?' said Elizabeth.

'Don't rise to the bait,' said Annie, clattering pots in the dishwasher, 'It's not worth it. Save your energy.'

'I haven't got much energy these days.' Elizabeth said in a sort of confession. She never admitted to anything that might sound remotely like a weakness. 'In fact, I've been thinking about selling the house and finding something smaller. Much smaller. It's all getting too much for me.'

Annie's heart warmed to her. Poor woman. She must be feeling bad. Annie felt a twinge of anxiety as it dawned on her how much she depended on Elizabeth nowadays.

'That sounds like a good idea,' she said, joining her at the kitchen table and propping her bad foot up on a chair.

'Particularly as Elsie is retiring soon. She'll be sixty next birthday.'

'Where will you be looking?' Annie tried to keep her tone light so as not to show panic in her voice.

'I thought I might look in Holmebridge.' That, Annie knew, was a tentative suggestion that needed encouragement.

'That would be great. Having you nearby.' She smiled for the first time that day.

'That's settled, then.' Elizabeth smiled in return. 'Now what about Jessica?'

Jessica's house was no more than a fifteen minute drive away but it was so different from the brick built boxes on the Riverside development it may as well have been co-opted from another continent.

The great round tower with its little slitty windows and the adjoining lean-to looked like the remains of a monastery on a Greek island; the sort you see in a Thompson's brochure perched on top of a high-rise hill. Mediterranean ceramic tiling on the gatepost bore the name Pharos. Stuck there at the end of a row of semis, it looked just about as ridiculous as a fairy cake in a butcher's shop.

Annie pressed the electronic doorbell and heard what sounded, for all the world, like a church bell tolling the dead. The wonders of modern technology. Jessica's mam opened the door in double force Damart slippers.

'I'm sorry to bother you, but I need your help,' said Annie, thinking she might appeal to her better nature.

'Help?' Jessica's mam looked startled, as though she might be asked to childmind.

'I wanted to ask you what happened yesterday. Bethany won't tell me anything. I hope you don't mind.'

'Oh,' Jessica's mam softened an inch. 'Come in then. I was thinking I ought to be having a word with you.' She led the way into a spacious circular room, made all the more spacious by the fact that there was hardly any furniture in it. Minimalist, you might call it.

'Have you just moved in?' said Annie.

'We've been here about five years,' said Jessica's mam,

drawing up what looked like a B&Q patio chair. 'Take a seat.' She pulled up a matching one and sat next to Annie, not exactly opposite but near enough to make her feel uncomfortable. There was no visible form of heating. Annie looked down at the bare wooden floor. No wonder they needed thermal slippers.

'I'm sorry, Mrs Neill,' said Jessica's mam, 'you're not going to like this.' Annie sighed. Here we go again.

'Call me Annie,' she said. It was ridiculous standing on ceremony after all those years.

'Did you know, Mrs Neill, your daughter logs on to pornographic websites?'

'What?'

'And I don't mean soft. The stuff she was showing Jessica was... well, disgusting by anybody's standards. Jessica was very upset, I can tell you. She's not been exposed to that sort of thing before.'

'Neither has Bethany.' Annie felt the breath knocked out of her. What was this all about? 'We monitor what she watches on TV and we have web guards on the computer. She can't have seen anything like that at home.' The room swirled slightly. She had to fix on the door to make sure she wasn't swirling with it. 'I mean, don't you have a web guard?'

'We have Norton Anti-virus,' Jessica's mam said stoutly.

'But that's not the same...'

'And,' she said, clinching her argument, 'We don't allow Jessica a credit card.'

'Credit card?'

'You have to pay to get on those websites, you know.'

'Bethany hasn't got a credit card either.' I mean, what eleven-year-old would have a credit card?

'Well, somebody did.' The air bristled with accusation.

'I don't know what to say.' Annie shook her head and swallowed.

'And what's more, there's evidence on our computer. If the police examine it... well, our name'll be mud.'

'Police? How d'you mean, police?'

'Well people have been arrested for that sort of thing.' Jessica's mam pursed her lips so hard they looked like somebody's bum. 'I mean, look at Barry Glitter.'

'You're not going to the police?' Annie couldn't credit it. 'That's a different thing altogether.'

'It might come to that.'

'In that case,' said Annie, 'can I see the 'evidence' so I know exactly what it's all about?'

'I'll have a word with Kenneth,' said Jessica's mam, standing up and heading for the door. 'Won't be a minute.'

She came back with her husband in tow. He was a chubby little man with sandy hair and a complexion like a knitted dishcloth. Annie stood up and shook hands.

'Mrs Neill wants to know what the girls were looking at on the Internet,' said Jessica's mam.

'I shouldn't worry too much,' said Kenneth, smiling. 'Jessica explained they were trying to email a friend and they got the wrong site by mistake.' He flashed Annie a wink. 'I blame the schools,' he said, knowing full well Annie and David were teachers, 'they don't teach spelling like they used to, ha, ha.' He rubbed his hands together to show what a jolly good joke it was. Annie was struck dumb.

'Just what exactly are you on about, Kenneth?' His wife was obviously used to him.

'Hotmail.com,' said Kenneth, spreading his hands wide. 'Hot Male! Get it?'

'Oh,' said Jessica's mam.

'Then,' he laughed, 'I suppose their curiosity got the better of them.'

'Just a minute,' said Annie. 'You said they paid by credit card.'

'Did they, Eunice?' Kenneth turned to his wife.

'You have to, to get on that sort of site.'

'What sort of site?'

'Not a public site.'

Both turned to look at Annie, as though an explanation might be forthcoming. Annie took a few deep breaths.

'What do you suppose,' she said, 'is the best thing to do now?'

'Check your credit card,' said Eunice.

Driving back home was weird. Annie remembered the panic attacks she used to have that made her feel as though she didn't know what was real anymore. She felt like that now. Only she couldn't summon up the energy for a panic attack.

One thing was real enough though. Her credit card was missing from her purse. It was the first thing she checked when she got in the car.

At one time she would have swallowed any old excuse. But only because she wanted to. There was always a warning voice, telling her she was too gullible, urging her to dig down to the truth, but she ignored it. People who hear voices usually finish up in a psychiatric facility unless, by some strange fluke, they happened to be somebody important like the President of America.

She was listening now, though. Too much had happened to keep sweeping under the carpet. Eventually, you run out of carpet.

Bethany had always showed an interest in sexuality,

sometimes too much for her own good. Like that phase she went through of groping little boys willies. She must have only been six or seven. And, even now, the way she got physical with men. Any old man. Even Horace. She was always sprawling herself over his knees and snuggling up to him. She was way too old for that sort of carry on. In fact, it had crossed Annie's mind to warn the teachers at Oldroyd, just in case she compromised any of them. It had been known. She'd been fawning round male teachers since she started school, using her prettiness to wield power, sometimes to the teachers' embarrassment. Now she was growing up, she was getting to be more than pretty. She was getting dangerous. Annie sighed. What to do? What in God's name could you do?

Sometimes she felt like driving into a brick wall.

On the spur of the moment, she took a right turn up the near perpendicular road that climbed over the moors to Keighley. She wasn't sure if she was just buying time or if she might bugger off altogether.

She stopped on the brow of the hill and parked up beside the crags. Bethany used to be taken up there in the holidays. She would leap fearlessly from rock to mossy rock, scaring Annie half to death.

She opened the window and breathed the sharp air. The sun exerted itself to shine wanly over the pinched rooftops below. She opened the car door to catch the odd warming ray on her face. Then, before she knew what she was doing, she was out of the car, stripping her coat off and throwing herself on the rocks like a moth to a light bulb. Good job nobody was there. They might have thought she was going barmy. Actually, that might not be a bad idea. You could say insanity would be an easy option. Then she could be forgiven for strangling the little witch.

A few minutes on the frozen rock soon brought her to her senses. The sun had given up and gone in. She could hardly feel her arms and legs, never mind her fingers and toes.

'I *must* be mad,' she said, taking comfort in the thought. 'Balm cake,' she said with a half-baked smile. She found her coat and, feeling a bit sheepish, put it on again. Then she sat in the car with the heater on full blast.

Thinking about it, no wonder she was acting daft. Folk had been known to be committed with less provocation than she had. They'd started out with such high hopes. A pretty little girl of their own to bring up, a purpose in life. When did it all go pear shaped?

Well, to be honest, right from the start. Bethany had never been what you might call normal with her secretive ways that made you feel she couldn't abide you and had to function behind your back. She kept herself to herself even before she could talk. She listened through keyholes and spied round corners and stored her findings for future use. You could love her all you liked and still come away with the feeling she was laughing at you. It made you feel stupid. It did. A full grown adult made to feel stupid just by the look on her face.

Friends? Forget it. Any friendship Bethany had was with people she could use. Like Omar, prey to her sexual curiosity or Jessica who had a computer without net guards. They saw through her in the end. Or their parents did. But she was growing up now, out of parental censorship, and so were her victims.

'I've got a psychopath on my hands,' said Annie and knew in her bones that it was true. She'd finally managed not to look the other way. It was quite liberating really, once you got used to the idea. Perhaps it wasn't all due to her bad mothering after all, in spite of what David might say. Perhaps she'd been damaged to begin with. They're not like puppies, though, you can't take them back when they don't develop the right traits. No wonder they never got to the bottom of her behaviour problems, there may well be no bottom to get to.

She caught sight of herself in the driving mirror. For a minute there, she looked like somebody else.

She found Elizabeth on her hands and knees in the kitchen. The smell of stale coffee hung sharp in the air. The soundtrack of 'The Sound of Music' annual rerun wafted through from the lounge.

'How d'you solve a problem like Maria...?'

Easy. Shoot her.

'Hello, dear,' Elizabeth was poking about under the kitchen sink. 'Have you seen my ring?'

'What ring?'

'You know, my engagement ring. I took it of to wash the coffee cups.' Annie never did cure Elizabeth of washing up behind her back. If she didn't grab the cups and stash them in the dishwasher, they'd be given the same hand wash treatment Elizabeth favoured for her mismatched collection of Coalport. That was more than they deserved coming, as they did, from Ikea.

'Sorry, no.'

'Oh, well. I suppose it will turn up eventually.' Elizabeth sighed and pulled herself to her feet by climbing up the sink unit. 'How did you get on?'

'How do you hold a rainbow in your hand?' enquired Mother Superior.

You don't. Bloody stupid woman.

234

'Where is she?' Annie's voice was terse.

'Bethany? In her room.' Annie stalked through the lounge, turning the telly off as she went, and clomped up the staircase as though she meant business. Elizabeth followed, looking anxious, like a hamster let out of its cage.

Bethany was lying on her bed, drinking lemonade and flicking through a copy of 17. She didn't deign to lift her eyes off the magazine when her mother walked in.

Annie registered the mess; drawers pulled out, surfaces swiped, floor littered with things broken and torn, including the crushed remains of the blessed Swatch spread over the floor.

'Oh! What on earth?' Elizabeth's hand went to her mouth.

'She's trashed her room.' Annie's voice was cold.

'But, why?'

'Because she can.'

Bethany levelled a hard stare from below her lashes.

'Where's my credit card?' Annie asked in the same frigid voice. Bethany shrugged.

'I know you've got it. Where is it?' Bethany didn't respond. Annie started sorting through the mess, through Bethany's slouch bag, through her coat pockets and, eventually, snatched the pillow from under her elbow. She pulled the case of the pillow and shook it. The credit card fell out.

Bethany sprang to her feet and hurled herself at Annie, thumping her round the head with a series of hefty blows. Annie, caught of guard, was stunned. She was well used to verbal fights, and they were exhausting enough, but this was a new ball game. She clapped her hand to her nose in an effort to stem the blood that gushed down her front and dripped in heavy blobs onto the brand new candy-striped rug.

'Bethany! How dare you?' Elizabeth's voice shook with fury. She pulled herself up to her full height and mustered her authority.

'Apologise to your mother. Then you can clean up your room. And I mean *now*.' There was a buzz of silence in the air then Bethany loped off. They heard the front door slam. Elizabeth snatched up the tumbler of lemonade that was perched on the edge of the bedside cabinet and took a swig. Annie thought she was dreaming.

'That's my gin,' said Elizabeth. The glass slipped through her fingers and landed on the corner of a cast-aside drawer where it smashed into pieces. Annie felt her legs wobble beneath her and sat down suddenly on the edge of the bed.

The darkness closed in. She was too tired to think. Too tired to hurt. Too heavy to move. The cloud that hung over her, haunting her, kept changing shape; Bethany shape, David shape, Madge shape, Uncle Ted. The colours were changing from grey to red, then black. She felt a tight ball of grief somewhere in the middle of her chest and a sensation like her blood was running out of every pore in her body. She knew if it went on long enough, she would die. But she wasn't all that bothered. Enough is enough. Enough is as good as a feast. And she'd had a basin full.

As her vision cleared, she made out Elizabeth tidying things into drawers.

'You told Bethany to do that,' said Annie, her voice weak and pathetic.

'I know,' said Elizabeth, on the verge of tears. 'I don't know what else to do.' So, it had come to that. Even Elizabeth didn't know what to do.

Annie roused herself to start tidying up too, a feeble attempt to put things in order, to restore a semblance of normality. To make things more like they should be.

'She's out without a coat,' she said, picking up piles of underwear off the floor.

'It's her own fault.'

'Do you think she'll come back?' said Annie, dumping mini-bras and knickers into the chest of drawers.

'I'm sure she will when she's hungry,' said Elizabeth, pulling the foil-wrapped package of turkey from under the bed.

'I'd better call the police? I mean, what if anything happens to her?' Elizabeth didn't answer, she was looking at something in the palm of her hand, her face screwed up as though she might scream any minute now.

'Don't tell me,' said Annie. It was the ring, Elizabeth's frail, worn, beloved engagement ring. The little emeralds had been prized out.

It was always the same. If Bethany wanted to get back at you she destroyed something that mattered. Annie had no end of belongings disappear over the years. It used to be things like her Channel perfume, scarves, necklaces, or a book she was in the middle of reading. They reappeared sooner or later, smashed or torn to bits. Now she was moving upmarket, credit cards and engagement rings. What next? Would she go and trash the car? Bethany obviously had no fear of trashing her own stuff either. Just to show she didn't care. Nothing mattered to her. That way, she was unpunishable.

'I'm sorry.' Annie put her arm round Elizabeth. Her shoulders felt skinny through her jumper.

'It's not important. Not really. It's only a ring. It's Bethany I'm worried about.' Poor woman. Why should she have to put up with the little devil's antics? Why should anybody?

'There must be somebody,' said Annie, burning with desperation. 'There's got to be *somebody* we can turn to.'

Why had she come back, she wondered, come back to worse than what she'd left? Perhaps she should just have buggered off after all.

Sure as eggs, she turned up at teatime. Sauntered in as though nothing had happened.

'Where've you been?' Annie tried to sound offhand. To tell the truth, she felt offhand. Looking at Bethany now, shrugging her shoulders, hands in her jeans pockets and bored look on her cold-chapped face, she realised with a shock that she didn't even like her any more. In fact, she resented her. A cuckoo in the nest, bullying her way to the centre of everything and grabbing all there was to be had. She was the kind of cuckoo that would happily starve its foster parents to death if there wasn't enough to go round. What crime against humanity could she possibly have committed in a former life to be landed with her in this? All she'd ever wanted was an ordinary life. It wasn't all that much to ask was it?

'I went to Maura's,' said Bethany, in a 'so there' tone of voice.

That's right, thought Annie. Go to my friends, telling your lies, poisoning their ears against me. She could already imagine Maura's forthcoming advice, wishy-washy psycho-crap about giving her respect. *You have to give respect to earn respect.* Where Bethany was concerned, that was a one-way highway.

How come she has to commandeer my friends?

Because she hasn't got any of her own, or because she wants to turn them against me, leave me on my own with nobody? Got to hand it to her, crafty little bitch.

She turned and hobbled out of the room.

Chapter 18 – Annie

The phone rang for long enough before Aire Valley Social Services deigned to pick it up. Probably on holiday, just when you need them.

'Social Services,' said a vague and distant voice.

'Hello.' Annie hardly knew where to begin. 'I... I want to talk to somebody.'

'Have you tried the Samaritans?' Samaritans? Since when were they supposed to substitute for Social Services? Didn't they have enough on their hands with all the seasonal suicides you read about in the papers. She must sound desperate.

'Well, no. It's more a Social Services matter.'

'Sorry love, I'm only the cleaner. Just a minute, I'll go and find somebody.' She disappeared for several minutes then efficient footsteps could be heard approaching the phone.

'Alison speaking. How may I help you?' Alison's voice was young and clipped in a 'don't even try to answer that' sort of way.

'I need help,' sighed Annie, 'with my daughter.'

'I'm afraid we're operating a skeleton staff over the holidays,' Annie had visions of long bony fingers wrapped round the phone at the other end and a lower mandible creaking up and down to ask, 'Is it urgent?'

'It's my adopted daughter.'

'Yes, but is it *urgent*?' How bad does it have to be to be urgent? What scale of urgency could you apply? There must be something like the Richter Scale of Urgencies stashed in the back of somebody's filing cabinet somewhere.

'Yes, it's urgent.' Her voice wavered. 'I'm at my wit's end.' A short pause followed. Time to let the idea sink in.

'When did the adoption take place?' Alison began to sound a shade more sympathetic.

'Going on ten years ago.' Ten years. My God. How had she survived?

'And was that in this area?'

'Yes. The social workers were Mrs Whitehead and Ms Blackshaw. If I could just speak to one of them...'

'I wouldn't know about that,' said Alison. 'We've been reorganised since then. Three times. They've probably been retired off by now.' That was obviously what happened in such circumstances. She sounded as though that was the end of the matter. Annie felt anger welling up inside her. Anger mixed with a generous dollop of self-pity. Fit to choke her.

'Who *can* I talk to, then?' she wailed.

'What's your address?'

'13 Brackenbed Drive, Holmebridge.'

Annie could hear a tap tapping as Alison busied herself with a keyboard.

'Sorry,' she said with obvious relief, 'it's nothing to do with us. You need to get in touch with your local office.'

'Which office would that be?' Annie said, wearily.

'Your nearest? Erm, Holmefield I should think. Try giving them a ring. I'll just get the number for you.' Annie put the phone down feeling like a traitor, surrendering her daughter to the mob. Still, that didn't stop her from punching in the number for the office in Holmefield.

'Social Services.' The woman sounded older than

241

Alison and her first two words were enough to betray a tone like that employed by GP's receptionists to protect harassed doctors by fending off demanding patients.

'Hello.' Annie felt better prepared the second time round. 'I want to speak to a social worker about my adopted daughter. I'm desperate.'

'I see,' said Madam. 'Name?'

'Annie Neill.' Tap, tap, tap.

'There's no record of that here.'

'Well, I do exist. At least most of the time.' That was probably a big mistake. Sarcasm doesn't go down all that well with women like her.

'Address?'

'13 Brackenbed Drive, Holmebridge.'

'In that case,' she said, with relish, 'in that case you're out of our area.'

'What area am I in, then?'

'Try Aire Valley.'

'But I've already...'

'Sorry.' That, thought Annie, was said with a smile. She redialled the Aire Valley number.

'Hello, can I speak to Alison?'

'Sorry.' It was a young man this time. 'She's in a meeting.' Probably in the lav. 'Can I get her to ring you back?'

'It's about my adopted daughter. I need to talk to a social worker.' She was practically pleading by now.

'Sure,' said the lovely young man. 'Just let me take some details then I'll find one for you. Where do you live?' She recited her address again. It was beginning to sound like a mantra.

'I don't know about that.' Doubt hung heavy in his voice. Tap, tap, tap. ' I'm sorry. You're out of our area.'

'I know. I've already spoken to Alison. She said try Holmefield and I did and they sent me back to you. I must be in *somebody's* area.' She felt exhausted.

'I expect so.' Agreed the young man. Tap, tap, tap. 'Here we are. Kingsbury and Shelf. Try Kingsbury and Shelf. Hang on, I'll get you the number.' At least he was trying, more than could be said for anybody else.

The Kingsbury and Shelf number rang six times before an answering service kicked in.

'Sorry, this office is closed until January 2nd 2000. In emergency, please ring the out of hours emergency team on the following number ...' Annie dropped the phone and subsided onto the unstructured sofa. Elizabeth and Bethany were standing there, mouths gaping like a Greek chorus ready to hold forth.

'I've had enough,' she sighed. 'Enough of your carryings on.' She nearly said 'enough of you' but stopped herself just in time. Bethany smirked with self-importance. Elizabeth's face was as white as a bleached sheet.

'I could do with a cup of tea,' said Annie, looking straight at Bethany. 'Shape yourself and put the kettle on. Make yourself useful for once in your life.' Bethany amazed everybody by doing as she was told.

Next morning Maura landed on the doorstep in a sweat. It took somebody of Maura's bulk to work up a sweat in temperatures hardly more than freezing.

'Shut that door behind you,' said Annie. 'You're letting the cold in.' Even as she said it she could hear a replay of one of David's lectures.

It's not a matter of keeping the cold out. It's a matter of keeping the heat in. Dear David. If only he hadn't gone to

243

Altrincham. Still, at least she didn't have to put up with any more of his lectures.

Maura shut the door and shrugged off her threadbare duffle coat. You could say it was vintage but that implied effort, appreciation and a close knowledge of the retro market. In Maura's case it was just that she'd never bothered to get rid of it.

'How are y'all, then?' she asked brightly, dumping a bag of mince pies on the table.

'Let's have a brew,' she said. 'With a drop of rum in it.' Annie busied herself brewing the tea.

'Sorry, we haven't any rum. Will brandy do?'

'Ah-hah!' sang Maura, producing a half bottle of Captain Morgan's out of her bag with a flourish. 'One of Horace's Christmas presents.'

'Doesn't he mind?'

'He doesn't know.'

'Oh well, that's alright, then.' Annie smiled.

'Where's everybody?' said Maura, looking round as though she was expecting a cast of thousands.

'Elizabeth's gone for a walk round the estate agents. She's looking for a little house round here.'

'Not surprised,' said Maura. 'She's getting a bit long in the tooth to be managing a country mansion.'

'Actually, it's a run down parsonage. But it's all the same, too big and too expensive.' Annie hovered over the kettle, encouraging it to boil.

'I though she was loaded,' said Maura, ripping the paper bag off the mince pies.

'She's never been loaded. She just gives off that impression.'

'Probably because she talks posh.'

'Probably.'

'What about Bethany?' said Maura, biting into one of the mince pies.

'Skulking in her room as usual.'

'What d'you mean, skulking?'

'I mean skulking.' Annie reached into the cupboard for a couple of Simpsons mugs. She was twisting the top off the Captain Morgan's when they heard a sharp rap at the door.

'Ring the bloody doorbell, will you?' Maura shouted loud enough to be heard.

'Shush. You never know who it might be,' fluttered Annie.

'Somebody half blind if they can't see the doorbell.' Annie opened the door to find a small plump woman with straight blond hair cut in a fringe.

'Mrs Neill?' she said. He voice was warm and soft. 'I'm Rosie Barker. Social Services. Could I have a word with you? It's about your daughter.'

'Oh, good,' said Annie. 'Come in.' Rosie Barker stepped into the kitchen with a puzzled look on her face.

'D'you think I could have a word in private?' she said, looking from one to the other.

'It's alright,' said Annie, smiling. 'This is my friend. Bethany's auntie. She knows all about it.'

'Oh,' Rosie Barker looked a bit flummoxed. 'Well, I'm sorry to have to tell you there's been a complaint against your daughter, accusing her of sending offensive text messages.'

'What?'

'I'm afraid so.' Rosie Barker looked suitably distressed.

'Who? What?' Maura demanded, sounding aggressive as a result of shock.

'Ms Kathleen Griffiths found offensive text messages

on her son's mobile phone. They came, she said, from Bethany. She says there's been a history of this sort of thing?' Annie was thrown.

'That's Kath,' said Maura. 'She's talking about Omar.'

'Kath? But she's not his mother.' It seemed a pointless thing to say at the time but it was all Annie could think of.

'She is now,' said Maura firmly. 'Doe ran off years ago with an aromatherapist from Rochdale.' As though that explained every thing.

'What's going to happen?' Annie needed something to hang on to, something that made sense.

'I can't say at the moment.' Rosie Barker's honey voice tried its best to break the news gently. 'You see, the thing is, the messages are sexually explicit.' Maura snorted with laughter, then thought better of it.

Annie felt a surge of anxiety. She knew, in her own mind, it was true. It was the sort of thing Bethany *would* do. And, in spite of Annie's careful monitoring, she had obviously gained enough sexual knowledge to be able to shock other kids her own age. And, what was even more chilling, was the realisation that Bethany obviously knew that gave her power. Sexual power can be a potent weapon, but in the hands of a girl who'd hardly entered puberty, it was a whole bloody minefield.

'What a fuckin' carry on,' said Maura as Rosie Barker left and Annie closed the door behind her. She slopped a generous slurp of rum into her tea. Then, as an afterthought, she slopped some in to Annie's as well. 'What do you make of that?'

'I thought it was about my phone calls for a minute,' said Annie in a deadpan voice.

246

'What d'you suppose will happen now?' Maura didn't look as cocksure as she usually did when discussing the subject of Bethany.

'God knows. It looks as though she'll have to be interviewed. I can't imagine what she'll say. I hope she doesn't...'

'What?'

'I hope she doesn't ...'

'Blame David? Don't be daft. He's not even here, is he?' Annie gave way to tears.

'Well, I don't know what more you could have done,' said Maura stoically. You showed that Rosie Barker all the books and DVDs Bethany's ever likely to get her hands on. She knows you ration the telly and she knows the computer's protected. They could examine it if they wanted.'

'Jessica's computer wasn't protected.' Annie sniffed.

'Well, it's everywhere, isn't it?' Maura said, as though porn was a virus, 'Just look at the newspapers, never mind the top shelf. Your average daily paper shows birds with their boobs hanging out. It's enough to give a bloke a heart attack.' Maura paused to sip her tea. 'You don't think she's been ... well, interfered with, do you?' She sounded tentative.

'No,' said Annie. 'I don't. She doesn't act like a girl who's been interfered with. Anyway, she doesn't come into contact with any men, except Horace. But I wouldn't put it past her to accuse somebody out of spite.' Annie hung her head and longed for David's solid presence. At least he wouldn't be implicated, being, as he was, in Altrincham.

'Well, I must say I don't know,' said Maura. She sounded forlorn.

'Now you know how I feel,' Annie sobbed. Maura put a sturdy arm round her drooping shoulders and squeezed her tight.

Whatever Bethany said in her 'little talk' with Rosie Barker and the child psychologist, it can't have been anything wild enough to have her taken into care, just enough to have her kept an eye on. She was given the privilege of twice weekly outings with Rosie Barker, and a social worker called Stu, to give her the chance to 'talk about her feelings' with the professionals. God knows what good that was supposed to do.

The first time they came back, with Bethany in a self-satisfied mood, praising her to high heaven. Annie got sick of hearing what a lovely girl she was. Course Bethany was given the choice of where she wanted to go and probably indulged when she got there. See how long that lasts.

Meanwhile Annie was trying to prepare for the new school term. Two days to go before the pre-term teachers' meeting and there she was with all her lesson planning to do. She set her school folders out on the kitchen table and tried to crank up parts of her brain that had been left rusting for far too long. It was a daunting prospect but exciting all the same. It gave her a little buzz. Made her feel more like a real person; like somebody who had a part to play in the scheme of things.

The second time they left in high spirits. Bethany was fair beaming with self-importance. Annie settled down to her work again, hoping for the best. The realist inside her, the one that had been battered too many times to retain any false optimism, said it would only be a matter of time. The best she could hope for was a respite long enough to

get herself established back in school. That's what she was
setting her hopes on now.

Chapter 19 – Maura

'If you ask me, it's a lot of fuss about nothing,' said Maura, poking vigorously at the fire.'

'You'll poke the damn thing out, if you're not careful,' said Horace, his eyes glued to the silent TV.

'But, what if there *is* something in it?'

'What?'

'For fuck's sake, Horace! What have I just been telling you?' Horace's eyes swivelled round to Maura whilst he made a visible effort to arrange his face into an expression of interest.

'It's not easy,' he said, shuffling in his chair. 'No, no, it's not easy.'

'What's not easy?' Maura challenged, ready to catch him out.

'This texting business.' Horace shook his head regretfully. 'Thing is, you see, you don't know exactly what was said.'

'Rosie Barker said it was explicit. Enough for the Social Services to take notice, to make them think she knew something she shouldn't at her age.'

'Knowing it and doing it are two different things.' Horace mused. 'Very different things.'

'But *how* does she know? You know how sheltered she's been.' Maura stared into the fire, feeling the heat in her face. A possibility was lurking at the back of her mind. Something to do with David and his going away. But that couldn't be right, could it? Still, you never know.

'Like you were saying, you can get hold of porn anywhere. Nothing easier. They pass it round at school.' Horace's voice held the authority of experience. He was right. It was simply natural curiosity, just as she'd thought in the first place. And, when all was said and done, she was hardly more than Bethany's age the first time she had sex herself. It was no big deal. If you wanted to know what it was all about you just fucked around until you knew what you were doing. It was expected. She gazed into the fire, hearing the sudden sharp scattering of hailstones on the window.

'There is one thing that bothers me though.'

'What's that, then?' Horace leaned forward, his kindly face closer to her. She noticed his nose hairs were getting out of hand.

'How can Annie be so sure that nothing's happened to Bethany? Do you think she could be in denial?'

'No, I don't think she's in denial,' said Horace gently.

'Well, then, how does she know?' Maura wasn't sure she wanted the answer.

'She knows because it happened to her. That's how she knows.' But how did Horace know that? Because that was the sort of thing Horace knew without asking. That's what made him so special. Maura felt a sob rise in her throat. Poor Annie.

'Now you've got that fire going, what about making a brew?' Horace smiled and turned back to the TV. The only thing that made it bearable was the fact that he watched it with the sound turned off. Maura stood herself up with a sigh and went over to the sink to fill the kettle.

'You know,' she said over her shoulder, 'I still can't get over her setting fire to Viagra.'

'That was years ago. She was only a kid,' Horace said

251

kindly. But then sometimes Horace was too kind for his own good. He believed the best of everybody. Not that he was let down very often. Probably because he didn't expect much in the first place.

'But it's not the sort of thing a normal kid would do.' Maura lit the gas. 'Just suppose there *is* something wrong with her. Something they haven't diagnosed.' She felt a wave of guilt. All those times she'd fobbed Annie off when she might have been right all along. Perhaps there *was* something wrong with Bethany and Annie had found nobody to believe her? What sort of a friend had she been? She'd better be more sympathetic in future.

Horace yawned. It was getting late. Maura decided to let it go. Just for now.

She logged on to Astradate at nine o'clock next morning, like she did every working day. Horace was still buried under the blankets, like he was every working day. It had only taken a month or two of co-habitation for him to revert to his old habits but they were too entrenched now for things to change. Maura did the work and Horace, well, it was hard to define exactly what Horace did other than potter round Holmebridge like an old codger. Still, it didn't really matter. Not like it would if they were younger. Like it or not, Horace was getting old. Thank God for Viagra.

Maura sighed. She spent her working life pairing up couples on the flimsiest of excuses. It worked out surprisingly well. She sometimes wondered if she could have done any better for herself. Horace was the man she got by default and made the best of. She was stuck with him now.

Would she have settled for him if she were ten years younger? Probably not. But she wasn't ten years younger, was she? It was countdown to retirement time. Thanks to Astradate, they would manage well enough. And Horace's house had proved to be a good little earner in rent. You could say, if you were being kind, that he earned a living without having to get out of bed. In fact, given their background, earning money could be classed as an embarrassment. You were supposed to be poor. Property is theft and all that.

Aries:
I am a young 58-year-old male, 6 foot tall with brown hair (brown? thought Maura) and brown eyes. I enjoy crosswords, food and wine and walking the dog. I am looking for a slim lady, 35 to 45, with an interest in cooking and a lively personality.

Yes, thought Maura, not your typical Aries, but then they never are typical. And, like most of the men, he's looking for more than he can offer in return.

Gemini:
I am a slim good-looking blond (blond?) in my early fifties who likes travel, theatre and restaurants. I would like to meet a male with similar interests, must like pets as I have two cats and a dog.

Yes, they had a lot in common. Well, they both liked dogs, and both looking for sex, no doubt. It was a farce, or a fantasy. Everybody was looking for somebody who might believe they were who they wanted to be. As she composed a couple of sympathetic emails that would drive them both into a state of anticipatory excitement, it struck her that her own life had been built largely on fantasy.

Take the Hippy myth for example. They were no more Hippies than they were Santa's Little Helpers. Truth be known, they were a pathetic bunch of northern working class dope addicts dossing on the dole. A rotting caravan gave them enough of an address to claim unemployment and a state of near-permanent trance enabled them to remain unemployed. Her mam and three blokes, she never knew which of them, if any, was her dad. She could well have committed incest without knowing it. She never thought about anything like that at the time. Anyway, something made her leave, cold, hunger and a growing sense of disgust. She didn't go far though. How could she? With hardly a rag on her back and not a bean to her name, she was a right little Orphan Annie. She was lucky to find somebody to employ a thirteen-year-old who, by rights, should have been at school. Mind you, the word 'employ' was stretching it a bit, slaving, as she did, for Old Clegg in his bakery. And he wasn't above demanding a hand job when he felt up to it. Still, he was clean. Bakery's a clean line of work. When Old Clegg dropped down dead with a heart attack and his shop sold to a draper he kept her on. They all did. Including Hamid. She'd had a lifetime of being kept on. She was glad to be independent; independent enough for a relationship with a lazy bugger like Horace to work.

She sighed and turned her attention back to the computer. Then, without really knowing why, she typed 'disturbed behaviour' into Google and got 1230000 results. Curious, she started browsing to see what she could find.

***

There she was, a skinny, scurrying figure looking as though she was trying to get herself down Main Street undetected. Maura thought she recognised her then thought better of it. That couldn't be Beccy hunched up in an old mac like that. She couldn't help staring all the same. Then Beccy looked back and saw her. She seemed to hesitate then stopped to let Maura catch her up.

'Hello, Beccy. What are you doing here?' she said, shocked at her pasty face, black circles round her eyes and no evidence of lip-gloss.

'I'm going to meet me mam,' said Beccy. She looked on the verge of tears.

'What's matter? You don't look very well.' Maura felt a surge of compassion along with her curiosity.

'I'm alright.'

'How's David,' Maura said airily, as though she didn't care one way or the other.

'He's having a hard time.'

'Is he?' Serves him right.

'This new school, it's really rough. He's exhausted.'

'Oh dear.' The rougher the better, thought Maura. 'And are you still with the Halifax?'

'For the time being.'

'Right.' For the time being. What's that supposed to mean?

'I'd better get going,' said Beccy, hunched in misery. 'Mam'll be waiting.' She managed a weak smile and scurried off down the street, a black stick-like figure in a Lowry landscape. Maura felt lonely on her behalf.

She crossed the road to catch the bus to Riverside to see how Annie was getting on. Anyway, she'd found something she wanted to show her.

***

Annie was sitting at a kitchen table piled up with schoolwork and half empty coffee cups.

'Is that your school desk now?' said Maura. Annie laughed.

'I know it's daft. I have a perfectly good desk upstairs and here I am, making do with the kitchen table. It must be my deprived childhood. Old habits die hard.' She stood up to clear the table, side the dirty cups and put the kettle on.

'How're you getting on, then?' Maura sat at the table and eyed the notebooks and folders, different colours for different purposes, as though they were something from the Starship Enterprise.

'OK,' Annie hesitated. 'It takes a bit of getting into when you've been out of it for so long. But I'm getting the hang of it.'

'That's good.'

'Yes, but...'

'What?'

'I can't help thinking... What's it going to be like in reality? Not just in the planning, on paper, but when I'm stuck there with thirty odd stroppy kids to cope with.' She wiped her hands down the front of her jeans. 'I suppose I'm a bit nervous.'

'Course you are,' said Maura. 'It's only natural.' Then she remembered David. 'I saw Beccy this afternoon. She says David's having a hard time. His school's a bit rough by the sound of it.' She hadn't meant to say anything. It had just popped out.

'Beccy?' She looked startled.

'On Main Street. She was meeting her mam.'

'How is she?' Annie was polite. No doubt about that.

'She looked like something the cat dragged in.' Maura

took a guilty pleasure in reporting this fact. Annie's face was impassive.

'How d'you mean?'

'She looked poorly. Skinny as a rake and white as a sheet and great black rings round her eyes.'

'Good God.' Annie gasped and clapped her hand to her mouth.

'What?' said Maura, alarmed.

'She's pregnant.' Annie's voice shook.

'How d'you know?'

'It would be just my luck.'

'What d'you mean?' Maura was heartily wishing she'd kept her big mouth shut. Annie sat down heavily.

'We didn't know who's fault it was. David wouldn't do anything about it. Refused point blank.' She wiped the back of her hand across her eyes.

'That's why...?'

'We adopted. Yes.' The kettle started steaming gently. 'It must be my fault. I'm not supposed to have kids. I'm not fit. Now I've got a psychopath on my hands, it serves me right. Bethany's my punishment.' Her voice was bitter.

'But you don't know for sure.' Maura said in a no-nonsense voice. 'What d'you want? Tea or coffee? I'll put a swig of rum in it.' She busied herself with mugs and spoons, trying to get back to some sort of normality. Annie was suddenly wracked with sobs that seemed to start deep inside before finally exploding out of her mouth. She looked for all the world as though she was possessed.

My God, thought Maura, what the bloody hell do I do?

'She won't let me do it!' Annie's voice was strangled. 'She'll do something to spoil it. She'll stop me teaching just because it's something I want to do.' Her chest heaved as she gasped for breath.

It's hysteria, thought Maura, wondering if she should slap her across the face. She grabbed the Captain Morgan's and slopped a good measure into a Harry Potter mug.

'Here,' she wafted the sickly dry fumes under Annie's nose, 'get that down you.' Annie took hold of the mug with trembling hands before Maura could pour its contents straight down her throat. She drank in little gulps.

A few minutes later, Annie was calm enough to hold a sensible conversation.

'I've been on the Internet,' said Maura. 'I've found stuff that might help.' She smiled an encouraging smile; the sort of smile you might give your demented old mother when she remembers what day it is. 'Tell you what, I'll come round tomorrow, when you're feeling better, and go through it with you.' Annie nodded.

The door opened. Elizabeth and Bethany came in. Bethany, wearing a blank expression, sauntered through the kitchen and made her way upstairs.

'Hello, dears,' said Elizabeth. 'Good news. I've found a little house to rent.'

'Rent?' said Annie.

'Oh, yes. I decided not to buy. I need the interest to live on, you see.' She smiled.

'Where is it?' said Annie. 'Is it nearby?'

'Wormald Street, number 57. The agent said I can move in at the end of the month.' She sounded quite chirpy.

'What!' Maura shouted with laughter. 'That's Horace's house. Poor old you, living at Horace's!'

'I'm sure it will be very nice,' said Elizabeth, looking better than she had in weeks.

Horace was up to something. He got up early for a start, donned his hat and coat, and was out of the house before Maura had chance to brew the tea. He came in again, carrying a plastic bag, just as she was finishing the morning session of Astradate. He walked straight through the kitchen and up the stairs. What's more, he had a smirk on his face. She could hear him banging about in the bedroom above. Curiouser and curiouser, she thought.

She logged off to make lunch. She knew it wouldn't take long for an explanation to be forthcoming. Horace was far too lazy to go to the effort of keeping a secret.

She took a fresh loaf out of the breadbin and, smiling to herself, sliced it up. A few cheese and onion sandwiches would soften him up no end.

'Internet Caff's up for sale,' he announced, appearing in the kitchen just in time for a sandwich.

'Is it now?' said Maura. So that's where he's been. 'Why is that then?'

'I expect everybody's got their own computer at home.'

'I expect so.' She took a bite. The onion was surprisingly sweet.

'Them's good onions,' said Horace, chewing with enthusiasm. 'Better than you get at the Flying Veggie.' He obviously didn't feel ownership of it anymore. Maura smiled, waiting.

'Been on the bus,' he ventured. It was a rare occurrence, worthy of mention.

'Have you now?'

'Aye, I have that.' He smirked again.

'Where to?'

'That'd be telling,' he said, reaching for another sandwich. She'd bide her time. It wouldn't be long. Not if she knew Horace.

'I've been doing some research for you.' Maura plonked a sheaf of paper onto the pile on Annie's kitchen table and sat herself down. She noticed a smell of stale fish and chips.

'Oh, yes?' said Annie, picking at her cuticles.

'You should read this,' said Maura, passing her an article entitled 'Advice on Positive Parenting'. 'It's by an American psychologist, you know.'

'I thought you'd no time for psychologists.' Annie's voice was deadpan.

'I don't, as a rule. But this one talks sense. Go on, read it,' she bossed. Annie skim read the article that dealt with modelling desirable behaviour, positive reinforcement of good behaviour, building trust and affirming self-worth.

'It's very nice of you to go to the trouble,' she said. 'But I did the teacher training. I know all this stuff already.' She looked weary.

'Well, did you try any of it?' Maura's voice was sharp on account of her feeling put out. It seemed to her that Annie hadn't done anything but moan for the last ten years and now she was here, believing her, she was getting short shrift.

'You don't get it, do you?' She sounded as though she could hardly rouse herself. 'You just don't get it.'

'What?'

'She's past all that. The stuff that normal kids respond to. It doesn't work with such as her. Because she's not normal.'

260

'What's wrong with her, that's what I want to know? And can you do anything about it?'

'I wish I knew. Jasbinder Kaur tried hard enough with behaviour modification but that only worked when Bethany decided it would. She calls the shots. She always has.'

'Why do you let her?'

'Because,' said Annie, as though explaining something very simple to a very unintelligent person, 'You can't do anything about it, short of murdering her.'

'Well there's lots of stuff out there on the net. I've been searching. Millions of results to look at. Why don't you have a go sometime? You never know.' Annie, staring into space, didn't reply. Elizabeth appeared in the kitchen doorway, wearing a cardigan buttoned up the wrong way.

'Hello, Maura. How are you?'

'OK, Elizabeth. I was just going.' Maura stood up and gathered the papers together to put in her bag. On second thought, she put them back on the table and left them there.

'You'd better pull yourself together,' she said, feeling bitchy, 'or you won't be fit to teach next week.' She regretted it straight away and was going to say sorry but Annie didn't seem to have heard.

Elizabeth let her out. As Maura stepped out into the early dusk, she laid a gentle hand on her arm,

'You will come again, won't you?' she said. Poor Elizabeth. She shouldn't have to be coping with all this crap at her age. The sooner she moved into Horace's the better.

***

Horace appeared at teatime.

'It's parky out there!' he came huffing and blowing through the door.

'It is the middle of winter, you know.' Maura smiled. 'Sit by the fire and warm yourself. I've got some carrot and lentil soup on the go.' It was simmering on the cooker, giving off a tangy smell of garlic and cumin. She put a fresh loaf in the oven to warm and set the dish of butter on the hearth to melt it enough to spread. Horace spread his hand to the flames, chuckling to himself. It won't be long now, thought Maura, before he tells me what's going on. He's full of it, whatever it is.

They sat down to a satisfying meal. Maura was just going to tell Horace about her conversation with Annie when she noticed Horace had stopped eating and was smiling at her. Horace did tend to smile a lot, he was that sort of person, but he didn't usually do it at the expense of his dinner.

'You know what day it is today?' he said.

'No.' Other than being Thursday, what day could it be?

'It's a special anniversary.' He nodded to emphasise the point then applied himself to his dinner.

What special anniversary? Maura didn't know what to think. Her mind spooled backwards through their relationship, trying to identify key points. There weren't any to speak of. They'd drifted together, then drifted apart and, twenty years later, drifted together again.

'What anniversary?' she said. 'We've never had an anniversary before.'

'All in good time,' he said, slurping his soup with appreciation.

All became clear when, after the pots were sided and

the tea on the brew, Horace sidled up to Maura just as she was reaching the mugs out of the cupboard. He put his arms around her, hands grasping her breasts, and whispered in her ear.

'It's the anniversary of our first fuck.' He nuzzled into her neck, squeezing her nipples. Was it? How did he remember that? It was donkeys years ago. The thought crossed her mind that he'd just made it up as a ploy for a bit of romance. That wasn't all that regular these days. Oh well, why not? She turned in his arms and gently kissed him on the mouth. He pulled her close, pressing himself hard against her.

'Come on upstairs, my little treasure. See what I've got for you.'

'You've been on the Viagra again,' she murmured, following his lead up the narrow stairway to their bedroom. It was an ordinary bedroom with a second-hand oak bed and a double wardrobe. The bed was covered in a quilt that somebody, a long time ago, had laboured over to pass the time. On top of the quilt was spread an enormous white cotton nightgown with a finely tucked bodice and picot edging.

'Bloody hell, Horace, where did you get that? Did you rob the Parsonage Museum?'

'No need,' he said, 'Brighouse Borough Market.' She might have known. Horace's taste in lingerie could be said to be a bit behind the times. She couldn't imagine what he'd make of peephole bras or split crotch knickers. But then, her earth-mother figure wasn't exactly made for such as that. 'It's a surprise,' he said. 'Don't you like it?' He obviously needed her to like it.

'It's beautiful!' she said. He smiled.

'Come on then, let's get you into it.'

It was like making love in a collapsed marquee, cumbersome but hilarious. Horace had obviously chosen a size that he thought was big enough for both of them but, for all his burrowing, there was only so far he could go. He emerged red in the face and breathless. Maura was hooting with laughter. He collapsed on top of her, chuckling helplessly. Eventually, they did it missionary style with the nightgown hitched up round Maura's bum in true Victorian fashion. Horace, considerate as ever, pushed into her in a rhythm that he knew would bring her to the edge. Then, at the last possible moment, he let go, folding in, exhausted, and Maura loved him because of it. When it came to sex, Horace might be old fashioned but he gave as generously as he possibly could. There was no way, she thought, she could have done better for herself on Astradate. She already had more than she deserved.

Chapter 20 - Elizabeth

It's good to have a real fire again, thought Elizabeth, staring into the flames. The living room of 57 Wormald Street was comfortable enough, not so draughty as the Old Parsonage, but it would be better when she could replace Horace's musty old furniture with her own. More like home.

The Old Parsonage was with an agent in Norwich, and at a good price. People, it seemed were moving out of London, snapping up rural properties as they went, but she couldn't see how she could possibly manage to sort out all her belongings without help. She sighed, feeling old and weary. But not useless, she told herself. She must be strong. She was needed. She went through to the kitchen to pour herself a gin.

The kitchen was much as it always had been, she suspected. There was a rough wooden dresser that someone, long ago, had painted utility green, a deep ceramic sink with a crazed glaze and a rickety gas stove that stood on four enamelled legs. But she would manage well enough, she thought. She was used to being old-fashioned.

She took her drink into the living room, sat down in the fireside chair and picked up the phone from the little table beside her. She peered hard at the buttons. Her arthritic forefinger painfully punched out David's number.

'Hello, David. How are you?'

'Alright, thank you, considering...' He sounded forlorn.

'Considering what, dear?'

'Well, you know…' Perhaps he didn't want to talk in front of Beccy.

'Is work getting you down?' she prompted.

'No, not really.'

'Is it Bethany?'

'I've had it with Bethany. I don't want anything more to do with the little bastard.' Elizabeth was shocked by the harshness of his tone.

'And where do you suppose that leaves Annie?' she snapped, then regretted it.

'She can cope. I can't.' Elizabeth was astonished. David would never reveal a weakness. He must be in a bad way. She heard a deep sigh, a voice in the background, a door slamming.

'That was Beccy. She's just gone out.'

'How *is* Beccy?' she ventured.

'She's a mess.' She heard a hard, dry sob and her heart went out to him.

'Oh, David, what have you done?'

'I don't know, Mother. I don't know.' His voice broke. 'What a bloody mess!'

'Oh, dear.' She longed to hold him, to kiss him better and wipe away the tears. If only she could.

'I'll call you later,' David croaked.

'When you feel better,' said Elizabeth. She replaced the phone and sighed. How could she ask David for help when he needed help himself? Who else was there for her to turn to?

It was no good. She couldn't rest. After passing a sleepless night tossing and turning on Horace's lumpy old mattress, Elizabeth determined to get herself to Altrincham, wherever that might be. Somewhere near Manchester, she thought. It couldn't be so far away.

She dressed, packed a small bag and left a message on Annie's voice mail. Then she walked to the railway station and bought an over 60's return to Manchester Victoria. As she had half an hour to wait, she went in to the station buffet where she sat on one of the three available chairs and tried to calm herself with a cup of muddy coffee. At least she was doing something. In Elizabeth's philosophy, whatever happened, there was always something that could be done.

By the time she had taken the train to Manchester Victoria, the bus to Altrincham bus station and a taxi to the Beijing Diner, it was the middle of the afternoon. She didn't expect anyone to be at home but she rang the top doorbell all the same, just to make sure, and was surprised to hear Beccy's voice on the intercom.

'Who is it?'

'Hello, Beccy. It's David's mother here. Do you mind if I come in?' The electronic buzzer sounded and she pushed the door open. Beccy was standing at the top of the flight of stairs that led up to their flat. She wore a pink satin dressing gown pulled tight round her skinny frame.

'What are you doing here?' Her voice was flat.

'I thought it was time I came to see David,' said Elizabeth, climbing the stairs. 'Are you alright Beccy? Are you ill?' Beccy turned away and Elizabeth followed her into a living room that was just about filled with an old leather sofa and smelled of fried onions. She perched on the edge of the sofa. She looked straight ahead, her face blank. Elizabeth took off her coat.

'Do you mind if I make some tea?' Elizabeth felt the need to bring some sort of normality to the situation and, if she didn't make the tea, she was sure Beccy wouldn't. Depression, was Elizabeth's guess.

Beccy didn't answer but Elizabeth went ahead anyway. She found some Earl Gray teabags in the kitchen cupboard. It was just as well it was Earl Gray because there didn't appear to be any milk.

'Here you are, Beccy.' She tried to sound positive. 'You'll feel better with a hot drink inside you.' Beccy took the steaming mug between both hands like a navvy sitting at a brazier. She made no move to drink. Elizabeth was worried. A mess, David had said. Couldn't he see she was ill?

'Beccy, will you drink your tea?' she said softly. Beccy raised the mug to her lips then put it down again

'I can't. I'm sorry, I can't.'

'What is it, Beccy? What's troubling you?' Beccy hung her head and wept.

'I thought I was pregnant,' she wailed. 'I was supposed to be pregnant. And I never will be now.' She sobbed great harrowing sobs. Elizabeth put her tea down and went to hold Beccy in her arms. It was like holding a sack of bones.

'Oh, Beccy. What's happened to you?' The poor child.

Becky was persuaded to lie down. The bedroom was dark and the air stale. When Elizabeth drew back the curtains to find a window that might open, she realised the reason why. The room was directly over the Beijing Diner's kitchens and the extractor that hoovered up the greasy cooking fumes spat them out on a level with the bedroom window. The smell was rancid.

Who in their right state of mind would leave a perfectly good house on Brackenbed Drive to live in a hovel like this? It seemed to Elizabeth that all David had achieved was to swap one set of problems for another. On balance, she thought, the former set was preferable.

268

She decided if she was to have any conversation at all with David, she would have to spend the night. Better find a hotel. She looked in the telephone book and found a Wayfarer's Rest nearby. That would, at least, be an improvement on the Beijing Diner.

It was a good thing she did. David didn't arrive until about seven thirty and that was with a briefcase full of marking.

'Mother! What are you doing here?' He looked round anxiously. 'Where's Beccy?'

'It's alright, David. Beccy's asleep.' Elizabeth went towards him, arms held out in embrace. David didn't move so she found herself embracing both him and the briefcase together.

'Why did you come?' He sounded put out.

'I came to see you, David. I thought it was high time I came to offer some help and support.' She smiled. His face softened. He dumped his briefcase and slipped his coat off.

'Well, I don't know what's to be done. I really don't.' He turned to hang it on the back of the chair.

'Let's start by making some tea.' Elizabeth started towards the kitchen, then remembered. 'I'm afraid there isn't any milk.'

'I'm not surprised,' said David. 'I don't suppose there's much of anything. I'll have to get a take-away again.' He sounded resigned.

'I'm staying at the Wayfarer's Rest tonight. Why don't the three of us go there for a meal? We'll be able to get something, even if it's only an overdone steak.' And then we can talk, she thought.

'You're joking.' His voice was sour. 'It's a waste of time taking Beccy anywhere.'

'What do you mean?'

'She won't eat a thing. She's anorexic.'

'Anorexic? How long...'

'Years, I expect. I wish I'd realised.'

'Is that why she lost the baby?'

'There wasn't any baby.' He laughed, bitterly. 'Her periods stopped because of anorexia, not pregnancy.'

'Poor girl.'

'Yes, poor girl,' he sniffed. 'The last thing I need is another neurotic woman. I had enough of that the first time round.' Elizabeth felt winded. She lowered herself onto the sofa.

'How can you say that? Annie did her level best, in trying circumstances. She still does. She never gave up on anyone.'

'She raised the little witch, didn't she?' He scowled. 'She was obsessed with her. She made her into a monster.'

'And what about you? What was your part in all that?'

'I was working all hours to provide for them. It was her job, not mine.' He pronounced the words carefully as though she might not understand. Or was he just trying to convince himself?

The bedroom door opened and Beccy appeared.

'It's alright,' she said. 'You two can go out if you want. I'll just stay here.'

'Are you sure?' said Elizabeth, 'Sure you want to be alone?'

'I'll give me mam a ring.'

'That sounds like a good idea.' Elizabeth retrieved her coat and bag. 'Come along, David.'

'Alright, Mother. If you say so.' He followed her out.

***

270

Elizabeth arranged herself in the strange bed. It was much bigger and softer than she was used to. She found she could soon put her limbs at ease and made a mental note to herself to find out details of the make and model. If she deserved anything, she deserved a decent bed. It was ridiculous to put up with an inferior bed at home when better ones were to be found in what was, basically, a chain of utilitarian motels that asked you not to use the towels for the sake of the environment.

Her thoughts dwelled on David. She had never before realised how selfish he could be. He had taken on two women, along with their hopes and dreams, and emotionally abandoned them both when the going got rough. Was it selfishness, though? Could it be an inability to face up to things? An inability to cope? And what about *his* hopes and dreams? Whatever they were he never spoke of them. Perhaps he should be pitied as well.

She thought of Francis. He had the support of an older and wiser woman, as well as his religion, but that didn't help him in the end. Men, she thought, were such frail creatures.

The telephone rang. She nearly jumped out of her skin. She switched on the bedside light and glanced at the clock. Twenty three fifteen. That means quarter past eleven, she thought. Who could it be at this time?

'Mother?' Who else? David was the only one who knew where she was.

'What is it, dear?' Her heart was racing.

'Beccy's gone.' He sounded matter of fact. She wondered for a minute why he'd bothered to disturb her so late at night to tell her something that clearly hadn't affected him.

'Gone?'

'Yes, she's packed up and gone. Left me.' So that was it. Wounded pride.

'Frankly, David, I don't blame her. I hope she's gone back to her mother. I don't think I would stay with a man who said I was neurotic.'

'Well...' was all he could find to say.

'Don't worry, dear.' That's what mothers always say. 'Everything will turn out right. You'll see.'

Eventually, she fell into a fitful sleep and dreamed of Blackie. The dog was on fire. Elizabeth tried to get to him, to douse the flames, but however hard she tried, she couldn't get her legs to work. They were stuck to the ground. And Bethany was there in front of her, blocking her path.

'Andrew,' she called, 'Andrew, help me!' Andrew appeared through the smoke, picked her up in his arms and laid her gently back on the bed.

'Don't worry Mrs Neill,' he said, stroking her hair, 'everything's alright now.'

'It's only a dream,' she said.

The train rattled reluctantly towards Holmebridge. Elizabeth, seated uncomfortably on smoke impregnated moquette, felt her spirits sink. She was, she thought, getting too old for the eternal soap opera of family life. It was like a film that went round and round in a remorseless loop. She had left behind a son who was becoming as troubled as his father had been, in spite of all her best efforts. And Goodness only knew what she might find on her return to Holmebridge.

It was the unpredictability that was so wearing. It was all well and good to look back and say Bethany had a good first term at Oldroyd, and that was something to be pleased about, but there was still the anxiety that something might happen at any time. In fact, something was *sure* to happen at any time. It was like waiting for... what was that phrase? Something about shoes? Yes that was it, waiting for the other shoe to drop. When you heard the first shoe fall to the floor, then you knew that, inevitably, you would hear the second. It was simply a matter of when.

Annie was doing well. She had overcome her initial nervousness and got off to a good start with her new class. Elizabeth hoped against hope that it would work out for her; restore her confidence. That was what she needed most of all.

Bethany seemed to enjoy her routine outings with Rosie and Stu. Whatever they talked about, it must be having some effect. Smiling and chatting with them, she seemed almost normal, unlike the distant creature that looked straight through her mother as though she didn't exist and behaved as thought the world was invented for her peculiar anarchic pleasure. But how long would it last?

Elizabeth sighed.

And what about herself? What was she going to do about clearing out the old life and organising the new? The answer came to her in the form of a hoarding at the side of the railway line. An ancient tattered poster showed a smiling slick-haired 'fifties man advertising Liver Salts. That was it! She would ask Andrew. He would help. She would get in touch with him as soon as she got home. That, at least, was settled.

Thinking of Andrew inevitably brought back the memory of poor Blackie and the feeling that Bethany was somehow responsible for his death. The train slowed, jerking and grinding to a faltering stop. Elizabeth arrived in Holmebridge with an anxious stomach and a heavy heart.

Chapter 21 – Annie

Annie sat in the middle of the Year 1 classroom, revelling in the busyness around her. The busyness of six-year-olds is a powerful tonic, she thought, it gave her hope for the future. A glance at the clock told her it was time to bring the lesson to a close. Shame, she thought. She was enjoying it.

'Finish the problem you're working on, children,' she said, 'then pack away.' Number rods were packed, colour coded, into their boxes, pencils collected in jars and a pile of books tidy on her desk. Tables were shuffled, chairs tucked under table and twenty-eight little people sat themselves on the carpet in the story corner for the favourite part of the day. After reviewing their number lesson, the children knew, one of them would get to choose a story.

Annie looked forward to it as much as anybody. She loved the children's wide-eyed gaze as she wove her spell. She loved the way they were captured by the power of story, their eagerness to enter into an imaginary world. She loved their ready responses. She was so used to talking to a brick wall, she couldn't get over the excitement of it all, watching children learn. It was so heartening.

If only life were a story, she thought; tidied up, topped and tailed, with good winning through and the weak raised up. But then, she told herself, her own story wasn't finished yet.

***

'Bethany,' she called, letting herself into the house. 'Are you home?' No answer. Well, there wouldn't be, would there? Bethany didn't speak to her any more. Not now she had Rosie and Stu hanging onto her every word. Annie would be reduced to searching the house for her when tea was ready but she wasn't about to do it just yet. She unloaded her work onto the kitchen table, poured herself a glass of chilled Sauvignon Blanc and sat down to update her class records before her energy gave out. No doubt about it, teaching was exhausting but it gave her a buzz that she hadn't felt in a long time. She just hoped she could last out until half term without falling behind.

When her records were up to date, she marked a pile of number books, then, feeling hungry, decided to cook tea. Tomorrow's preparation would have to be done later. She poured herself another glass of wine then scrutinised the contents of the fridge to see what she could concoct.

The cupboard was bare. Bethany foraged in the fridge behind her back and ate anything and everything she could lay her hands on. It was impossible to plan. You just had to manage. She decided to ring the Thai Bride and get a curry delivered. Being responsible for the education of twenty-eight six-year-olds, she had more to worry about than cooking meals.

'Bethany,' she called upstairs, maintaining the pretence that they were on speaking terms whether Bethany liked it or not. Then she went looking for her. She was in her bedroom, listening to her personal CD player and watching television at the same time. You couldn't say the child was neglected.

Placing herself in Bethany's eyeline, she smiled.

'I'm sending out for a Thai. What do you fancy?' Bethany's reply was the faintest of shrugs. 'Alright, then,

I'll just get one for me.' She smiled again, to show there were no hard feelings, the little bugger. She lingered a moment to see if Bethany's need for food would overcome her need to play power games but it didn't. Bethany didn't care. She wasn't going to give in for anything. You could starve her to death and she wouldn't give in. At one time, Annie would have bought her a meal anyway, even begged her to eat a morsel, but not now. No way.

She got herself a red Thai chicken curry, delivered by a Pakistani lad on a motorbike, and settled herself down in the fragrant steam to plan for the next school day.

'Hello Annie, are you there?' She found the message on the voice mail when she got home the next day. It was faint, as though coming from a long way off. Norfolk, as it happened. Elizabeth was seeing to her affairs.

'The agent thinks he's got a sale so I'm having to move quickly. Andrew is helping me to sort out my things and send the surplus to the salerooms. I'll be back at the end of the week. Goodbye dear.' Elizabeth never was comfortable with voice mail. She sounded like a bad actor rehearsing her lines.

Thank God for Andrew. With David out of the picture and herself at work, there was nobody else to help. Elsie was alright when it came to wielding dusters but she wasn't up to moving the big heavy stuff that filled Elizabeth's house. It would be a relief all round when she was settled in Wormald Street with her own furniture round her. Not that 57 Wormald Street would take a fraction of the stuff that inhabited the Old Parsonage. Elizabeth would have to pick and choose.

Annie dumped her schoolwork onto the kitchen table, jacked up the heating and looked in the fridge. There was half a lemon and a few crumbs of mouldy cheese. Her bottle of Sauvignon Blanc, she noticed, was nearly empty. Oh, well, nothing for it, she'd have to go to the shops.

'Bethany,' she called upstairs, 'I'm just going out to the Co-op. Is there anything you want?' She usually finished with a question to give Bethany an opening, a chance to respond. She rarely did. All the same, Annie went upstairs to look for her. She wanted the moral high ground. Nobody could say she didn't try.

Bethany wasn't there. She must still be out with Rosie and Stu, thought Annie. Hope nothing's wrong, any more than usual. She went out, leaving the door on the latch.

It was seven o'clock by the time they got back. They came shivering into the kitchen. Bethany went straight upstairs. Rosie and Stu hung about, obviously waiting to be asked in.

'Come in,' said Annie, leading the way to the lounge, 'Grab a seat. Everything OK?' Her heart was pounding. They didn't stand on ceremony as a rule. They more or less shunted Bethany through the door and disappeared off to deal with the rest of their impossible workload.

'Actually, Mrs Neill,' said Rosie, her gentle voice hesitant, 'we, Stu and me, well, we don't feel we're really getting anywhere.' Stu nodded his magnificent moustache in agreement. Am I surprised? thought Annie. No, I'm not.

'What d'you mean?'

'Well,' said Rosie, 'at first Bethany seemed to be responding very well. She talked to us quite a bit about how she was feeling and, you know, her views about things. It all seemed perfectly normal for a child in her situation.'

'What d'you mean, her situation?' Annie wasn't clear which, of Bethany's many situations, she was talking about.

'You know. Broken family.' Rosie said apologetically.

'Broken family?' Annie couldn't get her head round it. 'Is that what this is about? I thought it was about her sexual bullying of a little boy who was supposed to be her friend.' It's a miracle she hasn't been accused of racism, she thought.

'Well,' Rosie was looking uncomfortable and kept glancing at Stu. He was obviously the strong silent type.

'That's how it started out. But, after talking to Bethany, we realised that it was a symptom. A way of attracting attention. A call for help.' She looked ready to burst into tears. 'We were wondering if you might consider Family Counselling.' Stu nodded again. So, Bethany was playing that game was she?

'Actually, Rosie. You're wrong. Bethany's behaviour's been the problem from the start. Long before we were a broken family. As a matter of fact,' she warmed to the theme, 'she's the reason we *are* a broken family. She was the one who drove my husband out.' Her voice caught.

'D'you want to talk about it?' said Stu. Yes, but where to begin. By the time she'd finished her diatribe they'd be ready to lock her up for life. She shook her head.

Rosie and Stu went, leaving a feeling of faint disapproval behind them.

Thank God it's Friday, thought Annie, turning her key in the door. She was looking forward to a relaxing drink, a chicken tikka ready meal and an evening watching mindless television. She might give Maura a ring and arrange to see her over the weekend.

Bethany was home but, instead of skulking in her room, was sitting on the sofa with Rosie Barker.

'Hello, Rosie,' said Annie, her anxiety notching up by the second, 'any problem?'

'I'm sorry, Mrs Neill.' Rosie focussed her shortsighted blue eyes in Annie's direction.

'What?'

'I've come to ask your consent for Bethany to be interviewed by one of my colleagues on the Referral and Assessment team.' She paused to let the message sink in.

'Why?' What now, for God's sake? Annie's heart sank like dishwater down a drain.

'Would you like to sit down?'

Sit down! Isn't that what they say that when somebody's dead? Had the little witch gone and killed somebody? She plonked down on the chair arm.

'I'm afraid Bethany's accused one of her teachers of abuse.'

'Abuse?' Annie's head was spinning. Had she beaten them up? She knew from experience Bethany could pack a powerful punch.

'Sexual abuse.'

'Oh.'

'So, would you give your consent? For an interview?'

'Yes. No. I don't know.' Where was David for God's sake? Sod him, fucking off and leaving her with this.

'It may be as well if you did,' said Rosie, 'because of what happened with the text messages, you know? I mean, she could be interviewed without your consent.' She looked imploring.

'Alright, then. Perhaps it would be better if I did.' She

put her head in her hands, then started rubbing her eyes with the heels of her hands. 'When?'

'The sooner, the better,' said Rosie, briskly. 'I'll arrange it as soon as I can. I'm really sorry, Mrs Neill,' she said. Annie nodded.

'Who was the teacher?' she croaked.

'Mr Kaye.'

Tears came to her eyes and a great sob of pity welled up in her throat. Bethany handed her a tissue.

'You look a right mess,' she said. 'You've got mascara all over your face.'

Well, thought Annie, at least she's speaking.

Rosie laid a sympathetic hand on her shoulder. It just made her cry all the harder.

Needless to say, the weekend was nightmare. Talking to David, Elizabeth, Maura and, amazingly, Bethany, took it out of her. She felt wiped out.

Rosie rang on Saturday teatime to say that the matter was being considered as a child protection issue in the first place, with a disciplinary procedure pending. Mr Kaye, apparently, was on paid leave. Bethany could attend school as usual.

Her conversation with David was brief to say the least.

'I *told* you I'm finished with her,' he said. 'I've enough to cope with here. Will you just get it into your head? *I'm finished with her.*'

Elizabeth arrived on Sunday, looking frail and flustered.

'Will you come and stay with me,' Annie begged.

'I'm alright, dear,' said Elizabeth, obviously mistaking

Annie's need for concern, 'I've got Andrew with me. Fancy, he drove me all the way here.' She took him off to Wormald Street, leaving Annie exposed and raw.

She rang Maura.

'Can you come round?'

'Are you alright?' Maura's voice was sharp.

'Yes, I'm alright.' Annie didn't want to put her off by sounding too needy.

'Well, if you don't mind, I'll pass. I've got a backlog of Astradate to catch up on.'

'OK.'

'Are you sure you're alright?' she nagged. Annie couldn't be bothered any more and put the phone down.

Sunday evening, Bethany came into the kitchen when Annie was hopelessly trying to concentrate on her lesson preparation. She was working in the dark with only the kitchen counter strip lights on, enclosed in her own little world, practically hibernating. Bethany snapped the overhead lights on, went to the fridge and poured a glass of wine.

'Bethany...' Annie started, but then thought, oh to hell with her.

'It's for you.' Bethany plonked it in front of her. A weak 'thank you' was all Annie could manage. Bethany sat down and waited.

Bethany had the gift of waiting, like people you see at airports or in hospital outpatients. They don't sigh and shuffle about, click their tongues and search for something to read. They just sit as thought time made no difference to them. Some people make waiting into an active verb. Some make it into an art form.

'You can wait all you like,' they might say, 'but you can't out-wait me.'

'What happened with Mr Kaye, Bethany?' nothing ventured, nothing gained.

'He gave me a detention.'

'What for?'

'Well... It was her own fault. She told on me.'

'Who? What?'

'She said I spat on her.'

'And did you?' Bethany rolled her eyes and made a 'so what' gesture. That was it. It was more than Annie had been privy to in a long time.

'And what happened in detention?'

'He came on to me.'

'What?' Annie wasn't too sure what she was talking about.

'You know!' Bethany growled.

'I'm sorry, I don't.' Bethany jumped to her feet and flounced off in a huff.

Well, thought Annie, looks like I've blown it again.

Next morning, the sun was making a pathetic attempt at streaming through the window. Annie grudgingly opened her eyes and looked at the clock. Half past seven. She should have been up by now. The thought swam about in her head for a while then slowly disintegrated. Her eyes were heavy. Just another minute.

Some time later, she thought she heard Bethany moving about but she didn't come into Annie's room. She drifted away. She couldn't help it.

She was dreaming about Bethany when she was a little girl, six or seven, peeping down Great Aunty Janet's well.

'Look out, Bethany, be careful.' Her mind screamed the words but she couldn't get them out of her mouth.

'Look out!' She tried to run towards the child, to grab her, but her feet felt like they were buried in concrete. She tried to will herself to fly; sometimes she could fly in dreams, but, just as Bethany tipped over the side, Annie found that it was she herself who was falling down. Down through the Vortex, right into the lizard's eye. She knew she was going to die.

Then an infernal noise, like a train shrieking it's way to hell, raised her state of consciousness to a level where she realised she was dreaming. *It's only a dream, it's only a dream, it's only a dream, it's only a dream,* the train roared on.

'Annie, Annie, wake up!' The voice was insistent, through the sound of the train. 'Annie!' She felt somebody hold her hand, pulling her up. She surfaced enough to see a shadow of somebody leaning over her.

'It's alright. Don't worry, it's alright.' She heard the quiver in Elizabeth's voice. Her heart was pounding, her mouth was dry and her throat sore. She tried to focus, to get a grasp on what was going on.

'It's alright, Annie, you were having a nightmare.' Elizabeth stroked her hair, making soothing noises like you would to a disturbed child.

Gradually, Annie surfaced to find herself in bed in her own room. The air was thick and she could just about make out Elizabeth's face in the twilight.

'What time is it?' she tried to say but her throat was parched.

'Just a minute,' said Elizabeth, moving towards the door. 'I'll get a drink.' She came back with a glass of chilled water with a slice of lemon floating on it. Annie drank greedily.

'What's happening?' she said, her voice wavering.

'I think you're exhausted,' said Elizabeth, with authority. 'Your body shut down and made you sleep through the day.' She smiled comfortingly and held Annie's hand. 'I've called your doctor. You never know, she might be here before midnight.'

'You called Dr Parry? You shouldn't have bothered her. The poor woman works hard enough as it is.'

'She's your doctor and you need her.'

'What about school?' she thought protectively of Year 1. How could she let them down? Her heart sank and tears came to her eyes.

'I expect they got a supply teacher. And in case you're wondering about Bethany, she got herself up and off to school. It was only when she telephoned me after school that I realised something was wrong.'

If Bethany had got herself off to school and home again without a murmur and, only then, thought on to alert somebody, then something was very wrong. Annie was too tired to put it into words but she knew what was wrong was not so much with her as with Bethany.

Bethany appeared in the doorway with her coat on and a bag in her hand.

'Rosie Barker just phoned,' she said. 'She wants to see you tomorrow. You can give her a ring.'

'Bethany, why didn't you wake me up? Why did you bother Gran?'

'You were screaming your head off,' Bethany intoned, 'getting on my nerves.' Screaming? 'I'm going back with Gran,' she said.

'No, you are not, young lady,' said Elizabeth. 'I'm staying here with your mother tonight and, besides, Andrew is sleeping in the spare bed.' Bethany stalked out and they heard the door slam.

Dr Parry appeared two minutes later. She diagnosed stress, wrote a prescription for Prozac and a sick note for four weeks. If anybody knew anything about stress, it was Dr Parry.

Half an hour later, Andrew appeared with a sullen Bethany.

'How's Mrs Neill?' he asked, his face a picture of concern.

That's not the first time Andrew's brought her back, thought Annie, wondering if there was any significance in the fact.

Annie lay half asleep in the dark, thoughts swirling around in her head. Elizabeth had made her drink hot milk and tucked her up for the night. She hadn't the energy to toss and turn but would have if she could.

School was the main worry, the fact that she'd missed a day without a word of an explanation. It was Bethany's fault. Why hadn't she woken her? Was it spite, trying to get her into trouble, or was it that she just didn't care?

She would ring up tomorrow to apologise and explain, although God knows what she'd say. Perhaps they'd keep the job open for a few days, give her chance to get back on her feet. She did have a maternity contract, albeit short-term. If they could just fill in with supply until she got back. She had to get back. Getting back to school was the most important thing in her life. Bethany or no Bethany. School was her lifeline. She knew that.

She heard a noise beside her. She opened her eyes.

'Elizabeth?' but it wasn't Elizabeth. It was the great dark shape of Andrew that was leaning over her.

'Mrs Neill,' he said in a forced whisper, 'is there

anything I can do for you? I'll do anything. Anything at all.' She didn't find it strange at the time.

'I don't think so,' she said, 'but thank you.' He reached out and laid his great meaty hand across her forehead. It was strangely comforting, and surprisingly cool. She fell into an exhausted sleep.

Chapter 22 - Annie

'What's this multi-agency assessment? Who's involved in that?' Annie looked across at Rosie whose chubby little bottom was perched on the corner of a kitchen chair.

'It's a meeting of people like the head teacher, the education welfare officer, the school doctor and the educational psychologist, if he can make it. Oh, and me, of course.' Rosie smiled encouragingly. 'You'll be invited to come along to ask questions and say your piece.'

'The only piece I have to say is that she's lying through her teeth.' Annie's voice was bitter and tears came to her eyes.

'Well, that's what we need to assess,' said Rosie, gently. 'What if she's telling the truth?'

'You could find that out if you got a doctor to examine her,' Annie said, picking at her nails.

'We can't.'

'Why not?'

'Because she won't give her consent.'

'Does she have to?'

'She's considered to be a child of sufficient understanding. It's her right to refuse.'

'Well then, she's got it all tied up, hasn't she? How can anybody prove her wrong?'

'You'd be surprised,' said Rosie calmly. 'And we have to believe her until we're convinced otherwise.' She made movement to go, standing up, fiddling with her outsize handbag and sheepskin gloves, wrapping up against the cold. Annie made no move.

'I expect they'll blame me, everybody else does.' she said, deadpan.

'No they won't.' Rosie sounded unusually firm.

'What has she told you?' That was what Annie had wanted to ask all along.

'I believe it's the same as she's told you. At least that's what she says.' Rosie hovered near the door.

'And what's that?'

'Mr Kaye gave her a detention. She arrived before the other detainees and he took the opportunity to touch her up. How far he touched her up isn't clear. She keeps changing her story. She started talking about rape but I don't think she really knows what that means.'

Oh yeah? Pull the other one. As if a respectable teacher like Mr Kaye would rape a brat like Bethany with half a dozen other kids likely to appear at any time to catch him with his pants down. Do me a favour.

'Why was she in detention?'

'Didn't she tell you?' Rosie sounded surprised.

'What did she tell you?'

'Apparently, she was spitting on the pupil in front of her in class. The kids around her made a fuss and caught Mr Kaye's attention.'

'Well, then, don't you think she deserved detention?'

'Yes, but she didn't deserve to be abused.' Rosie's voice was hard. Annie had never heard her speak like that before. She minded her manners and stirred herself to let Rosie out.

As it happened the educational psychologist couldn't make it due to pressure of work. No doubt he had genuine cases to look into. A senior social worker was appointed to chair the meeting.

'Well, we're all here, then,' said the senior social worker, Mr Bland. 'Lets start by reviewing the situation.' He looked round the table in the school's stuffy office. There they all were, the head teacher, the educational welfare officer, the school doctor, the assigned social worker and the mother. His eyes lit on the head teacher, Mrs Johnson.

'It seems to me,' said Mrs Johnson, 'that there are two related problems here. There's Bethany's behaviour in general and the allegation of abuse in particular.' She looked eagle-eyed over her specs as though forbidding anyone to contradict.

'Actually,' intoned Mr Bland, 'it's the child protection issue that we are pursuing at the moment.'

'But not in isolation, I hope.' Mrs Johnson swept back her mane of white hair and looked down her nose at him. Mr Bland ignored her.

'Perhaps Bethany's assigned social worker could fill us in?' Rosie Barker took her cue.

'Mrs Johnson referred Bethany to the Social Services in early January this year when she was found to be bullying a fellow pupil by bombarding him with sexually explicit text messages. I, and a colleague, Stuart Lane, were assigned to her. We had regular meetings with her where she talked freely about her problems. What they boiled down to, in our opinion, was the fact that Bethany was feeling vulnerable after her parents split up and was trying to draw attention to herself. We were satisfied that nothing untoward was going on at home or at school. As far as the texts were concerned, she said she was just repeating things other children said because she knew they had shock value. Then, after several meetings she stopped talking to us.' She wiped the sweat off her forehead with the back of her hand.

'Why do you think that was?' said Mr Bland.

'We thought perhaps she's got it out of her system. She acted as though she wasn't interested in meeting with us any more. Then, the next thing we knew she accused a teacher of raping her in detention. When we talked to her again we realised her understanding of rape was vague to say the least but she was certain that inappropriate sexual advances had been made.'

That doesn't add up, thought Annie. The texts were sexually explicit but her understanding of rape is vague? She thought she'd say so when she got the chance.

'Then,' said Mr Bland, 'the school followed accepted child protection procedures by suspending the teacher and reporting the matter to Social Services.' He smiled at Mrs Johnson. Judging by her expression, she wasn't impressed. She probably always followed accepted procedures. It was her job.

'Dr Hussein?' Mr Bland addressed the small, balding man on his left.

'I cannot tell you very much,' he said. 'Bethany refused to be examined and did not say anything sufficiently specific to lead me to any definite conclusions. In my opinion, if a child cannot tell a coherent and consistent story then it is likely to be a case of attention seeking. But that, in itself, must be taken seriously. This kind of behaviour must *always* be taken seriously.' He wagged his head from side to side to emphasise his point.

Sounds about right, thought Annie, warming to the little man.

'The fact that Bethany's behaviour has been challenging does not mean that she's not telling the truth.' Rosie's voice was hard.

'Tell me,' said Dr Hussein, 'has Bethany never seen an

educational psychologist? I see no record of it.' He drew a large white hanky out of his pocket and wiped his face. He was obviously suffering from the unhealthy atmosphere.

'As a matter of fact, Bethany has been referred to a succession of educational psychologists during the course of her schooling. That is, when there happened to be one in post.' Mrs Johnson's voice was heavy with sarcasm. 'The fact that none managed to see her was beyond our control.' She had the look of somebody with an axe to grind.

'I shall write to her GP and suggest Bethany is referred to a paediatric psychologist.' He nodded sagely, as though agreeing with himself.

'And where will that get us? Will they be able to determine what happened any more than skilled social workers on the Assessment team can?' Mr Bland looked ready to be offended.

Dr Hussein drew himself up in his chair and suddenly looked quite imposing for a very small man.

'What happened on that occasion is a small part of the whole situation. Bethany's behaviour is not only challenging, as has been described, but is, in my humble opinion, extremely disturbing. When it comes to urinating on her victims it is more than a simple case of bullying. I am astonished that her behaviour has not been taken more seriously before now.'

What? This was the first Annie had heard anything about urinating on her victims. But she wasn't altogether surprised.

Dr Hussein, she thought, was the hero of the hour.

'It was surreal,' said Annie. 'Took me back to the Telly Tubby incident. She was always weeing on things and smearing shit when she didn't get her own way. I told them but nobody took any notice. She weed on that poor girl as a punishment for telling tales about Bethany spitting on her. Mr Kaye reported the whole thing in the incident file. Then Bethany accused him of abuse as a punishment for giving her a detention. Now his career's ruined and that little madam's got half a dozen professionals of one sort and another running round at her beck and call.' She took a sip of the skinny latte that the Community Café was obliged to provide, along with a ban on smoking, as part of its health promotion policy.

'How do you know?' said Maura. 'How can you know for sure?' She took a bite of her wholemeal Savoy leaf and sesame seed sandwich. For all she ate healthily, thought Annie, she could do with losing a few stones.

At one time, Annie would have put up a fight, or at least a semblance of one. Now she was worn out and could hardly bother.

'I know her,' she said. 'Just think about it, if you were Mr Kaye, would you take a chance like that?'

'You never know,' said Maura, darkly. 'You never know what goes on in peoples minds. And, to be honest, Annie, you ought to know that you have to listen to the child. I mean, why would Esther Rantzen waste her time setting up Childline and such if that weren't the case? You have to listen.' She applied herself to what was left of the organic challenge on her plate.

Annie felt an odd feeling of disconnection, as though whatever part she had ever played in the ongoing drama of human kind was history. The frail cord that connected her with the rest of humanity had eventually worn through and there she was, floating free like an escaped balloon at a fairground.

'I give up,' she said.

It was a weird dream. God knows what Freud would have made of it. Not that he would ever get the chance, being long gone. There was this light in the sky, flickering like flames in a hearth.

Maybe it was a star, exploding with anger. That's what they do, you know. Then they lose heart, burn out, and shrivel up. It's as though the life goes out of them. That's what anger can do. It can burn you up until there's nothing left but a charred and empty husk.

Then the stars collapse into black holes. Curl up in a ball. Turn in on themselves, trying to disappear. Annie knew how that felt.

Or maybe it was an asteroid on a mission to destroy the planet. David always said the earth would eventually be destroyed by asteroids.

Come to think of it, that's not a bad idea. Destroy the planet and start again from scratch. Start with the basic elements and get it right this time. What's the recipe for life? Can't remember.

The strange thing was, the light took on the shape of a dog. Some kind of terrier, the kind that grabs hold of your sleeve and won't let go. Funny, isn't it, a dog made of light? A dog star? Annie started to laugh but felt a great weight on her chest. The dog was coming for her. Wouldn't let her go. It bared its fangs and breathed its hot breath in her face.

Annie screamed. She couldn't imagine where she got the strength from, what with that weight in her chest. Suddenly awake, she sat bolt upright, gulping great lungfuls of air. Only the air was thick with smoke. It was seeping under the bedroom door. Her mind screamed at her to do something. But what? She couldn't remember.

There were rules you learned about what to do in a fire. She knew that from her teachers' health and safety training. But how are you supposed to think back to all that when you're caught in the thick of it?

Stay near the floor? Yes that was sensible. There was more air near the floor. Except for the ribbons of smoke worming up through the floorboards. And weren't you supposed to put a wet cloth over your face? She'd need to make it to the bathroom for that.

After a few moments' dithering, gathering her wits, she did what any mother would do.

'Bethany? Where are you? Bethany?' She threw open the bedroom door and ran through a black wall of smoke to Bethany's room. Her eyes were streaming. She was racked with coughing. Her outstretched arms found nothing but a row of attentive teddies. The bed hadn't even been slept in. Where was she? The bathroom? Maybe she'd gone to the bathroom. Turning to cross the landing, she was confronted by a sudden sheet of flame breaking through the floorboards. The fire came from below but was spreading hungrily. She knew she had no choice but to get out.

How could she go without Bethany? But Bethany wasn't there. Was she? What if she was? It was make or break time. Take the risk of leaving her behind or stay and be fried to a cinder. The thought stayed with her for a moment. The idea of letting it end like this. Her sins cleansed by fire, her failures forgotten; a seductive notion. Then her survival instinct took over.

Screaming inwardly, she backed into Bethany's room and shut the door. She tried the window. It was locked. Where was the key? It should have been in a little pot on the windowsill. The pot Bethany made at school last year.

They had it fired in the kiln to make it permanent. There it was. Her shaking hands unlocked the window, throwing it open to the night air.

There was Lynda from next door, her huge bosom bursting out of a black nylon negligee and pink fluffy mules on her size eight feet. Annie could have laughed if she'd had the breath.

'Jump, Annie,' yelled Lynda. 'Rod'll catch you. Won't you Rod?' Rod, thank God, was as big as a house end. He opened his arms, ready.

Suddenly, Annie experienced a moment of clarity. She darted back to the bed and grabbed Bethany's duvet. She stuffed it through the window thinking how much better it would have been to jump out of her own room with its big picture window and king size duvet to land on. She climbed out, letting herself down in some kind of crazy absail. Then, at exactly the same time as the upstairs window exploded, she let go.

She was floating, like swimming under water. She heard nothing but the whoosh of water in her ears. The faces she saw raised towards her were distorted by ripples. She felt morbidly calm. It was all very peculiar. Then she crashed.

The pain in her leg was crippling, but not as bad as the pain in her chest. Her eyes were throbbing and her throat was raw. Rod's face was hovering over her.

'Where's Bethany?' she tried to say. Then she heard Lynda's shrill voice rising over the bleating of the fire engine.

'You daft bugger! What are you playing at? You were supposed to catch her not drop her. You're good for nowt, you are. You great fat lump o' lard.'

Faces appeared around her, altogether too many. Some were asking questions but she couldn't make them out. A

296

siren sounded. A dog was barking in her ear. She was lifted onto a stretcher and, just before she passed out, Annie noticed a shadow dart across the driveway, under the trees.

She opened her throbbing eyes, relieved to see the light of day framed by the vast ward windows. What happened? Her thoughts slowly focussed. The fire. Bethany. What was it, though? What was it that made her heart squeeze and her mind lurch?

Then, there was something else. Wasn't Maura there? She thought Maura was there. She looked around and saw nobody. She snatched at the mask that was energetically puffing oxygen into her face and tried to call out but her throat was burning. Eventually the woman in the next bed noticed her and called a nurse.

'Hello, Annie! How are you this morning?' The nurse was no more than a young lass in a polyester trouser suite. How can she possibly know anything?

'Maura,' Annie mouthed

'What?'

'Her friend,' said the woman in the next bed. 'Her friend's called Maura. She's gone to get some breakfast.' She sank back, breathless, on her pile of weary pillows.

'Oh well,' said the nurse, as though a world crisis were suddenly and unexpectedly resolved. 'We'll give you a little wash. And then you can try a cup of tea.' Annie's mind was racing. She had to get up. She had to find Bethany.

'My daughter.' She mouthed to the nurse. 'Is she alright?' The nurse was busy splashing water into a grey plastic bowl. The tears flowed, easing Annie's scorched eyes. It felt like she had enough tears in reserve to put out any number of house fires.

Chapter 23 – Annie

Annie cried all the time. It was practically like breathing. She breathed and she cried. That was what kept her going. Both were necessary to life, and were just as painful as each other. But, in a funny sort of way, it was a comfort. Letting it out, as Maura said.

Sometimes her mind allowed her to worry about Bethany, about the house and whether or not David knew. But, most of the time, she just let go. Too tired to think.

Faces hovered over her. Faces came and went. Faces spoke to her but she couldn't make out what they said. Sometimes she dreamed and didn't always know the difference between dreams and reality. And there was always that itch at the back of her mind. If it wasn't for that, she could just curl up and die.

There was somebody, though, amongst all those faces, who wouldn't let her, somebody who talked to her, somebody determined to get through. Night and day, eyes open or shut, she could see the fine boned nose and the black liquid eyes. She could hear the lulling voice asking sharp questions. He wouldn't let her rest.

She woke up to find Maura sitting beside her, reading Astrology Now magazine.

'Maura?' Her voice cracked.

'Oh, hello!' Maura turned to her smiling, 'How are you feeling?' How was she feeling? She didn't honestly know.

'What time is it?' She tried to orientate herself, get a grasp on reality.

'Half past five,' said Maura. It didn't seem to make much difference. 'You've been out of it for a couple of days. They put you on some sedative or other. Anyway, it knocked you out.' So that was it.

'Am I alright now?'

'I don't know. Do you feel alright?'

'I feel all at sea.'

'Don't worry. Everything's under control.' Under control? Annie laughed, as well as she could. How could anything ever be under control? What a daft idea.

'Bethany?' There was something she needed to know, something that had been nattering at her, but she couldn't think what it might be.

'Don't you worry. Bethany's fine. She's staying with Elizabeth. Andrew's gone back to Norfolk to sort out the furniture removal.' That's alright then. Or is it? She closed her eyes and gave in to an overwhelming weariness.

Maura was still there reading the same magazine. Or had she gone away and come back again?

'What time is it?'

'Quarter to seven.'

'Is it still today?'

'Yes. You've just had a snooze.' She turned her head and looked around. The ward was much smaller than she thought. She could see three other beds with nobody in them. There was a table and four chairs in the middle.

Somebody had left an open colouring book and a pack of jumbo crayons scattered over it. Reminded her of school.

'It's a different room.'

'Actually,' said Maura, 'it's a different hospital.'

'Is it?' Annie couldn't think of another hospital apart from the General.

'It's St. Luke's.' Maura looked at her, sympathy written all over her face. St. Luke's. Had it come to that? A psychiatric facility. Miles away from home. What home?

'What about the house?'

'I'm sorry, Annie. It's a right mess.' Annie remembered the fire alright. She remembered Lynda's pink fluffy mules. She remembered jumping. She remembered pain. There was something else.

'What's wrong with me? Did I break a leg?'

'No,' said Maura, gently. 'You didn't break a leg. Lucky for you, Rod broke your fall. And you broke a couple of ribs, sprained your knee, and you have a lot of little cuts and lots of bruises but you didn't break a leg.'

That's aright, then.

'But how did you know?' How had Maura known to turn up at the hospital in the first place?

'Bethany. She knocked us up and told us the house was on fire. We called the Fire Brigade.'

'But...' There was something that didn't add up. She couldn't think. Let it go.

'When can I go home?' She realised, when she'd said it, she had no home to go to. That set her off weeping all over again.

'I expect it'll be up to Dr Bannerjee,' said Maura.

'Who's he?'

'He's the consultant psychiatrist.' Maura took Annie's

hand and gave it a squeeze. 'He'll be coming to see you again tomorrow.'

Psychiatrist. What a nightmare. How the heck had she wound up at St. Luke's? How come it was her that was suddenly the psychiatric patient when she was no more than the innocent victim of a psychopath? God. What a mess! She needed to get out. Get back in control. Soon. But not yet. She was too tired.

'Annie.' There it was again. That voice. 'Annie, are you awake?' She dragged her eyes open.

'You're the man in my dreams,' she said.

'Thank you.' He smiled, black eyes twinkling. 'I am Dr Bannerjee, and I have come to see how you are today.' How was she today?

'I don't know.' There she was, weeping all over again. He took her hand and held it for a few precious seconds.

'Don't worry. You will start to feel better soon.' He looked round at the nurse who was standing far away at the end of the bed. 'We will lighten the sedation and make an assessment tomorrow.' He smiled, showing strong white teeth. Annie found herself fascinated by his mouth. Funny isn't it? There you are, homeless and in the asylum to boot, and all you can think of is Dr Bannerjee's mouth. But she had to admit, the thought of Dr Bannerjee's mouth made her feel warm and safe.

As it turned out, he was quite a tall man, slender boned with strong black hair. He sat down at her bedside in a vinyl high seat chair. A nurse pulled the faded curtains round the bed to give an illusion of privacy that could tempt you to say more than you might want to, even though you knew there were people on the other side with their ears wagging. There's nothing like a hospital ward to plunge you into immediate intimacy with complete strangers. You finish up knowing more about folk than their spouses do. Certainly more than you'd want to know, unless you were an obsessive-compulsive nosy parker.

'How do you feel this morning?' murmured Dr Bannerjee. At least, to Annie, it sounded like murmuring. Or he might just have been trying to be discreet.

'A bit better,' she whispered, aware of the wagging ears. 'I think I'd better go home.' Home. She'd said it again. 'To mother-in-law's. There'll be everything to sort out and I can't remember who we were insured with.' She felt exhausted at the very idea, never mind actually doing anything about it.

'I'd like you to stay a little while longer. Give yourself time to heal.' He smiled tenderly. At least, to Annie, it looked like a tender sort of smile.

'How long does it take for broken ribs to heal?'

'I'm not thinking about your ribs.' He paused then looked her in the eye. 'You are suffering from trauma and you are in a fragile emotional state. I am going to prescribe some medicine that will help you. In a few weeks you will feel much better.' A few weeks!

'Tell me,' he said, moving closer, 'how were you before the fire happened?' What could she say to that? Might as well be honest.

'I was frazzled,' she said. 'At the end of my tether.' He nodded.

'Would you like to talk about it? Would that help?'

He smiled a quirky half smile. Annie felt a sudden

lightening, a kind of instant relief. Here, at last, was somebody she might be able to talk to, somebody who might possibly understand.

'I could talk to you,' she managed.

'Good girl.' He patted her hand. 'We'll talk tomorrow and see where that takes us.' Annie felt calmer than she had done in a long time and soon drifted off into a refreshing sleep.

The talks took longer than she thought. They seemed to be going on for weeks on end. It wasn't just a matter of telling him her life story, that would take long enough, but of analysing how she felt at every turn. It was amazing what came out. Better than Coronation Street. If it weren't her own life she was talking about, she would never have believed it.

As time went on, she began to see things more objectively. She realised just what a miserable childhood she'd been blessed with. She knew it was bad but hadn't grasped just *how* bad it was to be brought up with a feckless father, a terminally incompetent mother, not to mention a lecherous so called uncle lurking in the background. She developed a deep and abiding sympathy for the little girl that she had once been.

She began to understand why she'd married such an authoritarian know-all. He gave her the security she'd never had. He was supposed to make everything right. No wonder he'd failed her, poor bugger, she'd expected more than was humanly possible.

Finally, she even began to realise that Bethany's behaviour was not her fault. She'd kind of known it all along but hadn't quite believed it. There were too many people ready to say otherwise, including David. But Dr Bannerjee seemed to understand. The only one who had ever understood. He called it 'the notion of consent'. In other words, you can't mother a child who refuses to be mothered. Taking horses to water. Or something like that. It was a welcome idea that was slowly taking root, an idea that might save her sanity if she could let it.

And all the time, that itch was there in the back of her head. If she could get rid of that, she'd be alright. If she could tell anybody she could tell Dr Bannerjee, if only she could put it into words.

They say everybody falls in love with their psychiatrist, don't they? Audrey Hepburn married hers. If only!

Talking about marriage, where was David? Why didn't he come? Where was Elizabeth, come to think of it? And what about Bethany? She thought she'd better ask somebody next time she got the chance.

She was sitting in a high seat chair looking out of the window when David came.

'They wouldn't let me come and see you before. Said you were too upset.' He looked a bit shifty, like an innocent person taking part in a police line-up.

'Hello, David. Sit down.' She indicated the empty chair next to her. He settled himself as best he could on the vinyl seat. They looked out at the windblown crocuses struggling with climate change in the hospital grounds.

'They think it's spring,' said David. 'They'll be killed off as soon as there's a sharp frost.'

Well, there we are then. Annie was about to ask him how he was when she remembered *she* was the patient and *he* was supposed to ask *her* how *she* was. She waited.

'Mother told me about the fire,' he said.

'Do they know how it started?' After weeks of protective evasions, Annie was anxious to get her hands on some hard information. If anybody would have hard information, it would be David.

'Er, yes.' He fumbled with the Tesco bag on his knee. 'They think it was a cigarette left burning in the kitchen. Possibly set fire to some papers. There was the remains of an ashtray. I didn't know you'd started smoking.' He looked at her a bit sideways. She remembered that look well.

'You know very well I don't smoke.'

'Well, clearly, somebody did.' Guess who.

'And, of course, there could be difficulties with the insurance.' He looked like a saint about to be martyred.

'Why?'

'Well, if you did leave a lighted cigarette next to a pile of papers, they could claim that you hadn't taken reasonable precautions. I mean. You didn't even have smoke alarms, did you?'

David was there when they bought the house. David had taken at least an equal, if not dominant, part in making the decisions. Now, suddenly, it was her fault that they didn't have smoke alarms.

'Maura had smoke alarms,' she said. 'She had to take the batteries out because they went off every time she brewed a pot of tea.'

'It's not Maura's house that's destroyed, though, is it? It's ours.' So that's what he'd come for. To make sure he got his share of whatever was going to be had. They should have got divorced and settled things. She'd hung on though. Couldn't quite let go. Just in case. Now they were in a right mess.

'I brought you something to read,' said David, handing her the Tesco bag, 'to pass the time.'

'It passes well enough by itself,' said Annie, 'but thanks all the same.' She took out a second hand copy of 'The Killing Doll'. She'd read it before but, at the same time, she felt pleased he'd remembered that she liked Ruth Rendell.

She sighed and looked out of the window. She'd like to go out there, into the garden, feel the wind in her hair, but not today. Today she had some thinking to do.

Elizabeth came at teatime. Nobody had shut the windows and a sneaky draught crept through the ward.

'I've brought you some cherry scones,' she said. 'Home-made from the market.' Annie let that go. She couldn't be bothered with an insignificant contradiction in terms when there were more important things to make sense of.

They sat at the table in the middle of the ward. It had a checked cloth on, to make it look homely, but it was a hospital table all the same. Elizabeth busied herself cutting and buttering the scones ready for the tea round.

'How are you, dear?' she said brightly. Annie's stock answer was 'Alright'. She confined herself to that lately because she was frightened they might not let her out if she told the truth. Anyway, she wasn't sure what the truth was. And, come to think of it, didn't know if she wanted to be let out or not.

'It feels odd,' she said.

'What, dear?'

'Being in here.'

'In what way?' Elizabeth put the butter knife down and gave Annie her full attention.

'It's like being sealed up in a space station that's lost

contact with humanity... floating through the universe. '

'We *are* floating through the universe,' said Elizabeth. 'At least the world is, with us on it.'

'I'm out of the world in here. I feel safe. But I don't know what will happen when I get out.'

'What are you afraid of?' Elizabeth reached over the table and took her hand.

Annie thought for a minute, then it came to her.

'Anger. It's like I'd have to walk through a great wall of anger.' She found herself trembling but felt better for having put it into words. 'And I won't have the strength to do it.'

'Yes you will.' Elizabeth looked at her with such conviction on her face that Annie was tempted to believe her.

How thin she looked. How frail. And how strong she must have been.

'How's Bethany?' It was a subject that hadn't been much talked about for the last few weeks. Perhaps it had been best left alone.

'She's fine. She goes to school, does her homework, watches television and eats like a horse.' Elizabeth smiled.

'Does she ask about me?' Annie's voice was tight.

'Sometimes. I tell her you're getting better.'

'Does she still see Rosie?'

'From time to time.' She paused, then drew breath. 'They dropped the charges against Mr Kaye, you know. There was no firm evidence. She kept changing her story and finally said she couldn't remember what happened. Now, she seems to have forgotten all about it.' Elizabeth patted her hand reassuringly.

So, she's tired of that little game. What next, I wonder?

'Has he gone back to work?'

'No, I'm afraid he hasn't.' Elizabeth hesitated but Annie held her gaze. 'He had a nervous breakdown, you see, and I believe he's applying for early retirement.'

Annie caught her breath. Panic surged inside her. The public needed protection from Bethany.

'I need to get out of here,' she said.

Chapter 24 – Maura

Maura closed the computer down and sighed a weary sigh. She couldn't remember when she didn't feel tired. It seemed like a permanent state of affairs. All the same, she'd have to make shift and get herself over to see Annie.

She'd managed well enough when Annie was in hospital, going to see her every week and otherwise keeping her distance, but now Annie was installed in Wormald Street, practically on the doorstep, it was all too much.

Annie was needy. Well, she would be, having had a serious nervous breakdown, but Maura felt drained. There were times she could take Annie by the throat and shake her. God knows how Elizabeth coped with Annie's moods and Bethany's miserly silences. The house was too small for three at the best of times but, being as they were in a state of permanent tension, it was well nigh impossible for it to contain them.

A sharp pain caught her breath. She rubbed her midriff and grimaced. Bloody indigestion. Stress no doubt. She went over to the kitchen cupboard for one of her Flower Remedies. She was just reaching up to it when her chest was caught in a vice-like grip. Choking with pain and desperate to draw breath, she leaned against the kitchen sink for support. Her vision disintegrated and she felt herself go.

She came round to find herself lying shivering on the clammy mat, a dull pain in her middle and a sick feeling in her throat. She got up gingerly and managed to pour herself a good shot of Horace's rum. She sat down, leaning on the kitchen table, sipping cautiously.

Two minutes later, she was up on her feet again, vomiting into the sink. She turned the cold tap on full blast and tried to calm the violent retching. That was when Horace came in for his tea.

'Maura!' he dropped his carrier bags and reached toward her. 'What's up, my little treasure?'

'I don't know,' Maura moaned. 'I think it might be a tummy bug.'

'We'd better get you to bed.'

Horace supported her as best he could, his thin old man's frame nowhere near a match for her sturdy figure, and helped her into bed.

'I'll make you a potion,' he promised. Maura groaned at the very idea.

'Just get me a drink of water,' she said.

A couple of days later Maura felt more or less back to normal, to Horace's evident relief. It had crossed her mind that, if push came to shove, he might not be able to manage without her. But Maura was strong. She always had been. She would be alright.

'I ought to go over to Wormald Street,' she said.

'You could leave it a day or two,' said Horace. 'You don't want to go spreading germs, do you?' Well no, of course she didn't. She might just leave it a bit longer.

The thing was, sorry though she was for Annie, she was finding it hard going. For God only knows how many years she had supported Annie through her many and varied crises. And it was enough to finish anybody off having their house burn down round them. It was just that Annie kind of attracted trouble.

If anybody were to have a problem child, it would be Annie. If anybody were to lose their husband, it would be Annie. If anybody were to have their house burn down, it would be Annie. If only Annie had taken her advice over the years. Anybody could improve their Karma with a bit of effort. If she had bothered to work on her Astral bodies, she would have been so much more in control. Now look at her. She was a wreck. An emotional vampire. Maura herself had survived an impossible childhood to become a balanced personality because she had always taken the trouble to work on herself. If only Annie had.

Maura sighed. She was tired. Tired of working on herself. Tired of working on other people.

'D'you want a cup of tea, my love?' Horace was so loving, so there for her. She nodded her reply because her voice was choked up with tears.

Chapter 25 - Elizabeth

Elizabeth knew she was old. Of course she was old. Anyone who survived their allotted span of three-score-years-and-ten was, by Biblical definition, old. But now, she felt old. She felt it enough to believe it.

She knew that her body was wearing out. She'd known it for years. Now she not only knew it in her mind but felt it in her bones. She felt it in the rhythm of the train on the tracks. Old, old, old.

She was coming back from Altrincham, worried about David's emotional detachment and weary of his talk of insurance wrangles. If only they could sort it out, repair the house and make a fresh start. She sighed.

How they would manage the next few months was anyone's guess. True, Annie was improving. She spent much of her time in psychological research on the Internet in between Outpatient appointments. That struck Elizabeth as being somewhat obsessive but at least she was motivated to do something. Bethany was keeping quiet. It was a brooding quiet, the quiet of someone engaged in hatching a plot. There they were, the three of them, locked in a temporary situation that was threatening to become permanent. She sighed again.

The train arrived at Holmebridge in pouring rain and she decided to look for a taxi. In any case, it was far too far for her to walk to Wormald Street. She wondered if Annie had thought to prepare a meal or if that would be something else she would have to do. For the first time in years, in half a lifetime, she felt just a little sorry for herself.

She got back to find Annie sitting at her laptop. She looked up as Elizabeth entered. Her face was more animated that it had been for weeks.

'I think I'm on to something,' she said.

'Are you, dear?' said Elizabeth, distracted by the untidy room and lack of any meal preparation. Annie turned back to the screen. Elizabeth set about finding something to cook and something to cook it in.

Bethany appeared and, without a word, helped herself to a hunk of cheese from the fridge then disappeared. Elizabeth, throwing frozen burgers into the frying pan, felt an overwhelming sadness hanging over her like a malevolent blanket that was about to smother the life out of her.

They didn't get into conversation until they were washing up after tea.

'It was Maura that put me onto it,' said Annie, standing at the old pot sink. 'She left me a pile of stuff she found on the Internet weeks ago but I wasn't in a fit state to take any notice of it.' She paused.

'Yes, dear?' Elizabeth had only the vaguest notion of the Internet but she did know it was an endless source of information for those who knew how to go about finding it.

'There was lot of stuff to wade through concerning behaviour and none of it seemed right. But I think I've found it now.'

'Found what?' Elizabeth didn't like to ask whether Annie was referring to Bethany's problems or her own.

'Reactive Attachment Disorder,' declared Annie, as

though it was the solution to all her problems. Elizabeth turned the words over in her mind but try as she might, she couldn't find any meaning in them.

'What's that, dear?' she asked, brightly. Annie stopped scrubbing the plates and wiped her hands on the soggy tea towel hanging over the back of a chair.

'It's when...' she said, choosing her words, 'it's when new babies are neglected, they don't learn to respond. Their brain doesn't develop the ability to form relationships and that affects their social and emotional growth.' She stopped, shifting her weight on her feet, looking uncomfortable but also more involved than she had for a long time. Elizabeth waited.

'I printed something off,' said Annie. 'Do you want to look at it?' She sounded diffident.

'Yes, please,' said Elizabeth. 'I would like to have a look at it.' She sat down at the kitchen table and prepared to look at whatever it was that Annie wanted her to see.

Annie fetched two pages of print and put them in front of her.

'Just read that,' she said. 'It's an extract from a paper published by a Psychological Research Society in America.' Elizabeth read.

Symptoms of Attachment Disorder
In Infants:
Weak crying response
Rage
Constant whining
Sensitivity to touch / cuddles
Poor eye contact
No reciprocal smile response
Indifference to others

'My goodness,' she said.' That's just how she was, don't you remember?' She turned to Annie. Of course Annie remembered. She was the one who kept saying there was something wrong. Everyone else, herself included, kept saying Bethany would be alright.

'There's more,' said Annie.

In Children:
Superficially charming child
Lacks a conscience
Manipulates in order to control
Indiscriminately affectionate with strangers
Has poor peer relationships
Does not make eye contact (except when lying)
Avoids displays of affection
Cruel to animals
Engages in stealing or lying
Engages in hoarding or gorging food
Has a preoccupation with fire, blood or faeces

It was like a replay of Bethany's life. Elizabeth was shaken by the recollection of Bethany's inappropriate behaviour towards Andrew, of her manipulation of situations to get her own way, her thieving, her gorging, her bullying of other children, her cruelty towards Blackie. Then there was the fire at the scrapyard. Then there was the fire at 13 Brackenbed Drive. She shivered violently.

'Annie,' she said, 'there's something I should have told you.' She felt defeated, like a worn out bicycle tyre. Annie started.

'What?'

'You remember Blackie, don't you?'

'Yes.'

315

'I didn't say anything at the time because I found it difficult to even consider but, you know, Bethany went missing at the time the fire was started in Blackie's shed. I know it doesn't prove anything but, when she came back, she said she'd been to visit the pig farm. But, when I saw Mrs Beale, she said that was the first she'd heard about it.' Elizabeth covered her face with her hands. The smell of fried burgers hung in the air like the smell of burning flesh. Annie said nothing.

'I'm sorry,' Elizabeth whispered into her cupped hands.

'Don't be,' said Annie. 'I'm not surprised. She once set fire to Maura's parrot.' Then it struck her, like a bolt out of the blue.

'The fire... Oh, my God!'

Andrew came again. It seemed as though he couldn't stay away. He was a comfort, thought Elizabeth, but altogether too big for their small house. It was good, though, to see him sitting next to Annie, trying to be helpful.

It crossed Elizabeth's mind, as it had on more than one occasion, that it would be no bad thing to encourage his obvious affection for Annie. Elizabeth would not live forever and Annie would need a friend. A solid friend, that is, rather than one like Maura who lived in an alternative universe with no clear beliefs to guide her. It was crystals one week, angels the next and Goodness knows whatever next.

Elizabeth was old enough to know a good man when she saw one, old enough to see beneath the trappings. She just hoped Annie would have the good sense to see beneath the trappings too.

Chapter 26 – Annie

'That's when it all fell into place.' Annie watched Dr Bannerjee for signs of scepticism. They were sitting in his utilitarian National Health consulting room. It was small so they were obliged to sit comfortably close to each other. He smelled of cardamom and his face showed no sign of scepticism whatsoever.

'I have read something about Reactive Attachment Disorder,' said Dr Bannerjee. 'I believe there is someone in Leeds who specialises in it.' Annie stared. So far, in her conversations with teachers, social workers and doctors she might as well have been speaking Greek. Now, just when she was beginning to think she'd dreamed it all up, here was somebody who'd actually heard about it. Not only that, but he knew somebody who knew something about it. Her heart lifted.

'Who is it? Can you tell me?' He nodded slowly.

'Dr Rita Brown, I think, at St. James's. If you want to consult her, you will need a referral from your daughter's GP.' So, she would have to bully Dr Webster into referring Bethany for something he didn't believe in himself. Well, she could give it a go. She felt a thrill of hope course through her veins. And, there was something else.

'The thing is,' she said, 'the itch has gone. You know the one I told you about, at the back of my mind?' Dr Bannerjee nodded again, his beautiful mouth pursed as though ready for a kiss.

'Then tell me,' he said, so she did.

It was what she'd seen lurking in the shadows the night the house burned down. The outline of a figure in jeans and a baseball cap, it was Bethany. She was supposed to have gone to bed but her bed hadn't been slept in. She was up and dressed when the fire started. Annie had suspected her of messing about with cigarettes but now she believed she'd set the fire on purpose. She must have watched it take hold before she told Maura. It was well under way by the time the fire service arrived. Then she stood on the sidelines watching the action. Watching Annie fighting for her life.

'I'm convinced she tried to kill me,' she said, 'because I didn't believe what she was saying about Mr Kaye.' She shuddered violently, got up and started for the door. 'I'm going to be sick.' But she wasn't, She just stood holding onto the door handle, trying to get her breath. Dr Bannerjee took her arm and led her gently back to her seat.

'D'you believe me?' she said. It was desperately important that he should.

'I believe you.' She put her head in her hands and let the tears flow. Dr Bannerjee waited. There was a quality of kindness in his waiting. He didn't wait like an ordinary doctor, huffing and puffing, fiddling with his papers and looking at his watch. He waited as though they had all the time in the world.

Dr Webster, on the other hand, was what you might call 'crusty'. A short, balding man with a moustache like a dead rat, he was probably born middle aged. You never saw his pudgy face crack into a smile but, for some improbable reason, he was supposed to be good with children. To be honest, Bethany must have taken to him because she always managed to be nice and polite when she went to see him. Annie suspected that was the reason he was loath to believe what she was capable of getting up to.

Annie sat for half an hour in the surgery before a liquid crystal display informed the twenty-three people doggedly waiting there that Annie Neill was to see Dr Webster. Twenty-two pairs of eyes followed her progress to his door where she knocked and walked in.

It was a good fifteen minutes later that she walked out again into the collective gaze that was now, she felt, getting a bit hostile. It was worth it, though, to get what she wanted. Dr Webster finally agreed to refer Bethany, though he gave the distinct impression he was only doing it to shut Annie up.

Outside, the breeze was quite balmy for late March and the sun looked as though it might break through any minute. Annie decided to stop off in Holmebridge and have a walk round the shops.

She parked up Primrose Hill and walked down to Main Street. She hadn't shopped there much after going to live out at Riverside and it seemed to her the shops had changed insidiously behind her back.

Course the Veteran Clothes Cellar was long gone, along with Yesteryear's Antiques. Even the butcher's had morphed itself into a wine bar. Though how anybody could sit and drink a glass of red wine in a butcher's shop was beyond her. It was nearly as bad as drinking lager in the converted urinals in George Square. Maura's old shop was a discount bookstore that seemed to specialise in biographies written by people Annie had never heard of.

She turned into the former Community Caff, now known as the Flying Veggiebun, to see if Horace was around.

Janie was standing at the till, looking very pregnant. She'd have to be careful not to get wedged between the tables.

'Hello, Janie, how are you keeping?' Janie looked up.

'Terrible,' she intoned. 'I'll be glad when I've had it.' There was no answer to that.

'Is Horace around?'

'No, he's not been in. Maura's poorly.' Maura poorly? She thought she hadn't seen her for a bit.

'What's the matter?' she said. Janie shrugged. Other people's afflictions didn't interest her half as much as her own.

'Right,' said Annie. 'Bye, then.'

She walked on to Beechwood Rise and knocked on Maura's door. After some fumbling with keys, it opened a crack and Horace's weary face peered out at her.

'Annie!' He threw the door open and grabbed at her.

'What's up, Horace?' she said, hugging him tight, feeling his need. He was barely more than skin and bone.

'It's Maura,' he said and sighed. 'She's bad again.'

Annie drew away, concerned.

'What d'you mean?' She noticed the fire wasn't lit and the room was littered with dirty mugs. 'How long's this been going on?'

'It started last week,' he sounded on the verge of tears, 'and she seemed to pull round. But she's had another 'do'.'

'What sort of a 'do'?' Annie felt as though she was trying to squeeze blood out of a stone.

'Well, sick, like. You'd better go upstairs and see for yourself.' Tears came to his eyes and he looked much older than she remembered.

Maura was a great mound under the bedclothes, lying against a pile of pillows.

'Annie. It's nice to see you.'

'What's matter, Maura? What's wrong with you?'

'I had a tummy bug last week. Now I've got another one.' She looked pale.

'Have you seen a doctor?'

'You can't bother the doctor just for a tummy bug.'

'It might be something else. You don't know.' Truth be known, Annie was beginning to feel a bit helpless. She felt something was wrong and didn't want to just leave it at that.

'Aren't you with Dr Webster?' Maura nodded. 'I'll phone the surgery,' said Annie, hoping for the best.

She decided against telling Maura about the Reactive Attachment Disorder. She was probably too poorly to care.

Annie picked the phone up. The receptionist sounded as though she'd been asked to do something extremely unreasonable.

'The doctors only make house calls in case of dire emergency,' she said, 'and the next available appointment is early next week.' She sounded as though that was the end of the matter.

'But I think she might have something seriously wrong with her.' Annie felt her anxiety level rising at the very thought.

'Well,' she said, grudgingly, 'could you bring her to the surgery now? I can ask Dr Webster to see her at the end of his list.' That was as far as she was prepared to go.

'Yes, thanks,' said Annie.

But when she got back upstairs, Maura was vomiting heartily into a washing up bowl and could only groan at the very idea of getting herself into a car.

'If this carries on,' Annie told Horace, 'you'll have to call an ambulance.' Horace looked dismayed.

Before she went, she tidied up, washed the pots, made a cheese sandwich for Horace and brewed a pot of tea. She took Maura a fresh glass of water and told her to keep sipping it.

'I'll give you a ring later on,' she said to Horace as she left. 'See how she's getting on.'

When she did, after tea, Horace said Maura was fast asleep. He sounded as though he'd been crying.

Annie got a letter. It had been pushed through the door while she was out shopping. A note was scrawled across the envelope.

Dear Annie, them that bought your cottage on West Lane came looking for you. When they saw the state of your house they knocked on our door. They'd seen about the fire in the paper but hadn't realised it was you. There's this postcard come for you. Love Lynda x

The postcard inside was a picture of a fishing boat with an evil eye painted on the side. It was posted in Valetta and addressed to the cottage.

Dear Annie, Just to let you know your dad past away. It was an art attack in the ex-servicemen's bar. They don't do cremation here on account of being Catholic and graves are very deer due to overcrowding. I had him interd for five years but I had to swear he was Catholic and it took all his cash. Ted.

She didn't know whether to laugh or to cry. Oh, well. Trust Johnnie Smith to drop dead in a bar. It would have been the pub if he'd still been living here. Now he was in a box in a cemetery in Malta. Whatever would become of him in five years' time, she couldn't care less.

'D'you know of a Dr Brown at St. James?' said Annie. Rosie Barker called to see Bethany most Fridays after school. It was a pattern they'd got into when Bethany decided she was getting too old to be taken out for treats like a little girl. Sometimes Stu came along but mostly their workloads were too overwhelming for them to coincide. Annie thought she was wasting her precious time on Bethany who would never allow herself to benefit from anything that wasn't her idea in the first place. And besides, if anybody were 'at risk' in their household, it certainly wasn't Bethany.

'Do you know anything about her?' she said, as Rosie was on her way out. Rosie wrinkled her nose.

'I've read something about her,' she said. 'But I don't think she's mainstream. She's working on some American protocol.' She sounded doubtful.

'She's an expert on Reactive Attachment Disorder,' said Annie. 'I think that's what's wrong with Bethany. It explains everything.'

'Don't hang all your hopes on that,' said Rosie, kindly. 'Those American research papers describe behaviour that could be caused by a whole lot of other things, like autism, and even if it does turn out to be a valid syndrome, that doesn't necessarily mean you can do anything about it.' She looked sympathetic.

'At least you've heard of it,' said Annie.

'I've got a special interest in psychology.'

'Then, what do you make of Bethany?'

'I think, she's doing well. She's settling down.' Was that just wishful thinking?

'Bye, then.'

'Bye.'

'He says the insurance company is ready to settle.'

Elizabeth spent hours on the landline. She seemed to have set herself up as a go-between, shouting out David's comments to Annie and relaying Annie's back to him. It could get on your nerves if you let it.

'How much?' said Annie.

'How much?' said Elizabeth.

'He says he hadn't got a final figure.'

'OK,' said Annie.

'OK,' said Elizabeth.

'But he'll let you know when he gets one.'

'Right,' said Annie.

'Right,' said Elizabeth.

Wouldn't it be easier if they just talked to each other? Probably not.

'He wants to come over at the weekend,' said Elizabeth. She turned to look at Annie, pleading.

'Alright,' said Annie.

'She says alright,' said Elizabeth.

'But we've got nowhere to put him,' said Annie.

'I'll book you in at The Crown, said Elizabeth.

'My dad died,' she said. They were sitting together in his overheated consulting room. Dr Bannerjee shifted in his chair and turned his beautiful black eyes in her direction. He was sitting with his legs crossed, exposing six inches of smooth brown skin a few shades paler than his hands and face.

'How do you feel about it?' he said. Well, that was a poser. How *did* she feel?

'I don't know.' That was the honest truth. 'I haven't thought much about him. I don't think he was ever much of a dad. But I suppose I feel something. Perhaps I feel sorry for him.'

'Why is that?' Dr Bannerjee smiled the kind of smile that made you want to kiss him.

'Because he had to put up with my mam.'

'Tell me.' He leaned towards her, inviting her confidence. She'd talked about her family before, enough to make him understand. But now she trusted him enough to tell him the lot.

She told him about the inadequate, sour woman who blighted her early life; the woman who held her in dread of her death when she was at primary school; the woman who kept her short and left her to fend for herself.

She told him about the careless father who, ignoring her, admired himself in the mirror; the man who hardly had a word for her but spent all his spare time jawing with his mates in the pub; the man who only let her go to college when she threatened to expose Uncle Ted.

She told him about Uncle Ted who was always lurking, touching, insinuating, sitting her on his knee when he got the chance, and rubbing up against her, who eventually tried to fuck her, as best he could, with his little limp dick. Her mother did nothing. Her dad wouldn't believe her. Uncle Ted got away with it.

Sod the lot of them.

'But d'you know the worst of it?' she demanded, as

though he could. 'He was fucking my mam. When they were young. My dad was on permanent nights and Ted was in there with her. I could hear things. I didn't understand at the time but I knew it wasn't right. She had a little boy. He died.' Annie couldn't go on but there was one more thought forming itself ready to put into words for the very first time.

'Do you think the little boy was Uncle Ted's child?' Dr Bannerjee's voice was soft. She nodded. That was why Johnnie called him '*her* little lad' because it was nothing to do with him but he accepted it because Johnnie loved Ted more than he loved his wife.

'And what about me? What if...' she swallowed and looked into his eyes.

'What if what, Annie?'

'What if I'm his, as well?' She wanted to touch him, to feel his skin on her fingertips, to know he was real.

'Do you think you are?' He held her gaze.

Annie tried to think but her mind was reeling. She was on the edge of the Vortex. Look down and she'd see the lizard's eye. There would be no helping her. That would be the end. But, something seeped through to the front of her mind. Something she'd buried in the past that made a sort of sense of things.

'No, I don't,' she said. 'She loved little Edward and she didn't love me because she loved Ted and she didn't love my dad. That's what was wrong with her.'

'And how do you feel about that?'

That's when the tears came, first a trickle, then a great angry flood, then an almighty avalanche. Dr Bannerjee waited in his kindly way. He soothed her with his waiting until she cried herself out.

***

Annie had never wanted any man as much as she wanted Dr Bannerjee. She thought about him all the time. It was his presence she wanted as much as anything. She wanted to bask in his beauty, to feel his protection, to lay her head on his chest, to snuggle into his neck, to kiss his soft lips, to caress his stark white teeth with her tongue, to press herself against him, to be the one he loved. She would give everything she had for a man like Dr Bannerjee.

If only she had met him years ago, when she was at college say, what a difference it would have made. Even if she could never have married him she would have had the joy of being loved by him. Of that she was sure. As it was, she had been made to do with lesser men all round. The story of her life.

Chapter 27 – Annie

'The thing is,' said David, 'it appears the fire started in the kitchen and there was the remains of what could have been a glass ashtray along with a lot of ash that was probably a pile of your papers.' He looked at her meaningfully across the stifling living room at Wormald Street, a comedown from Brackenbed Drive, thought Annie, but it was a heck of a sight better than over the Beijing Diner of a Saturday night. Foisty was better than fried onions any day of the week.

'We didn't have an ashtray,' said Annie. 'There was a glass fruit bowl on the table though.' She hesitated, wondering how much she dare say.

'Well, they've decided it was probably an accidental fire caused by a lighted cigarette. Better leave it at that.' David looked resigned and crossed his legs. Annie suspected he wanted to believe she'd been smoking and left a tab end on a pile of her papers. He probably thought that was just the daft kind of thing she would do.

'If that's what will get us the insurance, then OK, leave it at that. But, you know, David. I know better.' He pulled a face. She decided to shut up for the time being.

'The damage isn't as bad as it looks,' he went on. 'It was mainly confined to the kitchen, the landing and Bethany's bedroom. Otherwise, it's more smoke damage than structural.' He looked at her as thought she ought to take comfort in that.

'So, how long will it take?'

'I've had a couple of estimates for about six weeks. That probably means three months. I'll have another look at it tomorrow.' He sighed, wearily.

'Right.'

'Then we'll need to decide what to do.' What was he on about now?

'What do you mean?' As far as she was concerned what she was going to do was move back into Brackenbed Drive.

'Obviously, it'll have to be sold,' David had the grace to look diffident, 'unless, we decide to get back together. Have a fresh start.' He couldn't quite meet her eye.

Get back together? You what? After all they'd been through? They'd been splitting up for years. You can't mend a split like that overnight, if at all. They knew too much about each other. It was too late.

'I'd like us to give it a try,' said David, in a small voice. 'I know I haven't always been easy to live with. And there's always been Bethany,' he said, then evidently ran out of speech.

'I'll give you a lift back to The Crown.' she said.

Annie decided to walk round to Maura's on Sunday afternoon, to see how she was getting on. With Bethany busy doing homework and Elizabeth at The Crown with David, she was at a loose end. Besides, walking helped her to think and she had that much to think about she didn't know where to start.

The weather was bright with a sneaky breeze that caught you off guard when you turned a corner. The wind funnelled along Main Street and up your skirt, if you happened to be wearing one. You could finish up like

Marylin Monroe. The thought made her smile. Good. She hadn't much to smile about lately.

She headed past the shops towards Beechwood Rise. It was quite busy even though it was a bit early for tourists. It was nice, though, being out mingling with the public at large. You could be anybody. You could be a person who mattered, a person who had a place in the scheme of things. One of these days, she might take courage and have a glass of red wine in the butcher's.

She walked along Main Street and up Beechwood Rise with a spring in her step.

She found Maura sat hugging the fire.

'I can't get warm,' she said. Her face was grey. Annie felt her anxiety level notch up a bit.

'Have you been to the doctors? I mean, now you're fit enough to go?' It was a matter of fine judgement, thought Annie.

If you were at death's door you might get an on-call doctor at a pinch. Most people resorted to phoning an ambulance with the result that A&E, already crowded out with drunken girls claiming date rape and young lads with bloody knuckles, was also lumbered with people who should, by rights, have seen their G.P.

If you were still alive, but too sick to get out of bed, you just had to put up with it until you were on the mend. At that point, and this was where the judgement came in, you could either make an appointment or decide to get better on your own. Annie thought, all in all, that Maura should go down the appointment route.

'I'm going on Wednesday,' said Maura. 'It was earliest I could get.'

'Good,' said Annie. 'D'you want me to come with you?'

'Thanks anyway.' She gazed mournfully into the fire.

Carry on like that and you'll turn into Madge, thought Annie.

'I'll put the kettle on, then,' she said.

She wanted to tell Maura about David and his suggestion of getting back together but she couldn't bring herself to. Not when Maura was looking like that.

'Oh dear,' said Elizabeth over breakfast, 'I don't know how to organise this.' She looked distracted, poking at her fried egg.

'What?' said Annie through a mouthful of toast as Bethany reached across her to grab the butter.

'Andrew wants to bring a vanload of my furniture this week. I don't know what to do with Horace's things and I don't know where to put my own.' She forked her egg around the plate, mixing the yolk with fried tomato.

'That's disgusting,' said Bethany, wolfing hers down in one bite. 'Don't you know all that cholesterol's bad for you, 'specially at your age.' Elizabeth put her fork down. She was near to tears. Annie had never seen her looking so helpless.

'Bethany, you'd better be getting going if you don't want to be late for school,' she said. Bethany stuffed her mouth with toast, grabbed her coat and bag then went, still chewing, out of the door. Thank God.

'Don't worry, Elizabeth. It'll be alright. I'll ask Horace to see to his furniture. He might sell it or put it in storage. There's no room for anything at Maura's.'

'But where shall we put Andrew?' Elizabeth was at a loss.

'Where we always put our superfluous guests, at The Crown.'

'Oh, don't say that, dear.' Elizabeth was shocked. 'I don't know what I'd do without Andrew.'

'Sorry. It's just that I could do without any extra hassle at the moment.'

'I know,' said Elizabeth, wearily. 'I know.' Poor old thing, thought Annie. But she could do without Andrew *again*.

'Still, you'll feel better with your own stuff around you.'

'Yes. I expect I shall.'

A couple of days later, Horace got a house clearance firm in and sold his stuff for next to nothing. He couldn't be bothered with it when he'd got Maura to worry about.

Annie and Elizabeth, inspired by the muck that was revealed when the furniture was moved from on top of it, set to, cleaning the place up. Elizabeth cheered up no end.

'I can't wait for Andrew to arrive,' she trilled.

'Well,' said Annie, 'we'll be sleeping on the floor if he doesn't.' Thankfully, it didn't come to that. Andrew arrived at teatime. Bethany bestirred herself and helped them unload Elizabeth's furniture from the hire van. Elizabeth busied herself making on-the-spot decisions about where to put it all.

'It looks naff,' said Bethany, when they'd finished. 'Too much.'

'It does,' said Elizabeth. 'I'll decide what to keep and what to get rid of when I get used to it.' Annie thought it looked cosy. A lot better than Horace's neglected old set up.

'What's for tea?' said Bethany.

'I was just thinking the same thing myself,' said Andrew, smiling.

'Fish and chips?' said Annie. 'I'll go and get them.'

She'd got as far as Main Street and was heading towards the In Plaice when she saw Maura coming out of the chemist's, clutching something in a paper bag.

There was something about the way she moved, that scuttling sort of motion, that made Annie catch her breath. She knew in her bones something was wrong. When had it started? When had she begun hunching over like that? Was it just this latest bout of sickness or was it something that had been creeping up on her? She should have taken notice ages ago instead of being wrapped up in her own problems.

'Maura! What are you doing?' Maura stopped suddenly.

'Oh, it's you,' she said. She looked distracted.

'What's matter, Maura?'

'Dyspepsia. I've just been to the doctor's. He's given me something for dyspepsia.' As she held out the pharmacy bag to show Annie, she stumbled, falling flat on her face. Annie reached out towards her but had the queer feeling that Maura had already slipped through her fingers.

She dropped down on the pavement and tried to roll Maura over onto her back. That was no easy job, given her bulk, but a couple of passing women, sensing a bit of excitement, came to lend a hand. Then, just for good measure, it started pouring down. Like stair rods, thought Annie, the sort of irreverent thought you get in a crisis.

'Call an ambulance, please,' she pleaded. One of them got her mobile out and faffed about with the buttons.

'Omigod!' shrieked the other one. 'She's a gonner!'

Annie took one look at Maura's face and shivered. It was practically navy blue. In a last ditch to do something useful for once, she applied herself to breathing into to Maura's mouth like she'd seen people do on Holby City. The second woman had obviously seen Holby City as well because she took to jumping up and down on Maura's chest.

'Art massage,' she said.

The first woman had eventually had some success because an ambulance appeared during the customer relations promised ten-minute callout window. Annie, without thinking twice, got into it with Maura.

It was a rocky ride with the siren going full blast. Maura lay under a pile of blankets with an oxygen mask over her face. A paramedic was thumping her chest.

Annie felt a surprising calm. It was the calm of acceptance before the grief kicks in. Then she got annoyed with the paramedic for creating havoc when it was already too late. It was as though they had to maintain the fiction that she was still alive until somebody in authority said she wasn't.

Maura was pronounced dead on arrival, although she'd obviously been that way for a good fifteen minutes before she was wheeled through the double doors into the sharp smell of sickness and disinfectant.

Lucky Annie was there, she could answer all their questions without them having to search through Maura's personal belongings to find out who she was. She could establish her identity as a deceased individual.

Annie's mind was in overdrive. Get to Horace before the police turn up. Police always turn up when somebody dies unexpectedly. And, if you lose somebody you love, you don't want to be told by the police. Then, at some point, let them at home know what had happened. She had a bizarre mental picture of them sitting patiently waiting for the fish and chips.

Remembering she'd left her mobile at home on the kitchen table, she eventually found a payphone that worked in the draughty foyer.

'Hello, Elizabeth?'

'Annie, where are you? We've been worried sick.'

'I'm at the hospital. I'm OK. It's Maura.'

'Has she had an accident?'

'I'm afraid it's worse than that. I met her coming out of the chemist's and she... she just dropped dead in the street.' She heard Elizabeth gasp.

'I know,' she said. 'I can't believe it either. And, I've got to go and tell Horace.'

'Poor thing.' You can say that again.

'Are you still waiting for the fish and chips?' Now why did she ask that? Maybe being responsible for the fish and chips was just one burden too many.

'No, dear. Bethany went for them. But neither Andrew nor I could eat a thing until we knew what had become of you.'

'I'm alright. I'll be back when I've seen Horace.' She was troubled by a feeling of unreality, as though she were some kind of angel hovering above it all; an angel that was about to make a traumatic visitation.

Walking back along Main Street, towards Beechwood Rise, Annie was possessed with a peculiar out-of-body experience. It was as though she was five years old again, busy with Small World Play. Not that she'd ever had a set of Playpeople, they'd probably not been invented when she was five, but she could see herself now, an omnipotent child, placing little plastic people on her Playmat.

There's a little old woman with pudding-basin hair and a bun stuck on top. Let's put her at the kitchen sink where she belongs. There's a little girl wearing a red plastic dress. Put her in the kitchen too. She can sit at the table and eat a plastic burger. That'll keep her out of mischief. There's a man with a hairstyle like a helmet. He's in the kitchen as well, standing near the window, watching out. They'll stay there as long as she likes, with their little dot eyes and little red mouths painted on their little round faces. They'll stay there until she's decided what to do with them.

There's another man. He's supposed to be old but he looks just like the rest. She could take his hair off. That would make him old. She put him in a different kitchen at the other side of town. He can sit by the fire and wait. And there's the woman he's waiting for. She's broken, split right in two, just as though she's been trodden on. She's in the hospital mortuary waiting for her big operation. She qualifies for medical attention now she's dead. A post mortem will be the biggest procedure she's had in her existence; her greatest demand ever on the NHS purse strings.

Now, who else is there? Let's see. There's a lonely man, wearing blue plastic trousers, in Altrincham. That's right on the edge of the Playmat, hardly on it all. Well, he can wait his turn. Leave him there for the time being.

And what about Annie herself, busy moving people about as though she had any control over people and events? It's an erroneous lesson you learn in childhood and it takes half a lifetime to sort it out. What would Dr Bannerjee think of her now? He'd probably section her before you could say 'knife'.

***

Horace crumpled like a wet paper bag. Like one you've brought fish home from the market in. Annie was loath to leave him and didn't know what to do for the best.

It wouldn't be so bad if he cried, or howled, even, it was just the way he slumped down lifeless in his chair that frightened her. Could people die of grief? Horace was doing a fair imitation. He wouldn't have a mug of tea or even a swig of rum. He was beyond all that.

She sat with him, holding his hand and stroking his brow; the things that you find yourself doing before you realise it. To treat an adult like a baby when they've had a nasty shock, it must be an inbuilt response.

After a bit, she phoned home.

'I can't leave him,' she said.

'What about you?' said Elizabeth.

'I don't know.'

Andrew arrived twenty minutes later and took it upon himself to give her a hug. He smelled of furniture polish. She relaxed into his comforting bulk and let the tears flow.

Then they stayed there together, the three of them, and sat the fire out.

The appointment to see Dr Brown plopped through the letterbox just as Bethany was about to leave for school.

'What's that?' said Annie, running the water for the washing up.

'Nothin',' said Bethany, stuffing it into her coat pocket. Annie darted across the kitchen, grabbing at the letter. She saw the St James Hospital crest on the envelope before Bethany grabbed it back and tore it in half.

'What's going on?' Elizabeth appeared, bleary eyed from a pain-wracked night, and automatically went to turn the tap off.

'This little madam's stealing my mail,' growled Annie.

'It's not your fuckin' mail!' yelled Bethany, 'It's mine. So there!' she screwed the remnants up and tossed them onto the fire.

'You needn't think I'm going,' she yelled, 'because I'm fuckin' not.' She flounced out and slammed the door.

Annie darted across to the fire. It had only just been lit and was more smoke than flame. She snatched as much as she could of the charred remains, straightened them out and tried to piece them together.

'The little bugger,' she said. 'No wonder it took so long.'

'What do you mean, dear?' Elizabeth looked completely flummoxed.

'This is a second appointment. She didn't turn up for the first. They've only sent this one because Dr Webster was chasing them up.'

Elizabeth eased herself onto a kitchen chair, her face a picture of weariness.

'But why didn't she keep the first appointment?'

'Because she didn't want to. I knew nothing about it. She must have stolen that letter as well. And,' she had a flash of understanding, 'no wonder we never heard anything more about the paediatric psychologist. She's been censoring the mail all along.' Annie sighed a sigh that came out like a groan and buried her face in her hands.

'But why would Dr Webster chase them up?' said Elizabeth. Annie pulled a face.

'After his big cock up with Maura, I should think he'll

be chasing everything up.' She tore a piece of kitchen paper off the roll and blew her nose.

'What are we going to do?' Elizabeth was practically wringing her hands.

'Get her there,' Annie's tone was grim, 'even if we have to bind her hand and foot. It's my only hope.'

'Hope for what, dear? What are you expecting? She raised a pale, tremulous face towards her.

'Treatment,' said Annie. 'Before she kills somebody.'

Elizabeth looked at her sideways as though she didn't know what to make of it.

The phone went at lunchtime. She didn't expect it to be David. He was supposed to be at school, come what may.

'I've been thinking,' he said. Nothing new in that, David was always thinking.

'Aren't you at school?' Annie was curious.

'No. I've taken the day off sick... to think.' It must be serious.

'What?'

'I've been thinking about us getting back together. Will you consider it?' His voice was heavy, like somebody who'd been up all night weighing the odds. If it took that much thinking about, she didn't have the energy.

'I can't get my head round it, David,' she said. 'It's all I can do to keep myself going. God knows what Bethany's going to do next.'

'Bethany!' he made it sound like a swear word. 'It always comes down to Bethany, doesn't it?' Yes, David. It does. 'What about me?'

'Sorry,' she said, 'I can't even begin thinking about you. I can't think about anybody. I don't have the strength. It's all I can do to keep myself alive. I have to keep remembering to draw breath.' She took advantage of his silence to put the phone down.

He hadn't mentioned Maura. How could anybody who was supposed to think anything at all about Annie not mention Maura?

She dropped her school bags by the door and headed towards the fridge without even taking her coat off. Annie was chopping onions ready for a lamb stew.

'Bethany,' she said, as reasonable as she could muster, 'you have to keep that appointment.' Bethany's eyes slid sideways in a pained expression that they seemed to learn at school these days, along with other expressions like 'whatever'.

'I'm not joking, Bethany. I've had enough of your lying and stealing, and manipulating. You can't carry on like this. You'll finish up in big trouble. You've got to face up to it before it's too late.' She dropped the knife on the draining board and held her hands out, entreating. 'Listen, you had a bad start in life. No wonder you don't trust people. But if you could just get some help and let yourself be loved,' she gestured for emphasis, 'I think you would be a much happier person.'

Annie realised she had said it all. There was nothing more she could say. For a moment, a split second, she hoped for some kind of response. Then her hands fell to her sides. It was the same as it had been all along. Bethany didn't even bother to laugh. She smirked the merest of smirks. It was a red rag to a bull.

Annie felt as though a rubber band had been wound up tight in her brain and now, after years of tightening, it snapped. She found herself screaming, plunging into the vortex, nearer and nearer to the lizard's eye. This time, she would surely be sucked in. Then she felt the etch of the knife blade down her face, a sickening blow in her stomach and the hefting of a force that threw her sideways. She wasn't entirely surprised. Bethany had tried to harm her before, thumping, pushing and shoving, poking with a screwdriver, leaving bits of broken glass in her shoes, but she'd never been like this before.

She tasted blood, the sharp metallic taste of blood. What was it, she thought, stigmata? She felt it flowing freely from her eyes into her mouth. Surely you can't weep blood, was the bizarre thought that formed itself in her head. Perhaps there was something in it, after all.

She surfaced to find Elizabeth lying in a crumpled heap.

'I'm sorry,' she sobbed. 'I tried to help... she knocked me down.'

Annie exerted herself. Shivering from head to foot, she reached for the landline and dialled 999.

'I've been knifed,' she croaked. 'It's my daughter... she tried to kill me.' She felt herself go. The last thing she remembered was the receiver falling to the floor.

'Hello...?'

'I'm sorry, Annie,' said David. He was weeping. 'For everything.' He screwed up his eyes and knuckled them, sniffing back the tears like a brave little boy.

'It's alright,' she breathed, from her hospital bed. Now, why had she said that? He stroked her face, where the stitches were, right from her eye to her mouth. She'd been lucky enough to be painstakingly stitched up by a Chinese

341

casualty officer who had nimble fingers and aspirations in the field of plastic surgery.

'I love you,' said David. 'I've always loved you.'

Yes, she thought, but Bethany always got in the way.

What if...? How would it have worked out? They might have jogged along together, never finding reason to test each other.

You can know too much about somebody, more than is good for you, more than is good for a relationship. You have to keep up some illusions, don't you? Otherwise nobody would love anybody. For all you admire somebody, once you've seen the ugly bits, you can forget the rest. Weaknesses you can forgive, but downright ugliness kills love dead. The worst of it is, we've probably all got ugly bits in us. Except Dr Bannerjee. Or maybe even Dr Bannerjee.

But, even if they had got on together, she would always have been left with the longing, the wanting a child of her own. That would always have been there between them.

She felt the gentle pressure of David's fingers on her face and realised he did love her after all.

Spring 2001

Chapter 28 – Annie

'You want the place decorated, don't ask me. Go ahead and get a decorator. You can afford it.' It was a sore point with David, Elizabeth leaving Annie all her money. Well, it wasn't that much, really, it was just a matter of principle. Unbeknown to them, Elizabeth had made a new will when she came to live in Holmebridge and left Annie the lot, to help her in raising Bethany. Then she died of pneumonia, after her 'fall', before she had chance to change her mind.

Funny, isn't it, how wills bring out the worst in people? Choose who gets what, there's always a bad taste left behind no matter how great, or well directed, the generosity of the deceased.

'If I have anything left, I'll leave it to a cat's home,' Annie told David. 'Then everybody can be upset.'

They were mooching about in the lounge at Brackenbed Drive, drinking tea.

'I'd forgotten how nice and sunny it is in here,' said Annie. At last, after more than a year, the house was fit to live in. The question was, who was going to live in it? Annie could no more make her mind up about that than she could about the colour of the walls.

'I don't know whether to go for the buttercup or the beige,' she fretted. 'Yellow is more cheerful but beige is more classy.'

'There'll be a lot more decisions to make before it's finished,' David warned. 'What about furniture, carpets, curtains and so on?' He shook his head in a *you'll never manage without me* sort of way. Not that he ever did much in the way of carpets and curtains at the best of times.

Annie found herself wanting to stay at Wormald Street out of sheer inertia. Horace didn't want it. He was still haunting Maura's old house.

'We'd better sell it,' she said, suddenly, realising in a moment of clarity that she'd made her decision.

'What?'

'This place. Take half each. I'll stay on at Wormald Street for the time being.'

'What about me?' said David, in a hurt tone of voice.

'You can move into Wormald Street as well until you find somewhere else to live. You might want to buy a new flat.' There was a rash of new flats appearing round Holmebridge on every random patch of spare land, even on the riverbank where you could guarantee flooding at least once in a generation. God only knows how they got insurance.

'This is supposed to be a joint decision, Annie. You sound as though you've already made your mind up.' He clenched his jaw.

'Oh, I don't know,' she sighed. She always did when pressed. She wasn't as strong as she used to be. She still missed Dr Bannerjee but he thought she was well enough to refer back to Dr Parry.

'Anyway,' said David. 'One thing's for sure. There's no way I'm going to live in Wormald Street.'

There they were, then. Bethany couldn't be blamed this time. She was twenty miles away with a very-nicely-off-thank-you couple called Derek and Angela who specialised in fostering difficult children. Mind you, Annie and David still paid for her keep. But Derek and Angela had the pleasure of buying her whatever she set her scheming little heart on next. They were talking about taking her to Majorca. Let them. They had their work cut out. It would only be a matter of time.

'I'm sorry, David. We can still be friends. But the marriage, it's over isn't it?' There was a silence like one you would hear the tick of the clock in, if there was a clock, that is. 'It's been over a long time.' There, she'd said it. Whatever the repercussions, she felt better for having said it.

David stifled a sob. She was just about to go to him, to fold him in her arms, when he turned on her.

'He was gay, you know. He went off and left us. With a man.' Annie's mind was reeling.

'What?'

'My father. He fell for a curate from Norwich. Mother never blamed him. But I did.' He was working hard to keep his emotions under control. Annie stared.

'Why are you telling me this? Why now? Elizabeth's gone. Can't you let it rest?' What had this to do with anything, for God's sake?

'My – father – was - gay. There might be something wrong with me!' He covered his eyes.

Well. So that was it, was it? Was that what was behind all that refusing to go to the fertility clinic, some irrational fear about something wrong with him?

She could have felt sorry for him but, there again, it was all about him. Let's face it, it had always been all about him.

Annie walked down Main Street, thinking about Elizabeth. Poor old Elizabeth, lying thin and frail in the hospital bed, the light dying in her eyes, apologising for not having been much help.

'You should have been *my* mother,' Annie had said,

stroking her hand. 'I could have done with a mother like you.' Elizabeth smiled and closed her eyes. Annie wept.

Looking back over Elizabeth's life, Annie felt ashamed of her own weakness. If she had half of Elizabeth's strength, what a difference it could have made.

She could have been a better wife, seen how needy David really was. She could have helped him gain more confidence instead of being so dependent on him.

She could have been a better mother if she hadn't been so tired. She could have exerted more discipline. She used to think love was enough. How daft can you be?

Carry on thinking like this, she said to herself, and you'll be back at square one.

She was on her way to meet Rosie Barker. Good thing too. That would snap her out of it, if anything would. She turned into the bistro. Rosie was already sitting at the narrow bar, leaning on her elbow and holding a large white wine aloft.

'There you are!' she said. 'I didn't get one in for you in case it warmed up enough for you to taste it. I'll get you one now.' She waved at the barman who nodded back and reached for the two-litre bottle he kept on ice in a plastic bucket.

'It's alright, this retirement lark, isn't it?' Rosie chirped as Annie climbed onto the bar stool beside her. Annie liked sitting on bar stools. There was something mildly decadent about it. She looked round at the splendid Burmantofts green tiled walls. She couldn't quite get over the feeling it was really a butcher's shop.

'Hanging about in bars all afternoon, there's nothing like it.' Rosie smiled and unlike most people, left a space for her to say, or not, whatever she wanted to.

Annie liked the quiet friendship that had grown

between them since Rosie had decided to take early retirement due, she said, to repetitive strain injury of the brain. Now the professional barriers were down, they found a good bit in common. In a funny kind of a way, although they were so different, it helped to fill the void caused by Maura's massive heart attack.

'How're you?' said Annie.

'Good. We're going out Saturday night, Stu and I, dancing. Why don't you come with us?'

'Dancing?' Annie panicked, 'I haven't been dancing since college. I don't do dancing.' Rosie smiled.

'Well, it's not disco, you know. It's belly dancing. It's getting quite popular now. Good for the abdominals. And you don't have to dance if you don't want. You can just sit and watch.' She watched Annie for her reaction.

Belly dancing! Whatever next? Holmebridge, the capital of exotica! Well, I never. Annie's mind was racing around, trying to find another excuse.

'No,' she said, dropping on one, 'I'm not going to play gooseberry. You can forget it.' Rosie laughed.

'There's no gooseberry about it,' she said. 'Stu and I are just good friends.'

'Well, I'll think about it,' said Annie. It was all she could think of to say.

Walking back down Main street, she realised she hadn't thought about Bethany, David, Elizabeth or Maura for a good hour. As for herself, she felt better. She knew she'd done her level best to be a good wife and mother. That's a lot more than some did. She might not have been perfect but, in her heart of hearts, she knew she'd been good enough.

An hour with Rosie Barker, she thought, was as good as a tonic.

***

The phone rang just as she was biting into her toast. Saturday morning, nine o'clock, it had to be Andrew. She sighed.

Andrew kept on turning up. It was normal enough to start with. He'd been close to Elizabeth, and became something of a mainstay in her old age, but he kept on coming even after she died. At first, it was to do jobs, help Annie sort things out and, to be honest, when Bethany was going through the courts en route to a life of luxury with Derek and Angela, and David was away in Altrincham earning their living, it was just as well she had somebody to turn to. Poor old Horace wasn't up to much. In fact, half the time, she felt responsible for him as well. So it had got to be a habit. And you can't put folk up at The Crown when you've got two spare beds, now can you?

'Hello, Mrs Neill, how are you getting along?' He didn't introduce himself, he'd no need.

'I'm alright, thanks. In fact, I'm going out tonight.' Why had she said that? She'd no intention of going belly dancing with Rosie and Stu, or with anybody else for that matter. Maybe a forlorn hope that it might put him off?

'Are you now?' His interest picked up. 'Matter of fact, I'm something of a dancer myself,' he chuckled.

'Not this kind, you're not,' said Annie, 'I don't expect you've done much in the way of belly dancing.' Andrew and belly dancing were as remote from each other as it was possible to be.

'Belly dancing? Well now, you're right there. It was Morris dancing and such, when I was young, like.' Annie didn't know where to take the conversation next. She'd no need to bother.

'I'll be on my way, shall I?' he said. 'I'll be there by tea time.'

'But I'm going out.'

'Don't let me stop you. You go out and enjoy yourself. It's high time you started enjoying yourself. Goodbye now.'

So there she was, expecting Andrew, again. She'd better make a bed up and clean the bathroom.

The most striking thing about Stu was his hair. At an age when most men struggle to keep their head decently covered, Stu had hair in abundance. It fair strained to thrive. His magnificent moustache only underlined the point that, in the hair department, Stu had everything going for him. So, even in the well-packed venue of the Belly Dance Spectacular, he was not going to be overlooked.

Andrew made a poor comparison. He'd gone uninvited. Annie hadn't the heart to say otherwise when he showed up willing to go with her to the 'do' at the Leisure Centre. Next to Stu, his beefy frame, sweaty complexion and number two haircut left a lot to be desired. He settled himself next to Annie with a pint of Newcastle Brown and watched the dancers avidly.

The dancers weren't what you might call the most skilled exponents of the genre but they were doing their best. Women of all ages, shapes and sizes were flaunting their assets. Busts, bellies, hips and thighs were taking advantage of hitherto before unknown opportunities to show themselves off in the name of culture.

It was a revelation, thought Annie. All this sexuality trapped in ordinary women's bodies. All this sexuality ready to let rip. No wonder the atmosphere was so steamy. Where were the men, though, who deserved it?

Looking round at Stu, sitting in front of a pint of Sola Cola, engrossed in a crossword, and Andrew, openly gawping at the displays of flesh undulating before him, she despaired.

There was something about belly dance, she thought, after a pint of white wine, that released the woman within. She stood up and joined in with the others in the free-for-alls. Rosie danced with her.

Andrew took her home. She was thankful for that. She couldn't have managed without. She thanked him kindly at the foot of the stairs.

In her happily inebriated state, she thought about Dr Bannerjee. When did she ever not think about Dr Bannerjee? She imagined his soft touch in her intimate places. In fact, she spent large parts of every day imagining his soft touch in her intimate places. It was something of a shock, then, when Andrew's big fingers closed round her crotch. He pulled her close against his chest, so close she could hardly breath. He didn't say anything. Good thing too, when you think about it, whatever Andrew could have said on that particular occasion would have ruined it altogether. She didn't know if Dr Bannerjee could have made her feel so wanted, so womanly, so downright sexy, but Andrew was making a good go of it. He lifted her off her feet and carried her up to bed.

He was possessed of that kind of strength that made you give up and let him get on with it. If you were hewing coal, for example, you could just stand by and let him do your bit as well without him noticing the difference. It was so refreshing, not having to try so hard. Not having to try at all.

When she made love with David she was always conscious of trying to please him, trying to make him pleased with her, trying to be good enough for him.

In her fantasies with Dr Bannerjee she was always the adoring one, the one who was allowed to kiss his feet, and other more private parts of his beautiful body, but she was never satisfied. How could she be? Who could be satisfied with a flimsy fantasy?

Now, with Andrew, she didn't need to lift a finger, or anything else for that matter. He managed to spread himself around her so that every part of her was in his loving embrace. His sheer persistence persuaded her to relax and give herself up to him. She could soak him up to her heart's content. He bided his time until she was more than ready then pushed into her like a pile driver. The harder he pushed the more she liked it until, eventually she came in a long sloppy orgasm that lasted for longer than she thought possible.

'Oh, God, Mrs Neill,' he sobbed into her ear.

For some unfortunate reason she found that funny. She couldn't help it. The bubbles of laughter surged up from her stomach and out of her mouth. She gasped helplessly. Andrew drew back, looking at her, then, realising she was laughing, turned away, covering his face with his hands. Annie realised he was hurt but couldn't stop herself laughing long enough to explain herself. The more she thought about it, the funnier it became. The more she laughed, the more Andrew withdrew. What man can stand to be laughed at anyway, never mind when he was overweight and stark naked?

He grabbed his clothes and went. Annie wanted to go after him. She wanted to explain. But she couldn't get herself off the bed. She fell asleep, still laughing, and dreamed about Stu, drinking Sola Cola and doing the crossword.

***

The next morning dawned late. About eleven o'clock. Annie woke in a panic. What about Andrew? Part of her said 'just let him go' but the rest of her felt ungrateful. Whatever his shortcomings, he'd aroused her out of androgyny and made her feel like a woman.

She found him in the kitchen, in his dressing gown, frying eggs.

'Morning, Andrew,' she said in a small voice. He didn't turn round. She came up behind him. 'I'm sorry if I upset you. I wasn't laughing at you, honest.' No reply. 'It was the relief, I expect. I never thought I would feel... like *that* again.' She reached out on hand and stroked his broad back until he turned to her. 'Thank you,' she said. She kissed him softly on the lips. He didn't move a muscle. She let go, disappointed. Then he caught her, pulling her roughly towards him and locked his mouth on hers, his tongue reaching down her throat. She thought she would faint for lack of air. He forced her back against the kitchen table, pressing himself between her thighs, moving against her. When, at last, he pushed into her she opened herself up, welcoming him in and coming at the same time. She heard his panting in her ear and felt his heart thumping against her chest.

An acrid smell filled the air.

'Andrew,' she gasped, 'the eggs!'

Horace was in his usual fireside chair. The fire was out.

He looked as though he hadn't stirred since last time she saw him.

'Are you alright?' said Annie.

'Aye, I'm alright,' said Horace, his voice flat.

'Have you had anything to eat?' She was beginning to sound like a home help.

'Nay, I'm not hungry.'

'Well you will be when I've cooked you a good fry-up,' she said. 'It's a bit cold in here.' It always was in those old stone houses no matter how hot it got outside. 'You get that fire going while I go down the Co-op.' She went before he could argue.

By the time she got back with a carrier bag full of eggs, bacon, black pudding and baked beans, he'd got a fire started in the grate. And by the time, he's waded through his fry up and a pot of tea, Horace was warming up.

'That's better,' said Annie. By way of conversation, she told him about Andrew burning the eggs that morning. 'He's still there,' she said. 'I don't know what to do with him.'

'Hang on to him,' said Horace, 'if he's worth having.' He chuckled.

'What d'you mean?' said Annie, her cheeks blushing bright red.

'What you need is a good man. Aye, that's it, a good man to look after you.' Horace nodded sagely.

'I've had enough of men,' said Annie, without much conviction. 'Anyway, I couldn't settle down with Andrew.'

'Why, what's up with him?'

Annie thought of quite a few reasons but couldn't bring herself to say them out loud. He's a scrap metal merchant, drinks too much, not educated, he's overweight, too old, he..

'He thinks a lot about you, ye know. That's what matters in the end. Aye, that's what matters.' Annie felt a bit ashamed of herself.

'Well, we'll see.' She started clearing the pots. 'I'll just sort these out before I go.' Horace watched her with a know-all expression on his face.

'I take it he's up to it, then? Tackle's in working order?'

'What d'you mean, up to it? Up to what?'

'You know what I mean,' Horace chuckled.

The scar had healed nicely, she saw in the bathroom mirror, but it was still quite red and a bit puckered at the corner of her mouth, giving her a quirky smile. Most of the redness could be covered up with cosmetic make-up. Plastic surgery had been mentioned as a possibility, just to even her mouth up, but she wasn't sure if she'd bother. Dr Yee had done a brilliant job and, she thought, ought to be promoted on the strength of it.

It was just that she'd started thinking of herself as a woman again. Maybe a bit of vanity was no bad thing.

David wasn't bothered by it, nor was Andrew, but then, perhaps she wanted better? And what about the children; the ones she was going to teach when she finally made her way back into the teaching world, didn't they deserve her at her best?

She cleansed her face carefully, exfoliated and toned. Then she massaged three layers of rejuvenating night cream into her skin and finished with a touch of lip plumping gloss.

It wasn't that she *expected* Andrew as such. It would be unfair to lead him on. All the same, she dug out a nightdress that was marginally more feminine than the One Size Fits All T-shirts she usually wore in bed.

It seemed like hours later when she gave up on him and turned over to go to sleep. It was probably for the best.

356

God knows what sort of a mess she could be getting herself into. Probably one she wouldn't be able to get out of. Then she heard what sounded like the creak of a floorboard outside her door. Nothing happened for at least three minutes. Then the floorboard creaked again. Annie got up, crept across the lino and opened the door. Andrew was lurking outside, just as she thought he might be.

'Oh,' she said. 'I was just going to the bathroom.'

'Yes,' said Andrew, 'so was I.' They smiled, even laughed in a quiet sort of way.

Annie made a show of flushing the toilet and running the taps. When she went back to her bedroom, Andrew was in the same place as she'd left him.

'Bathroom's free,' she smiled. He didn't move, except for his breathing. He sounded as though he'd just run a mile. Slowly, she walked over to the bed and stretched herself out, leaving the door wide open. It was, she thought, up to him.

He approached cautiously, as though he might be laughed at again, then he laid himself carefully on top of her. It was not the kind of thoughtless lying on top that might smother her beyond recognition, but a delicate balance of his bulk so that he covered her without her taking his weight.

Thank God, she thought.

When she'd taken him in, she let him lie on her, stroking his back. This is what love is, she thought.

In the morning, she thought better of it. She was glad when he went home. He kissed her goodbye and set off with a sloppy smile on his face. She panicked.

***

Monday morning, Stu appeared on the doorstep.

'Sorry, Annie,' he said. Now what? 'Can I come in?'

'Course you can.' She led him into the poky kitchen where a small fire smoked in the grate. 'What's the problem?' As though she didn't know.

'I'm sorry, it's Bethany.' He sat down heavily on a kitchen chair. Annie went to fill the kettle.

Of course it's Bethany. When isn't it Bethany? The course of Annie's life for the last God knows how many years had been determined by the antics of Bethany. She put the kettle on the hob and lit the gas. Would it ever change? She'd be fooling herself to think otherwise. She only had to think about herself for a single minute before Bethany started playing up again. Her life would never be her own. Never.

'Yes?' she said, folding her arms in front of her.

'I'm afraid she's accused her foster father of rape. He's been charged.'

Tell me why I am not surprised, thought Annie. Even Derek and Angela, experts though they may be, have been caught out. It was only a matter of time.

'What happened?'

'They went to Majorca. She got mixed up with a waiter. Says she's going to marry him. Derek and Angela wouldn't let her stay over there. The next news, she's saying Derek raped her. She's had to be placed with a single female foster parent for her own protection.'

'What happens now?' She dreaded to think.

'Well because she had sex with the waiter, Manuel is his name, I believe, it's not so cut and dried. She can't be proved to be a virgin.'

'She couldn't be proved to be a virgin last time because she wouldn't let herself be examined,' Annie said wearily.

'So, what happens now? What about this waiter? She's underage. He could be accused of being a paedophile.' Trust Bethany to make other people's lives a misery. Everybody she came into contact with suffered for it sooner or later.

'I don't know about that,' said Stu. 'She told him she was sixteen. He took her word for it whether he believed her or not. Anyway, being so tall, she looks older than she is. And she didn't want to bring any charges against him.'

'What about Derek? What's going to happen to him?' She'd brought charges against him and would probably stick to them this time, having had some practice in the matter, she thought, remembering poor Mr Kaye.

'Plea bargaining, I expect,' said Stu.

'Plea bargaining? What's that for God's sake?'

'It means he pleads guilty for a lesser offence, like indecent assault, for example, rather than pleading not guilty to rape. That would mean a shorter sentence.'

'But only if he lost! Why should he plead guilty to something he didn't do? What kind of justice is that?'

'Sometimes,' said Stu, 'justice has very little to do with it.' He stood up, held his arms out to Annie and circled her shoulders.

'I don't believe it,' said Annie, against his sweatshirt. 'He's got to plead guilty because he'll be worse off if he tries to prove he's innocent? She's lying again.'

'I know,' said Stu. 'Believe me, I know.'

'How many people,' asked Annie, out of the depths of her soul, 'are going to be dragged down because of her?'

'I don't know,' said Stu, letting her go. She respected him for his honesty. She took a deep breath and rinsed the teapot out.

'I was wondering,' said Stu, leaning his backside against the draining board, 'if Derek could use this RAD business in his defence.'

'Reactive Attachment Disorder? You mean it's becoming recognised?' Annie's heart quickened.

'Well, some professionals are taking it seriously, trying out holding therapy and so on.'

Holding therapy? What good was holding therapy? Bethany would never consent to being held. Even as a toddler, she'd refused to be held. She would fight to the death rather than give somebody the satisfaction of holding her. Annie ducked to reach the milk out of the fridge.

'But,' said Stu, 'you know how conservative the Law is. And she'll melt everybody's hearts, as usual.'

'Won't she just.'

'David?' She'd rung him up at school. It was unforgivable. It was the height of embarrassment to be rung up at school. It was as though your mind wasn't on the job. As though you had other priorities. Fortunately for Annie, he had a free period that hadn't been commandeered to cover for somebody who was off with stress.

'We need to talk. It's Bethany.' She hardly knew where to begin. She knew he'd be furious with her but she couldn't leave it until after school, could she, not when it was so important?

'Yes, I know. The social worker called me this morning.'

Did he now? Would that be before or after he'd been to see Annie?

'What are we going to do?' She felt all at sea.

360

'What *can* we do? As far as Bethany's concerned, it's the end of the line. She's not our responsibility any more.'

Not our responsibility any more. That was a heavy thought, one that she hadn't grappled with as yet. After all those years, how could you suddenly not be responsible any more? It was an ingrained habit. How could you let it all go?

David's voice was cool, not hostile like it usually was when he talked about Bethany. He was, she could see, already moving on. Well, she was moving on as well, but she was still Bethany's mother.

'What are *you* going to do, David?'

'I expect I'll buy an apartment over here. At least I've got a job.' She felt the sting of criticism.

'I'm going on a course,' she said, annoyed that she felt obliged to justify her existence. 'An update. Back into teaching.'

'Oh yes? Again?'

'Yes, again.'

'Let me know if you need help.' It was that *you'll never manage without me* tone again.

'Yes I will. But I won't.'

'Goodbye, then. By the way, Bethany's life story, what happened to it?' Now why had he said that?

'It was destroyed in the fire.'

'It wasn't real, you realise that.'

'What do you mean?'

'You made it up as you went along. It was nothing to do with Bethany.'

She put the receiver down.

David had put his finger on it. Annie had tried so hard to make a life story for Bethany, done her best to give her a life like any other little girl.

Elizabeth, Maura and Horace, even Andrew gathered together to make a family for her, appearing on milestone photos of birthdays and holidays.

She kept samples of schoolwork to show Bethany's progress, even her bizarre efforts at artwork as well as little poems she had written on subjects like autumn leaves.

She kept the presents Bethany made for her at school; fancy shopping lists, pincushions, calendars and other such paraphernalia children traditionally produce at Christmas time.

She kept beautiful photos; little Bethany holding a teddy, holding Maura's hand, with the children at playschool; photos of schoolgirl Bethany singing in the Summer concert, playing hopscotch in the playground, riding a pony with the sun lighting up her copper hair.

She'd valued everything about her and kept it all together to show Bethany that she was somebody, she was special and that she amounted to something.

And Bethany had destroyed it. Well, it wasn't Annie's fault. It wasn't Bethany's fault either, although that wasn't always easy to admit. It was something that happened when she was born and there was nothing Annie could do about it.

'So, how d'you like it?' said Rosie Barker, looking round Annie's new living space.

It was six weeks on, the house on Brackenbed Drive was sold and Annie had found a brand new apartment in Acacia Court, far enough up the hillside to be out of flooding distance, and was installed in no time.

Acacia Court was built on the site of a former HGV scrapyard and was still referred to as such by the locals.

'You live up at t'scrapyard, then?' was a common response when Annie gave her address. People in these parts had long memories. It might take a generation or so.

The apartment was what you might call bijou. The living area just about accommodated a sofa, a bistro table, two patio chairs and a twenty-six inch TV. The kitchen occupied a corner behind the counter top. It was companionable. You could chat with one foot in the lounge and cook with the other foot in the kitchen all at the same time, like Annie was doing now.

'Fine,' said Annie pushing a pepperoni pizza into the oven. 'A bit short on space, but it's so new and clean. I'd forgotten how nice it is to feel so clean!'

'How many bedrooms?' said Rosie, innocently.

'Two,' Annie enthused. 'But the second bedroom is so small there's hardly space for a bed. I've set it up as an office to do my schoolwork in. Come and have a look.'

It was the expected thing to do a tour of somebody's new home, however modest. Visitors would be offended if they weren't offered a formal opportunity for nosiness. So they went through the motions of touring the bedroom, bathroom and office and in no time at all were back where they'd started.

'Where will Andrew stay, then?' Rosie smiled a twinkling smile. Annie blushed bright red.

'He can stay at The Crown, if he wants.' She managed to keep a poker face. 'And, if Bethany ever comes to visit, you never know, there are twin beds in my room.' She looked at Rosie with a 'so there' sort of expression. That didn't stop Rosie laughing, though.

'The Crown, didn't you know it's closed down? It's got planning permission to convert into yet more luxury apartments.'

'Am I surprised?' said Annie. 'If you threw out an old packing crate somebody would convert it into apartments. And isn't it funny, how they're all called *luxury* apartments? Nobody ever says 'bog standard flat with running hot and cold' which, when you think about it, is all they really are.'

'That's right,' said Rosie.' It's a metaphor for life.'

'You can say that again. You never get what you're promised. You're always short changed along the way.' Rosie nodded, lips pursed. She reminded Annie of Horace in one of his philosophical moods.

'Well, you can say what you like,' said Annie. 'It may be hardly more than a shoe box but it's mine, not anybody else's, mine. And you're my first guest.' She delved into the fridge and brought out a bottle of champagne.

'Welcome to my humble abode,' she said, holding it aloft.

It *was* humble compared with Brackenbed Drive but she had that same feeling now as she did then, when they moved in there all those years ago. It was, she thought, all about leaving your old rubbish behind and starting out afresh, a feeling that fills you with hope for the future.

'Let's drink.'

They sat side by side on the sofa like old friends.

'How d'you feel about Bethany, now?' Rosie's voice was a bit tentative but it was a question that would have to be asked sooner or later. Annie took a deep breath.

'I'm mad with her for getting Derek into trouble.' *And the rest. What about the rest? She couldn't even talk about the rest. In fact she might just put the rest to bed and never think about it again.* 'I'll probably never get over being mad with her even though I know why she's like she is.' Annie paused, thinking. A cloud passed over and a ray of sunlight beamed through the patio window, flooding across the floor, bathing their feet. 'There's no way I can manage her. I gave it my best shot but I keep thinking I could have done it better. I think that'll always nag at me. As it is, Bethany's way beyond me.' Then, miraculously, a penny dropped. 'Way beyond anybody I shouldn't wonder.'

'I'm glad you realise that,' said Rosie, smiling.

'It's taken me long enough. And, you know, the worst thing was being on my own. Nobody believing me. People looking at me sideways. Honestly, Rosie, I began to have serious doubts about my sanity. Course, when I saw Dr. Bannerjee, I knew I was in the madhouse!' Annie grinned and raised her glass.

'Here's to the future.'

'The future.' They drank.

'And here's to Andrew.'

'Why Andrew?' Annie affected a bored expression.

'He'll feel at home here, won't he?'

'Why should he?' All this talk about Andrew was getting past a joke. Everybody she knew kept mentioning Andrew. Did they think she couldn't manage without a man? She'd managed without David for long enough. Ever since she got married, in fact. Alright, he'd supported them financially, and she was glad of that, but emotionally, she'd been on her own. She'd been on her own all her life.

'Because it's a scrapyard, isn't it?' Rosie looked as though she expected Annie to know what she was on about. Annie didn't get it for a minute, then, suddenly, she did. For some reason, it seemed excruciatingly funny. She opened her mouth and laughed a great loud laugh like she hadn't done in years. Rosie joined her. They let rip, doubling over with stomach cramps brought on by the force of unaccustomed hilarity.

'Some people,' Annie said between sobs, 'are born to scrapyards.'

'Some achieve scrapyards!'

'And some have scrapyards thrust upon them!'

Poor Andrew. How could they laugh like that, at his expense? But it wasn't really. After all, she'd chosen to live at the renovated scrapyard. Maybe it was an omen? You never can tell.

At least she could have a laugh.